For James:

As always, thanks for the support and enthusiasm.

Bear Hugs (always!)

Nick Pobb

May, 2008

For James:

As always, thanks for the support and encouragement.

Best wishes (always!)

Nick Jobb

The Handyman's Promise

BY

NICK POFF

authorHOUSE®

AuthorHouse™
1663 Liberty Drive, Suite 200
Bloomington, IN 47403
www.authorhouse.com
Phone: 1-800-839-8640

© *2008 Nick Poff. All rights reserved.*

No part of this book may be reproduced, stored in a retrieval system, or transmitted by any means without the written permission of the author.

First published by AuthorHouse 4/14/2008

ISBN: 978-1-4343-7054-9 (sc)
ISBN: 978-1-4343-7055-6 (hc)

Library of Congress Control Number: 2008902464

Printed in the United States of America
Bloomington, Indiana

This book is printed on acid-free paper.

Grateful acknowledgment is made to the following for permission to include copyrighted material:

Darling, Be Home Soon
Words and music by John Sebastian
Copyright © 1967 by Alley Music Corp. and Trio Music Company
Copyright renewed
International copyright secured All rights reserved
Used by permission

ALSO BY NICK POFF:

THE HANDYMAN'S DREAM

THE HANDYMAN'S REALITY

ACKNOWLEDGMENTS

Blessings and thanks go to my good ole guardian angel, Skip Carsten, whose guidance and encouragement pushed me forward when my confidence was flagging, and whose inspiration enriched this book in ways I could not have imagined.

I'd like to thank Kenna Fast and Scott Roddy, both good friends and two of the funniest people I know, who occasionally allow me to steal some of their best lines.

Heartfelt thanks and hugs are in order for Murray Hunt, Kerry Mills, and Steve Van Anda, whose friendship and support have kept me afloat through some stormy seas.

I'm indebted to the late Randy Shilts, whose book *And the Band Played On* refreshed my memory in regards to the gay community's reaction to AIDS in the early 1980s.

Once again it's my pleasure to thank Eileen Chetti for her fine editing work on the manuscript.

And finally, I'd like to thank again the many readers of the *Handyman* books, who pleaded for more of Ed's story. Thanks so much for sharing your own stories and lives with me. Your enthusiasm and kind words regarding Ed and Rick and the rest of the characters in these books fill me with awe and gratitude. Believe me, your support made this book possible.

For Mom

THE HANDYMAN'S PROMISE

CHAPTER ONE
AUTUMN 1983

"Three years, baby. Can ya believe it?"

Ed Stephens smiled. His face was buried in Rick's neck, the gold chain he had given Rick two years earlier tickling his nose.

"Three years," Ed said with a sigh. "And you're still the Dream Man."

"Am I? Really?" Rick gently pulled Ed's head away from his shoulder and looked deeply into his eyes. "Now. Look at this face and tell me I'm still your Dream Man."

As they slowly rocked back and forth in each other's arms to the music coming from Ed's old stereo in their carriage-house apartment, Ed returned Rick's deep gaze.

I guess beauty really is in the eye of the beholder, he thought. He knew there wasn't anything particularly extraordinary about Rick's looks, but in Ed's eyes, Rick was still the most handsome man in the world. Rick's brown eyes were as compelling as always, although the tinted contacts probably helped, Ed admitted to himself. He noticed upon closer inspection that a few threads of gray could now be seen in Rick's short, dark brown hair, and the equally dark, neatly trimmed beard. *When did* that *happen*, he wondered, thinking thirty-two was a little early for that kind of aging evidence, but also thinking that as hard as Rick had been working for the past year or so, he might have brought it on himself.

Still gazing into Rick's eyes, Ed allowed his mind to drift back three years to that bright, sunny day when he first saw Rick Benton delivering mail to his house, and the gloomy, overcast afternoon when he finally met the new mailman face-to-face. *I knew then*, he thought. *Don't ask me how I knew, but somehow I knew he was the real-life version of the man I had been dreaming about. I fell in love with him, and I still love him just as much. Maybe more. Oh, it's not the same; I'm not all excited and distracted all the time, but it's . . . warm . . . comforting. It's not perfect, but it's good, and probably better than some people get.*

A hand suddenly waved in front of Ed's face. "Ed? You still with me?" Rick's face crinkled into the mischievous grin that still managed to get an answering grin out of Ed. "Where the hell did you go just now?"

Ed sighed and returned his head to Rick's neck. He softly kissed the skin above the golden chain—his symbol of commitment to Rick and whispered, "I just went back to the day I first saw you and knew you were the Dream Man. And yeah, darlin', you are still the Dream Man."

"Really? You're not"—Rick nodded toward the stereo where the harmonies of the Association's "Never My Love" were smoothly serenading them—"tired of me yet?"

"Nope. That's why I put this record on. This heart of mine has not lost its desire for you. At all."

Rick's arms tightened around Ed. "I'm glad, baby. 'Cause you're still my dream man, too—the cutest handyman in Porterfield, Indiana. Hell, the whole world, for that matter."

Rick reached for Ed's left hand. He rubbed a finger over the ring he had put on Ed's hand shortly after they had made their mutual decision to bring their lives together. "I still love you so much. I'll admit, some days I still wanna kick you down the stairs, but I love you. And I can't imagine my life without you."

Ed snickered. "Yeah. I may throw a hammer at you yet, but I wouldn't trade you for anyone or anything."

"I'm not about to trade you in either." Rick gave Ed an appraising look. "You're still so handsome to me—even more, if that's possible. You're holding up well for an old man of thirty-one."

Ed's face went red, as it always did when someone complimented him. Still, even if he reacted to the praise with his usual embarrassment, it was true.

Since his teen years Ed's face had hinted at the possibility of a certain masculine maturity. Whether age itself had finished the job, or the experience of life and lessons learned had enabled him to grow into adulthood gracefully, Ed's appearance had indeed fulfilled its earlier promise.

The once skinny, awkward teenager was now a physically confident man; his six-foot frame was now fully filled out (a little too much in the gut, he sometimes ruefully thought, vowing to switch from regular to Diet Pepsi at some point), and even if his face wasn't one to turn heads, it looked good—probably better than it ever had. His light brown eyes reflected the wisdom he had acquired. At his sister's suggestion he'd allowed his sandy brown hair to grow into an acceptable eighties style, and though it was definitely thinning at the rate Rick's was going gray, he didn't have to worry about it—yet. He had come to the conclusion that his thick mustache—so in fashion back in the late seventies—made him look a little too much like someone impersonating one of the Village People, especially when combined with his handyman clothes, so he had trimmed it down short and was pleasantly surprised with the results. He was even considering a goatee to go with it these days.

"I guess we're doing okay," Ed murmured as the record changer on the stereo clicked and another one of his old 45s dropped onto the turntable. "Despite the fact that the last year has been kind of cruddy, these have been the best three years of my life."

Rick's grin disappeared. "Necessary cruddiness," he gently chided. "Right?"

"Yeah. I know it's for the best, but I do miss you sometimes, darlin', with you just being here on the weekends, and sometimes not even that much." And sometimes Ed worried about Rick as well, but he wasn't willing to admit that out loud.

"Well, I'm here now," Rick whispered. He pulled Ed's head to his and lightly kissed him. "I'm here for the whole weekend. I am not in Indy but right here, and I promise I'm gonna show you how glad I am to be here as often as possible before I have to leave on Monday morning."

Ed responded to Rick's kiss, pulling his Dream Man closer to him. Rick's tongue began to tease his mouth, probing between his lips. Ed felt the stirrings within that told him they'd be down the hall and on the bed shortly, unless, he thought lustfully, it happened right there in the living room, on the sofa or even the floor. As Ed reached for the first button on Rick's shirt, a loud *meow* rose above the music from the stereo.

Startled, the two men's kiss ended as they both turned toward the apartment door. Jett, their black cat, was on his hind legs; his front paws against the door. It was his signal that it was time for him to go out for his nightly patrol of the property. He let forth with another *meow* that let them know he meant not in a little bit, not at their convenience, but *now*.

They both began to laugh. "Yet another romantic moment torn to shreds by that cat," Rick roared, shaking his head. "Damn, he just knows, doesn't he?"

"You know, he has me to himself most of the time," Ed said, still laughing. "I think he's gotten jealous of you."

"Well, we can't have that," Rick said, heading for the door. "So I'll walk downstairs with him. While I'm at it, I think I'll put the car away." He gave Ed a very lustful glance. "I don't think we'll be going out anymore tonight."

Rick grabbed his keys from the hook Ed had placed near the door and trotted down the stairs with the impatient cat. A few moments later Ed heard the engine of Rick's car, which let him know that Jett had not paused to admire the cool autumn evening with Rick, but had quickly darted off on business of his own. Ed parted the curtains at one of the living room windows and watched as Rick drove his new-to-him, blue '81 Buick Regal into the garage under their bedroom. He thought nostalgically of the beat-up burgundy Monte Carlo Rick had had when they met. That shiny, respectable car rolling out of sight beneath him seemed to symbolize more than anything the changes in their lives over the past two years. Of course he also had a new pickup truck now, and that change had been quite unexpected, but still . . .

Ed let the curtains fall back into place and thought back two years ago to the day Rick had excitedly announced he had a job offer from a Realtor in Indianapolis. *That* had been unexpected, certainly to Ed. In Ed's mind it was the day things changed forever—the beginning not only of this period of time when they were moving forward with the plans they had made for their future together, but also of a time when their commitment to each other was being tested by distance, hard work, and the passage of time itself.

In the spring of 1981 Ed and Rick had made their marriage-like commitment to each other. Not long after that, Mrs. Hilda Penfield, Ed's former high school English teacher, favorite handyman client, and good friend and confidant, had made them an offer that had, in a way, truly signified the beginning of their life together. Mrs. Penfield had asked them to move into the second-floor apartment of the carriage house behind her stately Victorian home. In exchange for their work maintaining the buildings and the grounds, and occasionally assisting the elderly woman herself, the entire property would belong to them upon her death. It was a hard offer to refuse, and they eagerly accepted—moving from Ed's little house on Coleman Street into the newly renovated apartment within months.

After that, Rick insisted on taking the classes that would enable him to acquire a license to sell real estate, the first part of his plan to eventually give up his job with the postal service and become a full-time real estate agent. Ed assumed that once he had the license he wouldn't move forward with his plans until the local real estate market improved, and Vince Cummings, Rick's mentor in the business, was able to hire him. So Ed had been truly astonished when Walt Granger, a Realtor in Indianapolis with a thriving clientele of gay men, and gay himself, had, through Vince, offered Rick a job as his assistant.

Rick had been thrilled with the offer, but Ed was horrified at the idea of leaving Mrs. Penfield and their families in Porterfield. Ed and Rick had argued heatedly—probably the worst fight they had ever had, Ed thought—but settled the issue with the compromise that if Rick were to even consider the job offer, it had to be a mutual decision on their part. Rick, too, loathed the idea of abandoning the woman who had been so good to them, and the idea of not being available for his sister and her children when they needed him. However, he was eager to acquire the knowledge and experience that would enable him to successfully sell real estate in Porterfield and throughout Stratton County as well.

Over time they discussed the possibilities and finally arrived at a workable plan. They determined that instead of pulling up stakes and moving one hundred miles away to Indianapolis, Rick would give up his job at the Porterfield Post Office and more or less commute to his new job in Indianapolis, spending as much time as necessary there, and coming home when he could to be with Ed. Meanwhile, Ed would continue with his thriving handyman business, shoulder Rick's responsibilities at the Penfield place along with his own, and make himself available to Claire and the kids whenever they needed a helping hand.

It had taken about six months for everything, including the financial details, to fall into place, but in the spring of 1982 Rick had begun his new career as assistant to Walt Granger in Indianapolis.

And although the past year and a half hadn't been "cruddy," as Ed had said earlier, it had been tough. While Rick was working hard in Indianapolis, Ed was working hard in Porterfield, keeping everything running smoothly. There were plenty of nights when he came home to an empty apartment, save for the cat. If his mother didn't call and insist on him coming to her house for a good meal, he relied on his own less-than-inspired cooking. Then he and Jett would sprawl on the couch as Ed watched TV and petted the cat, feeling bored, restless, and lonely. Rick would call every night, but the conversation—"I wish I was there, baby"; "Yeah, I wish you were here, too"—seemed to only intensify the loneliness and his longing to have Rick next to him. *This is all going to work out for the best*, he'd tell himself as he settled into bed with one of Rick's books—books he'd never really had any desire to read until Rick was gone. Somehow Ed felt closer to Rick reading the stories he knew Rick enjoyed.

But now, much to Ed's relief, the end was actually in sight. The real estate market had improved, and Vince Cummings had offered Rick a job at home, confident that Rick would be an asset to his well-established business. Over the years Rick had volunteered for the Porterfield Historical Society when he could, and had earned the respect and admiration not only of its leader and a staunch pillar of the community, Eunice Ames, but of a good many other people as well. Ed had no doubt that Rick would be successful working with Vince. From that point, Ed and Rick would be able to move on to the next phase of their long-term goals—buying houses that needed work, which Ed would restore with his handyman talents, and Rick would then sell for a profit.

And as for the gay thing, Ed thought as he heard Rick's steps on the stairs, it didn't worry him as it once had. Over time the fact of their relationship had become something of an open secret in Porterfield. Those who accepted it did so; those who didn't kept their distance, or at least didn't have the nerve to confront them. The town did have a rather live-and-let-live philosophy, as Mrs. Penfield had once said, and although Ed and Rick were probably grist for the constantly grinding gossip mill as much as any other Porterfield citizens, it didn't seem to hurt them in any way that mattered.

Rick came through the open door, slammed it shut, locked it, and even put the safety chain on. "There! The rest of this evening belongs to you and me."

Ed smirked. "Yeah, until Jett starts hollering under our bedroom window to be let in."

Rick put his keys back on the hook near the door. "Well, I guess I can live with that, as long as he's the only one who interrupts us this weekend."

"And soon you'll be here all the time again," Ed said, walking to meet Rick halfway across the living room floor.

"Oh, yeah," Rick whispered as he slid a hand under Ed's T-shirt. "And then," he continued as he began to tickle the hair on Ed's belly, "I will be able to molest my wonderful handyman husband whenever I want to."

Ed pulled Rick's shirt out of his pants and began doing some exploration of his own. "I don't think it's molesting when it's consensual."

"Umm, okay. Whenever you want to make consensual love, I will be here, instead of a hundred miles away. I will," Rick said after a lingering kiss, "be very eager and willing." He took Ed's hand and slowly brushed it against the already swelling crotch of his dress pants. "And ready. Very ready."

The last record on the stereo ended, leaving as the only sounds in the room the faint hiss of the stereo speakers and the thud of a belt still wound through the loops of a pair of pants hitting the floor. Ed's jeans fell to the floor soon after, and as he stepped out of them he beckoned Rick toward the sofa.

"Now that all of those records I picked out for tonight have played," he said, stroking Rick from head to foot, "it is time for the two greatest one-man bands the world has ever known to make some of their own music. Care to rock the charts with me, darlin'?"

"Oh, yeah," Rick moaned. "I have a feeling this might be one loud song, baby."

"Well, you want to write it here, or in the bedroom?"

"Hmmm. How about a compromise? How 'bout the hallway?" Rick asked as he struggled to remove Ed's now bulging jockeys.

Ed kicked his underwear beneath the coffee table and stood up. "The hallway acoustics should be okay," he said before firmly planting his mouth against Rick's.

Yeah, it's almost over, Ed thought.

There had been times when, relieving himself with only the touch of his own hand, he had longed for his husband so much, it almost hurt. There had been times when, frustrated with the demands of his work, Rick's nieces and nephew, and his own family, he wanted to call Rick and insist he quit that damn job and just *come home*.

But somehow we got through it, he thought before completely surrendering to the moment. Somehow they had muddled through the hard compromise they had made, and surely they could, together, bat away any of the curveballs life decided to pitch toward them from now on.

Hopefully, anyway.

CHAPTER TWO

When Ed awoke on Saturday morning, Rick's side of the bed was empty and breakfast smells were wafting down the hall from the kitchen. Ed stretched under the covers and experienced a pleasant moment of déjà vu. In a way it was like when they were dating. Rick had been living with his sister, Claire, and her kids, but had spent most of his weekends with Ed. Although this current arrangement had been going on for a year and a half, the feeling of waking up in a bed mussed on both sides, with breakfast sounds and scents in the air, seemed somehow fresh.

Absence makes the heart grow fonder. Distance lends enchantment. Ed chuckled to himself as he rolled over to Rick's still-warm side of the bed. *I guess all those tired old words are true. Who knew that living a hundred miles apart during the week would bring the passion and excitement back into our marriage?*

He couldn't help but wonder if all of the current energy between them would fade once Rick was back home for good, but rather than worry about that he decided to enjoy the moment. He slid out of bed, eager to answer the siren call of pancakes and warm maple syrup.

After breakfast Rick walked across the yard for a visit with Mrs. Penfield to see how she was doing and to let her see with her own eyes that he had survived another week in the big city. When he returned, he told Ed that unless something important he didn't know about was going on, he was willing to spend the rest of the weekend at home—just the two of them. Ed agreed. He had spent an exhausting week getting caught up on fall chores for the bulk of his elderly clients, so a quiet weekend seemed in order for both of them.

"I suppose," Rick said with little enthusiasm, "that I should run over to Claire's and see how the kids are doing, but since I haven't heard about any new crises, I guess I can get away with blowing it off."

"Feeling a little guilty, Uncle Rick?" Ed gave him a teasing slap on the ass. "Don't worry. They're too busy with their own stuff to care about what you're doing."

It was true. When Rick first began working in Indianapolis, the children had usually demanded to see him on weekends, but as time went by they had adjusted to him being around less often. As they were all quite fond of Ed, they had easily accepted him as a substitute for Uncle Rick. Ed generally didn't mind being hauled into their squabbles and dramas, but he drew the line at helping Judy with her algebra homework. And as Ed said, they were indeed busy with their own lives these days.

Judy was completely consumed by the teenage soap operas developing in her freshman year. As Ed had predicted, once her braces had come off and she had made it through the horrors of puberty, she had begun showing signs of being a potential teen queen. With high school popularity imminent, her social life had gathered momentum, to the occasional alarm of Claire. More than once Ed had found himself mediating curfew battles between mother and daughter.

Eleven-year-old Josh had become quite a nature fiend through projects in his 4-H club and was now predicting he would be a forest ranger when he grew up. He was happily away for the weekend with his friend Eric's family on an autumn campout in southern Indiana.

And little Jane, who wasn't quite so little anymore, was totally involved with her new best bud, none other than Lesley Ames, Ed's niece. The girls had both landed in the same third-grade classroom at Porterfield Elementary. As a result of their earlier acquaintance through their uncles, they had immediately latched on to each other. These days they were involved in the plans for a huge double wedding ceremony for their Barbies. The only men they seemed to have time for were the dull but necessary plastic grooms.

So the day passed uneventfully. Ed was even spared any emergency calls from his regular clients. By evening, though, the two men, who had become used to being so busy, were both a little restless.

"Nothing but the usual junk on TV." Rick tossed the television listings on the coffee table in disgust. "Almost makes me think about driving to Fort Wayne for a movie."

Ed's eyes lit up. "There's a new *Halloween* movie out."

Rick frowned at him. "I'm not that bored."

Ed shrugged. He had known it would be a long shot at best, considering Rick's distaste for gory horror movies. "Oh, well. Jamie Lee Curtis isn't even in this one, so how good could it be?"

"I know one thing," Rick said as he slumped on the sofa, idly surfing the channels on their new remote-controlled television. "The number one request on our Christmas list this year needs to be a VCR. Surely the price has come down on them, and wouldn't it be great to watch whatever we want, especially on nights like this, when there's nothing but crap on HBO?"

"Yeah," Ed agreed. "They've got lots of movies on tape now at the library you can borrow. I even heard a rumor that a video store might open up here in Porterfield, so we really wouldn't have to go to Fort Wayne to see movies anymore."

During his time in Indianapolis Rick had become used to the new phenomenon of stores that rented out videocassettes. He smiled affectionately at Ed—the smile Ed had always privately referred to as "Rick's warm and tender special." "Well, how 'bout that? A video store in Porterfield! This town may make it into the eighties after all. I guess we made the right decision in staying here."

"I just wish Gordy and Doug had decided to stay." Ed sighed. "I miss spending Saturday nights with them, playing cards and just goofing on each other."

Rick nodded with a sigh of his own. "I know. Me, too. But they're not that far away, and you'll get to see them when you come down to Indy for that closing party. But," he said, getting up from the sofa and heading for the hall, "there's no reason why we can't have a rousing game of our own tonight."

Ed groaned, assuming that within minutes he'd be passing Go and collecting two hundred dollars. He was surprised, therefore, when Rick reappeared with a battered Clue box, the very same game set Ed and his sister, Laurie, had routinely fought over as kids.

"What's this?" Ed asked with raised eyebrows. "You mean we aren't going to be arguing over the B&O Railroad tonight?"

"My life is all about selling and buying property during the week," Rick said firmly, plopping the game on the coffee table. "The last thing I want to think about tonight is collecting rent or going to jail for real estate fraud. I'm much more in the mood for a murder mystery."

"Okay," Ed agreed, opening the box and placing the board on the table. "I guess I can handle that, as long as you don't cheat like Laurie always did. You know the reason the game board is bent is 'cause I hit her with it once."

"You two." Rick snickered as he sorted through the cards. "It's no wonder your mom is as bossy as she is. Riding herd over you two monsters was probably tougher than keeping track of a real herd of cattle."

"Humph," Ed grumbled, just like his mother, Norma. "She was plenty bossy long before the Ed and Laurie wars. I'll tell you one thing: she thought Dr. Spock was the biggest fool to ever publish a book, and she proved it by spanking us with a Ping-Pong paddle whenever we started attacking each other."

"And yet you kept torturing each other, right? Picking on your poor, defenseless younger sister!"

"Defenseless? Ha," Ed said with great indignation. "She was a terrorist before I ever heard the word or knew what it meant. And anyway," he said with a sheepish grin, "Mom never spanked us that hard, just hard enough to let us know she was sick of our nonsense, and it was time to calm down."

"Well, I guess Claire and I weren't any better. I don't know what my mom thought about Dr. Spock, but I do remember her trying to reason with us, and treating us like her students at school. That always worked, but not why she thought. Claire and I hated her treating us like a teacher did, so we'd get over being mad at each other and get mad at her." Rick paused and stared into space for a moment. "Maybe that was the point," he mumbled. "I'll have to ask her about that."

Ed giggled. "Well, we both survived it. And like we always say, we're pretty lucky to have the parents we do, 'cause there are plenty of guys out there like us who don't really have parents anymore 'cause of being gay."

Rick nodded sadly as he handed Ed the dice, and Ed was sure they were both thinking the same thing: wouldn't it be nice if Gordy's parents were like their own?

Rick had become friendly with Gordy Smith when they were both working at the Porterfield Post Office. Ed had known Gordy most of his life. Two years older than Ed, Gordy had been one of the popular jock types in school, and nothing had ever led Ed to believe Gordy was gay until the day he surprised both Ed and Rick by coming out to them. He quickly became a good friend to both of them and managed to surprise them again later that year by beginning a hot and heavy relationship with Doug Morgan, the handsome young mortician who was renting Ed's house on Coleman Street. From that point on the two couples had spent a good deal of social time together—not just Saturday night dinners and card games, but day trips to amusement parks, and one highly successful trip to San Francisco, "Queer Capital U.S.A." as Gordy called it, before Rick began his job in Indianapolis.

Gordy had surprised them one more time when a year later he announced that he and Doug would be moving to Indianapolis as well.

As Ed moved the green game token from the library to the billiard room, he remembered the day last May when Gordy had dropped that bombshell on him.

Ed had been working at his desk in his workshop/office on the ground floor of the carriage house. He was bent over his calculator working on client invoices when Gordy strolled in, beer can in hand, and parked himself on the workbench after first brushing away some sawdust.

Ed wasn't surprised to see him. With Rick in Indianapolis most of the time, Gordy had made it his duty to frequently check up on Ed and hang out with him during the evenings when Doug was busy with wakes at the funeral home. As a result, Ed, who considered Gordy his best friend other than Rick, had found himself growing even closer to Gordy—grateful for his company, his patient ears when Ed felt like bitching about Rick being gone, and the genuine empathetic compassion usually hidden under Gordy's aging-jock bluster and bullshit.

"Hey, what's happenin'?" Ed glanced at Gordy as he reached to turn down the volume on the radio, which was playing "Billie Jean" for what seemed to be the ten millionth time.

Gordy shrugged. "Doug's workin'. Thought I'd see if you were up for some supper."

"Cool. Just let me finish this and let's go out to the P & J for some Spanish dogs or something."

"Okay." Gordy peered over Ed's shoulder. "'Mrs. Nadine West,'" he read, snickering. "Hell, is that old battle-ax still kickin'? If I had to put a bet on the next one of your Old Lady Brigade broads to land on Doug's embalming table, it'd be her."

Ed sighed. "She's gonna outlive us all. She just gets older and weirder. You know how all my old clients have trays full of pill bottles? Hers are all vitamins and herbs and stuff. I don't know what she's doing, but it's working."

He folded Mrs. West's invoice and jammed it into an envelope. "There! That's everybody—Abbott to West." He pushed the envelopes to one side of his desk and pulled down the rolltop lid. "I'll stamp and mail 'em in the morning. I'm hungry, so let's go. Your car or my truck?" He looked expectantly at Gordy.

Gordy pushed Ed back into his chair. "Uh, before we go, I kinda need to tell you something," he said, looking apprehensive.

Oh, God, Ed thought. *Here it comes. It's finally happening. Someone I know is gonna tell me they have that awful AIDS thing...*

"It's not what you're thinkin'," Gordy said, shaking his head. "Shitfire, Ed, don't worry about that until any of us has to."

He settled back on the workbench. "No, I'm fine. Doug's fine. But . . . well, we're moving to Indy."

Ed stared at Gordy, his mouth open. He was glad Gordy had sat him down for this news. "What?" he exclaimed. "What the hell for? Is everyone I know gonna end up moving down there?"

"Now, Ed, don't pretend you didn't see this comin'. You know the kind of stuff Doug and I have been talkin' about ever since that trip to Frisco."

"I know; I know," Ed grumbled. "I guess I was just hoping . . . well, that somehow it'd all work out."

The two men looked at each other, a good deal of unspoken communication passing between them. Gordy folded his arms across his chest. "It hasn't," he said flatly.

Unlike Ed's and Rick's families, neither Gordy's family nor Doug's was aware of their sexual orientation, nor of their serious relationship. With Doug's family located in the western suburbs of Chicago, it didn't seem to matter as much where they were concerned, but Gordy's family was right there in Porterfield, and Mr. Smith's intolerance was no secret. When he had come to the realization that Gordy was friends with both Ed and Rick, he had made endless jokes about limp wrists and butt buddies. However, it was so unthinkable to him that his son, the former football player, could be "one of those goddamned faggots" that Gordy had somehow managed to maintain his friendship with Ed and Rick without being tarred and feathered from the same bucket Mr. Smith reserved for Ed, Rick, and any other gay man. As for Doug, as far as Mr. Smith was concerned, he was just his son's best friend, as in his eyes there was no way an ex-army man would be gay, and being an undertaker wasn't the kind of job a queer would have either.

"Shows how much he knows," Doug had once said, laughing.

But laughter on that subject had become scarce as time went by. Doug had begun lobbying for Gordy to move into his house several months into their relationship, but Gordy had stalled indefinitely, refusing to let go of his apartment on Stratton Avenue. He had confided to Ed on numerous occasions that he wanted very badly to live with Doug but simply wasn't prepared to deal with his father's reaction, or the reaction of anyone else in his family or at the post office.

Ed had no doubt that Gordy could take care of anyone who gave him grief on that subject. He was still big and strong and had the potential to be a seriously mean fightin' machine when he needed to be, but Ed also knew that Gordy didn't want to deal with that kind of crap unless he absolutely had to. Ed, who'd had a few tense moments over the years with the less tolerant citizens of Porterfield, understood that. He also knew that Gordy dreaded losing his father's respect. Mr. Smith's thinking on the subject of sexual orientation was certainly messed up, but in many other ways he'd been a good father.

"Hell, he's old and not in the best of health anymore," Gordy had said to Ed in one late-night conversation. "I s'pose after he's gone I'll regret not bein' honest with him, but I just don't want him goin' to his grave hating my guts. Can you understand that?"

"Yeah, I understand. Everybody has to make their own decisions on that stuff, no matter what all those gay pride people say. It's hard"—Ed sighed—"and I don't think there are any easy answers."

Looking at Gordy, seated on the workbench hunched over as though expecting a blow, Ed lost his desire to protest the move, knowing it wasn't something Gordy really wanted to do. Instead his heart all but broke as he thought of his friend's inner struggle.

"Look, Doug's tired of hidin'," Gordy said heavily. "I can't blame him. I don't think he could come out at Reimer and Bayless and keep his job. And let's face it—he's only twenty-five. He wants to have a job where he can be out, and as much as he loves hangin' out with us old farts, he wants to go out and have the kind of fun guys his age have. Not that kind of fun," Gordy stressed, seeing the skeptical look on Ed's face. "At least I hope not." He shrugged. "There's just lots more for guys like us to do in Indy than there is around here."

"Yeah, lots more bars," Ed sneered.

"There's other stuff, too—lots of clubs and social things. Despite all the crap Rick carries on about where gay bars are concerned, it's not all about sex, especially with all this AIDS shit goin' on. There's just more freedom. You know that. Remember Frisco last year?"

Ed did. He remembered the joy of walking hand in hand with Rick on Castro Street and feeling like part of a majority and not a minority. He'd had his own thoughts about living in such a place, but Porterfield was home, and despite Rick's current job in Indianapolis, it was the place they had decided upon for their future. He just wished it could be the same for Gordy and Doug.

"Does Doug have a job lined up there yet?" he asked quietly.

"Pretty much. He's interviewed at a couple of funeral homes, and there's one he's sure is gonna hire him. It's run by a couple of brothers, and one of 'em's gay, so it should work out great. I've put in for a transfer with the post office, and believe it or not, looks like I'll be workin' for the same office Rick worked at on the north side before he moved up here."

Gordy shrugged again. "I s'pose I should have told you about this sooner, but I didn't want you worryin' about it until it looked like it was really gonna happen. You've had enough on your mind the past year."

Ed slumped in his chair. "Well, crud. Double crud. When are you leaving?"

Gordy reached over and put a hand on his shoulder. "First of July, after Doug's lease on your house is up. He would have told you himself, but he's afraid you're gonna blame him for all of this."

Ed shook his head. "No. I don't blame him. As much as I hate to say it, I really do understand. And you're right: I should have seen it coming. The thing is, Gord, Indy's only a hundred miles down I-69. What makes you think your dad isn't going to put it together when you and Doug both leave town and end up living together *there*?"

Gordy laughed. "For years he's been telling me I need to get out of this burg, that I'll never find a wife here. Hell, he told Doug the same damn thing. So as far as he's concerned, he thinks we're two wild-and-crazy guys, goin' off to the big city to get laid and find some respectable pussy to marry. We'll rent a two-bedroom apartment just in case he and Mom decide to drop in, but I don't think that'll happen too often. By the way, I've noticed Mom givin' me some funny looks. I wonder if she's figured it out. But even if she did, I don't think she'll say anything."

"Okay. Sounds like you got it all figured out, too."

"Yeah, right!" Gordy snorted. "Ed, you know me well enough to know that under this hard shell of mine I'm a total cream puff. I'm scared. I've lived my whole life in this stupid town. Who knows how it'll be down there? Sure, Doug'll be with me, but who knows if that'll last? I love that guy so much, and I know he loves me, but he's still eight years younger than me. Who's to say he'll still love me when he's in that city with all those hot guys runnin' around? I feel like I'm taking the biggest chance I've ever taken, and . . . well, shit, I'm just scared."

Ed got up from his chair and put his arms around his friend. "In the first place, if Doug is stupid enough to let go of you, he's just that. Stupid. And he'll be dead, 'cause I'll kill him."

Gordy squeezed Ed. "Oh, hell, I can't worry about that. It's just life. All guys are cockhounds, and if it happens, I'll deal with it. But you know what? It's kinda like Rick goin' down there for that real estate thing. You guys talked about it, and you decided it was the best thing to do for your future. Doug and me have talked about this, and this is what we're gonna do for our future. It sucks, but Rick bein' gone so much sucks, too."

"Yeah, and I'll be here alone, kind of like I was before Rick moved here. It almost makes me feel like I'm going backward, not forward."

"Ah, bud, we'll still be gettin' together—lots of times, especially with Rick down there so much." Gordy increased his grip on Ed. "I know what you mean, though. All of this shit—movin' and a new job and everything—the hardest part is gonna be missin' you. You're the best friend I've ever had, Ed," Gordy whispered, sounding a little choked up. "Finding you and Rick when I did, well, sometimes I think it saved my life. You probably don't want to hear it right now, but I wouldn't have Doug if it wasn't for you."

Ed giggled weakly. "Oh, you probably would have stumbled over each other eventually."

"No. Well, maybe, but I would have never had the guts to make a move on him if it hadn't've been for all the time I spent with you guys. And I don't think I'd'a allowed myself to fall in love with him the way I did unless I saw how it all worked out for you and Rick. You know how I used to say you guys are an inspiration? Well, you are. I may be moving away, but you guys are still my best buds, especially you. I need you to keep remindin' me that things work out sometimes."

Ed buried his face in Gordy's T-shirt. "You asshole. You're gonna make me cry."

"Beat you to it." Gordy sniffed, squeezing Ed even tighter. "Promise you'll always be my best bud?"

"I promise," Ed choked out in a big gulp.

And then they both sat down on the workbench, knocking over Gordy's empty beer can, and had themselves a good cry.

"Mrs. White in the dining room with the revolver," Rick sang out in triumph. He peeked in the envelope. "Ha! I was right. I win," he added smugly.

Ed threw his cards on the table. "Yeah, you did. I guess my mind wasn't really on it. Let's play again, and this time I'm gonna concentrate."

"What's on your mind? You worrying about Gordy and Doug?"

"Yeah, a little bit. I haven't even talked to Gord since I went down there last month to spend my birthday with you guys. You see them more than I do. Are they doin' okay?"

Rick shrugged. "Yeah, sure."

Ed looked at him with suspicion.

"Really," Rick said, sorting the cards. "Look, I've been busy with that damn O'Connor deal, so I haven't really seen much of them either. And like I said, after that stupid closing party Frank O'Connor insists on having, the party where I have been commanded to show up with the *faaa-bu-lous husband* I keep talking about, we'll go over to their place and spend the rest of the weekend in that unused second bedroom of theirs. We'll have two whole days for you to study them, interrogate poor ole Gordy, and probably make 'em glad they moved away."

Ed sat back on the floor, leaned on his hands, and pouted. "You make me sound like my mom."

Rick grinned at him. "Well, sometimes the apple doesn't fall too far from the tree. Don't worry, baby. A big move like that is an adjustment for anyone. I oughta know. But I'm sure they're okay, and once I'm back here for good, I'll be missing them as much as you do."

"Still," Ed said thoughtfully, "I keep remembering that weekend we helped them move down, how hot and miserable it was, and how tense Gordy was. Doug, too, for that matter."

"The whole summer was hot and miserable," Rick grumbled, shuffling the cards. "And I spent most of it in dress clothes. Boy, did I miss my mailman shorts! What I remember is you playing that damned 'Too Shy' song over and over in the truck. I was about ready to rip the cassette out of the tape deck."

Ed giggled, remembering. "It was my favorite song of the whole summer. Be glad you weren't here to hear me play it over and over on the stereo. Hush, huuuush," he added just to tweak Rick.

Rick rolled his eyes. "What did I yell at you that day? 'That your new theme song, shy boy?' Gawd, what a day that was. I guess we were all a little tense from the heat and having to move them into a new place so far away." He dealt the cards. "You wanna be Mr. Green again?"

Ed reached across the board for the red token. "Nah, I think I'll be Miss Scarlet this time. Nothing shy about her."

"Hmmm. Well, I have to admit, there are definitely times and places when you are not in the least bit shy, stud, and I may just have you prove it after this game."

"Really?" Ed mock-gasped. "Twice in one weekend?"

"Baby, by the time I have to go back to Indy, we may be up to three or four."

Rick put his cards facedown on the table and reached for Ed's hand. "Maybe it's 'cause I'm getting close to the end of this whole thing, but I've just been missing you like crazy lately. And not just when you're naked either. I've just been missing you, period, so I guess Mr. Greedy here wants as much of you as I can get before I have to leave."

Ed looked at Rick's hand on his and moved his foot under the table so it was touching Rick's. "No problem," he said with a grin. "You can have as much of me as you want."

What he didn't say was how relieved he was to hear how Rick felt. Yes, he shared Gordy's concerns about young, handsome Doug running around a city filled with hot, available men. What he had never allowed himself to say out loud, though, was that occasionally he worried about his own husband spending so much time alone in such a place as well. Logically he knew better than to worry, but Ed was human, and any gay man in his situation would worry. As Gordy had more or less said months ago, it was natural to worry, and very natural for guys to screw around. He couldn't really imagine a man as honorable as Rick doing such a thing, but . . .

He quickly glanced at Rick's eyes and easily saw, as he always did, the love Rick had for him. He'd been seeing that love in Rick's eyes for three years now. It reassured him, and he turned his mind to the game, determined to win this time.

All in all, though, he would be very glad when Rick was home to stay.

CHAPTER THREE

On Monday morning Ed was up early, as he usually was on Mondays, to see Rick off for the week. Ed and Jett sat on the edge of the bed watching Rick place a couple of books in his overnight bag. "Did I forget anything?" Rick mumbled as he looked distractedly around the room.

"Just this." Ed got up, put his arms around him, and gave him a soft, lingering kiss.

"Oh, I hadn't forgot that," Rick said, returning the kiss. "I was just saving the best for last, as they say."

Ed picked a piece of lint from the shoulder of Rick's suit jacket. "I know you're looking forward to being done with all of this in a few weeks, but are you going to miss it? The job, being in Indy, and all that?"

Rick gave that some thought. "Oh, a little bit. It's been one hell of a ride learning the real estate game, and Walt has really been good to me. I'm not in the least bit worried about going to work for Vince next month with everything I know now." He laughed. "Of course, sometimes I miss being a mailman, too. I don't have any regrets, though. Just think: when I get my commission from this last sale, I'll be able to live easily on the draw income Vince'll pay me, and we'll still have enough money put aside to buy some wreck of a house here in town that we can fix up and sell. Remember that day at Spruce Lake when we first talked about doing that? It's really happening! These past two years have been hard, but it's all falling into place, baby."

"All because of your hard work."

Rick gave Ed an affectionate knock against his head. "Your hard work, too. I never, ever could have survived any of this without knowing you were here taking care of everything and everyone. We've both worked hard, and now it's going to pay off.

"Still," Rick continued with a thoughtful frown, "I guess I will miss being so open. So many of the clients I've handled for Walt have been gay, I've been able to be completely myself. You know, talk about you and our life. Now I'll have to be a lot more professional, not quite as chatty as I've been with these guys."

"Even Frank O'Connor?" Ed snickered.

"Shit, who can get a word in edgewise with that motormouthed queen?" Rick shook his head. "I'm grateful for his trust fund and that huge house he's buying, but I definitely will not miss him. I just hope he doesn't back out of this deal at the last minute. I'm sure I'll spend most of this week answering his phone calls and holding his hand until it's all done."

"Maybe he has a crush on you," Ed teased.

Rick shuddered. "Well, it ain't mutual." He looked at his watch. "I s'pose I should hit the road. Wanna walk me downstairs?"

Both Ed and Jett accompanied Rick down to the garage. Jett wandered off to sniff the white mums blooming on the side of the carriage house while Ed watched Rick get comfortably settled in his car for the long drive.

Ed leaned in the open window, straightened Rick's tie, and smiled at him. "I love you, darlin'. Be careful, okay? And say hi to your mom and dad." In Ed's opinion, the most surprising aspect of Rick taking the job in Indianapolis was the fact that he was actually staying at his parents' house during the week.

Rick's warm and tender special was glowing as he cranked the ignition. "I will. I love you, too, baby. Always. I'll call you tonight, okay?"

"Okay."

Ed watched Rick back carefully down the driveway to Race Street. He paused at the corner, then turned west onto Spruce. The car's wheels kicked up a puddle of rust-colored oak leaves as it picked up speed and moved out of sight.

Ed waved at Mrs. Penfield, who appeared briefly at the kitchen window in the main house, obviously preparing to settle at the table with her coffee and the Fort Wayne morning newspaper. He shivered a bit as he gazed across the garden, wishing he had grabbed his jacket on the way out. There was a definite autumn nip in air. He thought about putting away the lawn furniture for the season, wondered whether he should get busy planting the new tulip bulbs that had arrived from Holland, and frowned at Jett, who seemed to be chewing on the mum stalks.

"If that makes you barf, you better do it outside, bud," he called to the cat.

Jett gave Ed a disdainful look and marched around the side of the carriage house, where he could do his nibbling without observation.

"As if I didn't spend enough money on cat food," Ed mumbled to himself.

He tried to refocus on lawn chores but found himself picturing Rick heading out of Porterfield in the Regal, making his way across Stratton County to I-69. Ed had gotten so used to Rick leaving on Monday mornings that he usually didn't give it much thought once he was gone, but for some reason today he was feeling a little wistful. He hoped for both his sake and Rick's that the O'Connor deal would go through on schedule. Despite everything that had happened in the past year and a half, Ed somehow felt as though their lives had been on hold since that spring day Rick left for his first week in Indianapolis. He was definitely ready for Rick to return home once and for all and begin his job with Cummings Realty.

It had been a warm, sunny day in early May when Rick left for the first time. The lilac bushes along the driveway had been in full bloom, and Ed had carefully clipped and packed a fragrant bouquet for Rick to give to his mother.

He fussed with the flowers more than necessary as Rick wandered from the apartment to his car to make sure he had everything he needed. Both of them were nervous about this new adventure Rick was beginning, but neither one of them would cop to it.

Ed had accompanied Rick on all of his preliminary excursions to Indianapolis; had frequently met Walt Granger and liked him, and had been secretly pleased when the first thing Rick had placed in his new office was a picture of Ed he had taken in San Francisco. He had helped Rick reestablish his old bedroom at his parents' house, and had actually been the one to negotiate that particular miracle.

Rick had been dead set against staying with his parents, John and Vera, because of their earlier objections to his decision to leave the postal service for a career in real estate. Feeling a bit like Henry Kissinger, Ed had managed to get all of the "battling Bentons," as he called them, to see reason. John and Vera had come around and were actually impressed by Rick's new job, and Ed had convinced Rick that their rent-free offer of a place to stay was the best solution to his housing problem.

Everything had fallen into place, and now it was time for Rick to leave. Finished with the flowers, Ed turned around from the kitchen counter to see Rick stroking the cat as he gazed out the living room window. Rick turned to find Ed's eyes upon him and gave him a halfhearted smile as he hugged the cat.

"'Bye, Jett. You behave while I'm gone, okay?" He gently set the cat on the sill of the open window. Jett immediately began his morning wash, obviously unconcerned about Rick's leave-taking, unlike Ed.

Ed and Rick looked at each other from across the room. There seemed to be so much to say, but surely it had all been said in the six months since Rick had first received this job offer. Ed almost winced as he remembered his furious initial reaction to the idea of Rick going to work in Indianapolis. Oh, they had made up from that fight a long time ago, and Rick wouldn't be leaving today if they weren't in one hundred percent agreement about it, but Ed knew Rick well enough to know that the only thing keeping him from walking down the stairs and getting into his car was his fear that Ed was still unhappy with the situation.

"I guess it's time for me to go," Rick said tentatively.

Ed nodded. "Yeah, I know. There's just something I need you to hear first."

Rick looked puzzled as Ed walked across the room to the record cabinet his father had made for him so many years before. Ed slid open one of the doors, pulled out a 45, and carefully placed it on the turntable.

Rick's warm and tender special spread across his face. "'One Man Band,' baby?" he asked, referring to the Three Dog Night record that was "their" song. "For good luck?"

"No." Ed started the turntable. "There's something I needed to say to you before you leave, but I couldn't seem to think of the right words. Well, it finally hit me that John Sebastian wrote exactly what I want to say to you years ago."

Rick shook his head as the Lovin' Spoonful's "Darling Be Home Soon" began to play. "Oh, baby, I will be. Home soon, that is."

"I know. But there's more."

Ed put his arms around Rick and held him close as the song continued. When it reached the final verse, Ed whispered the lyrics to Rick as they played.

Go
And beat your crazy head against the sky
Try
And see beyond the houses and your eyes
It's ok to shoot the moon

"It really is okay to shoot the moon, darlin'," Ed whispered. "I needed you to know that if I'm not there in person, I'm there with you in spirit, and you have my total blessing. I'll be cheering you on the whole way and the whole time."

Rick drew a shuddering breath. "I am not going to cry. I am not going to cry," he murmured. "Ah, baby, I love you so much. Thank you. Thank you for loving me, and for agreeing to all of this. I wouldn't give a damn about any of it if it wasn't for you and the life we have together, and the thought of spending the rest of my life with you. I just want all of our dreams to come true, and I'll work like hell at this so it can happen for both of us."

"I know, darlin'. I know. And I love you, too, more than I can say."

They stood there together, in each other's arms, eyes closed, and quietly allowed their mutual love to strengthen them both for the hard work and solitude of the weeks and months ahead of them. Ed's hand reached under Rick's shirt collar, and he was comforted by the links of the gold chain he had placed around Rick's neck as a sign of his love and commitment. It was still there, and Rick would indeed be home soon. Ed was nervous, even a little scared, but he knew his darlin' would be home as soon as he could be.

Rick gave another shuddery sigh and slowly stepped away from Ed as the record began to play for the third time. He gave Ed a hopeful grin, went to the kitchen for the package of lilacs, and headed for the door.

"No, baby," he said quietly as Ed went to follow him. "Let's leave it like this. I'll be home Friday night. I promise."

And with that he was through the door and down the stairs. Ed turned his back to the window as he heard the car roar to life below him. It wasn't until the sound of the car had faded away that he went to the window and petted the cat, listening to the end of the song one more time.

So darling
My darling be home soon
I couldn't bear to wait an extra minute if you dawdled
My darling be home soon
It's not just these few hours but I've been waiting since I toddled
For the great relief of having you to talk to

Ed was jolted back to the present by the sound of an ancient pickup truck coming to a halt in the driveway. The driver's-side door squeaked open, and Effie Maude Sanders, Mrs. Penfield's housekeeper, alighted. She pulled off a white windbreaker as she glanced at Ed.

"'Lo there, Ed," she said in her rusty voice. "You okay? Looked like you were a million miles away."

"Yeah. I was just thinking about all the stuff I need to do around here."

Effie Maude folded her jacket over her arm and gave Ed a shrewd look through her bifocals. She had been Mrs. Penfield's housekeeper for more than forty years, and in the past two of them she had come to consider looking after Ed and Rick as much her responsibility as tending to Mrs. Penfield.

Counting Effie Maude, Mrs. Penfield, and his own genuine mother, Norma, Ed sometimes felt he had three mothers instead of one.

"Rick gone already?"

"Yeah."

She nodded. "Well, he'll be done with that big city foolishness soon; then you'll probably get tired of havin' him underfoot."

Ed grinned. "I suppose."

Effie Maude rearranged the white-and-blue-striped housedress around her decidedly ample frame, and touched a hand to her head to make sure her gray hair was in its usual untidy bun.

"Well, I need to get to the warsh," she announced. "Anything you want me to throw in the machine?"

"Hmmm?" Thinking of mothers had reminded Ed that Norma had called the night before and insisted on seeing him first thing in the morning. Norma, an early riser, was probably at home tapping her foot and wondering where on earth Ed was. "No, no laundry for us. I got it done yesterday. I need to get over to Mom's," he called over his shoulder as he headed for the carriage-house door.

"Your cat's eatin' the flowers again," she hollered after him.

"I know; I know," he muttered as he hit the stairs at a dead run.

A few minutes later Ed's new-to-him, dark blue Chevy pickup was rolling to a stop in front of his childhood home two blocks away on East Walnut Street. As he was getting out of the truck he saw, much to his surprise, Laurie's car pulling up behind his truck.

Laurie got out of her sedan and shot Ed a suspicious look. She was dressed for her secretarial job at the law offices of Mason and Schultz in downtown Porterfield. Ed returned her look of suspicion. Something was definitely up if they had both been summoned.

"All right," Laurie called as she walked toward him. "What's she up to now?"

Ed looked down at her. Laurie was short like their mother but dark haired like their late father. "Hell if I know. She just called and told me to be here this morning."

Laurie frowned. "Me, too. I'm taking a very early coffee break so I can attend this royal command meeting."

They looked at each other silently for a moment. "You don't suppose," Laurie said slowly, "that something's wrong with her, do you? Remember how the whole family got called out to the farm when we were kids to be told Grandma Beale was dying of cancer?"

"Oh, I don't think so," Ed said uncertainly. "I mean, as often as we see her, wouldn't we know if she wasn't feeling good? It's not like she really keeps anything to herself."

Laurie's face brightened. "Maybe it's Clyde." She grabbed Ed's wrist. "Maybe he popped the question!"

Ed guffawed. "Now you're really reachin', Shortshit! She's been keeping a ten-foot pole between them ever since he came to town."

Ed had met Clyde Croasdale two years earlier. He had become good friends with the older man when they discovered a mutual enjoyment of woodworking. Ed had been astonished to learn shortly after meeting Clyde that he had grown up on a farm near Norma's rural childhood home. Although she adamantly denied it, Ed and Laurie had learned that Norma had had quite a schoolgirl crush on the handsome farm boy from down the road.

Clyde was now a widower, living with his older spinster sister Claudine in Porterfield after an early retirement from the Milwaukee Police Department. With Ed and Clyde spending so much time together conferring on and sharing so many woodworking projects, it was inevitable that Clyde's path would cross Norma's. Sure enough, he had taken a gentle interest in the widow Stephens, much to the secret delight of Ed and Laurie. Whenever either one of them had the nerve to ask about him, though, Norma routinely stated that there was nothing, absolutely *nothing*, going on between her and Clyde Croasdale, and they needed to get their minds out of the gutter and back on their own disorganized lives.

Ed and Laurie both missed their father, who had been gone more than five years now, but they enjoyed the idea of Norma having some occasional male companionship, especially since the man in question was Clyde, a man they both liked and respected. However, if Clyde and Norma had spent any time together other than for a restaurant meal or some other very public social event, it was news to Ed.

"Well, you know she always refuses to talk to me about him when I ask," Laurie said. She wouldn't admit it, but as far as Ed was concerned, Laurie was just as nosy as their mother. "Maybe they've been hiding out in Fort Wayne or something so we don't know what they're up to."

"You've been watching *All My Children* too long." Ed rolled his eyes. "I see enough of Clyde to know nothing has changed. I mean," he added doubtfully, "he'd tell me, wouldn't he?"

"Maybe not. Maybe she swore him to secrecy. I'll bet—"

Laurie was cut off by the sound of the storm door slamming shut behind them. Ed and Laurie both turned to see Norma standing on the front porch, hands on hips, glaring at them.

"What are you whispering about out there?" she barked at them. "Honestly, the sight of the two of you with your heads together on the front sidewalk? What will the neighbors think? Probably that I've jumped my trolley tracks and you're figuring out how to haul me off to the nut barn!"

Ed's hands involuntarily went to his own hips. "Well, *honestly*, Mom! Have you jumped your trolley tracks? What's this little secret family meeting about, anyway?"

"Oh, get in the house. Both of you. Come on!" She shooed them both through the front door and down the hall to the kitchen like a couple of vexatious chickens. Laurie poured herself a cup of coffee while Ed headed for the pumpkin-shaped cookie jar that had sat on the counter next to the refrigerator since he was a boy. Norma slapped his hand away from it.

"You don't need to be eating cookies first thing in the morning," she grumbled.

"Laurie's having coffee," he whined; "don't I get anything?"

"Well," Laurie began in the smart-ass voice she had always used with him when they were teenagers, "if you'd *learn* to drink coffee like the *rest* of us grownups . . ."

"Don't start with me," he said, raising a threatening hand, "'cause whatever you start, I'll finish."

"I'll be the one to finish both of you," Norma stated as she poured Ed a glass of orange juice. "Now, sit down and hush up. Drink this." She slammed the juice on the table in front of Ed. "That's more than enough sugar to keep you happy."

"So, what's up, Mom?" Laurie sipped her coffee. "Now I can honestly say I'm having a coffee break, but I do need to get back to work."

Norma sat at the table in her accustomed place. She sipped slowly from her own cup of coffee while Ed and Laurie fidgeted with impatience. "I have an announcement to make," she said after a very theatrical throat clearing.

"We're all ears." Ed sighed, wishing she'd get on with it.

Norma glared at him. "I have decided," she said in her most dignified tone, "to go back to work. I have a job starting tomorrow."

Ed and Laurie stared at her. "*What?*" they both exclaimed.

"Is it such a surprise that someone might want to employ your mother?" Norma assumed a wounded expression.

"Mom, you haven't had a job outside of the house since you got pregnant with me," Ed said. "So why all of a sudden do you want to go to work?"

"Yeah," Laurie added. "You've never said one word about getting a job. Of course we're surprised."

A troubling thought occurred to Ed. "Mom," he said uneasily, "this doesn't have anything to do with money, does it?"

"Of course not!" she snapped. "Your father certainly didn't intend to die so young, but he had already seen to making sure I'd be taken care of if anything happened to him. You just get that thought right out of your head, young man. I don't need your money. Or yours." She glared at Laurie as well.

"So then why go to work?" Laurie wanted to know.

Norma traced the pattern on her coffee cup with a finger. "I'm bored," she finally said in a soft voice.

Ed and Laurie looked at each other across the table. "Oh," they said, more or less together.

Ed glanced at his mother as she stared into her coffee cup, a rather wistful expression on her face. He noticed, perhaps really noticed for the first time, the gray roots and the wrinkles that betrayed her fifty-four years of age, despite the Miss Clairol and the Merle Norman makeup. He thought of her living alone in this house for the past five years, missing their father as his children did. He suddenly realized that her interference in his and Laurie's lives may have had less to do with her take-charge attitude than with loneliness and, yes, maybe even boredom.

"So where are you going to work, Mom?" he asked quietly.

Norma looked up and smiled. "I'm going right back where I left off in 1952," she said proudly. "Right back to Patterson's Bakery."

"How did that come about?" Laurie asked, looking at her in wonder.

"Well, you know that place just hasn't been the same since Old Man Patterson died," Norma began, sounding more like her usual self. "That son of his?" She snorted. "Why, he couldn't run a pushcart, let alone a bakery. So Mrs. Patterson came out of retirement and kicked him to the curb, where he belongs. Spends all his time over at that tacky house he bought near the country club, playing in his yard while that cheap second wife of his plays golf. Have you seen it? Humph! That place looks like one of those newfangled cemeteries. Patterson Memorial Gardens, they ought to call it."

Ed mustered his patience to get her back on track. "So what does all this have to do with you?"

"Well, I stopped in there a while back to see if they still had those good caramel rolls your father liked so much. I just got hungry for one of them, and I wondered if that worthless son had managed to wreck all their recipes. I got to talking with Mrs. Patterson, and she told me everything that had been going on, and how she got Midge Boylan's daughter in there to manage the place. Now, there's a girl with a head on her shoulders. I asked Mrs. Patterson why she was still working if she didn't have to, and she said to me, 'Norma, after all these years of being covered in flour, I just can't seem to sit at home and watch *Good Morning America* when I should be baking. I'll probably be here until they carry me out feet first.'

"That got me to thinking. You know she always was the real brains of that place. We got to talking about how she was still using some of my mother's cookie recipes, and how much she and the old man had liked the work I did for them, and how sorry they were when I left. So without giving myself time to really think about it, I said, 'Mardell'—daring to call her by her first name, something I would have never done thirty years ago—'Mardell,' I said, 'how would you like me to come back and bake some of those cookies for you?' 'Why, Norma, I think that's a wonderful idea.' So I start tomorrow."

"So how were the caramel rolls?" Ed had gotten hungry for one himself just thinking about how their father had enjoyed them.

Laurie groaned. "Is *that* all you can think about?" She shook her head at him, and then turned to Norma. "I think that's great, Mom. Congratulations!"

"Yeah, congratulations," Ed hurriedly added.

"Humph! You're just not going to be happy until you have something that'll rot your teeth this morning, are you?" Norma got up from the table and handed him two sugar cookies from the jar. He smirked at Laurie in triumph.

"What about me?" Laurie asked Norma indignantly.

"At almost thirty years old with two pregnancies behind you, *you* need to watch your figure, Laurie Margaret!"

"Yeah, Laurie *Margaret*," Ed taunted her.

Laurie gave him a disgusted look. "Beats being called Shortshit."

Norma gasped. "Edward, are you still using that filthy nickname for your sister? I thought I told you when you were fifteen that you were never to call her that again!" She rapped him across the back of the head the same way she had sixteen years earlier.

"Owww . . . ouch!" Ed put a hand to his wounded head.

"Serves you right. Maybe you'll learn your lesson this time. Honestly, the two of you will send me to my grave yet."

Ed rubbed the back of his head. "I suppose now if Rick and I want chocolate-chip cookies we'll have to go to the bakery and buy them like everyone else."

"Oh, of course not. I'm still your mother, and I'll still do what mothers do for their children. If you behave," she added with a stern look at both of them. "But you know," she said in a softer tone, "with everything going so well with your job, Laurie, and Todd making a name for himself at the bank, and both of your children in school full-time, and with Rick coming home for good soon, I just feel like I need something else to do other than keep an eye on everyone."

"We're fine, Mom; everyone's doing great." Laurie laid a reassuring hand on Norma's. "Don't worry about us."

"Don't worry! Humph. I'll be worrying about you two fools until the day I'm lying under a stone that reads: HERE LIES NORMA BEALE STEPHENS—DIED BECAUSE HER CHILDREN DROVE HER CRAZY!"

CHAPTER FOUR

Ed was sprawled on the sofa that evening after a busy afternoon of handyman appointments. When the phone rang he lowered the volume on *Wheel of Fortune*, sure it was Rick making his usual daily check-in.

Ed's news about Norma's new job made for lively conversation. When that topic had been thoroughly discussed, Ed said, "Since I've got a quiet afternoon tomorrow, Clyde's coming over. He's going to let me help him make that rocking horse he's giving his granddaughter for Christmas."

"That sounds like fun."

"Yeah, since our nieces and nephews are a little old for rocking horses, it'll be something different for me. Oh, and this morning Laurie told me Clyde's son's divorce is final, and it looks like he really is moving to Porterfield to go to work with Mason and Schultz."

"How 'bout that?" Rick laughed. "A newly single man moving to town, *and* a lawyer. That should jack up makeup sales and hair appointments in town."

"Oh, it already has. Laurie said that secretary in the investment firm next door has already joined Weight Watchers and frosted her hair."

"Good timing for me, too. With your connection to Clyde, maybe I can sell the guy a house."

"That's true. I hadn't thought of that. I'll be sure and say something to Clyde tomorrow. I think that's all the Porterfield news. What have you been up to all day?"

"Oh, nothing out of the ordinary. Shuffled through some paperwork, and I showed a couple of houses to one of Walt's new clients."

"No Frank O'Connor today?"

Rick snickered. "Nope. He has a tendency to spend Mondays recovering from the weekend. He'll probably call tomorrow, once his hangover's gone. I tell you, though; that'll actually be a nice change of pace from today. That new client of Walt's? I don't think she has any intention of buying anything. She's just some bored society matron who tours houses the way other women kill time at Ayres trying on dresses they'll never buy."

As Rick continued to describe the woman and her irrelevant questions about the houses he had shown her, Ed's eyes drifted back to the television, where Vanna White was perkily turning over several *L*s on the puzzle board. "*All Creatures Great and Small*," he suddenly blurted, pleased to have come up with the answer before the contestant.

There was an abrupt ringing silence on the phone. "Edward, are you watching *Wheel of Fortune* again?" There was both amusement and disgust in Rick's voice.

"Busted," Ed said with a sigh. Although Ed and Rick were compatible in many ways, they were definitely at odds when it came to game shows and television in general. With Rick gone so much, Ed had slid back into the habit of watching a good deal of television. He didn't talk about it much, assuming what Rick didn't know wouldn't hurt him (or irritate him), but Rick knew Ed well enough to suspect what was going on while he was away.

"Oh, well. At least all the As Mrs. Penfield gave you in English are coming in handy for something," Rick said in that slightly superior tone he occasional used that provoked no small amount of irritation in Ed as well. "I guess it's a good thing I'm coming home soon so I can get you away from the tube and back to some good reading."

"Yeah," Ed replied without much enthusiasm. He was tempted to tell Rick that he and Laurie had wasted a few minutes that morning discussing *All My Children* and whether Greg and Jenny would ever come to their senses and get back together, but he didn't really want to give Rick a reason to continue his lecture. *Scarecrow and Mrs. King* was coming on soon.

A few minutes later they finished their conversation. Ed returned the TV volume to its earlier level just as some poor bastard with a pile of money in front of him hit Bankrupt.

"Them's the breaks, buddy," Ed muttered at the TV as he got up to let the cat out.

Ed was tidying his workshop when Clyde arrived the next day. Clyde deposited the wood he had purchased at Rankin's on the workbench, and together the two men happily studied the sketch Clyde had drawn for the proposed rocking horse. Ed thoroughly enjoyed spending time with the older man. Clyde's easygoing attitude and general patience with Ed's reticence to kick on the saw and tear into a new piece of wood reminded Ed a good deal of his father. Although Clyde bore no resemblance to the late Tim Stephens, Ed could see the qualities they shared that had obviously drawn Norma to both of them.

Clyde Croasdale, shorter than Ed, was a powerfully built man in his late fifties. There was still evidence of an earlier rugged handsomeness in his rather careworn face. Clyde had seen and experienced a lot in his life. He'd become a policeman after his stint in World War II, and his early retirement was due in part to a bullet wound in his left knee that still troubled him from time to time. His wife had died after a short and dirty battle with cancer three years earlier, and although his three daughters seemed to be doing fine, Ed knew Clyde worried about his son, Matt, whose marriage to a woman neither Clyde nor his late wife had particularly liked had finally ended in an acrimonious divorce. Ed hoped Matt's decision to move to Porterfield would bring some comfort to Clyde.

Ed was certainly comforted by Clyde's easy acceptance of Ed's relationship with Rick. When they had begun spending time in each other's workshops, Ed had worried whether the fact that he was gay would end their budding friendship. One day, when they were sanding the wood for a cedar chest Clyde was building for his sister, Ed had decided to be honest about it, timidly telling Clyde that Rick was more than just his roommate.

Clyde's slow and steady strokes with the sandpaper never faltered as he nodded. "I thought so," he said. "From what I've seen of Rick, he seems to be a good man. Considering the problems so many people have these days, I'd say you're both pretty fortunate."

"It doesn't bother you?"

Clyde put down his sandpaper and stared into space for a moment. "Ed, with everything I've seen in my life, between the war and working for a big-city police department, the last thing I'm going to do is waste time judging people for who they love."

He shook his head as he returned to his work. "I remember one night about ten years ago. My partner and I got a call to go to one of those bars fellas like you go to. There was a young man stretched out unconscious in the alley next to some garbage cans. He was a bloody mess because some punks had jumped him. They didn't take his wallet. They just beat the hell out of him because that's what they did for fun, ambush faggots. I remember looking at the poor boy's face, covered in blood, his eyes swollen shut, thinking how that could have been Matt lying there if he were different. I wondered about that boy's parents, and how I didn't want to be the one to call them and tell them their son had been beaten nearly to death because some stupid bastards thought it was a good way to prove how manly they were.

"I try not to dwell too much on all the human ugliness I've seen, but it does get to me still, even today. I'd rather think about the good I've seen, and you're a good man, Ed, just like Rick. So don't worry about it. Just keep doing what you're doing. But watch your back. I'd hate to see some jerks do to you what they did to that boy."

Ed was moved by Clyde's acceptance, and by the thought of that man who had been so savagely attacked—a man who could have easily been Ed, Rick, Gordy, Doug, or any other gay man he knew. He nodded as he picked up a fresh piece of sandpaper. "I do. And I will. Even though things have gone good for Rick and me here in Porterfield, I know we're not totally safe. I guess we'll always be watching our backs."

Clyde put an arm around Ed's shoulders and gave him a quick squeeze. That had ended any further discussion on the subject.

Ed and Clyde had made a good beginning on the rocking horse when Mrs. Penfield appeared at the carriage-house doorway. "I thought I heard that saw buzzing," she said with a grin. Although Mrs. Penfield moved very slowly from the crippling arthritis she struggled with, her hearing and other senses remained keen.

"What do you think?" Ed showed her Clyde's sketch.

The old woman nodded. "Very nice indeed. I've no doubt your granddaughter will cherish it, and no doubt her own children will cherish it as well someday. The two of you are a wonderful team." She beamed at them.

"We do our best, ma'am," Clyde said modestly, brushing sawdust from his hands.

"Well, after all of this hard work, perhaps I could interest you gentlemen in some supper. Effie Maude has a chicken baking, and there will surely be more than I need. Clyde, I finally unearthed those letters George Junior sent me from Korea." Mrs. Penfield's only son had died during the Korean conflict. "I've been meaning to show them to you for months."

Clyde smiled. "I would like to read those, and I'm certainly not dumb enough to turn down Effie Maude's cooking. Claudine has a women's society meeting tonight, so it would have been a TV dinner for this man."

"I'm in, too," Ed said, glancing at his watch, "but right now I need to get over to Mrs. Tucker's house. I promised to show her how to run her new microwave." He shook his head and sighed. "Right now she's afraid to touch it, let alone try to cook anything."

Mrs. Penfield chuckled. "I must admit, I understand her reluctance. For those of us who remember baking with stoves that didn't even have thermostats, today's technology is both exciting and a bit alarming."

"It's not that hard," Ed grumbled, putting his tools away. "But I have to admit, what with microwaves, answering machines, and VCRs, my older clients are keeping my income steady. If everyone starts buying home computers, I'll probably be set for life."

Clyde turned toward Ed with a teasing grin. "What do you think about these newfangled CD things they have for music now, Ed?"

Ed shrugged. "I don't know. Probably just a fad, like eight-tracks. I can't imagine anything replacing records."

Mrs. Penfield chuckled. "Considering your sizable record collection, I certainly hope not."

"Have I been playing the stereo too loud again?" Ed blushed.

Mrs. Penfield laughed outright. "Oh, no. As I've said in the past, it doesn't really bother me. However, there were days this past summer when I was in the garden that I would puzzle a bit over some song you kept playing, a tune with a young man crooning about being 'too shy.'"

"Aw, crud, am I the only one who likes that song?" Ed muttered. The sound of affectionate laughter from both Clyde and Mrs. Penfield followed him as he walked to his truck.

As he crossed Main Street on his way to Mrs. Tucker's house, Ed reflected on the work he had completed with Clyde on the rocking horse. The time he spent in his workshop was a wonderful distraction from his handyman work and life's general worries. It had become a pleasant and satisfying hobby for him, but nothing more than that.

Since the early days of their relationship, Rick had strongly encouraged Ed to use his talent for woodworking as a possible career in the hopes of scaling back on his handyman services. Ed had agreed at the time. As Rick began his own work in changing careers from mail carrier to real estate agent, Ed had taken his father's tools and re-created Tim's basement workshop in the carriage house. He had started slowly with some Christmas gifts of his own—a spice rack for Laurie; a dollhouse for Lesley, and a bookcase/storage unit for her brother Bobby and one for Josh as well. Rick had observed this activity with enthusiasm and continued to nag Ed about attempting some paying work. In fact, Rick had told Eunice Ames about the cedar chest Clyde and Ed had constructed for Claudine, and Eunice had called Ed, imploring him to create one for her as well, offering a handsome price for the finished product.

So Ed had bought the necessary supplies, and with Clyde's help had gone to work. One bitterly cold winter day Ed had taken care of the snow-removal chores for his elderly clients and had come home determined to do nothing more than crawl under a blanket on the couch and relax. However, the deadline for that cedar chest weighed heavily on him. He bundled up against the chill that no amount of heat seemed to dispel from the ground floor of the carriage house and slowly went to work. As he cranked the volume on the portable stereo louder and louder to distract himself from his irritation with the whole situation, he discovered an important fact: the work simply wasn't any fun for him when he had to do it, only when he wanted to do it.

He stood there, level in hand, while Stevie Wonder's "That Girl" blared from the radio. He pondered the truth of his thoughts and recalled the times he had asked his father why he didn't quit his job at Marsden Electric and do woodworking and carpentry jobs full-time. Tim had always said he didn't think he was good enough to make a career of it, but Ed suddenly realized something else. The fun Tim had with his projects was just that—fun. Making an actual job of it would have turned a way to relax and put aside stress into nothing but one more chore.

"Well, shit, Dad, why didn't you ever tell me that?" Ed thumped the level on his workbench and shut off Stevie in midchorus, shaking his head.

He pondered the situation as he went to the window to watch the wind re-create a drift of snow across the back walk he had dug out earlier. Thanks to his new snowblower, he didn't really mind dealing with the winter-weather chores at home or for his clients. Although some of his clients and the jobs they gave him could be genuine pains in the ass on occasion, he liked being a handyman. He got a great deal of satisfaction out of helping people with the routine problems that cropped up in any household.

"I could be a handyman from now until the day I die, and it wouldn't bother me a bit," he mumbled, staring across the snow-covered garden. "Especially if I can come in here and play around when it gets to me. Dad knew that. I think Clyde knows it, too. But how do I explain it to Rick?"

Part of Rick's desire for Ed to create cabinets and chests to sell was related to the potential disapproval people might have about Ed's sexual orientation. It was a valid point, especially in a little town such as Porterfield. By that time, however, Ed had begun to see that most of the folks he worked for were willing to ignore that information and the ring Ed wore on his left hand that bound him to another man. Oh, he had lost a client or two since had joined his life to Rick's—Ed had survived an unpleasant scene with one woman he had never really liked anyway, and a few other people had stopped calling him for work after that—but his regulars, the older Porterfield citizens who depended on him as much as if not more than on their own children, openly praised him and routinely showed their gratitude by spreading the word about his services. As some clients eventually passed away, there always seemed to be at least two new ones entering their senior years who were eager to hire him. The still lingering occasional worry of homophobia aside, Ed suspected he'd have plenty of business until the day he too was a senior citizen.

As far as money was concerned, Ed wasn't worried about that. His income was modest but sufficient. Like his father, Ed had no desire to be so busy with work that he had no time to enjoy what he had. Mrs. Penfield's generosity had allowed Ed and Rick a cushion of comfort that many men their age didn't have. When the property became theirs—main house and all—whether they kept it or sold it didn't matter as long as they used their mutual good sense to manage their financial affairs.

Ed turned from the window and quietly went back to work on the cedar chest, determined to have it done within a week's time. As far as he was concerned, it would probably be the first and last commissioned piece he would do. As he worked, he planned in his mind how to explain his decision to Rick, wondering whether Rick would understand.

"It's all part of the man he married," Ed whispered to himself as he rechecked a measurement. "He'll just have to understand that I'm still perfectly willing to fix up the houses he buys, but somebody else is gonna create the furniture that goes in them."

With Clyde's help, the cedar chest was finished and delivered to Eunice Ames, who exclaimed over its beauty. Then, over Ed's protestations, she overpaid him and carried on about how envious her friends would be. Ed returned home with a feeling of both relief and satisfaction.

Rick admired the check Eunice had given him. "Maybe we should frame it," he said to Ed with his mischievous grin, "considering it will probably be the last check you ever get for that kind of work."

Ed's mouth fell open. "What? How did you figure that out?" he sputtered.

Rick led Ed to the sofa and settled them both comfortably. "Baby, I've been watching you the past few weeks. I began to see that you weren't really enjoying this project, and I also began to see that you wouldn't have ever gotten involved with it if it weren't for me being my usual pushy, bossy self. When you first rebuilt your dad's workshop downstairs, the main thing I wanted was for you to have fun there. Let's face it: this whole thing about you building furniture was my idea, not yours. Right?"

Rick gave Ed a rather sheepish grin. Ed smirked and nodded.

"Well, you humored me and tried it, and we've both discovered that it's a great hobby for you, but not such a hot career move. I know you sometimes think I work harder than you when it comes to building our future, but you work just as hard as I do. Harder even, sometimes. The last thing I want is you thinking that you don't pull your weight on that concern. We worked that all out a long time ago, as far as I'm concerned. I still think we'll be a hell of a team when it comes to buying and remodeling houses, but when that becomes stressful, you can come home and mess around in your workshop the same way I retreat into a good mystery book."

Ed leaned over and kissed him. "I knew there had to be a good reason why I love you so much."

So it was settled. Despite several pleas from friends of Eunice Ames's for cedar chests of their own, Ed politely explained to them that Eunice's chest was an "Ed Stephens One and Only." He was out of the furniture-building business. This raised Eunice's already high esteem for him, and actually increased his handyman workload, as several of her cronies hired him for routine chores in the hope of persuading him to change his mind.

Now, as Ed brought his truck to a halt in front of Mary Tucker's house, he felt a burst of optimism. *We will be a hell of team when it comes to those houses,* he thought. *We've learned an awful lot about each other these past three years, and we've sure learned how to live together. We may have some rough moments, and I may have to threaten to hit him with my hammer a few times, but we'll be okay.*

Ed jumped from his truck and made his way up the Tucker front walk with a bounce in his step. He didn't feel comfortable seconding Rick's claim that he was the cutest handyman in Porterfield, Indiana, but he knew that when it came to his good fortune regarding a life partner, he was without a doubt the luckiest one.

⋄•⋄

The rest of the week passed quickly. On Friday evening Ed eagerly awaited Rick's usual jubilant arrival at the carriage-house apartment. Rick indeed was in a good mood when he came through the door, jauntily tossing his overcoat on the clothes tree near the door and sweeping Ed into his arms for a big hug.

"I am home, and very happy about it. And, baby, when I come home next weekend, I will be home to stay."

"Really? Everything's set with the O'Connor deal?"

"Yep! Barring the unforeseen, the closing will be a week from today. So whatever you do, don't take any jobs for next Friday. You will be too busy driving your truck to Indianapolis to help me clean out my office. Then we'll go to my parent's house, where we will change our clothes, and then to Frank O'Connor's party, where he will be celebrating his new house and we will celebrate my very lucrative commission check. *And*, once that social obligation is behind us, we will spend the rest of the weekend with our best friends celebrating whatever we want to celebrate.

"And then," he continued, hugging Ed harder, "we will return to the quaint little town of Porterfield, where I will spend a week doing jack-shit nothing, 'cause I am one exhausted real estate mogul."

"You look it." Ed scrutinized Rick's face. He looked rather haggard, in Ed's opinion. "Have you been taking care of yourself? I can't decide whether to be worried about you or not."

"Ah, it's just nerves. Once this is all over with, I'll be fine."

"If you say so," Ed said doubtfully. "Do you really promise to relax that week before you go to work for Vince?"

"Yes, dear, I will relax. Well," he said with a wince, "except for meeting with Eunice about this year's holiday home tour for the historical society. I'm sure she's chomping at the bit to get me to work on that."

"Don't let her take advantage of you." Ed gave him a good shake. "You let her know you'll do your part, but you're not gonna end up running the whole damn thing like you did two years ago. Hell, I'll volunteer again if it means keeping you sane and rested."

"Okay, okay. I'll behave. I promise." Rick grinned. "Shit, once I'm here all the time, are you going to turn into a nagging husband?"

"If I have to." Ed pulled away from Rick, folded his arms across his chest, and smirked. "Now that I'm gonna have you home where you belong, I sure the fuck don't want you dropping dead of exhaustion."

"Well," Rick said softly, prying Ed's arms apart. "I guess it is part of your job to look after me the same way I keep an eye on you."

"You bet it is." Ed allowed Rick to pull him back into his arms. "I've spent the last year and a half waiting for the day you could call out, 'Baby, I'm home,' and really mean it. I've felt like your worrywart mother all this time, wondering if you're taking care of yourself and worrying about you spending so much time on the road. You coming home for good is just one more dream come true, as far as I'm concerned."

Rick sighed, and again Ed could see that despite what Rick said, he was genuinely tired. "I know. In a lot of ways this time has been a huge detour in what Gordy calls the Ed and Rick Adventure, but we're almost back on track. Winter may be coming, but I predict nothing but sunny days ahead."

He kissed Ed, and then kissed him again for good measure. Ed nestled his head into Rick's neck and let go of a sigh of his own, allowing the familiar comfort of being close to Rick dissolve his worries.

"How 'bout I call Gino's for a pizza," Ed whispered against Rick's neck. "Then I'll park you on the couch and wait on you hand and foot so you can get a preview of what that week of relaxing is gonna be like."

"Mm-hmm," Rick assented, stroking Ed's hair. "That sounds great." He snickered softly and turned to blow his words directly into Ed's ear. "I knew there was a reason I loved you so much."

CHAPTER FIVE

The following Friday, Ed was on the road by early afternoon. It was a beautiful day; the woods along the highway were a riot of autumn color, and here and there Ed could see a few farmers industriously harvesting the last of the corn crop. After the many trips both he and Rick had taken to Indianapolis and back, he felt both excitement and satisfaction in thinking their mutual, intimate knowledge of every billboard, exit, and speed trap on I-69 could be shelved for a while.

He frowned as he punched through the presets on the truck's radio, passing by yet another single from Michael Jackson's *Thriller*, a noisy heavy-metal song, and a country crossover ballad that was too sappy even for him. He began to twist the dial and finally landed with relief on the Grass Roots' "Midnight Confessions." He cranked it up and bellowed his way through the chorus.

Geez, I'm getting old.

Ed hated to admit it, but he did seem to be losing touch with the current pop music. *Thriller*-mania had left him less than thrilled, and that Police song they had been playing endlessly for the past few months was downright creepy, in his opinion. He did seem to be enjoying most of the other hits that were flooding out of Britain these days, and he snickered to himself whenever he heard Culture Club on the radio. He got a big kick out of Boy George and loved the idea that such an outrageous drag queen was riding high on the U.S. charts. Despite the gloomy shadow and suspicion the disease now known as AIDS was casting upon the gay community, maybe intolerance was finally transforming into a tentative acceptance.

Unlike Rick's niece, Judy, though, he wasn't bothered a bit that MTV was not available on Porterfield cable TV. He was mystified by the popularity of music videos. In that respect, he thought, he was definitely a generation or two behind the times.

The Grass Roots faded out, followed by a fast-talking DJ and a long string of commercials. Ed reached for an *Oldies but Goodies* tape Judy had given him for his birthday, slid it into the cassette deck, set the cruise control at about sixty, and settled comfortably in his seat, feeling a trifle smug about the luxuries and comforts of his current ride. He couldn't help but think he'd probably still be driving his old, white, option-free pickup if it hadn't have been for that cold Saturday evening and that damned chili powder . . .

Two years earlier, Ed and Rick had taken a trip to Mackinac Island in Michigan. While they were gone, Ed's truck had been left behind at Wagner Chevy/Olds to have its malfunctioning transmission repaired. Upon their return, Ed collected his truck, sighed over the amount of the bill, and drove away hoping the truck would remain in good shape for the foreseeable future. A decision hadn't been made regarding Rick's future in real estate at that time, but Ed wasn't happy with the idea of adding the cost of a new truck to their expenses when they were already contemplating a new car for Rick.

That next weekend was the coldest one of the season so far, and the chilly weather gave Rick a hankering for some homemade chili soup. He called Norma and wheedled her recipe out of her. After he had the hamburger browning, he discovered there wasn't enough chili powder in the cupboard. Ed, who'd been sprawled on the couch reading Stephen King, reluctantly agreed to run out to the IGA for some more.

He was heading south on Race Street, bopping his head to Lindsay Buckingham's new solo hit on the radio, when he noticed an old lime green sedan heading toward him on Nash Street. Confident the car's driver would obediently halt for the stop sign, he entered the intersection and suddenly realized to his horror that the sedan was *not* stopping. In fact, it was moving quite fast, considering the low speed limit for narrow old Nash Street.

Ed hit the gas and twisted the steering wheel in an attempt to avoid a collision, but the rusty sedan plowed right into the truck's driver's-side door. Ed's left knee slammed into the window crank, sending a jolt of pain up his leg. Stunned by the impact, Ed lost control of the truck, which careened toward the corner, the right front wheel smashing into a wooden utility pole. The truck, with its wheel alignment now in complete disarray, lurched over the sidewalk and thumped back onto Race Street. Ed's foot scrambled for the brake as he wildly grabbed for the steering wheel, which had been knocked out of his hands by the encounter with the utility pole. His hand brushed the radio volume knob, and the bass beat of the song playing was pounding in both the speakers and his head when the truck finally rolled to a halt.

"Jeee-zus Christ!" he hollered, trying to shake the dizziness out of his head.

Lindsay Buckingham blithely crooned over and over again that he thought he was in trouble, oblivious to the troubling drama in the banged-up truck.

"You think?" Ed growled, snapping the radio off.

Rubbing his knee, he glanced in the rearview to see whether the villain who'd run into him was still at the scene. He saw the lime green car, the chrome on its front bumper crumpled, parked on Nash Street about thirty feet from the intersection. Ed's eyes narrowed. Something about that car seemed awfully familiar. When the driver's-side door opened and a stocky, gray-haired woman stumbled out, he groaned. The driver was Camille Van Vleet, his former across-the-street neighbor.

Mrs. Van Vleet and Ed did not care for each other. They had somehow gotten off on the wrong foot when Ed had first moved into his house on Coleman Street and had pretty much avoided each other from that moment until the day he moved with Rick to Mrs. Penfield's. Ed had thought perhaps it was simply a personality clash, but once Doug had moved into the house, he had quickly established a similar rapport with the older woman.

"If the day comes when I have to cut into her on the table, I swear nothing but pure poison will spurt out and hit the ceiling," Doug often said.

And now, seeing her piggy little eyes reduced to slits as she huffed and puffed back to the intersection in her usual knock-kneed stagger, Ed suspected that even though she was clearly at fault, some of that internal poison might be directed at him.

"Just what do you think you're doing?" she demanded in an unusually severe Hoosier twang. "You trying to kill me? What kind of a hooligan are you?"

By now she had reached the rear of the truck, and as she stopped to catch her breath, she got a good look at her victim. "Oh," she said flatly. "It's you. I might have known. I always knew you didn't have any sense, and this just proves it."

Ed shoved open his door and limped out of the truck, favoring his left leg. The pain in his knee combined with the shock of the moment and his absolute rage at being unjustly accused of being at fault rendered him almost speechless.

"Why, you . . . ran that stop sign . . . old menace . . .," he sputtered. He gasped and caught his breath. "You should be put in a home! Who taught you how to drive, Helen Keller?"

They glared at each in silence until they both noticed a Porterfield police cruiser coming to a halt on Nash Street, its lights flashing. Office Ron Marlowe, who'd been a classmate of Ed's, stepped out.

"That was fast," Ed called to him.

Ron shrugged. "I was about a block away and heard it. So what happened?"

Mrs. Van Vleet pointed a fat finger at Ed. "That juvenile delinquent ran right into my car! Look at it. I could have been killed! Officer, arrest him. Cart him right off to jail. He's probably drunk as a skunk!"

Ed, who'd seen plenty of empty gin bottles poking out of Mrs. Van Vleet's untidy trashcans in the past, gave her the look she deserved.

Ron nodded and turned to Ed. "Ed?"

Ed took in a deep breath and slowly let it out. "I was coming down Race when she blew the stop sign on Nash and plowed right into me."

"I did not! Officer, don't listen to a word he says. Why, he's been bleeding old folks in this town dry for years, stealing their money and doing lousy work besides. He should be put in jail for that, too!"

Ron, whose grandmother was one of Ed's occasional clients, grinned briefly. Ed, however, was in no mood to see the humor in Mrs. Van Vleet's outlandish accusations.

"I was on my way to the IGA for some chili powder," he continued. "Considering the package store is just a block away on Main Street, I'd like to know where *she* was going when she about blasted me to kingdom come!"

Mrs. Van Vleet gasped. "I was on my way to my usual Saturday night dinner at the Wood Haven with my cousin Doreen. We always get the country ribs special. You can call there and ask. She's waiting on me right now, probably worried sick."

"They don't serve booze at the Wood Haven," Ed said in a mean voice. "Sure you weren't gonna stop at Spirits of Porterfield for some hooch to hide in your purse?"

"Now, calm down, both of you." Ron held his hands out in a peaceful gesture. "I'm going to need to see license and registration for you, ma'am. You, too, Ed."

Mrs. Van Vleet waved her navy blue patent leather purse at Ron. "What for? It's his fault."

"Procedure, ma'am." Ron continued to argue with the old woman as Ed painfully crawled into his truck and fumbled his official Indiana vehicle registration out of the glove compartment. He pulled his wallet out of the back pocket of his jeans for his driver's license as Mrs. Van Vleet, who'd been on the verge of hitting Ron with her purse until she apparently thought better of it, hobbled back to her car, mumbling under her breath.

Another police cruiser stopped at the intersection. "Must be a slow night," Ed remarked as Ron studied his license.

"Nah, I called for backup after I heard the crash in case there were any injuries." Ron looked up. "Damn, Ed, she really did a number on your truck. I think I'd better call Hammond's Wrecking and have this towed away. I don't think you should try to drive it."

He glanced down at Ed's leg. "Did you know you're bleeding?"

Ed looked down. His knee's impact with the window crank had ripped a hole in his jeans, and there was a patch of very bloody skin visible. Now that he thought about it, he could feel blood dripping down his leg. "Aw, crud," he moaned, wincing again at the pain.

"Jay," Ron called to the officer in the other police car. "Why don't you take Ed here off to hospital so he can have his leg looked at. Is there anything you want out of your truck before I call Hammond's?" he asked Ed.

"Not right now. I'll worry about it tomorrow," Ed muttered as he limped to the police car, where the other policeman helped him into the front passenger seat.

Ron came over and squatted by the window. "Don't worry about this. I'll take care of it. Just have your insurance company call the station on Monday for the report." Ron scratched his head as he glanced back at Mrs. Van Vleet, who was watching their huddle with great suspicion. "Just who is that old buzzard anyway?"

"Camille Van Vleet, my former neighbor." Ed sighed.

"Oh, yeah. Now I know who she is. I don't think this is her first wreck. Can't wait to run a check on her license. Good luck at the hospital, Ed. Call me if you have any questions."

The police car pulled away, and Ed slumped against the seat as the shock of the event finally caught up to him. Twenty minutes later, an emergency room nurse at Porterfield General allowed him to use the phone.

"Where the hell are you?" Rick demanded when he answered. "And where's my chili powder?"

"I'm at the emergency room. You'll have to get that damned chili powder yourself!"

⋘•⋙

Needless to say, Mrs. Van Vleet, who was forever after referred to by Ed, Rick, Doug, and Gordy as "Hurricane Camille," was found to be at total fault for the accident, and was also in hot water for driving with an expired license. And that wasn't all: she confessed to her son in a weak moment that she hadn't stopped because she was trying to "save the brakes." Upon closer inspection, it turned out the brakes on the old sedan were almost completely shot. Ed learned of this when Mrs. Van Vleet's son called and meekly apologized for his mother's actions. He also reassured Ed that her auto insurance was paid up. "So you'll be taken care of, but this time I'm taking away her keys for good," he grimly added.

X-rays showed no serious damage to Ed's knee, but his truck was declared a total loss. When the anticipated insurance check arrived, Ed and Rick went truck shopping.

"What kind of truck do you want this time?" Rick wanted to know as they cruised through the Porterfield car lots.

"Blue," Ed responded firmly.

Rick rolled his eyes. "Well, that sure narrows it down."

He finally chose a gently used '79 Chevy, similar to his old truck aside from the dark blue paint job, and with a lot less mileage and all the options available at the time. He'd been happily driving it ever since. Despite the aggravation and the pain in his knee that lingered for several weeks, he was secretly grateful to ole Hurricane Camille for solving the truck situation before it became an actual problem. When it came time to buy a reliable vehicle for Rick to drive back and forth between Porterfield and Indianapolis, they'd been able to absorb the payments into their budget with no problem.

Ed entered Indianapolis and confidently navigated his way along streets that not long ago had been a confusing maze to him. He rolled to a stop in front of the Bentons' comfortable brick home on the northeast side, pleased to see Rick's car in the driveway. Obviously the O'Connor closing had gone as scheduled. A glance at his watch told him John and Vera would still be at work.

After an enthusiastic greeting at the front door, Rick led Ed upstairs to his room. Flopping on the bed, Rick told him he'd already cleared away what little there was to take from his office. For all intents and purposes, his job at Granger Realty had come to an end.

"We'll have to come back here after the party to spend the night," Rick said with a sigh. "Mom's all freaked-out about me not being here anymore, so she insists we stay here, and then have breakfast with them tomorrow. I already called Gordy and told him we'd come over tomorrow afternoon."

Ed nodded. He was well acquainted with Vera's occasional "smothering mother" moods. He'd learned it was best to just give in and let her have her way.

He sat on the bed next to Rick and gazed around the room. "You gonna miss staying here during the week?"

Rick frowned. "No, I don't think so. I think all of my boyhood angst is still alive and well within these walls. There would be mornings when I'd wake up and think I was facing another day at Broad Ripple High. I'd have to remind myself I was an adult and going out into the adult world. So, no, I don't think I'll miss being here. I'm anxious to get home where I belong."

Rick changed the subject. "So what did you bring to wear to this party tonight?"

Ed giggled. "Well, I asked Laurie to help me pick something out, so she came over after work last night. She poked around in my closet and finally told me nobody would know I was a gay man if they checked out my wardrobe."

Rick grinned. "Neither one of us has much fashion sense, that's for sure."

"So anyway, she threw me in the car, drove downtown, and picked out a whole new outfit at Gibson's." Ed opened the garment bag Laurie had lent him and showed Rick a pair of black slacks, a dark gray sweater, and a crisp new white shirt. "She even made me get new shoes. They're down in the truck."

"Umm, nice." Rick felt the sweater. "You're gonna look so good, I'll have to keep an eye on all those hungry men who'll be hitting on you."

Ed carefully laid out his new clothes, thinking of the evening ahead. "So why do we even have to go to this party anyway? Your job with Walt is done. Frank O'Connor has his new house. Why can't we just spend time with your parents and our friends, and then go home?"

"Believe me, that's what I wanted to do. When I first told Frank we'd come to this party, I had no intention of actually going once all the papers were signed. But I got to thinking—thinking a lot."

Rick sat up and put an arm around Ed's shoulders. "For strictly business reasons, I need to go to this party. Walt will be there, and we both know how good Walt has been to me, giving a job to someone with no real estate experience. I've learned a lot, and I wouldn't want to do anything that might offend him. As for Frank O'Connor, even though he's a pain in the ass, the day may come when his good impression of me might come in handy. You never know what connections in this business might pay off someday. And let's face it: sometimes you just have to be nice to people you don't like for business purposes. You know that."

Ed nodded. He'd certainly learned that over the years.

"There's another reason I want us to go. You know, we have a great life in Porterfield, but it's kind of isolated. Sometimes I think we're probably better off that way, but then other times I wonder if we aren't too isolated.

"Remember when I first moved to Porterfield, and all the nasty cracks I made about the gay guys I had known down here? Well, I knew if I was going to come back to Indy and try to sell houses to those guys, I was going to have to change my attitude. And I'll tell you, coming back here as a happily married man, and with a firm resolve to drop my judgmental attitude, really opened my eyes. Oh, sure, I've had to deal with guys I'd never want to put up with otherwise, but I've also met some really nice guys. Remember that couple, Kevin and Tom, I helped get that house just off Pennsylvania Avenue? I really liked them. We have a standing invitation to visit them, and I'd like us to go over there sometime."

Rick shrugged. "I'll grant you, I doubt Kevin and Tom or any of those other nice guys will be at this party tonight. With Frank being a trust-fund baby, he has a tendency to run with a pretty fast, bitchy crowd, but it's not gonna hurt us to get a look at that side of gay life. If nothing else, it'll remind us how good we've got it."

"I thought we got a good look at some of that when we were in San Francisco."

"Yeah, I know, but this is the Hoosier version, which is actually kind of funny. I mean, these queens would like to *think* they're as hip as gay guys on the coasts. Every now and again, I can't help but think they have to be on to themselves, and how silly and pretentious they are, but they seem to have a sense of humor about everything other than themselves. So us going to this party tonight should be entertaining in that respect, and also kind of a . . . well, a sociological observation."

"Oh, brother." Ed snorted. "Should I bring a notebook and a pen?"

Rick ruffled Ed's hair. "No, smart-ass. Just keep your eyes open and check your judgment at the door. I've had to alter my perspective a lot in the past year, and I don't think it'll hurt you to see what I've seen. This marriage of ours is all about sharing, isn't it?"

Ed had to agree with that, and thought perhaps Rick had a point when it came to their isolation in Porterfield. Ed suspected he'd grown a trifle smug about the stability of his relationship with Rick over the past few years. Maybe stepping out of his comfort zone would give him some fresh insight into their marriage, and even increase his already fervent gratitude for what they had.

"Okay. I understand where you're coming from, so we'll go and hobnob with Indy gay society. But promise me if it gets too bitchy we'll leave."

"Yes, dear." Rick gave him a quick kiss and a squeeze as a door slammed downstairs. "Now let's go see Mom so she can fuss over you for a while."

Vera was indeed in the mood to fuss over "her boys." Even though she had obviously had a tiring day dealing with a classroom of unruly fifth graders, she insisted on settling them in the kitchen for coffee and a snack. She was tall and still thin, but seemingly a bit grayer since the last time he had seen her, Ed thought, and he watched her search through the cupboards for a box of cookies with his usual gratitude that he had in-laws who actually accepted him and considered him part of the family.

"This should hold you until dinner. John will be a little late because of some counseling appointments he has," she said as she poured coffee for Rick and tea for Ed. "Then I thought we'd all go out to dinner before this party you have. My, I'm going to miss Rick's help in the kitchen! I'm afraid I've gotten lazier than usual in that regard."

Ed grinned. Vera had little enthusiasm or aptitude for cooking. Rick often said that Campbell's soup had been one of his best friends while he was growing up in this house. Rick had taught himself to cook over the years and rather enjoyed it, so he had earned his free room and board this past year and a half by taking over most of the culinary chores.

"Of course I'm just going to miss him, period. It's been so good to have him here again. I shouldn't admit it, but I was somewhat hoping this job might lead to the two of you moving here permanently."

"Oh, Mom," Rick groaned.

"I know; I know. But a mother can dream, can't she? I still wish Claire would consider moving back here with the children. I worry about them so."

"Now, Mom," Rick said patiently, "we've been over that and over that. Claire has a good job and great benefits with Dr. Wells, and the kids would be one big mass of resentment if they were pulled away from their friends. Besides, the cost of living is cheaper in Porterfield. If you and Dad are so determined to keep us all under your microscope, you should consider moving north when you retire."

Ed stirred in his chair uneasily at the thought of so much parental attention, but Vera smiled and nodded. "Well, it's certainly something to think about."

"So, how was school today?" Ed asked, wanting the subject changed—quickly.

Rick glanced at him with a secret smirk as Vera began a story about one of her star pupils. Rick obviously knew exactly what Ed was thinking.

After John arrived and had a chance to relax, they all piled into Rick's car and drove to a neighborhood steak restaurant. Over celebratory cocktails, they discussed Rick's career. Ed was amazed at the 180-degree turn John and Vera had taken on that subject. They had originally been dead set against Rick's plan to leave the postal service for a career in real estate, but Rick's success working for Walt Granger had convinced them he wasn't making a mistake. Relations between John and Rick had been especially tense for some time, and Ed was relieved to see they had obviously returned to their former easygoing give-and-take with each other.

"So, tell me what all led up to this shindig you're going to tonight," John requested as he sipped his Rob Roy. As always, Ed felt he was observing an older, grayer version of Rick. "I've been so busy getting the counseling office squared away at school, I'm afraid I haven't been paying too much attention to my son's big deal."

Rick grinned, pleased at his father's admiration. Rick told of the warm afternoon shortly after Labor Day when Frank O'Connor had breezed into the office requesting information on a house that had caught his eye.

"When he told me the address, I couldn't believe it," Rick said. "It's a big, old, turn-of-the-century pile not far from the governor's mansion. It had been on Walt's listings for over a year, and I didn't expect to see it sell while I was working for him. I thought Frank was full of crap, but since I was the only one in the office, I grabbed the keys and drove him over there."

Rick had shown Frank the house both inside and out, expecting little of the experience other than a chance to get out of the office for an hour. Much to his surprise, Frank exclaimed rapturously over the place, saying he "absolutely loved it," and it was "the house of his dreams."

Rick had remained skeptical until the subject of financing came up. "Turns out his dad had been a big shot at Eli Lilly," Rick said, nibbling on an appetizer. "He made a killing on the stock market and set all of his kids up with trust funds. I don't think Frank has worked a day in his life, not that he has to as long as some old family retainer type keeps an eye on his investments. Frank said that since he's turning thirty and getting older, it was time he had a respectable address, and the proper sort of place for gracious entertaining."

"Since when is thirty considered old?" Vera wanted to know.

Rick chuckled. "A lot of gay men consider thirty to be the kiss of death. From what I've seen of Frank, I suppose he thinks if he has this elegant home, he'll be able to keep other guys interested in him. Lord knows his personality isn't enough to win over too many people. Anyway, Walt was so thrilled at the idea of unloading that white elephant that he told me if I saw the deal through from start to finish, I could keep the entire commission."

"I think that's wonderful." John beamed around the pipe clenched between his teeth. "I'll admit I had my doubts about this real estate thing, but I'm very happy to sit here and eat crow and say I was wrong."

"If only crow was on the menu here," Rick teased him. "I'd make sure you got a double order."

"So, is this party at the new home?" Vera asked as she distractedly waved pipe smoke away.

"No. It's at the condo he has now downtown. It's really an up-and-coming neighborhood, but I guess Frank wants to stay a step ahead of his friends with this new place. This party is to celebrate the purchase of the house. Actually, I don't think Frank needs much of an excuse to have a party. We've spent so much time together over the past month that I kept talking about Ed to keep from having to listen to too much of his obnoxious chatter. The minute he decided to have this party, he demanded I come and bring Ed so he could see him for himself."

John glanced at Ed. "I can just imagine how excited you are about this party."

"Oh, yeah," replied Ed. "I've been more excited about dentist appointments with Dr. Wells."

They all laughed. "Still," Ed said after the merriment died away, "you do what you have to do for your spouse's business. Rick's been awfully patient about times when a handyman emergency has ruined plans we had, and taking those rambling phone calls from some of my clients. I feel a bit like those wives on those old TV shows we watched when we were kids. You know, how they'd have to get all dressed up and entertain their husband's clients? But I don't mind going tonight if it'll be good for Rick's career."

Vera reached across the table and squeezed Ed's hand. "My woman's intuition told me the moment I met you that you were going to be good for Rick, and you've never let me down yet. I still worry about the two of you choosing to stay in Porterfield, but I have a much better feeling about that than I used to."

"Mrs. Penfield wants you both to come up for Thanksgiving this year," Ed said, hoping to derail Vera from that tired old subject. "So in just a month you can come and see for yourself how good we're doing."

"We gladly accept." John glanced at Vera. "I'm sure we'll all have plenty to be thankful for this year. But now," he said as he raised a glass, "how about a toast to Richard's continued success in real estate?"

As Ed raised his glass with the others, he realized that Chicago's "Beginnings" was playing on the restaurant's audio system. He thought back three years to his first date with Rick. That same song had been playing on his stereo when Rick walked through his door that night. Ed marveled at the fact that they seemed to be beginning all over again, and quietly thanked the universe that so far all of their endings had been happy ones.

CHAPTER SIX

After dinner, Ed and Rick dropped Rick's parents off at their house before proceeding south. By this time Ed actually found himself looking forward to the party, thinking with slightly inebriated amusement that the two drinks he'd had before dinner were probably responsible. He was glad Rick was driving.

An elevator whisked them off to the tenth floor of a high-rise building on the east side of the downtown area. As they stepped off, Rick pointed out Frank O'Connor, who was at the open door of his condo receiving guests.

"*That's* Frank O'Connor?" Ed exclaimed in a low tone, his eyes open wide.

"Yep. What do you think?"

Ed studied the man who was flinging his arms around two well-dressed men, shouting with joy at seeing them. "He looks like the kind of man who dresses up like a clown on the weekends."

Rick turned his back and tried to contain the laughter that was bubbling out of him. "Oh, baby, that's priceless. But I think you've nailed him."

Frank O'Connor was shorter and a good deal wider than Ed had imagined, with thick, bright red hair cut in the most fashionable style of the moment. His rather large nose and chubby cheeks were equally red, but Ed suspected that redness came from intimate companionship with the bottle as opposed to the Indiana sunshine. He was obviously several drinks ahead of Ed, but his pale blue eyes remained clear and shrewd. Despite the images of Ronald McDonald, Bozo, and Emmett Kelly that floated through Ed's mind, he quickly determined that he wouldn't want to find himself on the wrong side of Frank O'Connor. Ed guessed Frank had learned to hold his own with the general cattiness of gay society, and probably would not hesitate to sink his well-sharpened claws into any convenient victim.

"Mom always said the Irish drink a lot," Ed whispered as they made their way along the hall. "He looks like a classic example."

Rick took Ed's hand as they approached Frank. "I'm not gonna argue about ethnic traits, but it's true that this will be not be an AA meeting tonight."

"Rick!" their host shouted as he spotted them. "Faaa-bu-lous job at the closing today! And this must be Ed."

Ed held out his right hand for a customary handshake but found himself instead in a whiskey-smelling hug against Frank O'Connor's ample belly. "Well, just look at you," Frank cooed. "Now I can see for myself why Rick is such a happy man." The appraisal Ed received from those cool blue eyes and the noncommittal tone of the words belied their graciousness.

Ed was determined to remain polite. "It's certainly a pleasure to meet you. Rick's very excited about your new home."

"As am I. I can't wait to get settled. You *must* come for a visit the moment I've redecorated."

Must we? Ed thought, but he smiled cordially.

Rick gave Frank's shoulders a brief but affectionate squeeze. "Congratulations again, Frank. I'm sure you'll be very happy in your new place."

"Oh, yes, of course, but if I could only find a cute little handyman like yours to help out." Frank had turned his back on Ed and was eyeing Rick seductively. "I'm sure your little handyman here has taught you *all* of his tricks."

Rick glanced at Ed, and then took a step back. "Well, I doubt that I'll ever be as skillful as Ed."

"And I'm sure there's someone local who's just as skillful," Ed said as he moved closer to Rick. "If you look hard enough, I'm sure you'll find someone. It's truly amazing what money can buy these days," he added, smiling kindly at Frank. *Horny bitch*, he thought. *Touch my husband and your fat ass is going out of one of these tenth-floor windows.*

Frank's smile froze in place. "Why, yes, dear, it certainly is, isn't it?" His eyes swept Ed from head to toe once again, but there seemed to be some grudging respect in this new appraisal. Ed returned the look with a challenging gaze that clearly expressed what he was thinking. *I may be from the boondocks, honey, but I've been around the block more than once with queens like you. Watch your step.* Ed sensed Frank's acknowledgment of this and breathed a little easier.

"But where are my manners," Frank cried, ushering them into the crowded living room. "The bar is set up in the dining room, so do help yourself. And enjoy, enjoy, for it's a beautiful day in the neighborhood."

Because you're leaving it? Ed almost laughed, wondering what Mr. Rogers would have to say about this gathering.

Ed and Rick politely eased their way through the throng toward the dining room. Ed's eyes slowly adjusted to the dim lighting and the smoky air. "So Many Men, So Little Time" was pounding through hidden speakers, and the guests were almost shouting to make themselves heard.

"Hey, there's Walt," Rick said directly into Ed's ear. He turned and saw Rick's now former boss chatting amiably with a much older gentleman near a bookcase filled with glass figurines. Rick led him in that direction.

Walt Granger was an attractive man in his early fifties—slim and well toned with a perpetual tan. Ed had always been impressed with Walt's easy grace and sincerity. He had been a good and patient teacher where Rick was concerned. The two men had shared an excellent working relationship, and Ed was sure Walt regretted Rick's departure.

"I'm going to miss this boy." Walt confirmed Ed's thoughts with an affectionate but sad glance at Rick. "You take good care of him, Ed, you promise?"

"Oh, I will." Ed gave Walt a grateful hug. "Thanks so much for what you've done for Rick. We both really appreciate it."

Walt returned the hug but graciously denied any credit for Rick's progress as a real estate agent. "Best assistant I've ever had. He's a natural. He should do just fine working with Vince."

He turned and introduced his companion to Ed and Rick. Ed didn't catch the man's name, as he was distracted by the way the older man was staring so lasciviously at him. *Geez, how obvious can you be*, he thought, once again moving closer to Rick.

"So where's Ray?" Rick asked Walt, seemingly oblivious to his husband's admirer. Ray was Walt's longtime boyfriend.

"Oh, he's here somewhere." Walt glanced around the room. His gaze rested on a handsome young man in a black leather jacket who was definitely not Ray. Ed stirred uneasily. He'd always suspected that Walt had both a roving eye and hands to match. Still, as Walt had never shown that kind of interest in Rick, he'd never let it bother him, assuming that was Ray's cross to bear.

As Rick and Walt continued to chat, Ed deliberately turned his back on the older man, who was still sending loud and clear signals. "So Many Men, So Little Time" faded out and was followed by "It's Raining Men." Ed was beginning to detect a theme in the party's music, and in the party itself. Despite the location and the cocktail party atmosphere, he felt as though he were dead center in the hunting grounds of any gay bar on a Friday night.

His throat felt parched from all the smoke, so he excused himself and headed into the dining room for something to drink. Behind the bar, a dark-haired, muscle-stud type was clumsily mixing the complicated drink the man in front of Ed had ordered. He had obviously been hired for the evening based on his appearance rather than his bartending skills.

"Pepsi?" Ed inquired after the other man stepped away. The bartender nodded and reached for a two-liter bottle. Ed glanced away and groaned as he realized the old man had followed him and was smiling at him from across the room. "On second thought," he said to the bartender, "throw a shot of rum in there, too."

"Who's that?" Ed heard someone whisper nearby. He discreetly turned and saw two effeminate men delicately smoking and sipping their drinks as they checked him out.

"I don't know," one of them said. "She's kind of cute, but *someone* needs to take her shopping."

Ed felt his face go red. *Fucking queens*, he thought, remembering Laurie's eagerness to pick out an attractive outfit for him, and knowing, despite what that one creep had said, that he looked fine that evening. He accepted his drink from the bartender and turned to the pair, callously appraising their outfits.

"I'm so sorry, ladies," he said with a fake smile, "but there's no outlet of the Faggot-Go-Round where I live."

Watching the surprise cross their faces, Ed was silently grateful for the nights spent in Carlton's bar in Fort Wayne, and the involuntary classes he'd taken there in Bitchery 101.

He turned away and went to inspect the eats spread out on the huge dining room table. He was about to reach for a canapé when he felt a nudge on his shoulder.

"Hey there, good lookin'." It was the old man from the other room, leering at him.

"Hello." Ed's eyes darted around, looking for a quick escape.

The old man caressed the crotch of Ed's black pants. "How 'bout a blow job, sweetie?" He clicked his dentures. "I'll even take my teeth out for ya."

Ed's mouth fell open. He stared in disbelief at the old man, who was now rubbing his tongue over his gums. "Uh . . . ," he muttered. He searched his paralyzed brain for a comeback but simply didn't have one for this situation.

"Uh . . . no thanks," he finally spit out and pushed his way back to the living room. He found an empty spot near the corner and sagged against the wall. A woman's voice was wailing through the speakers about the boys coming to town around midnight. He glanced at his watch and sighed.

Midnight was still a long time away, and he was ready to blow town and this clambake of a party right now.

He sipped at his drink, which turned out to be quite strong. He relaxed a bit as he watched the crowd mingle. He saw Rick and Walt in deep conversation with a couple on the other side of the room and contemplated joining them. However, as he finished his drink he realized a visit to the bathroom might be in order first.

He wandered through the condo and had to admit to himself that Frank O'Connor might be an asshole, but he certainly had good taste. The rooms were decorated with the utmost care but were still warm and inviting. He joined the short line in front of a bathroom near the kitchen, admiring his surroundings.

"So, Frankie, tell us about your new house," Ed heard a voice say in the kitchen.

"Oh, it's absolutely divine, almost as divine as the man who sold it to me."

Ed glanced in the kitchen and saw Frank O'Connor's broad back. He quickly stepped back out of sight and continued to eavesdrop.

"He's here tonight," Frank continued. "Wait 'til you see him. Tall, dark, and handsome, with a big, butch beard, and the dick of death! *God*." He sighed dramatically.

"How would you know?" Frank's friend responded in an amused voice.

"Well, how do you think we closed the deal?" Frank giggled.

The bathroom door opened and a woman who bore a frightening resemblance to Nancy Reagan stepped out. Ed slid by her into the room and quickly locked the door behind him. He stared at himself in the mirror over the sink, shaking his head, replaying the conversation he'd overheard.

First of all, Ed had intimate knowledge of Rick's private parts, and although he'd never had cause to complain, he felt "dick of death" was quite an exaggeration. Secondly, he simply could not imagine that Frank O'Connor shared that intimate knowledge. He knew Rick well enough to know that attendance at this party was about as far as Rick was willing to go to pacify a man like Frank O'Connor. There was no way Rick would lower himself to sleeping with such a man as a way to pursue and seal a business deal. Ed knew that. He *knew* that.

But the seed of doubt was planted. He admitted to himself that in his darkest thoughts over the past year and a half he had wondered whether Rick would be bored and restless enough to actually go cruising for sex while alone in the city. Ed couldn't really imagine Rick cheating on him, but Rick had a normal gay man's healthy sex drive, just as Ed did. And the disturbing fact was that the two of them had never really talked about monogamy. Ed had always assumed it was implicit in the commitment they had made to each other, but Ed had been around long enough to know that when a man started thinking with his dick and not his brain, all bets were off.

Feeling quite sober despite the strong drink he'd tossed down, Ed finished his business in the bathroom, took a reassuring look at himself in the mirror, and rejoined the party. Frank and his friend had disappeared from the kitchen, but Ed saw Walt's boyfriend, Ray, standing alone by the refrigerator. Relieved to see a familiar face, Ed walked over and greeted him.

Ray was what Ed privately referred to as a "pretty boy." His handsome face and nicely sculpted body showed careful attention. However, Ed suspected that Ray wasn't more than a few years younger than himself, and his age was beginning to show a bit. Ed knew Ray enjoyed a rather indolent lifestyle, thanks to Walt's lucrative income. Despite that, though, Ed had always enjoyed Ray's company and his casual but genuine warmth.

Ed couldn't help but wonder how Ray had managed to maintain his pleasant disposition in such a viper's nest. As they chatted, Ed thought he had a clue. While Ray was friendly and attentive with Ed, he wasted no time in disparaging and dishing on some of the men who wandered in and out of the kitchen.

That's it, Ed thought in gratitude. *He's like me. He knows a phony when he sees one.* The self-mocking smile on Ray's face as he told Ed about drinking too much at a similar party and making an ass of himself let Ed know that Ray was not one of those men Rick claimed had no sense of humor about themselves as well.

The shock of Frank O'Connor's boast was beginning to fade from Ed's mind, but it was still troubling him. He decided to confide what he'd heard to Ray as a way of confirming the impossibility of Frank's claim.

Ray nodded. "That doesn't surprise me. If that silly bitch had really had all of the men he's claimed to have had, he wouldn't have time to sleep, let alone throw parties like this. I'm sure he'd like everyone to think that his money could buy someone like Rick, but you know what? That's no different than buying a hustler for the night, so the joke's really on him."

"But you don't think it's true, do you?"

Ray snorted. "Oh, get real, Ed. Rick wouldn't go near him for any reason, let alone to sell a house. Walt wouldn't either. However," he said as an especially handsome young boy strutted through the kitchen, "when Walt's off work he's been known to stray quite a bit. I oughta know. That boy? That was me seven years ago when Walt first picked me up. Somehow I managed to last for more than one night, but I'm not dumb enough to think I've been the only one all this time." He laughed sardonically. "Especially considering that he brings 'em home sometimes and wants me to play as well."

Ed looked at Ray in disbelief. "It doesn't bother you?"

"Wouldn't matter if it did." Ray shrugged. "Walt does what he wants. I like the life he can give me, so I keep my mouth shut."

"Do you love him?"

Ray looked wistful. "Yes, I love him. I've had plenty of opportunities to leave him or even trade up to something better, but I stay with him 'cause I really do love him. And his fucking around, well, it's just something I have to accept as part of the package."

"I don't know if I could do that."

"Well, hopefully you don't have to," Ray said with a cryptic smile.

Uneasiness slithered through Ed's mind. "Ray, if you knew anything, you'd tell me, wouldn't you?"

"Of course!" Ray gave Ed a big hug. "We real estate widows have to stick together. But no," he said, shaking his head, "I don't know anything. As far as I know, Rick doesn't do anything except hang out with those friends of yours who moved here. I don't think you have anything to worry about. Every man has his moments, but it seems to me that Rick saves his for the weekends with you, you lucky bitch."

Ed giggled with relief. He was about to ask Ray to join him at the bar for another drink (and another look at the hot bartender, he devilishly thought) when Rick and Walt entered the kitchen.

"There you two are," Walt said. "We've been looking all over for you. What have you been up to?"

"Oh, swapping secrets about you two," Ray said demurely.

"Oh, really? That must have been one juicy conversation." Walt glanced at Rick, who mock-frowned at Ed, who gave Rick a wouldn't-you-like-to-know look.

"Well, I hate to break up your information exchange," Walt said with a shrug, "but Rick and I were thinking of heading back to our place for some coffee and dessert. I think we've done our duty by this party and Frank O'Connor. A few more belts and he won't even know if we're here or not."

"Sounds good." Ray glanced at Ed. "Ed?"

"Sure. I'm ready to go."

"Me, too," Rick muttered. "This smoke is killing my contacts. I feel like I'm in some damned bar. And Walt and Ray have chocolate cake at home."

"Well, then, I'm definitely in." Ed laughed and took Rick's hand as they went in search of their host.

They found Frank O'Connor at the bar, drunkenly flirting with the bartender. They all thanked him for a wonderful evening.

"Oh, it's a shame you have to leave," Frank said, stroking the bartender's bicep. "And, Rick, are you really going back to that pitiful little town?"

Rick chuckled modestly. "Yes, I am. I'm more than ready to live full-time with my husband again."

Ed looked at Frank's hand on the bartender, then directly into Frank's eyes. "And sometimes that pitiful little town gets pretty hot."

Frank's hand fell away from the hunky bartender. "I'm sure it does," he said as he reached for his drink. He slugged it down and held out the glass for a refill. "You must allow Rick to come here occasionally and see his old friends, though."

Not if I can help it, Ed thought. "Of course. Thank you so much for inviting me, Frank. It was real treat, to say the least."

A few minutes later, as Ed and Rick were following Walt and Ray to the elevator, Rick whispered into Ed's ear. "What was all that about back there?"

Ed grabbed Rick's hand. "Nothing. Let's just say this sociologist is ready to go back to isolation."

Rick glanced back at the party, still loudly in progress, and gave Ed's hand a good squeeze. "Me, too, baby."

⟨☙•❧⟩

Late that night Ed lay next to Rick in Rick's boyhood bedroom. Rick was sound asleep and lightly snoring as usual. Ed tossed and turned, kept awake by both the change in environment and his thoughts.

He replayed the evening over in his head. He had to admit that he wasn't particularly proud of his behavior. Oh, he hadn't done anything to disgrace either Rick or himself; he had, in fact, blended right into the gathering. And that's what was bothering him.

Should he have risen above the whole thing, declining to join those queens in their bitchy reindeer games? He wasn't sure. His first instinct had been to defend himself. He had also wanted Frank O'Connor to know damn good and well that Rick belonged to him, and that Ed wasn't some mealymouthed fag who would stand aside while another man made an obvious play for his husband. It was, he supposed, a natural response, but he wondered if it showed a lack of faith in Rick. He muffled a groan and rolled over to the side of the bed. That was probably the thing that was bothering him the most.

Rick had said he wanted them to attend the party to remind them of how good they had it, and as far as Ed was concerned, it had worked. He realized anew how blessed he was to have both Rick and the life they led in Porterfield.

He couldn't help but wonder what his life would be like now if Rick hadn't walked through his front door three years earlier. Ed saw himself alone, getting older, spending more and more time at Carlton's in Fort Wayne. He saw himself paying more attention to his appearance, maybe spending more money on clothes meant to impress, perhaps even joining one of the many health clubs that were sprouting up around Fort Wayne.

He could see himself enduring long nights at Carlton's, drinking more as the years went by, enviously watching the couples and their obvious displays of affection. Ed would be just another man along the bar rail, drink in hand, maybe even a cigarette in the other, his face carefully arranged in an I'm-too-cool-for-you look, an expression Ed suspected usually hid nothing but loneliness and desperation, and occasionally a little self-loathing as well.

His classes in Bitchery 101 would eventually evolve into a master's degree; he'd feast away, along with all the other bitter vultures, on the carcasses of anyone who dared to be himself. Ed kneaded the pillow under his head, thinking that being a catty bitch didn't solve anything, but it probably did ease some of the discontentment. Or did it? Maybe it only made it worse.

Why are we all so mean to one another? Hasn't everyone else been mean enough to us already?

He didn't know, couldn't even begin to answer those questions.

Rick gave a snort in his sleep. He rolled over, taking the covers with him, and sighed. Ed turned to his side and molded himself against Rick's back, carefully putting his arms around him.

The life he had with Rick had saved him from endless nights in a dark bar, and the occasional one-night stand full of sex without affection. Ed felt that their love for each other was as strong as it had ever been, but he knew that love alone was not enough to keep them together. It took patience, understanding, and the constant hard work of compromise. It meant support for decisions that weren't always unanimous, and with that, a certain amount of courage to allow each other to experiment with new choices, to grow and change. *Time doesn't stand still, and neither do we,* Ed thought, knowing it had been one of the hardest lessons he had learned in his life with Rick.

His apparent lack of faith in Rick made him feel guilty and ashamed. He thought of the past year and a half, and the occasional times he had allowed self-pity to drown him, thinking how unfair it was that Rick was a hundred miles away instead of with him. He realized now that some of the men at that party would all but kill to have it so good. He thought of Ray and his stolid acceptance of Walt's prowls for younger men. Ed knew that was not an issue with Rick, at least at this point. The fact that some weak, possessive, jealous part of his character was determined to make it an issue was keeping him awake, and bringing on a little self-loathing of his own.

We have got to talk about it, he silently told the man sleeping next to him. *We need to discuss whether this ring I wear and that chain around your neck are signs of fidelity along with commitment. Guys get horny, guys get bored, and guys eventually end up fucking around. I need to know if that's an option for either one of us. I don't want it to be. No matter what my dick tells me when a hot man catches my eye, I don't want to share that with anyone else but you, 'cause love and affection are the best parts of my sex life with you, and I can't imagine having that with another man, no matter how attractive he may be.*

Ed sighed, finally feeling sleepy. He made a vow to himself that once they were back in Porterfield, back on their comfortable home turf, he was going to sit Rick down and talk about it. He didn't want to, and he dreaded the discussion that would evolve, but he knew he couldn't let his doubts and lack of faith lurk in his brain. If he did, they would continue to fester there, eventually growing into something just as ugly as some of the behavior he had seen that night.

And Ed wasn't about to ever let something as beautiful as the love he shared with Rick become ugly.

CHAPTER SEVEN

The next day Ed and Rick took off in Ed's truck for the mile drive north to the apartment complex where Gordy and Doug were now living. After the falseness of the previous evening, Ed especially relished their welcoming hugs and the comfort of being with good friends.

Since it was unusually warm for late October, they settled on the small balcony of Gordy and Doug's apartment. As they sipped iced tea, Rick brought them up to date on his dealings with Frank O'Connor, and in rather wicked terms described the party.

Ed sat back and observed his friends. It seemed so odd seeing them in their new surroundings, and he was surprised to see that they had both already changed somewhat. Gordy either hadn't shaved or was growing a beard to compensate for his thinning blond hair. Ed was hoping for a beard, as he thought it would compliment Gordy's aging but still attractive face. His tall, broad body showed the results of once again walking a mail route. At least on the surface Gordy seemed to be flourishing in his new environment.

Doug had cut his thick blond hair quite short. Ed figured Doug could shave his head bald and he'd still be one of the best-looking men he knew. Unlike some of the drop-dead gorgeous men Ed had met over the years, Doug had no conceit about his good looks or the superior attitude to match. He was warm, friendly, and funny; Ed had liked him from the moment he had rented his house to him two years earlier. Considering Doug's age and slim build, he probably would have caught Walt Granger's eye, but Ed couldn't call him a pretty boy. He suspected time served in the army and the things Doug had seen as a mortician had given Doug a maturity many men his age had yet to achieve.

"So, we were thinkin'," Gordy said once their laughter over Rick's party tale had subsided. "Maybe we could all go to the flicks tonight. Doug here wants to see *Brainstorm*," he added with less enthusiasm. Obviously it wasn't his movie of choice.

"I just want to see how they pulled it together after Natalie Wood died." Doug shrugged.

"Ah, poor Natalie," Rick said with a dramatic sigh. "Such a tragic early death. Do you suppose Robert Wagner pushed her off that boat?"

"You sound like those queens at that party last night," Ed teased him. "Next you'll be reading the tabloids in the supermarket checkout."

"Well, I always did like her," Rick said sheepishly. "But I think if I was going to watch Natalie Wood, I'd rather sit through *West Side Story* again."

"Oh, man," Gordy scoffed. "Now you do sound like a show-tune queen. If you start singin' 'Maria,' our friendship is over."

Rick laughed. "Okay, how 'bout *Miracle on 34th Street*?"

"It's almost Halloween, not Christmas," Gordy said, draining his glass of iced tea. "So I think we should see something appropriate. There's a theater here in town that's doin' an old horror movie revival. They've got *Night of the Living Dead* on tonight."

"Yeah!" Ed said happily as Rick rolled his eyes and moaned. "Oh, c'mon, Rick, you told me yourself once that you liked that one. And you have to admit it's a classic."

"I don't know if I'd call it a classic, and I don't remember saying I liked it, just that it scared the shit out of me in college."

"I've never seen it," Doug said. "What's so scary about it?"

"You've never seen it?" Ed turned wide eyes to Doug. "Well, that's it. We've got to see it, then, right, Rick?"

"Okay." Rick surrendered. "I know when I'm outnumbered. But you've got to promise to hold my hand when those zombies start swarming that house." He shuddered.

"Promise," said Ed, grabbing Rick's hand to prove it.

They drove back to Gordy and Doug's after the movie that night acting like a carload of teenagers as they relived the more frightening moments of the film. Gordy ghoulishly supplied details of where George Romero had gotten his props for the flesh-eating scenes and repeatedly leered at Doug, exclaiming, "They're coming to get you, Dougie!"

"Oh, stop," Ed said in a prissy voice, trying to imitate the girl in the movie. "You're just being ignorant."

"Yeah, stop already." Doug, in the driver's seat, gave Gordy a good-natured shove.

"So, what do you think, Doug?" Rick asked from the backseat. "As a mortician, that whole movie probably didn't freak you out as much as it does us."

"Actually it does," Doug admitted, turning into the apartment complex. "Having a corpse on my table coming alive while I'm working on it is probably one of my biggest nightmares."

"So that's what's goin' on in your sleep when you start moaning and rollin' around," Gordy said, grabbing his neck affectionately. "Zombies are on the prowl, huh?"

"Sometimes." Doug gave him a brief smile as he angled the car into their reserved spot in the carport.

They filed into the building, Ed bringing up the rear with a thoughtful frown on his face. On the one hand, it was just like old times, but on the other (which had warts, Norma always said), there was something different tonight. Ed thought it had to do with Doug. He seemed to be enjoying himself and their company, but there was some sort of reserve Ed had never felt from him before. What made him truly uneasy was that he suspected this reserve had more to do with Gordy than with Ed and Rick.

"So how 'bout a game of euchre before bedtime?" Gordy suggested.

"I guess," Doug said, going into the kitchen. "But if we're going to play cards, I want some ice cream, and I think we're all out. Damn!" He slammed the freezer door. "Nothing but boring old vanilla. I'll bet you guys want chocolate something." He gave Ed and Rick an expectant look.

"Of course," Ed shrugged, "but don't go to any bother on our account."

"It's no trouble." Doug felt in his back pocket for his wallet. "There's a market not far from here. I won't be gone long. Gordon, my man, why don't you get out the cards while I'm gone."

"Okay," Gordy assented, "but why don't you take Rick with you for company, and to see you don't get mugged."

"My small-town guy." Doug shook his head at Gordy with a smile. "I can take care of myself out there, you know, but if Rick wants to shotgun, that's cool."

"And I'll make sure he gets some coffee going," Ed said to Rick, anticipating Rick's beverage request upon their return.

"Okay, okay," Rick sighed as he followed Doug to the door.

Once the coffee machine was perking, Gordy suggested they step outside. He led Ed to the balcony, where Gordy lit a cigarette and took a deep drag, blowing the smoke into the cool night air. Ed realized it was one of the few cigarettes he'd seen Gordy with all day. He said as much.

"Yeah." Gordy took another deep lungful of smoke. "Doug's still naggin' at me to quit. If we were still home, I'd'a probably quit by now."

Ed leaned against the railing and looked closely at his friend. "But you are home, aren't you? Isn't this your home now?"

"I s'pose. Sure is different, though. Doug loves it, but it's tougher for me, maybe 'cause I'm older."

Ed shifted his weight and looked away from Gordy. "What's going on between you two?" he asked bluntly. "I've had a weird feeling all evening, and it's not 'cause of that movie."

"Hell, I'd rather be fightin' off zombies than what I'm fightin' in my mind these days." Gordy sighed. He gazed off toward the city skyline. "I think he's cheatin' on me."

"Oh, Gord," Ed whispered, feeling a little sick to his stomach and in no mood for ice cream. He put an arm around Gordy's shoulders. "What makes you think so?"

"I don't have any evidence—not really, anyway. But he's been working a lot of late nights. You know better than anyone how early a mailman goes to bed, so there are nights when I go to sleep alone, wonderin' where he is. He's always there when I get up in the morning, but I have a feeling he's been out most of the night doin' something other than embalming dead people."

"Maybe you're just being paranoid."

"No. He's changed. Oh, he still loves me. I know that. But there's . . . a distance. He was so crazy about me when we first got together. I know that doesn't really last, but I get the feelin' that if I told him I was gonna move back to Porterfield, he'd just shrug and say, 'Cool,' the way he does about so many other things. Sometimes I think he's just goin' through the motions, ya know? And hell, our sex life ain't what it used to be."

"Well, all couples go through different stages with that."

"Maybe," Gordy allowed, "but I just get the feelin' that he'd move on if he could, or that he wishes he'd moved down here alone."

Ed shivered from both the chilly air and the conversation. "Do you think it's one guy, or is he just tricking around?"

"Oh, I don't think it's any one guy. Doug's prime beef, ya know, and not only that—he's new meat in town. He could get picked up after five minutes in Talbott Street. Shit, I saw that the first night we walked in there together."

"Don't you guys talk about this stuff?" Ed thought about his own planned discussion with Rick. "I mean, geez, with all that AIDS stuff going on, it's just not smart to be screwing around these days."

"I know. Oh, believe me, I know. What's the line in that damned song of Divine's they play at the bar? Something about being careful who you sleep with 'cause you don't know where it's been? Believe me, I think about that sometimes when we're together, and it, uh, affects my performance, if you know what I mean."

"But do you talk about it?"

Gordy shrugged. "We have. I guess we've always kind of left it that if something happened, we'd just keep it to ourselves. So Doug's doin' that, but I guess I'm not as cool with it as I thought."

"Gord, you can't do that. Not with this AIDS shit. Remember when we thought it was just in California or New York? Remember the stuff we heard in San Francisco? It's gonna be in Indiana. Shoot, it probably already is. I don't want you getting that. I don't know what I'd do if something happened to you."

"I know," Gordy said miserably. "But, shit; I love the guy. I'm fuckin' thirty-three years old, and he's the only guy I've ever really loved. Do I just give him up 'cause I'm not enough for him? He comes home every night. Isn't that enough?"

"I don't know. Is it? And what happens the first time he doesn't come home?"

"I guess I'll deal with it when it happens." Gordy lit another cigarette and slumped against the railing.

Ed pulled Gordy into a tight hug. "You promise me you'll call me if you need me," Ed said fiercely. "No matter what. If you need me to come down here and talk, or if you need me to kick his ass, I will. Don't ever think you're dealing with this alone. I'm always here for you, you got it?"

"I got it," Gordy whispered, returning the hug. "Thanks, bud. I know I always can count on you, even if I can't count on him."

Over Gordy's shoulder, Ed saw Doug's car pulling into the parking lot. "They're back. So let's go play cards and try to have a good time. I hate it that we're going home tomorrow. I wish we could talk some more."

"I've got some time off comin' up. Maybe I'll drive up and see you."

"Yeah, do that, okay? I miss having you around."

"Me, too, bud." Gordy gave Ed a good squeeze and let him go. He pitched his cigarette over the railing and went inside. "I know you'll probably spill your guts to Rick about this, and that's okay, but keep your mouth shut around Doug, at least for now. And don't hold it against him, let it ruin the rest of our weekend." Gordy looked Ed right in the eye. "He's just bein' a guy, doin' what guys do. A part of me can't blame him for that."

Well, I can, Ed thought as he followed Gordy inside, but he nodded in agreement. Ed liked Doug. He didn't want to think unfavorably of him, but he also had a strong desire to shake him. *Don't you see what you've got?* Ed wanted to scream at him.

Maybe it wasn't enough for Doug, Ed thought as he watched Doug and Rick enter the apartment, laughing together about the inept cashier at the grocery store. Unlike Ed, maybe Doug simply wasn't ready to make that kind of commitment to one man.

Ed was rather quiet as the ice cream was dished out and the card game began. No one seemed to really notice, and he was grateful. He wondered if the good times the four of them had had together we're coming to an end. Again time and change seemed to be stealing something precious from him. There wasn't anything he could do about it, he reflected as he distractedly jammed the jack of clubs next to the ace in his hand. He closely examined the cards he had been dealt, thinking that for at least this hand he could do one thing. He could be the one taking all the tricks, not Doug.

So he did, with a little help from Rick's cards. The only problem with his satisfaction at winning the hand was that Doug's partner in the game, Gordy, was also left in the dust. And the last thing Ed wanted to see was Gordy being hurt for any reason, even in a stupid card game.

◇◆◇

Early the next afternoon Ed was back in his truck heading north on I-69. Rick was somewhere behind in him in the Regal. They intended to stop at a roadside rest area about fifty miles north of Indianapolis to share the picnic lunch Doug had thoughtfully packed for them so they wouldn't feel the need to stop for fast food. Ed couldn't help but think that Doug really was a nice guy; he just wasn't nice in the way Ed wanted him to be.

"Talking in Your Sleep," the new hit from the Romantics, was playing on the radio. Ed winced as the lead singer smugly told of the secrets revealed by his lover during slumber. He wondered whether some of Doug's secrets would eventually be exposed in the same way. Not wanting to think about that, Ed twisted the radio dial and relaxed against his seat as he heard the familiar voice of Lesley Gore. Lesley was singing in a world-weary voice about how "That's the Way Boys Are."

"Yeah, they sure are," Ed agreed, speeding up to pass a slow-moving semi truck.

Still, Ed reflected, ole Lesley may have put up with her boyfriend's macho male nonsense in 1964, but he couldn't help but think in 1983 she'd tell him to get lost. A lot had happened over the years where male-female relations were concerned. The concept of a man loving another man may have inched a little closer to acceptance, but the men involved in such relationships had not seemed to have made the same strides in self-respect as women had. Gay men appeared to be stuck in the same old leaky boat when it came to putting up with shit from their lovers. Even with the quiet fear the AIDS epidemic was spreading, nothing was really changing in that respect.

Geez, when will we learn to keep it in our pants? When we're all dead and buried from whatever this damned disease is? Ed shook his head in disgust.

He slowed the truck and exited the interstate, rolling to a stop in the far end of the rest area's parking lot, near some picnic tables. Rick pulled up next to him a moment later. They took their lunch to a splintery table under a few trees with some lingering autumn leaves. The breeze blowing across the now empty fields ruffled Ed's hair and flapped Rick's unzipped windbreaker. Ed was glad for the comfort of his jean jacket as they settled down to eat.

"It sure was nice of Doug to fix us some sandwiches," Rick said as he tore into a roast beef and Swiss.

"Yeah. It was."

Rick looked at Ed through narrowed eyes. "What's bothering you? Something is. I noticed it after we got back from the store last night. I was going to say something when we went to bed but decided I should wait until we were really alone."

With some reluctance Ed repeated his private conversation with Gordy.

Rick closed his eyes and sighed. "Well, shit," he said as he put his sandwich aside. He looked at it with distaste. "I don't know if I can finish this now or not. I can't believe Doug's fucking around. It's a good thing I didn't know this earlier. I probably would have pushed him off their balcony."

Ed picked up his sandwich. "You might as well eat it. He may be a dog, but he's also a good sandwich maker."

Rick slowly chewed for a moment. "So what do we do?"

"What can we do? We just have to be there when Gordy needs us. He said something about coming up to Porterfield on one of his days off. We can talk to him then, and at least give him our support."

"I guess the era of the four musketeers is over." Rick opened a can of Pepsi. "But then, maybe it ended when they moved away. I didn't want to admit it, but in some way I saw this coming. I just never saw them lasting the way we have. I didn't say anything because I didn't want to jinx it, and let me tell you, I sure hate being right."

"You think they'll break up?"

"Oh, Ed, do you see Gordy putting up with that for very long, the way Ray puts up with Walt?" Rick grinned at the surprised look on Ed's face. "What, you think I didn't know about that? I've been working with Walt for a year and a half. I've seen him in action plenty of times. I just assumed that's what you and Ray were talking about at the party the other night."

"Yeah, we were."

They ate in silence for a minute.

"Rick," Ed said tentatively, "about that party, I heard something else that kind of bothered me."

"What's that?"

Ed shifted on the hard bench. He didn't know if this was the time or the place to get into it, but he knew the longer he waited, the harder it would probably be. "I overheard Frank O'Connor tell one of his friends that you two had been together."

Rick snorted. "That asshole. Thank God that deal's over with." He looked over at Ed. "Oh, for Christ's sake, you didn't believe it, did you?"

"Of course not! It was . . . well, it was just such a surprise to hear another man talking about you that way. I know you wouldn't fuck Frank O'Connor for a business deal, or any other time for that matter. But put yourself in my shoes. Wouldn't you have been a little freaked-out to overhear that?"

Rick swallowed a gulp of Pepsi and gazed across the fields. "Yeah, I guess I would. Oh, well. I'm coming home now, so we don't have to worry about it anymore."

"Do we? Not have to worry about it?"

Rick turned and looked at Ed in silence for several moments. "I can't decide," he finally said, "whether to get really pissed off or just kiss you out in the open here, and tell you how much I love you. Ed, are you worried that I was joining Walt on his adventures? Do you really think I could or would do that?"

Ed was hoping for a kiss, but he couldn't blame Rick for being angry. "No," he said quietly, "I don't really think you could or did do anything like that while you were working in Indy, but with everything I've heard and had to think about this weekend, do you blame me for wondering a little?"

Rick got up from the table. He paced around its perimeter and finally sat on the table itself, facing Ed. "No, I don't blame you, probably because I was wondering the same fucking thing during those lonely nights at Mom and Dad's. There may not be a lot of available men in Porterfield, but Fort Wayne's just thirty miles away."

Now it was Ed's turn to be a little pissed off. "You think I'd do that?"

"No, but can you blame me for wondering?" Rick asked with a mocking smile.

They looked at each other for a moment before they both began to laugh.

"What a pair we are." Rick slapped the table for emphasis.

"So much for faith and trust," Ed sputtered through his giggles.

Rick shook his head as he watched the trucks roaring along the highway. "Baby, just for the record, I have been one hundred percent faithful to you since the day we met. Oh, I've looked, but as we always say, lookin' is free."

Ed laid a gentle hand on Rick's knee. "I know. I've done my share of looking and lusting in my heart, too, just like Jimmy Carter. But I've never really thought about acting on it. I can't imagine there's a man out there who can give me what you do." Ed stroked Rick's leg. "I can't imagine another man loving me the way you do."

Rick looked at the hand on his leg and smiled. "I know. Don't they say something about 'forsaking all others' in traditional wedding vows? Maybe we should have said something about that when I put that ring on your finger."

"Maybe. Maybe we should say something about it now so we know for sure."

"That's not a bad idea." Rick hopped off the picnic table and went down on one knee in front of Ed. "Edward Stephens," he said in a solemn tone, "I do hereby forsake all others for you. Other men may have open relationships, but I would like to declare ours closed, because I love you, and God help me, I don't want to share you."

Ed kneeled next to Rick on the cold grass. "Richard Benton, I also forsake all others because you are the love of my life, and as God as my witness, I sure as hell don't want to share you either.

"And that's a promise," he added, leaning over to kiss Rick, not caring who might be watching.

"I promise, too," Rick said as he softly returned the kiss. "I love you, baby."

"I love you too, darlin'." Ed smiled at Rick, not noticing the cold seeping through his jeans to his knees.

"Baby, as much as I hate to end one of the most tender moments we've ever had, maybe we should get up and finish our lunch before some state cop comes by and thinks we picked each other up over there in the men's room, huh?"

Ed laughed and, groaning a bit, got to his feet. He settled back on the bench with his sandwich, feeling a peace within that he hadn't felt, he thought, since the day Rick first left for Indianapolis.

"We're gonna be okay," Rick said confidently as he drained his pop can. "As long as we can always talk about this stuff and not let it make us crazy, we'll be fine. A lot's happened in the last three years, and I know there's a hell of a lot more to come, so you gotta make one more promise, okay? Promise me if you ever worry about me taking off with some other guy, you'll come to me first, and not our friends, okay?"

"Okay." Ed nodded and bumped his Pepsi can against Rick's. "It's a promise, but it goes for you, too, right?"

"Right."

Ed wadded up his sandwich wrapper and looked around for a trashcan. He noticed a particularly hunky looking truck driver as he jumped down from his cab and made his way to the restrooms, his boot heels clicking on the cement walk.

"What do you say, darlin'?" Ed nudged Rick so he could see the trucker. "Wanna go meet him in the men's room and ask about a three-way in his truck?"

"Aw, shit!" Rick exclaimed, slapping Ed upside the head as he began to roar with laughter. "Get back in that truck of yours," he commanded. "We are going home, where we will live the rest of our lives together, no studly truck drivers included."

"Yes, dear." Ed giggled as he cleared away the debris from the table and followed Rick back to their vehicles.

Home, he thought. *What a beautiful word that is.*

CHAPTER EIGHT

And so they returned to Porterfield with the promise of a renewed commitment creating an eagerness in both Ed and Rick to move forward with their lives. As always, Ed couldn't help but reflect on how much had changed, but instead of reacting with his usual thoughts of *What the hell is going on*, he relaxed and accepted it. He enjoyed his relief at having Rick at home full-time, and he did his best to put his worries about Gordy on the back burner of his mind as he plunged into a busy week of appointments.

Within a few days, it seemed as though Rick had never been away. One especially cool morning Ed was lingering under the spray of the warm shower when Rick pounded on the bathroom door.

"Hey! I need to get in there, too. I have to meet Eunice for the holiday home tour today."

"Aw, crud," Ed muttered as he killed the shower. He stepped out and grabbed a towel. "You suppose you could pick up some cat food while you're out today?" Ed asked once Rick was established in the tub.

"Oh, do I have to?" Rick groaned, splashing water against the curtain. "I just know Eunice is going to give me about eight thousand things to do. I don't want to have to worry about cat food."

"Yeah, but you'll probably end up near the IGA, and all of my appointments are on the north side."

Ed heard an exasperated sigh from behind the curtain.

"It will help you rebond with Jett."

This elicited an equally exasperated snort from behind the shower curtain.

Ed grinned at himself in the mirror. "Besides, now that you're home all the time, you need to pick up some of the chores you dumped on me a year and a half ago."

"It's not working, baby."

Ed stifled a giggle. "Yeah? Well, then I'm going into the living room. I am going to turn on the television. I am going to turn it up very loud 'cause *Sale of the Century* is probably on. They may even have an Instant Bargain going on."

"Okay, okay!" Rick surrendered. "I'll pick up the damned cat food!"

Ed smiled happily as he combed his hair. Yes, it was good to have Rick home again.

As Ed had expected, once Eunice Ames had her hooks into Rick, what was supposed to be a week of relaxation for him turned into a whirl of what did seem to be about eight thousand chores. Eunice belonged to a great many organizations and clubs in Stratton County, but the historical society was her pet project, and she ruled it with an iron hand. She took full advantage of Rick's interest in local history and architecture when it came to the holiday home tour, the society's biggest annual fund-raiser.

Every year Eunice talked as many owners of older, stately houses as she could into opening their doors for a weekend in early December so those who paid for the privilege could tour their appropriately holiday-decorated homes. Ed thought of it as the annual Ames-Penfield war, as Eunice was determined to get the Penfield place on her list of tour stops, and Mrs. Penfield was equally determined to keep her doors firmly closed to such activity.

"I suppose it is uncharitable of me," Mrs. Penfield said every year, "but with my health as it is, I simply cannot tolerate all the disruption it would cause. Not to mention," she would add with a twinkle in her eye, "I lost so many battles with Eunice Ames during her years on the school board that I mustn't allow her to win this one."

At that point Rick would report his failure to persuade Mrs. Penfield to Eunice, who accepted this yearly defeat with a certain amount of gracious dignity but used it as a way to guilt Rick into more work. There was no sigh of relief to have this traditional polite fight put to rest for Ed. He somehow always managed to end up as a tour volunteer and was usually cajoled by Eunice into buying some god-awful Christmas craft from the bazaar that was always held in the historical society building itself.

"God bless us, every one," Ed would grumble once it was all over, knowing full well that once Mrs. Penfield had passed away and the house belonged to them, it would become a stop on the holiday home tour whether they wanted it to or not. Ed and Rick simply did not have Mrs. Penfield's strength of will when it came to Eunice Ames.

Ed came home for lunch on Friday of that week to find a note from Rick saying he was drafting a press release with Eunice and would be home for supper, and would Ed please check on the pork chops he had left thawing in the sink? Ed rolled his eyes, hoping they would indeed have pork chops for supper as opposed to a Gino's pizza because Rick would get home too late to cook. He was poking at the chops when the phone rang.

"Hello?"

"Hello? Is this Ed or the other one? This is Althea Klarn."

"It's Ed, Mrs. Klarn," Ed said, trying to keep the despair out of his voice.

Much to Ed's dismay, Althea Klarn had become one of his regular clients. He had first been called to her home on the southwest side of Porterfield six months earlier when she had broken her arm in a fall. Mrs. Klarn, who was about his mother's age, had required some help with routine house chores until the cast was removed. Once Ed was acquainted with the woman, he found himself counting the days until she had full use of both arms again, as he found her to be one of the most tedious human beings he had ever met. However, Mrs. Klarn seemed to so enjoy Ed's company that she continued to call him on a regular basis with all sorts of trivial activities for him. Ed could only assume that she needed someone to listen to her nonstop stream of chatter more than she needed a regular handyman.

"I was watching TV this morning," Mrs. Klarn droned in her usual monotone, "and they were talking about cleaning the lint out of your dryer hose. I never thought about that. I just thought the lint went out the hose and into the air. You know how you can always smell it when the dryer is running? Now, I would have thought that was the lint from my clothes freshening the air. Do you suppose that causes air pollution? I never thought about that. Do you suppose we're polluting the air when we run our dryers?"

"Uh . . ."

"Well, I don't know if it's air pollution. Even if it is, it can't be as bad as those factories and their smokestacks. I suppose I could hang the clothes out to dry, but a dryer is more convenient. Especially since I broke my arm, you know. It still pains me from time to time. My son says I'll have that at my age. It really is easier to use the dryer, so I just won't think about air pollution."

She paused, and Ed, who had been watching Jett wash his whiskers, tried to snap to attention.

"Is that why you called, Mrs. Klarn? To ask about air pollution?"

"I don't think so. Why are we talking about air pollution? Oh, yes. We were talking about my dryer. Well, on TV this morning they said that lint lingers in the hose and can start a fire. I never thought of that. Why, I've never even looked in that hose since the dryer was installed. That was when Paul was in high school. I think it was his junior year. That was the year he won the chemistry prize. I was so proud of him. I still am, of course, but I was so thrilled when Mr. Stieglitz told me Paul was the best chemistry student he'd ever had. Such a nice man, Mr. Stieglitz. Paul did enjoy his class, and it's certainly come in handy, hasn't it? Paul being a doctor and all."

In addition to her endless ramblings about most any topic, Mrs. Klarn had a tendency to drift off into repeated praise for her son, Paul. Ed, who barely remembered Paul Klarn from school and who had hated Mr. Stieglitz's class, stifled a sigh.

"So you're worried about your dryer hose?"

"Well, yes, I am. I just never thought that something like lint could start a fire. How could it? It's just lint. But then I suppose most anything could start a fire, couldn't it? Usually, though, I think about frayed electrical cords. I do worry about them. That's why I don't put lights on my Christmas tree anymore. I just can't think of anything sadder than a fire at Christmas. I just don't trust those cords they use for Christmas lights. Of course I remember my grandparents putting lit candles on their tree. Can you imagine? Oh, it was pretty, but you couldn't have them lit for very long. My *goodness*," she moaned, her voice actually rising a notch. "I worried so the year I got my Raggedy Ann doll. Wouldn't that have been a shame if it caught fire before I even got to play with her?"

"Oh, yeah," Ed said as his gaze went to the pork chops in the sink. He wondered if Rick planned to bread them and bake them, or perhaps cook them on the stove with some kind of sauce.

"So do you have some free time this afternoon?"

"Huh? For what?" Ed asked, his mind full of pork chops, Christmas trees, and Raggedy Ann dolls.

"Why, to clean out my dryer hose! Isn't that what we were talking about?"

I don't know, were we? Ed thought. Unfortunately he did have time to stop by Mrs. Klarn's that afternoon and couldn't think of any reason not to. *Aw, crud*, he thought, telling her that he'd stop by at about three o'clock.

So that afternoon Ed found himself in the Klarn basement disconnecting her dryer while Mrs. Klarn leaned against a rusted sink and carried on a one-woman conversation about everything from the weather to the current plotlines on *As the World Turns*. Ed muttered an occasional *uh-huh* to let her know he was listening. Kind of.

When she mentioned something about her son returning to Porterfield, he actually removed his head from the bowels of the dryer and said, "Really?"

Paul Klarn had taken his chemistry prize and his general gift for science to a college out of state, and then to medical school. He was finishing his residency at a hospital in New York City, Ed had learned. He remembered Paul, two years younger than himself, as a slight, slim fellow who was even nerdier than he was in high school. He didn't know much about Paul's father. Apparently the Klarns were divorced, one of the few topics Mrs. Klarn avoided. Ed couldn't imagine why someone who'd achieved what Paul Klarn had (and was blessed with the mother he had) would voluntarily return to Porterfield. He somehow managed to arrange those thoughts into a polite question for Mrs. Klarn.

"Well," Mrs. Klarn said importantly, "you know how well he's done with his residency. I'm just so proud of him. He was all set to begin his practice in New York, but he's found out he's just not a big-city man. That doesn't surprise me. You couldn't pay me to live in a big city. I always knew Paul would come home where he belongs. With Dr. Weisburg retiring, it just seems like fate has brought my boy back to me."

Dr. Weisburg had been the Stephens' family physician since before Ed was born, and in fact had been the doctor who brought Ed into the world. Despite Norma's constant predictions that the day would come when Dr. Weisburg's stone-cold body would be hauled out of his office, his stethoscope dragging on the ground behind him, the old doctor had decided his own health issues were a good reason to at last hang up that stethoscope. Ed had been informed of this in a letter sent to all of Dr. Weisburg's patients. His practice was being absorbed into a new medical group at Porterfield General. Ed had just assumed he'd select a new doctor once he actually had a good reason to see one. By then, he figured, he would know from his clients' gossip who was the best of the bunch.

"So Paul is going to join that new medical group?" Ed simply couldn't imagine having a doctor who was younger than him. It was yet another sign that he was getting older and would probably be cursed with more reasons to seek medical help as his own body began to fail him. He didn't even want to think about some guy he'd known in high school giving him a prostate exam.

"Oh, yes. The moment Dr. Weisburg decided to retire, he called Paul. Wasn't that nice of him? I always did like Dr. Weisburg. He was so supportive of Paul. I always knew Paul wanted to have a practice just like Dr. Weisburg's, and now he will. I'm so happy that Paul is coming home."

Ed was mystified as to why Paul would want to take on the responsibilities of a large medical practice and at the same time be at his mother's beck and call. He pondered that as he finished cleaning out the dryer hose. Fortunately Mrs. Klarn's phone rang and she went upstairs, leaving him to complete his job in beautiful silence. He found forty-three cents in the bottom of the dryer and considered pocketing it himself, but instead dutifully went upstairs to hand it over to Mrs. Klarn, who thanked him repeatedly for his work, and also managed to remark on Paul's homecoming several more times.

Rick arrived home on time that evening, and as they sat down at the table to feast on baked pork chops, Ed told him about his day and his time at Mrs. Klarn's. Rick snickered as he usually did when Ed spoke of Mrs. Klarn, and shared Ed's mystification as to why Paul Klarn would want to return home.

"I don't know." Ed mashed some butter into his baked potato. "I can only hope that with him around she won't call me so much, but I s'pose with him being a doctor he'll be too busy to spend time with her."

"Since we have to sign up for a new doctor, do you think we should choose this Klarn guy? He's the only one we know anything about."

Ed shrugged. "Beats me. I say wait until one of us gets sick; then we can worry about it."

"Yeah, I guess. I have enough to think about these days as it is." Rick helped himself to some peas. "I can't believe I'm starting a new job on Monday. Happy Halloween! Do you suppose that's bad luck, starting a new job on Halloween?"

"You could always wait until Tuesday. Vince wouldn't care."

"That's true," Rick admitted, "but he's taking me to that Jaycees lunch on Tuesday, and I'd really like to see what all is going on in the office before I have to talk to any of those guys. Not to mention I somehow got roped into taking Jane and Lesley trick-or-treating Monday night. Josh claims he's too old to be dragged around by a grown-up, so Claire's letting him go alone with Eric, but she and Laurie refuse to let the girls go out alone."

"How'd you get stuck with it? Can't Claire or Laurie or Todd take them?"

"You'd think, but the girls don't want to be seen with their parents. Jane insisted that I be the one, since I'm home now. That little minx knows just how to work Uncle Rick's guilt, so after my first day at my new job, I'll be walking the streets of Porterfield, just like I did in my mailman days. Oh, well. Maybe it'll give me a chance to check out the competition's listings."

"Okay. I guess I'll spend the evening over at the main house, handing out candy for Mrs. Penfield. Still, trick-or-treating is over at nine, so if you make it home early enough, I'll promise to save a treat for you."

Rick smirked. "Oh, yeah? You gonna hold back one whole fun-size Snickers bar for me?"

"Oh, maybe," Ed said airily, waving his fork. "I had something a little more provocative in mind, though."

"Such as?"

"Well, remember that black leather jockstrap we bought in San Francisco just for the heck of it? Halloween seems as good a time as any to actually wear it."

"Hmmm." Ed definitely had Rick's full attention. "And what do I get to wear, since we only bought the one?"

"Oh, you can dress up as a real estate agent who's checking out a new house. Come to the bedroom door, holler, 'trick or treat,' and we'll see what you get aside from a Snickers."

Rick's mischievous grin spread across his face, mixed with a little bit of lust. "And if I don't?"

"Then I'll pull my jeans on over that jock strap, go downstairs, and soap the windows on your car!"

⋘•⋙

On Halloween night, Ed was sitting in the front parlor of the main house pouring a bag of Snickers bars into a large antique bowl when Mrs. Penfield entered the room. She carefully settled herself in a corner of the sofa with a sigh.

"Rough day?" Ed asked as she leaned her cane against the end table.

"Somewhat. My joints seem to be going through their annual adjustment to autumn. I seem to feel my old friend, arthritis, chuckling with a certain amount of glee. I suspect that this winter, unlike the last, will be a good deal colder."

"Well, that's bad news for you, but good for me," Ed said, thinking of the income he had lost the previous winter, which had been relatively snow free.

"Indeed. Well, we'll muddle through it as we always do." Mrs. Penfield settled into the sofa, a tired expression on her face.

Ed spent so much time around older people that their complaints of constant ill health usually went in one ear and out the other. However, Mrs. Penfield, who generally kept her complaints to a minimum, had his full attention. As he ripped open a bag of Milky Ways and stirred them into the bowl with the Snickers, he looked at her out of the corner of his eye.

Mrs. Penfield was now in her mid-seventies. The ravages of arthritis and several other minor health problems had definitely taken their toll on her appearance. Ed had always been fond of the old woman, but living in such close proximity for the past two years had increased that fondness to genuine love. His own grandmothers had died when he was young, and Mrs. Penfield had done much more than fill their roles. She had become a trusted friend and mentor, someone Ed could always count on when he needed to talk for any reason. In many ways she had become something of a substitute for his late father. Her presence in his life had lightened his grief over Tim Stephens's untimely death. The fact that the bulk of her estate, including this beautiful 1898 brick Second Empire home, would belong to Ed and Rick upon her death was something he refused to think about any more than he had to. Her trust, support, and guidance were worth much more than that to Ed.

He looked at her now as she reached out a gnarled hand for a Milky Way. He wondered if she really was feeling any worse than usual, or if she was simply experiencing one of her occasional "blue spells," as she called them.

Oh, well, he thought. *I guess we'll muddle through, just like she said. There's not a whole lot I can do about it except be here for her.*

"I remember," Mrs. Penfield was saying, her face a bit brighter, "when Effie Maude would spend the whole of Halloween day in the kitchen making caramel apples. We would have lines of children at the door, eager for the taste of those wonderful treats. Even some of my students, who considered themselves much too old and dignified to participate in Beggar's Night, would stop by for one."

Mrs. Penfield chewed slowly through her Milky Way. "I suppose that's no longer practical, considering those awful rumors of razor blades in apples and such. I do my best to remain optimistic, but what is our world coming to? Is it just me, or does there seem to be a greater need to protect our children these days?"

Ed thought about Claire and Laurie's insistence that an adult accompany their daughters for trick-or-treating, and how he and Laurie, at Jane and Lesley's age, had run the streets like hoodlums on Halloween night, their only fears the ones they made up to scare each other.

"Rick says he doesn't know if there's more danger, or just more paranoia. Sometimes I think we just know too much."

"Ah, yes. Ignorance can indeed be bliss at times." Mrs. Penfield carefully folded her candy wrapper and placed it on the table. "Well, I shan't dwell upon it. You've seen to it that we are well supplied with candy, and I'm sure we will have plenty of visitors this evening. The children always seem to enjoy taking the walk to the front door of this 'spooky old house.' I'm sure those jack-o'-lanterns you and Rick carved over the weekend and put on the front porch will attract several more as well."

Ed grinned. "Yeah, that's the weird thing about Rick and me. We don't have kids of our own to do the things we did as kids with, so we still do them just for ourselves. I'm beginning to wonder if that's why so many of those guys I met through Rick in Indy don't seem to grow up. Maybe it takes kids to make you realize you're an adult."

The doorbell rang. After Ed had handed candy to an E.T. and two Luke Skywalkers, he returned to the parlor.

"I've been thinking about what you said, Ed." Mrs. Penfield eagerly accepted another Milky Way from him. "I do believe that having children does greatly increase the maturity of some adults. However, I believe Rick and yourself have done an excellent job of achieving your own maturity. Yes, you occasionally enjoy boyish pleasures, but most grown men do. There's nothing wrong with anyone of any age carving jack-o'-lanterns or waving sparklers on the Fourth of July."

"We do that, too," Ed said, unwrapping a Milky Way for himself. "And hang stockings on that fireplace over there for Santa every year. I guess you're right. We know we're grown-ups with grown-up responsibilities, but it's fun to do that stuff. I think I'd hate to feel too grown-up to have that kind of fun."

"I always said facing rooms full of adolescents every day kept me young for years," Mrs. Penfield said with a chuckle. "Although there were days when I felt old before my time dealing with them. Still, I feel the cheerfulness you and Rick have added to this house has done wonders in recapturing that youthful feeling for me. You certainly don't see me objecting to a stocking with my name added to the fireplace mantle at yuletide."

Ed chuckled with her as the doorbell rang again. He faced down yet another E.T., wishing he'd thought to buy some Reece's Pieces. He had figured the E.T. craze was over, but apparently not. As *Thriller* was still every kid's favorite album, he had a bet going with Rick as to whether someone would show up at the door wearing one glove like Michael Jackson.

Before he could settle himself once again on the sofa by Mrs. Penfield, the doorbell rang again. He picked up the bowl of candy and returned to the door, but he jumped back when he saw who was outside. Among a group of assorted goblins was a kid dressed up like Jason from the *Friday the 13th* movies.

"Geez!" he exclaimed, honestly startled.

"Trick or treat!" they yelled in a ragged chorus, the little Jason clone remaining silent.

Ed quickly handed over the goods; not wanting to mess with a kid whose idea of fun was to dress up as a maniacal movie murderer. "You don't have a big knife in that bag, do you?" He eyed the youngster with apprehension.

Jason shook his head, obviously choosing to remain silent, as the character did in the movies.

"He had one, but his mom took it away from him," a glow-in-the-dark Darth Vader volunteered as he accepted a Snickers.

Well, thank God for that, Ed thought as he threw an extra candy bar into Jason's bag, just to be on the safe side.

After some loud thank-yous, the mob crowded down the front steps, eager to get to the next stop. Ed returned to the parlor shaking his head. "Whatever happened to ghosts and witches?" he mumbled.

"I've been wondering," Mrs. Penfield said as he finally sat down. "With Rick now home, are you feeling calmer these days? I know the past year and a half was tiring for you, but I can't help but think the time apart had value in regards to both of you obtaining some of that maturity we were discussing."

"Yeah," Ed said with a sheepish smile. "I feel kind of stupid now about all the worrying I did. I mean, everything's changed, but in some ways it's like we've gone back to where we were before."

"Oh, trust me: As an avid bystander, I can tell you that both of you weathered the separation quite well. I'm proud of you, Ed, and Rick as well. The distance the two of you endured could have broken up a pair of lesser men. Of course I always had faith in you, but I'm still glad to see all is well."

Ed sighed. "Turns out we were both worrying about each other being alone," he admitted. In between trips to the door he told Mrs. Penfield of the conversation they'd had at the rest area the previous week.

She nodded. "I suppose you think your talk of monogamy was unique in the fact that your relationship isn't the traditional one between a man and a woman. Perhaps it is. Monogamy is supposedly a given in such a relationship, but as we both know, infidelity is as common among heterosexuals as it is in exclusively male relationships. I can't help but think that such a discussion would benefit a great many marriages."

"I'm glad we talked about it," Ed confessed. "I think we had reached a point where we couldn't just assume it anymore, you know?"

"Yes, I do." Mrs. Penfield frowned in thought. "You and Rick have now been together long enough for that first wonderful flush of passion to have faded. You needn't worry, though. It happens in all marriages. You and Rick, however, are blessed in the great companionship you share with each other. I strongly suspect that even if you were no longer lovers, you would certainly remain friends."

"You think so?" Ed wasn't so sure. He knew of too many couples whose relationships had broken up in the most permanent of ways. He couldn't help but worry that something similar might happen to Doug and Gordy. He said as much.

"Oh, that's not what I meant at all," Mrs. Penfield said, "although I share your concern about Doug and Gordon. No, I can't see you and Rick actually breaking up for any reason. What I am saying is that if you no longer desire each other physically, the relationship will endure based on your companionship, your common interests, and the deep love you have for each other."

Ed looked unconvinced.

Mrs. Penfield took his hand, accurately interpreting his skepticism. "Love is a great mystery, Ed. Everything from sonnets to popular songs has been written about it. Why? Perhaps because it does remain such a mystery. We all spend our lives looking for the clues that will solve the mystery of love, but I suspect we never really solve it. I'm certain I will go to my grave with the mystery intact. I'm quite grateful for that."

"Why?"

Mrs. Penfield began to knead her fingers as she often did in times of great thought. "I guess I don't want to know all the answers about love. It's the genuine mysteriousness of a mystery that compels us forward in a search of clues. It is what keeps us turning the pages of a whodunit, or allows us to sit patiently until the end of a poorly filmed suspense movie. Once the mystery is solved, we can move on with our lives. If you understood the total mystery of your love for Rick, do you think it would endure?"

Ed shrugged.

"Think about it a moment, Ed. You and Rick have a tremendous attraction for each other, but do you think that alone has kept you together? Of course not. At some point you both decided to be obedient to the feelings that bind you together. Many couples disregard that call for obedience and casually end their relationships. You and Rick, however, have given in to the mystery, have shown your willingness to be obedient to your feelings, and have formed the sort of communication so necessary for a long-lasting marriage. It doesn't matter if you're homo- or heterosexual in this regard.

"I fear some people wrongly interpret obedience as slavery, as well. There is a mighty difference. You have not been forced into loving Rick, or staying faithful to him and your feelings for him. You have chosen to be obedient to love, chosen to do the hard work necessary to maintaining a successful marriage. That is why I feel that your marriage will last in the longer run. It is also why I so confidently bequeathed my home to you both. I know this place, which I have loved so mysteriously for so many years, will continue to be a place where the mystery of love thrives in two pairs of very capable hands."

Ed stared into space, digesting her words. It was true. Even though he felt he knew Rick about as well as anyone could, there was still some element of mystery, some unexplainable *something* that drew him to Rick. It was much more than a desire to not be alone, and more, too, than the comfort of having a partner beside him to face life's battles. No, despite their occasional spats and the frustration Ed felt with Rick at times, he was almost always willing to do what was needed to keep their love alive and flourishing. Maybe he really was simply being obedient to the mystery of love.

Ed reached out to fold Mrs. Penfield into a careful hug. "You know, you're still my favorite teacher. Just when I think I know it all, or you've explained everything to me, you come up with something else to make me think, and make me feel better."

Mrs. Penfield returned the hug. "That has always been my chosen profession—to share, teach, and guide. I cannot tell you what a joy it has been to have you as such a bright and enthusiastic student in these golden years of mine. You and Rick have truly made them golden indeed."

"Thanks, Mrs. P.," Ed whispered, using Rick and Effie Maude's nickname for her.

"And thank *you*, Mr. S." Mrs. Penfield chuckled, giving him one last squeeze.

They sat in silence for a few minutes, each drifting away on his or her own thoughts until the doorbell rang once again. Ed grabbed the candy bowl hoping they were nearing the end of the night's visitors, as there wasn't much left. He opened the door and glanced around. The porch, lit only by the eerie glow of the candles in the jack-o'-lanterns, seemed to be empty.

"*Boo!*" Rick jumped up from a hiding place by the front steps. Jane and Lesley popped out from behind the shrubbery with similar exclamations as Ed fell against the door with a genuine gasp.

"You dork," he muttered to Rick with a smile as the girls came forward, hauling their overfilled goody bags. "Mrs. Penfield," he called, "here are two goblins you need to see for yourself."

As he waited for her to join him at the door, Ed had a chance to study the girls' costumes. "Well, well, well," he marveled as he took in Jane Romanowski's get-up, a dead-on salute to Michael Jackson, single glittering glove and all.

Rick shook his head in disgust. "I almost didn't bring them here. I knew you'd never let me live it down, my own niece dressed up like Michael Jackson. I guess this means I lose the bet, huh?"

Ed nodded with great smugness. "You lose, my friend. You have to do the dinner dishes for the rest of this week!"

"C'mon, Uncle Ed," Lesley demanded. "Are we gonna get any candy or not?" She was dressed up as a princess, and she waved her bag at him in a truly imperious fashion.

"Yeah, hand it over, Uncle Ed," Jane said as she did a very bad moonwalk across the porch floor.

"My gracious," Mrs. Penfield said as she came to the door. "What have we here? Come in, girls. I believe Effie Maude left behind some special treats just for you."

As the girls followed Mrs. Penfield to the kitchen, Ed and Rick shared a look of amusement and affection. "It's almost nine o'clock," Rick said with a wink. "Do I still get my treat tonight?"

"Tell you what," Ed said in a low voice, glancing behind him. "Once you pry those girls away from Effie Maude's cookie jar and get them both home, you come right back to our place. I'll be waiting."

"Leather jockstrap and all?" Rick's hand gently brushed the front of Ed's jeans.

"Leather jockstrap and all, darlin'," Ed said after a quick kiss.

As Rick wandered off to the kitchen for some cookies of his own, Ed walked onto the porch to blow out the candles in the jack-o'-lanterns. He paused and allowed both the childlike wonder of Halloween night and the enchanting mystery that was his love for Rick to sweep through him. They were both mysteries he didn't particularly want to solve. If enjoying the love he shared with Rick meant being obedient to its mystery, than he was more than willing to continue behaving.

CHAPTER NINE

The next evening at dinner, Rick was full of news and observations from the Jaycees lunch he had attended with Vince Cummings. "Turns out they really are going to build that pharmaceutical plant on the south side. It'll be announced officially tomorrow. So some new, major industry is actually coming to Porterfield."

"Wow," Ed said as he stacked the dishes for Rick to wash. "We may actually get a video store in this town yet. Maybe even a Chinese restaurant."

Rick's warm and tender special spread across his face. "That's my handyman, thinking big. Actually it could turn out to be very lucrative for Vince, which in turn would benefit us. Apparently this drug company is importing a lot of their upper- and middle-level management to Porterfield from both Illinois and Missouri. So about six or eight months from now, a lot of new folks will be moving to town, looking for houses. Talk about a jackpot! If Vince and I stay on top of things, 1984 could be—sorry, George Orwell—a very good year indeed.

"Which brings me to a related topic," Rick said as he squeezed some Ivory liquid into the sink. "What's up with the Mouse?"

The Mouse was the current occupant of Ed's house on Coleman Street. Her name was actually Wendy Fox. She was a shy, pale little woman in her mid-twenties, definitely more mouse than fox, hence the nickname Ed and Rick had given her. She was a kindergarten teacher at Porterfield Elementary. Ed simply could not imagine her in front of a classroom, but his spies at the school (Jane and Lesley) had reported that she seemed to be well liked. Ed assumed she was one of those people who were more comfortable with children than adults.

The strained but polite relationship Ed had with Wendy Fox was a big comedown after the easy camaraderie he'd had with Doug the past two years. Fortunately Wendy spent most of her weekends in Portland, Indiana, visiting family, so Ed usually scheduled his chore time at the house for when she was away.

"There's nothing new going on with the Mouse," Ed said now. "Why do you ask?"

"Well, considering how you don't particularly like being a landlord, maybe it's time to sell that place. What do you think?"

"What I think is that you're determined to make a commission no matter who you have to talk into selling." Ed swatted him affectionately with a dish towel. "Yeah, I have to admit I've thought about it a lot more since the Mouse moved in, but her lease isn't up 'til August, and I don't have any reason to throw her out. She may not be the liveliest person in the world, but she's been a good tenant so far."

"I sure would like to have some extra listings by the time those new people start moving here," Rick murmured as he rinsed a glass. "August just isn't going to cut it. I know you're gonna say I'm moving too fast again, but if I found a place for us to buy and fix up between now and spring, would you be willing to take it on as a project?"

"Whoa," Ed said, putting up his hands. "Are you sure you want to take on something like that just when you're getting settled into this job?"

Rick shrugged. "You gotta strike while the iron is hot, ya know. And the Porterfield real estate market is about to get very hot."

Ed frowned in thought as he pulled on his jacket to walk downstairs with Jett. Outside, he stood quietly as the chilly autumn breeze blew around him. The maple tree next to the carriage house was quickly shedding its leaves. Ed listened to them land delicately on the ground as he contemplated Rick's suggestion.

It was a good thing he liked roller coasters, he thought. At times his life with Rick seemed to be one long descent on the first hill of the Blue Streak at Cedar Point. He'd gotten used to the idea that Rick was a good deal quicker to jump into new action than he was, so he wasn't too startled by the idea of moving forward with their plans to renovate run-down houses and sell them.

He had to admit that in addition to the good timing for the local real estate market, the timing was good for him as well. Aside from snow-removal work, winter was always his slowest time of the year. Despite Mrs. Penfield's prediction of a cold winter ahead, if the upcoming season was anything like the previous year's one, Ed would spend a lot of time twiddling his thumbs or looking for projects to amuse himself in his workshop.

"I guess if we're gonna try to work together on this plan, now is as good a time as any," he mumbled, kicking at the leaves in front of him. He couldn't help but worry that working so closely together on a project that involved a lot of time, effort, and money would strain their marriage.

But he had agreed to it a long time ago, and for Rick the past two years of hard work had, for all intents and purposes, been leading up to this moment. Ed realized the time had come to see if this plan was a viable one in regards to building their financial independence.

"Well, cat," he said to Jett, who was sniffing at the fallen leaves, "it looks like you might not be seeing as much of me as you did last winter. I think I'm gonna be spending it turning some wreck of a house into a showplace."

He went back upstairs, where Rick was finishing the dishes. Ed put his arms around him, carefully avoiding the wet spots on Rick's shirt.

"Okay, darlin'," he said softly. "Just tell me when to get out my hammer and paintbrushes. I'm ready when you are."

A few days later Ed was finished with his appointments by midafternoon. He came home determined to call Gordy and find out what was going on with him. Ed hadn't heard from him in more than a week, and he was more worried about the current strain on Gordy's relationship with Doug than he was about the possible future strain on his own with Rick.

"I'm fine," Gordy grumbled when Ed began to question him. "Nothin' has really changed, and I'm dealin' with it."

"You're not drinking, are you?" Ed decided to be blunt about one of his biggest concerns. Gordy had a tendency to overindulge when he was depressed.

"No, I am not," Gordy distinctly said. "I suppose I should thank you for being my best bud and asking, but no, I'm not boozing it up. I'm a big boy now, and I decided I needed to get through this without the help of my other bud, Jack Daniels."

"Well, that's good to know." Ed sighed, taking Gordy at his word.

"Listen, remember when I talked about goin' up there on a day off? How about Thanksgiving weekend? Doug's goin' to Chicago, and I think I can get one of the guys here to cover my route. I'll have to hit my folks' house for the turkey, but then maybe I could sack out on your couch for the rest of the weekend. What do you think?"

"I think it's a great idea," Ed replied, pleased at the idea of spending so much time with his friend, and sad to realize he was also pleased that Doug wasn't involved. *I guess Rick's right*, he thought. *Maybe the four musketeers have bitten the dust.*

"You're welcome to the couch, but I gotta warn you, you might have to share it with Jett."

"Shit," Gordy said with a snort. "I might end up getting more affection from the cat than I have been around here lately. Doesn't bother me. So if I can swing it, I'll be over late that Thursday night, okay?"

"Okay. We've got a big Thanksgiving at the main house with the Bentons and the Croasdales, but it should be done by then. John and Vera are staying in the main house for the night, then going back to Indy in the morning, so we'll have the whole weekend to goof off and hang out."

"Awesome," Gordy said, using the current choice word of the younger crowd. "Just save a little leftover bird for turkey sandwiches, and we'll be good to go."

Ed hung up the phone feeling relieved. Gordy had sounded a good deal more like his old self, at least toward the end of their conversation. Ed hoped that spending some time away from Doug and with his best friends would go a long way toward lifting Gordy's spirits, and perhaps even help him find a solution to his current dilemma with Doug.

Ed had just settled onto the sofa with a couple of Effie Maude's cookies to tide him over until dinnertime when the phone rang. He sighed, assuming he'd shortly be leaving the apartment for a handyman emergency. To his surprise, the caller was Rick.

"I'm glad I caught you at home. You busy for the next hour or so?"

"Nope. I'm done for the day," Ed said with his mouth full.

"Well, swallow whatever it is you're eating and come down to the office. I've got something to show you."

"Aw, crud, have you found us a house *already*?"

"Maybe. Meet me out front here in ten minutes, and we'll see what you think."

Ed smothered a groan as he hung up the phone and went to pull on his jean jacket. He should have known Rick wouldn't waste any time in putting him to work on some local hovel, determined as he was to help Ed make it beautiful, and then sell it to one of those new factory executives next year.

Geez, I hope we know what we're doing, he thought as he backed his truck out of the driveway.

Ed tapped his fingers to the music on the radio, Culture Club's "Time (Clock of the Heart)," as he headed downtown. Both the overcast autumn day and the song were making him feel a bit pensive and gloomy. Gordy and Doug were still on his mind, and as Boy George sang of lovers thinking they have something real, Ed couldn't help but think that the something real Gordy and Doug once thought they had apparently wasn't quite so real after all.

He was also disturbed by his negative thoughts about Doug. He had always considered Doug a good friend, but Ed knew his loyalty was, first and always, with Gordy. It was inevitable, he supposed, that friends ended up taking sides when a couple was having problems. It sucked, but he couldn't see any way around it. If the crack in Gordy and Doug's relationship became wide enough to split them up, Ed knew both he and Rick would be there for Gordy, and Doug would possibly fade out of their lives.

"Time," he sighed as he braked for a red light. "I know it can't stand still, but why does it have to hurt so much when it goes forward?"

Having no answer for that question, he was relieved when Duran Duran replaced Culture Club on the radio and Rick's office came into view.

Vince had established Cummings Realty on the west edge of downtown Porterfield, on Clark Street in a renovated Victorian home. Vince's business was on the first floor, and he rented out the two apartments on the second. As Ed saw Rick waiting for him on the front walk, he shuddered at the idea of remodeling such a huge house and converting it into both a business and a commercial residential property. He hoped Rick had something a good deal smaller in mind.

Rick jumped into the truck and gave Ed an address on Elm Street, a few blocks west of Todd and Laurie's house. Ed pelted Rick with questions as they drove south, but Rick refused to say anything until they reached their destination.

"What do you think?" Rick asked once they were parked in front of 418 West Elm.

Ed studied the run-down, peeling-paint, two-story house with an expression of great skepticism on his face. "It looks like the Myers house in *Halloween*," he finally said.

Rick rolled his eyes. "I suppose you're gonna tell me some kid killed his sister here back in the sixties, right?"

"I don't know about that, but it sure wouldn't surprise me if this place turns out to be haunted."

"Well, let's go see for ourselves." Rick jingled the house keys as he stepped out of the truck.

Ed joined him on the front walk, and they slowly approached the house. Up close, Ed could see the house wasn't in as bad shape as he had first thought, but it had obviously been sitting empty and neglected for quite some time.

Rick opened the front door, and they gingerly entered a front hall with a wide staircase leading up, what appeared to be a closet underneath the stairway, and entrances to rooms on the left and right.

"As Bette Davis once said," Rick commented in a dry tone, "what a dump!"

"Actually," Ed said as he inspected the hardwood floor beneath his work boots and reached out to stroke the attractively carved banister on the stairway, "it's not that bad. I can't see anything a little hard work and paint won't fix. Still, I want to see the rest of the place before I get too carried away."

Rick shook his head in disbelief. "And here I thought I was going to have to be the one to convince you!"

They walked through the rest of the house, Ed wearing his handyman's frown as he looked closely at the plumbing, the electrical outlets, and the general condition of each room. They looked through the three bedrooms upstairs and admired the built-in bookcases in the living room. Ed stomped hard on the floors and banged his fist against the walls, pleased with what he felt and heard. He even ran out to his truck to get a flashlight so he could snoop around in the basement and check out the furnace and look for damp spots. He finally came to a halt in the kitchen, peering out a window that overlooked a ragged backyard filled with brown ash and maple leaves.

"I'll bet the neighbors just love that," he said, noting some deadwood that needed to be pruned from the trees.

"Vince'll have a lawn service come in and clean it up before winter," Rick said absently as he opened and closed the kitchen cabinets. "The expenses of maintaining the yard will be charged against any profits the owner gets from the sale."

"Who *is* the owner?"

"Some woman named Diane Kirschner. Vince has been out all day, so I haven't had a chance to ask him about it. I found this place in a pile of old listings. That sign he has out front has been there so long, it's beginning to rust."

"Hmmm." Ed glanced at what seemed to be a relatively new refrigerator. "That makes me wonder. This really is, or was, a nice house. There's gotta be a reason why nobody local has bought it. Maybe we should go back upstairs and look for bloodstains. Maybe someone really was murdered here."

"Oh, c'mon, if something really bad happened you'd know about it. You've lived here all your life."

Ed shrugged. "Yeah, but I'd still like to know the whole story before we do anything."

Rick took a small spiral notebook out of his suit jacket pocket. "Okay. I promise to get the whole story from Vince. For now, though, give me all the bad news. How much work and money would we have to put into this place to sell it for a nice profit?"

As Rick took notes, Ed listed what he felt were the most necessary repair jobs for the house. "I can take care of the little stuff, no problem," he said. "If I run into problems bigger than I suspect with the plumbing and the wiring, I can always call Gene Woeber. He's the one who did all the work on our apartment, and he and Dad were good friends, so he'd probably cut me a deal.

"The biggest two things I can see are the roof and the furnace. It really does need a new roof, and that's something I've never attempted. I really think we should have it professionally done. As for the furnace, it looks old to me and probably should be replaced. Also, after the hot summer we just had, it probably wouldn't hurt to put central air in, too. Again, that's something I've never done, and it may require some new ductwork. All in all, that stuff isn't gonna be cheap. Do you think if we dump all the money you have saved from those commissions into this we'd actually end up with a good enough profit to make it worth the time and aggravation?"

Rick tapped his pen against the notebook. "Let me put down some estimates here. I'm using numbers I used in Indy, and the work might actually be less expensive here. What do you think about these kitchen cabinets?"

"Not much." Ed grimaced at the plain white metal cabinets. "They remind me of the cabinets we had in our kitchen growing up, before Mom and Dad had the kitchen remodeled. I'd vote for all new wood cabinets. And before you say it, no, I don't think Clyde and I are up to the job. We should call Sam Carmichael for that. He's the best cabinetmaker in Stratton County. It won't be cheap, but it'd be worth it in the long run."

Rick wrote another figure in his notebook. He added some numbers, crossed something out, and then added again. He squinted at his notebook, shook his head, and moved over to the window for better light. He finally looked up with a tentative smile on his face.

"I think if I can lowball the asking price by about five or six grand, we might actually be able to get in and out of this with the money I have on hand, which would mean no trips to the bank to talk to your brother-in-law, Todd, about a loan. Then if we can sell it for what I think it'll bring next spring or summer, we'd have a profit of, oh, maybe ten grand, maybe even fifteen."

"You really think we can do all of this without going into the red?"

Rick nodded. "Yeah, I do. Even with the roof and the furnace and the kitchen cabinets. We'll save a ton of money with you doing the rest of the work. And just think: if you decide to sell your house when Wendy's lease is up next summer, we can pay off the mortgage on that, and then we'll have enough money to either do a bigger house project, assuming we don't kill each other on this one, or even buy some lake property like we've talked about. What do you think about that?"

"Geez," Ed whispered, trying to digest the possibilities.

Rick dropped his notebook on the counter and pulled Ed to him for a hug. "When we first came up with these ideas, I figured it'd be years and years before we could do anything like this. I could have never imagined that Mrs.

P. would secure our future by giving us a nice place to live, and the promise of her house someday. But since we have that security, and since I did so well in Indy, this is doable. Oh, it'll take a lot of hard work, sweat equity, and patience, but I really think we can do it."

"And if it blows up in our faces?"

Rick sighed as he stroked Ed's back. "Well, that's just the chance we have to take. You gotta spend money to make money. And I think we've been together long enough to know how to deal with each other in a working situation. Oh, I'm not as confident as I was back in the beginning. That's why I wouldn't even think of looking ahead to another project until this one is done and sold. I have to admit, two and a half years of marriage have taught me a thing or two, but I think we can pull it off without either one of us screaming for a divorce."

Ed giggled weakly. "I sure hope so."

"So what do you think, baby? We in or out of this?"

Ed gave him a quick kiss. "I don't suppose it'll hurt to look into it. Nothing's official 'til we sign the papers. You go talk to Vince. I wanna check out my own sources to see if this place is the Amityville Horror in disguise."

"Oh, yeah? Who's that?"

"My mom. If this place is haunted, she'll know about it."

◆

Early the next morning, Ed drove over to Patterson's Bakery on Main Street. As he parked behind the white brick building, he appreciatively sniffed the air, grateful he'd already had a good breakfast; otherwise, the smell of fresh doughnuts would lure him directly into the front of the store as it had so many people for more than forty years.

Patterson's Bakery was a local institution. Porterfielders had displayed such an allegiance to the baked goods available there that no chain doughnut shop or bakery had ever attempted to open a store in Porterfield, accurately assuming that any such endeavor was doomed to failure. Even with a good cook and baker like Norma for a mother, over the years Ed had become just as addicted to Patterson doughnuts, cakes, and pies as anyone else in town.

He peered in through the back screen door. The main door was open to let out some of the heat, and he could see Norma fussing with some cookie dough while Mrs. Patterson delicately iced what appeared to be a birthday cake. Norma caught sight of him and frowned.

"What are you doing here?" she barked. "Do I bother you at work?"

"Well, yes, Mom, sometimes you do," he said, opening the door.

"Oh, Norma, hush," Mrs. Patterson scolded, giving Ed a big smile. "Why, after all the work he did for me on that fence out back, Ed is always welcome here."

Mrs. Patterson selected a glazed doughnut from a tray that hadn't yet made it into the display cases out front and handed it to Ed with a paper napkin. Ed gratefully accepted the treat and thanked Mrs. Patterson, giving Norma a very smug, triumphant look.

Norma scowled. "My, aren't *you* just the charmer," she grumbled as Mrs. Patterson returned to icing her cake. "Is there a reason for stopping by here other than grubbing free doughnuts from my boss? You have to remember I'm a liberated, working woman now. I don't have as much time as I used to for all of your nonsense."

Ed licked his fingers. "I'm sure Betty Friedan is somewhere applauding you as we speak."

"You watch your mouth, young man," Norma threatened, waving her mixing spoon at him.

"Actually, I came to ask you about some gossip."

"Gossip? Since when do you pay any attention to gossip in this town?" Norma narrowed her eyes. "Are they talking about you and Rick again?"

"I hope not. We've got enough to worry about without worrying about that."

"Well, then." Norma returned to spooning out cookie dough onto a sheet. "What is it you want to know?"

"What can you tell me about the Kirschner house on Elm Street?"

Norma looked up from her work. "That mess down the street from your sister's? Why on earth do you want to know about that?"

"Rick and I are thinking about buying it and fixing it up to sell to one of those new factory executives that'll be pouring into town next spring."

"Oh, for Pete's sake!" Norma shook her head in disgust. "Of all the harebrained ideas you two have come up with, this just beats all."

"Mom," Ed said patiently, "you know Rick and I have talked about doing this for a few years now, so don't pretend to be shocked. We looked at this place yesterday, and it isn't really in such bad shape. If we're going to do this, I think it would be a good place to start, but I want to know why it hasn't sold already. Is it haunted or something?"

"Humph. Might as well be. You know Elsie Sutter from the garden club lives right across the street, so I've heard all about it."

"I figured as much."

"That Elsie, she's carried on about that place for years now, what an eyesore it's becoming, and how she worries about her property value. Why, she even tried to talk Gloria Axelrod and her husband into buying that place when they were looking for a new house last year. Gloria said they weren't interested, but of course you know why she wouldn't even consider it. Gloria's hated Elsie for years now. Why, the things she says about Elsie behind her back, being just as nice as pie to her face! Calls herself a good Christian woman, and she says the things she does about Elsie, and half the rest of the club, too, for that matter. The things that go on in that club . . ." Norma shook her head in righteous indignation.

Ed calmly threw his napkin into a nearby trashcan, assuming Norma would at some point return to the subject.

"Anyway," she said, shoving her sheets of cookies into the oven, "that Kirschner house. Well, the Kirschners lived there back in the seventies. They seemed like a nice young couple, with two children, a boy and a girl. Turns out the husband wasn't so nice after all. He was having an affair with one of those awful bar tramps from Buck's downtown. When she found out about it, there was an ugly divorce, and eventually the husband moved up to Fort Wayne just to get away from all the talk.

"Things would have been okay after that, I suppose, but one weekend he came down here to get the kids for a visit, and on the way back to Fort Wayne, all three of them were killed in an accident on the highway. Those poor children." Norma sighed, wiping her hands.

"Oh, yeah. I kinda remember that now. That must have been about seven or eight years ago, though."

"Yes, it was. That poor Diane Kirschner was just beside herself, first watching her marriage go bad, then losing both her children. I can only imagine what she went through. Well, the truth is, she got a little loony. I don't blame her a bit. I probably would have, too. She pretty much locked herself up in that house and just let it go to rack and ruin. Some relative of hers finally got her out of there, and she was hauled off to some mental ward in Fort Wayne. Last I heard, she was doing better and moved up to Michigan to be closer to her family. Hasn't been back here since. I can't blame her for that either."

Ed watched Norma go to work on some new cookie dough. "Well, that explains a lot—at least why it's so neglected and why no one around here is all that interested in buying it. They probably do think it's haunted by those two kids, or they just don't want to live in a house where a crazy lady lived."

"Probably. Still, as sad as it all is, I'm sure that place would be fine if someone took the effort to fix it up. I guess someone from out of town who doesn't know the story would jump right on it."

"So it could be a good investment for Rick and me." Lost in thought, Ed absentmindedly reached for a pile of chocolate chips. Norma slapped his hand away.

"Are you sure you really want to take on this foolishness? Seems like an awful lot of work to me."

Ed rubbed his fingers. "Yeah, it will be, but if we can pull it off, we'll be set financially. I told Rick I was willing to give it a try, and I am."

"Well, Elsie Sutter would certainly be grateful. *If* you two know what you're doing," Norma added, giving him a doubtful look.

"Only one way to find out," Ed said with a shrug.

"Don't you think for a minute that you're going to drag me into this. I have a job now, so don't you go thinking I have time to be over there with a paintbrush helping you turn that sow's ear into a silk purse. Understand?"

Ed assumed his most pathetic look. "You mean you won't even bake us cookies when we're spending all of our weekends there, trying to make you proud of us?"

"Humph! We'll see. If I've a mind to, I might. Why don't you ask her?" Norma jerked her head in Mrs. Patterson's direction. "Since you're so cozy with my boss, why don't you get her to make you some cookies?"

"Because her cookies aren't as good as yours are, Mom. That's why she was smart enough to hire you back here."

Norma put down her mixing spoon and folded her arms across her chest. "You've been around that Rick too long. You're starting to sound just like him with all those smooth words."

Ed grinned. "And you love it, don't you?"

"Humph!" She sneered. "You'll never hear me confess to that."

However, Norma walked to a nearby table where a sheet of cookies had been cooling. Pulling on a plastic glove, she carefully picked the choicest ones from the sheet and put them in a paper bag. She handed it to Ed with a wink. Ed thanked her with a careful hug, avoiding her stained apron.

"Getting soft in your old age?" he teased.

"I s'pose," she grumbled, going back to work. "Just don't tell that sister of yours about this. I'll never live it down!"

CHAPTER TEN

Rick came home that evening with Vince's story of the house, which checked out with Norma's except for one attractive detail: apparently Diane Kirschner was so eager to get rid of the house and be done with Porterfield once and for all that Vince was certain she would accept an offer much lower than her asking price. Rick spent the weekend going over his figures and consulting Ed about probable supply costs. By Sunday evening they were confident enough in Rick's numbers to put an official offer on the house. Within a few days they had their response from Diane Kirschner: offer accepted. After that, the slow but steady-as-clockwork mechanisms of buying a house began to go into motion.

"Do you realize," Rick said one morning as he was getting ready for work, "that this will actually be the first time in my life I've owned property? How 'bout that, huh?"

"Yeah." Ed paused in tying the laces on his work boots. "You know, now that we're getting to be such big shots with all this land and stuff, maybe we should do something to protect ourselves legally, make out a will or something."

Rick looked thoughtful as he knotted his tie. "That's not a bad idea. If something did happen to one of us, the other one would be screwed since we aren't really married. I've known for a long time that it was something we needed to think about, but maybe it's time for some action. Maybe we could talk to Matt Croasdale about that at Thanksgiving."

Clyde's son, Matt, had arrived in Porterfield and had begun work at Mason and Schultz. Laurie reported that he seemed to be a pleasant man, eager to settle into the small-town law firm. She also mentioned that most of the single working women on East Commerce Street were, as Rick had predicted, in a dither about having a newly single lawyer in their midst.

It had been Mrs. Penfield's idea to invite the Croasdales—Clyde, Claudine, and Matt—for Thanksgiving. Ed suspected that Mrs. Penfield was curious about the man who was now a part of the firm originally begun by her father-in-law and run by her husband until his death.

"Geez." Ed snickered. "With Mrs. Penfield checking him out, you bugging him about buying a house, and both of us asking him about wills, that guy isn't going to have much of a holiday."

"I'll be subtle." Rick patted the pocket on his suit jacket. "I'll just slip one of my business cards under his plate, or maybe in his stuffing."

Ed looked at Rick standing before him, dressed in a well-cut navy suit, looking quite confident and businesslike. The tiny threads of gray in his hair and beard seemed only to add to his look of distinction. Ed thought back to the first time he had seen Rick in anything other than his mailman uniform. He had been wearing a t-shirt, jeans, a windbreaker, and beat-up tennies, Ed remembered. This new version of Rick still took him by surprise on occasion, and even made him a little uneasy. But now, as Rick turned to him with his warm and tender special aglow, obviously requiring a kiss from his husband before he went out in the cruel world of the Porterfield real estate market, Ed was comforted as he realized that his Rick was still alive and well under the image of a sharp-dressed businessman.

⊰•⊱

Rick was definitely not dressed for success when Ed found him in the kitchen of the main house on Thanksgiving morning. He was clad in one of Ed's old flannel shirts and sweatpants as he and Mrs. Penfield busily worked on the day's feast. A good deal of the meal preparation had been accomplished by Effie Maude before she left to visit family in Ohio, but there was still plenty to do. Ed was pleased to see Mrs. Penfield easily mixing cranberry relish. He suspected the thought of so much company did wonders in keeping her "old friend arthritis" at bay for at least one day.

Ed wandered about the kitchen, accomplishing nothing but getting underfoot. Rick and Mrs. Penfield finally kicked him out, instructing him to set the dining room table. Ed carefully laid out twelve settings of the first Mrs. Penfield's silver and Havilland china. The delicate gold trim of the china and the freshly polished silver glowed against a snowy white damask tablecloth. The crystal chandelier, dusted the day before by Effie Maude, sent prisms of color throughout the room. When he was finished, Ed stood and savored the quiet, comfortable elegance of the room, with the beautifully set table, the burnished glow of the built-in oak breakfront, the mellow age of the light green patterned wallpaper, and the handsome bay window overlooking Race Street.

He loved the old house. He could imagine warm family Thanksgivings in that dining room for many years to come. There were still occasions when Ed thought that perhaps Porterfield wasn't the best place in the world for Rick and himself to build their life together, but at those times he also realized how deeply his roots had sunk into this house and the land it occupied. Their trip to San Francisco had opened his eyes to a kind of freedom he had only imagined, but he knew the cost of that freedom would be abandoning the comfort, stability, and traditions they were only beginning to create and enjoy in their current surroundings. Both Ed and Rick had discovered a gentle serenity during their time living at the Penfield place, a warmth that neither one of them was willing to give up in search of potentially greener pastures. The Penfield place had become, in every since of the word, home.

Ed's contentment with the day and his surroundings continued as the guests began to arrive. Rick settled John and Vera, who were a bit road weary from their long drive, in the quiet front parlor with fresh coffee, as Ed took their overnight bags to the guest room upstairs. Claire and her children arrived next. Judy, Josh, and Jane were shooed into the study to watch the tail end of the Macy's parade on television. Ed wandered in after them, building a fire as an excuse to enjoy the annual New York City celebration as well.

After she had deposited two pumpkin pies and a plate of brownies in the kitchen, Claire joined Ed in the study near the fireplace.

"I want to see Santa Claus, too," she whispered to Ed. "That's how I know the holidays are really here."

She glanced at her children, who were exchanging comments on the floats passing by. "I wish they still believed," she said wistfully. "Seems like it takes some of the magic out of Christmas."

"I still believe." Ed grinned at her as he stuffed kindling under the logs.

Claire grinned in return. "I guess I'm beginning to believe again. For a while there I wasn't so sure."

Ed studied Claire as her gaze returned to the television screen. He was pleased to see that the stress and worry that had become etched in her face had begun to vanish. Her husband had abandoned Claire and the children almost four years earlier. It had been a rough road for Claire, and she often said that if it wasn't for the help of her brother and his partner, she might have thrown in the towel.

She hadn't, though. She had worked hard, was doing a wonderful job of raising her children without a father, and had achieved a dignity she had never really managed during the years Hank Romanowski was in the picture. It was quietly believed by everyone involved that Claire and her children were a lot better off without him, and her well-adjusted children and refreshed appearance now that her divorce was final were testament to that belief.

After Santa Claus had passed by on the television screen, the Croasdales arrived. Activity shifted to the front parlor as Mrs. Penfield, Ed, and Rick fussed over the guests and made sure everyone was comfortable.

Although Ed had been friendly with Clyde for more than two years, he hadn't spent that much time in the company of Clyde's older sister, Claudine. Despite several troublesome health issues, she was still the dignified and authoritative woman who had dealt with generations of children and their mothers in the ready-to-wear department of the Porterfield Penney's store. Ed had often found her to be rather aloof, but watching her in genial conversation with both Vera and Mrs. Penfield, he thought perhaps that reserve had more to do with her poor health than with her general disposition. Ed was pleased to see that she was apparently enjoying herself today.

Matt Croasdale turned out to be a man of average height and build in his mid-thirties with an open, friendly face topped by a shock of light brown hair. He blended into the room full of strangers with an ease and charm that Ed rather envied. Ed also sensed some of his aunt's dignity and authority in Matt's manner and thought it probably proved to be an asset in the courtroom.

Conversation moved easily from the front parlor and into the dining room as dinner was served. After a short prayer of thanks from Mrs. Penfield, Rick stood up to carve the turkey.

As the side dishes began to make their way around the table, Ed heard Matt tell John that he was currently staying at his aunt's house on Michigan Street until he could find more permanent quarters in Porterfield. Rick's ears pricked up at that, and Ed quickly frowned at him, so Rick smirked in return, mouthing the words *after dinner* at him. Ed grinned and accepted the green bean casserole that was being nudged at him by Jane.

"Ed, I thought we would be seeing your mother today," Vera commented as she helped herself to Effie Maude's secret-recipe turkey stuffing. "Where is she spending the holiday?"

"Oh, she went to Crestland to have dinner with Uncle Chester and Aunt Eleanor," Ed replied. "One of the Perfects is in town, so she wanted to get the update on his fabulous life."

"The Perfects?"

"My cousins," Ed explained. "When we were kids, they never seemed to do anything wrong, always got straight As, and always made Laurie and me look bad, so we started calling them the Perfects. Mom would always say, 'Why can't you be more like your cousins?' It drove us crazy for years."

"And here I thought you were the perfect one," John teased from the other side of the table. "Rick has certainly painted that picture for us these past few years."

"I'm prejudiced," Rick said with a shrug.

"Laurie and I just couldn't compete with everything they did so well, but we managed to do okay for ourselves, I guess."

Ed laughed as one particular memory came to mind. "The thing was, Laurie and I fought a lot when we were kids—a heck of a lot more than the Perfects did, that's for sure. One Christmas when our families got together, Laurie and I got in a knock-down, drag-out over our presents, and Mom was embarrassed and absolutely furious with us. She locked all of our presents in a closet, and I don't think we got to see any of them again until almost New Year's Eve."

"Hey, Mom, we're not as bad as that," Josh piped up. "You've never had to take our presents away from us."

"There's a first time for everything," Claire responded with a stern look.

Matt Croasdale gave Josh a conspiratorial grin. "Oh, I'm sure neither Josh nor his sisters would ever do anything so bad as to deserve that kind of punishment."

Judy, next to Mrs. Penfield at the head of the table, rolled her eyes. "Oh, yeah? You wouldn't believe some of the stupid stuff those two argue about sometimes."

Rick laughed. "Getting so old you think you're above all that, Jude? I don't think so!"

"Yeah," Jane seconded, leaning across Ed to give her sister a righteous glare. "You're just as bad as we are."

Judy seemed prepared to make a snotty retort to her younger sister but obviously decided to shift gears before she fell into Jane's trap. "When you get older," she said to Jane with a condescending smile, "you'll realize how silly all of that is."

"Oh, brother!" Josh groaned.

As the rest of the table chuckled, Vera commented, "I must admit, it takes me back to the days when Claire and Rick were young."

That drew attention away from the children long enough for Jane to get away with sticking her tongue out Judy. Judy made a nasty face at her in return, which Mrs. Penfield caught out of the corner of her eye.

"Since I never had daughters of my own, it certainly gives me an idea of what I missed," Mrs. Penfield said, the twinkle in her eye aimed at Judy, who looked chagrined at being caught in such a childish act.

Claire's mother radar had also picked up on the interplay between her girls. "This is the day for counting blessings, Mrs. P. Make sure you add that one to your list." She gave Judy and Jane a look that plainly let them know to knock it off.

"Girls can be a handful sometimes," Claudine put in. "But then, so can boys. I remember times at the store . . ."

The conversation and the meal continued until everyone began to complain of overeating. Chairs were pushed back and Mrs. Penfield suggested they move to the parlor for coffee. John headed for the front porch with his pipe, and Clyde, pulling a cigar out of his pocket, eagerly joined him. Ed sighed, knowing his time as head cleanup person had come. He quickly drafted Judy, Josh, and Jane to help him clear the table.

Once they had the worst of it moved into the kitchen, he made an announcement. "I'm too full to worry about this now. Let's wait until after everyone's ready for dessert. Maybe I can talk your mom into helping me then."

Josh and Jane hurried off to the study and the television before Ed could change his mind. Ed slowly walked to the parlor, Judy trailing him.

Rick looked up from his conversation with Matt when Ed entered the room. "Mom and Dad want to see the house we're buying. How 'bout we go over there before dessert? If we wait too long, it'll be dark."

Ed, who was much more in the mood for a nap than for a drive across town, smiled and nodded as agreeably as possible.

On their way to the garage to get Rick's car, Rick told Ed he had spoken with Matt about their legal concerns. "Matt said we're definitely doing the right thing in that respect. I mean, you'd expect a lawyer to say that, but he said he read an article in a law journal recently about so many of these men dying of AIDS without any legal protection for their assets. Even if they've been with another guy for years, the families just come in and take whatever they want, and the guy who survives can't do anything about it."

"Geez."

"Yeah. So Matt wants us to come in sometime next week and talk with him about how we can protect our assets and provide for each other in case something happens to one of us. Oh, and yes," Rick added with a grin, "I'm gonna take him around town to look at some of the houses that are available, too."

"That's good," Ed said absently, his mind still on their potential legal problems.

John and Vera seemed impressed with both the Kirschner house and their plans for it. Ed found himself watching them, wondering if something did happen to Rick, would they feel they had the right to come in and take what they felt belonged to them as Rick's parents with no consideration for Ed? And to be fair, would Norma, in one her bossier moments, do the same thing if something happened to Ed?

He was rather quiet in the car on their way back to the Penfield place as he pondered those possibilities. John and Vera said they considered Ed to be part of the family, and Norma was certainly fonder of Rick than she was willing to admit, but did their parents really take Ed and Rick's relationship seriously? Or, since they were both men and not legally married, did they consider it some sort of casual arrangement—something less than their own marriages? Ed hated to think such negative thoughts about their parents, who, after all, had been much more accepting of the situation than most, but as a gay man, Ed was used to people thinking of him as a second-class citizen. He couldn't help but wonder what would happen if the polite veneer of their parents' acceptance was stripped away. Ed didn't want to think about anything bad happening to either Rick or himself but decided the upcoming meeting with Matt was probably a very good thing indeed.

His thoughts had the unfortunate side effect of taking away some of the glow he'd felt all day. It had been a wonderful family holiday so far, but he suddenly found himself restless with the day and the company. He was now looking forward to Gordy's arrival more than he already had been.

Maybe we do spend too much time around straight people, trying to fit in, he thought as he listened to Rick telling his parents about his work with Vince. For the first time that day, Ed found himself questioning their decision to remain in Porterfield.

The minute I think I've got it figured out and think we're okay, something else comes along to make me wonder if we're doing the right thing. He realized with a smothered sigh that he would probably continue to question and second-guess that decision as time went by.

As they piled out of the car and walked toward the main house, Ed shook his head, determined to let go of his negative thoughts and enjoy the rest of the day. At least for today he had no reason to question the loyalty of Rick's family or his own. It was still Thanksgiving, and Ed decided to just be grateful for what he did have.

Everyone seemed to be ready for dessert when they returned, so the pumpkin pies were brought out. As Ed went to fetch the dessert plates from the breakfront, Judy grabbed his arm and pulled him into the study.

"You won't believe what happened while you were gone," she whispered, still clutching his arm.

Ed rolled his eyes at her. "Okay. What did Josh and Jane do to make you mad this time?"

Judy shook her head impatiently. "No, no, it's not about them. It's about Mom. That Matt guy asked her out on a date!"

Ed's first reaction was pretty close to the astonishment showing on Judy's face. After he thought about it for a moment, though, he said, "Well, what's wrong with that?"

"Mom? On a date? Get real, Uncle Ed!"

"No, you get real, kid. Your mom's a young, attractive, single woman. I know you don't see her that way, but any straight guy in his right mind would. Matt's not stupid, so why wouldn't he ask her out?"

"Yeah, I know, but . . ."

"Your mom is a divorced woman now. She's been through hell since your dad took off. Don't you think it's time she had some fun, or even a little male companionship?"

Judy grimaced. "I guess. Somehow it's just different when it's your own mom."

"What, you think she's gonna turn into some wild, swinging single girl, running around all the time? I don't think you have to worry about that. Your mom's first priority is you three kids, and I think she's proved that in the last four years."

Ed's curiosity got the better of him. "So did he ask her in front of you? Where are they going?"

"No, I overheard them talking when I went to kitchen to get Mrs. Penfield a glass of water. He was saying that he'd been working so hard he hadn't had any time for fun, and he needed to do something about it. Then he asked her if she'd like to go to Fort Wayne for dinner and a movie this weekend. Mom seemed a little surprised, but she said she'd love to go."

"And did she know you were listening?" Ed crossed his arms and gave her the hairy eyeball.

"I don't think so," Judy admitted. "After that I cleared my throat really loud and walked in to get Mrs. Penfield's water. They weren't touching or anything, but they seemed to be smiling a lot."

Ed snickered. "Well, I'm glad to know they weren't passionately making out in the kitchen. Matt's a brave man, asking out the mother of a snoop like you."

Judy seemed a little embarrassed. "Well, I didn't mean to listen. It just kinda happened."

"Hey, Ed," Rick called from the kitchen. "Where are those dessert plates?"

"I'll be there in a minute," he hollered back.

Ed put his hands on Judy's shoulders. "Listen, will you make me a promise? You're almost fifteen now, and you're getting old enough to understand some of what your mom's been through. Will you promise me to support her on having a social life of her own, and run interference if the other kids give her a hard time about it? You're interested in boys and dates now, so you should be able to see how she feels."

Judy thought for a moment. "Okay. I guess so. Unless this guy turns out to be a loser."

"Don't get ahead of yourself. It's just one date. So we're cool?"

"Yeah, yeah, we're cool. Go get those plates before Uncle Rick totally freaks out."

As Ed carried the plates into the kitchen, he found himself watching Matt and Claire. He'd never even considered the possibility of the two of them being interested in each other, and he hoped Claire didn't think he and Rick had been playing matchmaker.

He had the opportunity to find out late that afternoon. As he had hoped, Claire joined him in the kitchen for cleanup duty. They settled in for the long haul, Ed carefully washing the china, crystal, and silver while Claire dried.

"You know, it's really been a good day," Claire said. "Not once did Mom and Dad start in on any of us about how badly we're running our lives. It must be true what they say about that chemical in turkey. We need to make sure they always get turkey when they come to visit."

Ed giggled. "I thought sure they'd blow a gasket when Rick told them he was buying that house, but they actually seem to trust his judgment for a change. Oh, well, whatever got into them, I hope it lasts."

He handed her some clean knives. "So do they know about your little excitement coming up this weekend?"

Claire gave him a dirty look. "My, my; good news sure does travel fast in these parts, doesn't it? I'm sure my eldest daughter, who was eavesdropping, probably blabbed to Mom the way she obviously did to you, but Mom hasn't said anything. Besides, what's to bitch about? Matt's a lawyer and he's single. Mom's probably keeping her mouth shut so she won't jinx it!"

The both laughed. "Well, you do know that I'm as surprised as Judy was. I mean, no one here was trying to fix you up or anything."

"Believe me; no one was more surprised than I was." Claire slid the knives into their slots in the silver box. "I didn't suspect you guys of anything at all. Matt seems like a nice guy, though. Actually, he's probably the first guy I've met since Hank took off that I'd consider going out with. That's why I said yes. Still, I'm not getting my hopes up. It's just dinner and a movie. No biggie, as Judy says."

"No fireworks, huh?"

Claire snorted. "I had fireworks once, and see where that got me. No, I'm not so much looking for fireworks, but the idea of a nice, stable guy with a decent job who can put up with my three brats, and maybe keep me company in my old age, sounds pretty good these days."

She glanced through the open door into the dining room. Josh and Jane were at the table, hard at work on a jigsaw puzzle with a Currier and Ives sort of Christmas scene that Mrs. Penfield had unearthed. Ed turned around and was surprised to see both Matt and Claudine eagerly turning over puzzle pieces as well. All four of them seemed to be getting along famously.

"I happen to know from Clyde," Ed said to Claire in a low voice, "that one of the reasons Matt got divorced is because his wife didn't want kids. I wonder how he'd feel about a ready-made family."

"Well, that's all he'd get out of me." Claire patted her belly. "This factory has ceased production forever."

"Never say never," Ed teased.

"Yeah, I suppose you're right. I never would have foreseen how things would turn out with Hank, so I guess I'd better keep my mouth shut."

Claire dreamily wiped a dinner plate as she stared out the window into the early dusk. "Things have sure changed, haven't they? I mean from where we all were when Rick first moved here, and you guys got together."

"Yeah. Remember the first time I babysat for you, right after Thanksgiving three years ago, when I locked Josh and myself out of the house? Geez, I figured I was finished with you before I even had a chance to make a good impression!"

Claire put down the plate and laughed. "Yeah, I remember that. It didn't bother me. That's just the kind of stuff that happens when you have three kids running loose. I'd already decided you were a good guy, and probably the best thing to ever happen to Rick. I'm so glad you guys are still together. I hope we're all having Thanksgiving together for a long, long time."

"Me, too."

And Ed did hope that, despite the thoughts he'd had earlier. Now that he was inside its walls, the Penfield house once again seemed to be the place of family and tradition it always had been, and hopefully always would be. The magic Ed had felt earlier in the day had returned in full. The world, Ed knew, was an imperfect place, and his place in it as a gay man would continue to be a struggle. For now, though . . .

"What's that old expression?" he blurted. "Something about 'God's in his heaven, and all's right with the world?' It feels like that today, doesn't it?"

Even though a long line of dirty dishes still stretched the length of the kitchen counter, Ed and Claire exchanged smiles of contentment.

"Yeah, it does," she said.

CHAPTER ELEVEN

Gordy arrived late that evening. There wasn't much conversation, as they were all tired from the long day. When Ed got up the next morning, he was comforted to see Gordy sprawled on the sofa, sound asleep with Jett curled up next to him. They had the whole weekend ahead of them to get caught up on each other's lives.

While Rick was at the main house seeing his parents off for their trip back to Indianapolis, Ed and Gordy kicked around ideas for the day. They had discussed going to Fort Wayne for a movie but decided that dealing with the day-after-Thanksgiving shopping crowds swarming around the malls wasn't worth the hassle. Ed suggested going in the completely opposite direction. Since it was a nice day for late November, how about a walk in the woods? Gordy grumbled that it was his day off and he didn't see why he should spend it walking, but then he agreed that the quiet would be good after the raucous Thanksgiving Day at the Smiths'.

Rick returned to the apartment and enthusiastically agreed with the plan. After a late breakfast at Dottie's Diner downtown, they headed out to Stratton County Park, the closest thing to wilderness that could be found in their part of northeast Indiana.

The three of them quietly walked the narrow path through the nature preserve, shuffling through the leaves and thinking their own thoughts. Ed reflected on how nice it was to be with people you knew so well that there was no need for conversation. The solitude of the park was indeed a good choice after a day spent with crowds of family and friends.

They rounded a curve and came upon a wooden footbridge over Stratton Creek. Ed paused and peered as far along the creek as he could. He had heard a beaver colony had established a lodge somewhere on its waters. He saw plenty of squirrels and birds, but no beavers.

"Hell, some asshole with a shotgun probably got wind of them," Gordy said, stretching over the railing.

"I hope not," Ed sighed, "but it sure wouldn't surprise me. There are just some people who can't leave well enough alone."

"Ain't that the truth." Rick joined them on the bridge. "Still, if hunters had been in the park, I doubt *he'd* still be running around." He drew their attention to a buck crashing through the woods.

Gordy snorted. "Shit, most of the guys around here couldn't hit the broad side of a barn. I think the only reason they go huntin' is to have an excuse to drink beer and piss in the woods."

He pulled his cigarettes and lighter out of his pocket and lit up. The light breeze blew the smoke into Rick's face. He impatiently waved it away.

"We come out here for fresh air and exercise and you're gonna do *that?*"

Gordy exhaled smoke with a tired sigh. "Don't nag, Benton, okay? Let me enjoy one of the few things I have left."

Rick looked contrite. "I'm sorry, bud," he said as he put an arm around Gordy's shoulders.

"Oh, Christ, and don't go feelin' sorry for me either. So it didn't work out for me like it did for you guys. It was a long shot, but I took a chance. I'm glad I did, but now I have to figure out what the hell to do with my life."

Ed settled himself against the railing, turning his face to the pale sunlight filtering through the bare trees. "So you're telling us it's really over?"

"Might as well be." Gordy took another deep drag and then exhaled. "We're supposed to be 'thinking it over' this weekend while we're apart. Shit! I think Doug's mind is made up. I heard him talking to an old friend in Chicago on the phone, making plans to meet him on Halsted Street tonight. And here I am back in good ole Porterfield. What the fuck is there to think about?"

Ed looked at Gordy and saw the sadness and resignation on his face. The irony of it, Ed thought, was that underneath his sorrow, Gordy had never looked better. He was probably in the best shape he'd been in since high school, and the new, dark blond beard gave his already handsome face a ruggedness it had previously lacked. Ed knew that a lot of men would love to have someone like Gordy sighing over them. Unfortunately a dumb-ass mortician by the name of Doug didn't seem to be one of them.

"Oh, Gord." Ed leaned against him and put his head on his shoulder.

Rick leaned in from the other direction. "So what's being going on? From what Ed told me, I didn't know things had gone this far."

"I didn't want to talk about it on the phone. A lot's been going on lately. I finally confronted him about trickin' around, and sure enough he copped to it. We've been bitchin' at each other nonstop for weeks now. Our sex life is toast. He may still be interested, but I'm not. I don't feel like bein' with him, knowing he's been with other guys, and with the AIDS shit, who knows what's goin' on with him? Who knows if there's more than what he's tellin' me?

"He says that we made an agreement, that we could see other guys. Well, shit, we made that agreement when we were here in Porterfield, so I didn't think too much about it. I finally accused him of wantin' to go to Indy just so he could get laid more. He said that wasn't true. He just wanted to be out. I said lots of guys are out without fuckin' around on their lovers, and he said I wasn't bein' realistic, that all guys fuck around. I said that you guys didn't, and he said—are you ready for this?—he said that you guys probably were but not bein' honest about it."

"*What?*" Ed exclaimed.

"Oh, he just said that to try to make himself look better," said Rick.

"Yeah. That's what I said to him. Then he went into this long blah-blah about how he was only twenty-five, and he wasn't ready to settle down, and all that shit. So I asked him, did he always think of me as temporary? He said no, that he thought when we got together that it would be forever, but that he'd changed, and realized he needed to—and I quote here—'Live a lot longer and see a lot more before I'm ready to be with just one guy.'"

"Oh, brother," Ed said with a snort.

"He may not live as long as he thinks if he keeps doing what he's doing," Rick commented dryly.

"Yeah! He said he loved me, loved me more than any man he'd ever known, but maybe it would be better for us to split up now while we still loved each other, and maybe sometime in the future it would work out. Can ya believe that? It's like, 'Okay, when I get tired of fuckin' around, if you're still waiting I'll be ready.' Fuck that!"

Gordy gulped. "Can you see me doin' that? Can you see me sittin' around, waitin' for him to get his fill of dick out there? I love the stupid son of a bitch, but I'm not gonna do that. I love him, but if we can't . . ."

The cigarette dropped from Gordy's trembling fingers and fell into the water below with a hiss. His whole body began to shake, and finally the tears came.

Ed and Rick silently held on to their friend, letting him know they were there for him, trying to give him what little comfort they could. Gordy's sobs began to slow down, and he wiped his nose with the back of his hand.

"Shit," he mumbled. "Anybody got a Kleenex?"

Ed chuckled as he pulled a wad of tissue out of his jacket pocket. Rick began to chuckle as well when Gordy gave his nose a huge, honking blow. Gordy joined in and accidentally let the snotty tissue fall into the water.

"Aw, fuck; now I'm a crybaby and a litterbug, too!"

"You needed to get that out, bro," Rick said, stroking his back.

"Yeah, I know." Gordy sighed as he lit another cigarette.

"So what are you going to do? I mean, what do you want to do?" Ed asked when Gordy had once again settled himself against the bridge railing.

Gordy shrugged. He watched a squirrel jump from tree to tree above them and shrugged again. "I want to come home," he said softly. "I feel like a fuckin' failure, but I wanna come home."

"Oh, Gord, you're not a failure." Rick slapped him on the back. "It's like you said: you took a chance, and it didn't work out. It may hurt like hell, but at least you tried."

"It just sounds so stupid," Gordy grumbled. "I go through this big deal about movin' to Indy, and a few months later I turn around and leave with my tail 'tween my legs. Thing is, I would have never moved down there without Doug, so if I don't have him, why should I stay? Shit, I know there aren't any men around here for me, and it's back in the closet for this homo, but right now I don't give a good goddamn about that. I just want to be where I'm comfortable, and that damned city ain't it.

"Remember before Doug how I'd go to Indy or Chicago or wherever to meet guys and get laid? Well, I got that out of my system. It'll still be there if I change my mind, but for now I just wanna get back to my life, and despite my fucked-up dad, I'd rather do it here with you guys than down there where I don't have any real friends."

Ed smiled. "Yeah, you need to be here where we can keep an eye on you."

Rick looked thoughtful. "Do you want to go back to the post office?"

"I don't know. I guess so. I thought about lookin' for another job, but I don't know what the hell it'd be. I suppose I could go work in that new factory, but I don't really want to do that. If Don would take me back, I guess I'd go back to sellin' stamps in Porterfield like I've always done. Or maybe I could get a mail route here. That's been the one thing I've liked down there."

"Well," Rick said, scratching his head, "I happen to have some news I've been holding back. I was kind of waiting to see where your head was at."

"What's up?"

"I stopped in the post office the other day. Don came out to talk to me for a few minutes. Seems he finally fired Jim Murkland."

"Murk the Jerk? Really?" Ed turned to Rick with his mouth open in surprise. Jim Murkland was the only person at the post office who had ever harassed Rick about being gay. Don Hoffmeyer, the postmaster, had put a stop to it. Ed couldn't help but feel a nasty thrill of delight at Murk the Jerk's downfall.

"What happened?" Gordy wanted to know.

"Oh, the usual. I guess he came into work still drunk from the night before one too many times. Rumor has it he's moving to Fort Wayne where there are a lot more bars and liquor stores, and no one knows what an asshole he is. Anyway, Don was teasing me, asking if I was tired of selling houses and ready to come back to the post office. I told him no, I liked my job, but on an impulse I asked him what he'd do if you wanted to come back. He said he'd hire you back in a second."

"What do you know?" Gordy snorted. "How's that for timing? Maybe there is somethin' to that karma business after all. Hell, workin' there would be a lot nicer with Murk the Jerk gone. And if Don's got a job for me, it kinda gives me a good excuse to come back."

Rick crossed his arms, a big smile on his face. "How 'bout that."

"Shit, if I've got a job, then all I need is a place to stay."

"Too bad Ed's house is tied up with the Mouse right now."

"No!" Gordy said adamantly. "I don't want to go back there with all those memories. The Mouse is welcome to stay there as long as she wants."

"You could stay with us." Ed almost stumbled off the bridge in his excitement. "Oh, not in the apartment, but you could stay at the main house until you get a place of your own. Mrs. Penfield would love it."

Gordy looked very skeptical. "I don't know about that. Since you guys have been livin' there, Mrs. P. and me have learned to like each other, but I don't know how she'd feel about one of her C-minus students livin' in her house."

"Oh, Gord, she doesn't care about that." Ed shook his head. "Why, she's been as worried about you as we have. You know the only reason she teases you about doing crummy in her class is because she likes you so much. I think she'd love having you around to help out, especially when Rick and I get busy with that new house. Plus, it'd only be temporary. But you could get the hell out of Indy and come home to a job and a place to live with people who love you. It's perfect!"

Gordy looked from Ed to Rick, hope beginning to dawn on his face. "Well, hell. What are we doing in the goddamned woods, then? Take me up to the post office so I can get my job back!"

⋘•⋙

Ed and Rick dropped Gordy off at the post office. Once Gordy saw that Don was indeed working that day, he told them to go on home without him; he'd walk back to the apartment.

As soon as Rick pulled into the driveway, Ed took off across the yard to the main house. He'd thought the idea of Gordy taking temporary refuge there had been a great one while they were in the park, but now he wanted to know how Mrs. Penfield would really feel about it.

"Why, I think it's a splendid idea," she said firmly when Ed poured out the story to her. "Of course we need to do whatever we can to support Gordon now. I think his cheerful presence is just what this place needs this winter."

"He'll probably insist on paying you rent," Ed said, relieved that she was pleased with the thought of having Gordy underfoot.

Mrs. Penfield chuckled. "Oh, yes, I'm sure he will. I'll accept it, too. I wouldn't want to do anything to damage his self-respect. I'm sure paying for the privilege of taking room and board from his former witch of an English teacher will go a long way in assuaging his battered dignity."

Ed went to the apartment to wait with Rick. The suspense ended about a half hour later when Gordy came trotting up the stairs. He burst through the door with the first genuinely happy look Ed had seen on his face all day.

"I am good to go, buds. Don promised he'd hold on to the job until I can give notice and leave the post office in Indy. In fact, he says with the Christmas rush comin' up that he wants me back here ASAP."

"I already talked to Mrs. Penfield," Ed said with a big grin. "She's all but got you moved in. And you'll be here for Christmas! That's great."

"Man, who woulda thought the day would come that I'd be sharin' digs with that old broad?" Gordy roared with laughter. "Ah, well, I s'pose it won't be so bad for a little while."

Rick walked over and gave Gordy a bear hug. "It's gonna be great to have you back, bro. We've missed you. Hell, you can even help us work on our new house!"

"I shoulda known you'd have an ulterior motive, Benton." Gordy slapped Rick upside the head.

Ed watched them smiling affectionately at each other, feeling his own happiness at the unexpected turn of events bubbling up inside him.

"So what are you going to tell Doug?" he asked curiously.

"I'm gonna tell him that I am packin' up and goin' home. And he can do whatever the hell he wants."

A shadow crossed Gordy's face. "It's not gonna be easy," he said softly, "but it's time. I gotta let him go, and I gotta move on, too. But maybe if I'm here it won't be so bad. Maybe it'll actually be a merry Christmas after all."

"We'll make it as merry as possible," Rick whispered, repeating his bear hug.

"Hell, enough of this shit," Gordy mumbled, obviously moved by his friends' devotion. "We got the whole weekend to talk about this. How 'bout some three-handed, bid euchre? I'm suddenly feelin' very lucky."

"I'll get the cards." Ed jumped up from the sofa and went down the hall to the bookcase he'd made for Rick two years earlier. A deck of cards had been lying on the bottom shelf since the last time they had all played cards at the apartment, Doug included.

He and Rick and had arranged several framed photographs on top of the bookcase back when they'd first put it there in the hall. Ed picked up a five-by-seven of Gordy, Doug, Rick, and himself. The four men, all smiling proudly, were standing with their arms thrown across one another's shoulders, the Golden Gate Bridge in the background. Ed studied the photo, remembering the wonderful time they'd all had on that trip to California. He remembered thinking that it was probably just the first of many trips they'd take together over the years. He sighed wistfully as he carried the photo, frame and all, into the bedroom.

Gordy's right. It isn't going to be easy, he thought as he opened the bedroom closet. He carefully slid the framed photograph, face down, under a pile of T-shirts on the top shelf, wanting it to be out of Gordy's sight for the rest of the weekend.

I want it out of my sight, too, he thought as he slowly closed the door.

As Ed drove over to Mrs. West's house early Monday morning, his thoughts were still on Gordy. He had left for Indianapolis early Sunday afternoon, full of determination to bring his life there to an end and return to Porterfield, even if, as he said, it seemed more like going backward than going forward.

It may have been a stroke of good luck that Gordy could return so easily to his old job and slide into a comfortable place to live with close friends, but Ed knew that no amount of luck or comfort could do much of anything when it came to easing the pain Gordy was feeling. Ed sighed as Toto's hit from earlier that year, "I Won't Hold You Back," played on the truck radio. Ed knew Gordy was rearranging his life as much for Doug as for himself. Gordy felt that letting Doug go and allowing him to have the experiences he wanted was the best way to preserve what they had shared. Oh, that was all noble and gracious, but nobility didn't go very far when it came to repairing a broken heart. If it did, Ed thought, people wouldn't cry so hard over the ending of *Stella Dallas*.

Mrs. West was her usual fretful self. She nattered on and on about how the newspaper boy couldn't seem to get her paper on the front steps and how she was sure her furnace wasn't running properly. Ed allowed himself to be swept into her myriad concerns and did his best to put Gordy out of his mind for the rest of the day.

Gordy called that evening. He reported that his superiors at the post office were "shittin' their pants" about his leaving so close to Christmas.

"They'll handle it, though. They've got lots of guys on standby, lots more than Don has, so it won't kill 'em. I hate to do this, and I've probably ruined any chance I ever have of workin' outside of Porterfield ever again, but what the hell. Maybe I need to pull a Benton and find a new job anyway."

"How's Doug?" Rick asked. He and Ed were standing together with the phone between their heads.

"Weird. Very weird. I don't think he really expected me to leave. Maybe he's regrettin' it now. I don't know. He's quiet; doesn't say much. I just want to get through the next two weeks without any explosions. You guys still comin' down to help me move my crap?"

"Sure," Ed said, as Rick said, "Of course!"

"That's good. Thank God I put so much of my stuff in storage up there. It won't be so bad." Gordy sighed. "Maybe I knew all along this wasn't gonna work out."

"Don't worry about it," Rick counseled. "Just get through these two weeks, and we'll do what we can to help, okay?"

"And if you need to talk, call us," Ed added.

Gordy said he would, gave them a quick good-bye, and hung up. Ed and Rick looked at each other silently. Finally Rick gave a shrug and hung up their phone. They had done everything they could for the time being.

There wasn't much time to dwell on Gordy during the rest of that busy week. The next day Ed and Rick managed to squeeze in a meeting with Matt Croasdale among their work demands. Ed's confidence in Matt grew as he told them he had worked with a gay couple in Milwaukee dealing with the same issues. Matt talked with them both separately and together and by the end of the meeting had begun the preliminary paperwork on what he felt would protect their assets and interests.

"Since you guys don't have a marriage license, this will take care of a lot of aggravation if you decide to split up someday, in addition to covering yourselves if one of you dies," Matt said, scribbling notes on his legal pad.

Ed got a little queasy at either idea—death or splitting up with Rick—but with Gordy's ordeal fresh in his mind, he knew it was in their best interests to have signed agreements if the worst did happen.

"Kind of takes the romance out of the whole thing, doesn't it?" Ed commented to Rick once the meeting had come to an end and they were standing together on the sidewalk in front of Mason and Schultz.

"Even romantics have to get practical sometime," Rick said with a sigh of resignation.

That realization was reinforced the next afternoon when Ed and Rick met Diane Kirschner at Porterfield Title Company for the closing on the Elm Street house. Ed had been through the closing ritual once before with the Coleman Street house, and closings were business as usual for Rick, but they both were rather awed by the idea of signing papers that would make them property co-owners.

Diane Kirschner was a pleasant, reserved woman who showed no signs of her earlier troubles. Business proceeded smoothly, and at the end Ed and Rick were the official owners of 418 West Elm Street. Diane wished them good luck and quickly disappeared. Ed and Rick disappeared as well, not to admire their newly purchased property or to celebrate, but to go back to work. Rick had a house tour scheduled with a young couple new to Porterfield, and Ed had promised Althea Klarn he would do her exterior Christmas decorating.

Ed wearily untangled strings of outdoor Christmas lights while Mrs. Klarn droned on and on about their potential danger.

"I just worry so about these cords. I haven't had them out of the basement since Paul was in high school, but now that he's home I want the house to look like it did then. These lights are so cheerful, especially if it snows for Christmas. Do you think we'll have a white Christmas this year? I do hope so, now that Paul is home. I just don't know about these lights, though. Do you think they're safe, Ed? Do the cords look okay to you? I just don't know what I'd do if they started a fire. I hoped Paul would be able to do this, but he's so busy getting settled at the hospital. Wouldn't it be awful if the house burned down right after he moved back? Maybe I should just hang garlands and no lights. Do you really think those cords are safe?"

The electrical cords looked okay to Ed. He was more concerned about the numerous burned-out bulbs. He drove downtown to Woolworth's and purchased several boxes of replacements. On the way back to Mrs. Klarn's, he detoured down Elm Street for a quick look at their new house. He paused and began to mentally sort out the projects he was eager to begin at the place. The bag full of brightly colored Christmas lights on the passenger seat reminded him he had other work to do first, and he forced himself to drive back to the Klarn house.

Mrs. Klarn continued to hover as he strung the lights around her front porch. "I don't know why I'm going to all of this trouble when Paul decided to move into that little apartment on Stratton Avenue instead of moving back into his old room like I thought. But maybe doing all of this will make him want to come home. I'd hate to risk using these dangerous cords if Paul didn't appreciate it, but then Paul really does appreciate everything I do for him. I just don't know why he wanted his own place when I could take such good care of him here."

Ed had a pretty good idea of why the town's newest doctor had opted for his own digs instead of moving into his childhood home, but he kept his thoughts to himself.

Ed got his ladder from the truck and began attaching the cords to the gutters around the porch roof. Mrs. Klarn's concern shifted from possible electrical fires to the color of the bulbs. Would just red and green bulbs be more festive? What about those clear ones? Would they show up better if it did snow? Ed reassured her that the multicolored bulbs were fine—they were just the perfect seasonal touch—and (hoping it would shut her up) said, "You want it to look like it did when Paul was in school, don't you?"

That worked, much to Ed's relief. He managed to finish the job by dark and escape before she thought of something else for him to do.

Ed hoped he would be able to spend time at the new house the next day, but as he had long been expecting, he found himself suckered into working on the final preparations for the Stratton County Historical Society's annual Porterfield holiday home tour, scheduled for that Saturday and Sunday. The woman who had volunteered to take charge of decorating the historical society building had suddenly taken ill, so both Eunice Ames and Rick, stretched to the limit by their own responsibilities, managed to talk Ed into doing most of the work.

So once again Ed hauled his ladder out of his truck and spent Thursday arranging what seemed like miles of garlands and greenery throughout the nineteenth-century house on West Commerce Street that was home to the historical society. On Friday he carefully assembled and decorated a huge artificial tree in the front hall under the direction of a woman named Harriet Drinkwater, the society's vice president. Rick had told Ed that Harriet was angling for Eunice's post as president and was doing her damnedest to take as much credit for this year's tour as possible. Ed did his best to follow her arbitrary instructions, reminding himself that he was working for the good of Stratton County's historical preservation, but when Harriet told him the tree looked simply dreadful and rudely pushed him aside to rearrange the ornaments, Ed had to resist a strong impulse to strangle her with a leftover string of lights.

"Only the second of December and already I'm done with Christmas," Ed grumbled to Rick that evening over a takeout meal of burgers and fries.

"Bah, humbug," Rick agreed, weary as well from being caught in the middle of the Ames-Drinkwater power struggle.

Another volunteer called in sick the next day, so Ed resigned himself to a wasted weekend, put aside his usual Saturday work clothes, and dressed to impress, throwing a sports jacket over the outfit he'd worn to that party in Indianapolis. He was somewhat relieved to discover that his partner in the chore of selling and collecting tickets was Susan Cummings, Vince's wife. Ed liked Susan, who was just as friendly and laid-back as her husband. Susan, a festive red maternity dress covering the bulge of her first child, due within the month, greeted Ed with similar relief.

"Want to feel the baby kick?" She teased as Ed did most of the work in setting up their station inside the front door, allowing her to rest against the wall, her hands cradling her belly.

"Only if it's kicking Harriet Drinkwater," he said under his breath.

Susan giggled as he settled her in the most comfortable chair he could find. They exchanged conspirators' grins as they faced a day of being sunny and polite to the citizens of Porterfield—the good, the bad, and most likely the ugly as well.

Thanks to Susan's cheerful company and wry comments on the people passing their table, the day went quickly. Ed returned to his post on Sunday feeling more relaxed and at peace than he had in days. It would all be over by late afternoon.

"And if any of the cleanup crew calls in sick, they can damn well do the work when they're feeling better," he confided to Susan in a low voice.

"Amen to that," replied Susan as she took the rubber band off a roll of tickets.

Ed was busy directing people to the back of the house for the craft bazaar and bake sale when someone touched his arm. He turned to find Fay Smith, Gordy's mother, smiling at him tentatively.

"I know you're busy, Ed, but do you think we could talk for a moment?"

Ed glanced at Susan, who nodded, telling him to take five; she could handle it by herself. Ed shrugged his sports jacket on and followed Mrs. Smith out to the front walk, which was temporarily deserted.

Mrs. Smith seemed rather embarrassed. She shifted her purse from one hand to the other and turned away from Ed to watch someone trying to parallel park a Cadillac in a space that was too small for it.

"I'm not quite sure what to say," she said, turning briefly toward Ed. "I can't stay out here too long either. My sister-in-law is inside. But when I saw you, I knew I needed to ask you something—something I can't ask Gordy."

Ed shifted uneasily, wondering what was on her mind.

"Ed, I'm hoping you'll be honest with me. Is Gordy moving home because he's having problems with Doug? He told us he didn't like Indy, and that Don wanted him to come back to the post office here, but I'm guessing there's a lot more to it."

"Uh . . ." Ed jammed his hands in his pockets, not sure what to say. He didn't want to betray Gordy and wasn't exactly sure what Mrs. Smith knew and didn't know.

"I think I know what's going on between them." Mrs. Smith sadly shook her head. "I feel awful that Gordy won't confide in me, but I understand. He's worried about his dad. It was a terrible shock to me when I realized that Gordy and Doug were more than just friends, but I don't mind as long as he's happy. It finally all made sense to me, why he was so unhappy for so long. I hoped being with Doug would change that, but it hasn't."

Ed let out the breath he had been holding. As Gordy had suspected, his mother had figured it out. "Well, yes, Mrs. Smith, Gordy and Doug are breaking up. It just didn't work out."

Mrs. Smith sighed and shook her head again. "Those poor boys," she murmured. "I had such high hopes."

She turned again to watch the traffic on Commerce Street. "It breaks my heart that Gordy thinks he can't confide in me. I know he's afraid I'll say something to his father, but I wouldn't do that. Gordy should know I've spent years doing what I can to keep the peace in that house. Gordy's father is a good man, but he does have his blind spots. I suppose I would to, but Gordy's my son, and all I want is for him to be settled and happy.

"Ed," she said as she glanced through the door behind them. "Would you please tell Gordy that he can talk to me? Will you tell him that we've talked, and it's okay for him to come to me?"

"Sure," Ed whispered, moved by her sadness, and by the fact that her sadness wasn't because her son was gay, but rather because things hadn't worked out between him and the man he loved.

"Rick and I are going to help him move back next weekend," he said, trying to give her a reassuring smile. "I'll make sure he knows you're there for him."

"Thank you," she said simply.

She turned to go into the historical society but paused near the front steps. "I'm so glad Gordy has you for a friend. You're a good man, too, Ed. It helps me to know you're looking out for him."

Ed was about to reply, but she hurried inside and disappeared into the crowd. He lingered on the walk for a moment, feeling both unsettled by and optimistic about their brief talk. It had not been easy for Mrs. Smith to approach him, and Ed was sure it wouldn't be easy for her to talk with her son, but it was good to know that Gordy had at least one more person on his side.

Ed returned to his post for the rest of the afternoon. Promptly at five o'clock, the door was locked, and Susan and Ed turned their receipts over to

Eunice Ames, who thanked them profusely and sent them on their way. Rick had spent the weekend directing traffic through one of the tour stops, and Ed met him at home as planned. They both fell onto the sofa with groans of relief, thankful that the annual holiday home tour was behind them for one more year.

Rick admired the Christmas centerpiece that Ed had bought from the bazaar in a moment of weakness. "It's actually very pretty," Rick said, nudging Jett away from the arrangement of pinecones and holly surrounding a red pillar candle.

"It was the best of the bunch, believe me." Ed stretched out on the sofa with his head in Rick's lap. "Some of those women outdid themselves on tacky this year. We might as well enjoy it, 'cause the way I feel right now, it's the only Christmas decoration we're gonna have until I recover from this weekend. I'm too sick of it all to even think of putting up so much as a wreath."

"I know," Rick agreed. "But the spirit will get to us eventually, and we'll be putting up wreaths, decorating trees, and hanging stockings."

"Yeah, I know. I just need to detox for a few days."

Ed got up, grabbed a pile of 45s from the record cabinet, and stacked them on the turntable. He didn't care what they were as long as they took the sound of the Muzak-like Christmas music he'd been forced to listen to all weekend out of his head.

He returned to his place on the sofa. Rick, his eyes closed, leaned his head back as he stroked Ed's hair.

"Thanks, baby, for all you did this weekend. I know it was above and beyond the call of duty, and I really appreciate it."

"Umm," Ed sighed as Rick began to rub his temples. "It's just one more thing I do to help the man I love."

"Yeah? Just as easy as one-two-three or A-B-C, huh?" Rick laughed gently as Len Barry's "1-2-3" began to play on the stereo.

"Yep. And as easy as taking candy from a baby," Ed paraphrased the song lyrics.

"Hmmm. It's been a while since I've had any candy from my baby. If I wasn't so tired . . ."

"Don't worry, darlin'. I'm tired, too. Maybe later, huh?"

"Okay. It's just . . . well, what you said about romance the other day after our meeting with Matt. It kind of got to me, how busy we've been, and how we haven't had any time to enjoy the fact that we bought that house, or even spend any time just being together. I guess watching what's going on with Gordy, I don't want us to drift apart because we're so caught up in all of this stuff. I love you, baby, so much. I don't want you to forget that."

Ed looked at Rick in surprise. "I know you love me. You don't have to make love to me, or be doing romantic things every day, to prove that. I love that stuff, but like you said the other day, sometimes you gotta be practical."

"I just don't want to get so practical that we forget how much fun we used to have, just being together. Remember when that was enough?"

Ed smiled at him. "Look at us right now. Isn't this enough? For right now, anyway?"

Rick nodded, his warm and tender special chasing the fatigue from his face. He leaned over and kissed Ed.

"My handyman. Always so practical. But you're right. For right now, being here together where it's quiet is enough."

Ed listened as Len Barry proclaimed there was nothing hard about love. That sounded good in a pop song, Ed thought, but wasn't exactly true in real life. Falling in love was easy enough; maintaining it was something else altogether. He thought back to Halloween and the things Mrs. Penfield had said that night.

"Mrs. Penfield says love is a mystery, and that as long as we're obedient to it we'll be okay."

"Hmmm. Obedient to the mystery of love. That sounds good, but I'm too tired to figure it out right now."

"That's just it. I don't think you have to figure it out. She said if you figure out the mystery, you lose what's so cool about it. Or something like that," Ed added vaguely, not remembering her exact words.

Rick returned to massaging Ed's head. "In other words, know enough to know that we love each other, but also know enough to get out of love's way."

Ed chuckled. "Yeah, so stop trying to be a know-it-all."

"Yes, dear." Rick chuckled as well as he gave Ed's head a hard rub. "I promise to be obedient to the mystery of love without trying to be Miss Marple or Sherlock Holmes. Do you promise, too?"

Ed sat up so he could hug his husband. "Yeah, darlin'. I promise."

He relaxed again under Rick's soothing fingers. All of his jumbled thoughts of legal documents, house projects, Gordy's mom, feuding historical society members, and Christmas decorations began to fade away. Having the man he love doing what he could to help him unwind after a stressful week made that an easy promise to make, and he could only hope keeping that promise would be as easy as falling in love had been back when life was a little less complicated.

CHAPTER TWELVE

Ed awoke the next morning at the sound of Rick's alarm clock. He groggily watched Rick pull himself out of bed to get ready for an early appointment. Despite more than eight hours of heavy sleep, Ed felt disinclined to get out of bed. Grateful his first appointment of the day wasn't until ten o'clock, he rolled over and feigned sleep until Rick had left for the day.

The smell of Rick's morning coffee lingered in the apartment. Ed usually didn't mind the scent, but today it was downright offensive.

"I think I need a day off or something," he muttered to Jett when he finally stumbled into the kitchen.

Nothing sounded good for breakfast. He managed to choke down a piece of buttered toast before he headed over to Mrs. Ilinski's house to help her clean out her basement. He found himself moving even more slowly than the heavyset older woman, and the musty odor of her basement seemed to be increasing the nausea that had been churning in his stomach all morning.

He abruptly set a box full of canning jars down on a rusty old metal table. Feeling quite dizzy, he leaned against the table and cussed under his breath. He suddenly realized that whatever plague had spread among the holiday home tour volunteers had nailed him as well.

Apologizing quietly and quickly to Mrs. Ilinski, promising to finish the job the moment he felt better, he fled to his truck. Somehow he managed to make it home and into his own bathroom before the inevitable happened. Afterward he lay shaking on the cold tile floor.

Literally crawling, he made his way to the living room and the telephone. He canceled his appointments for the rest of the day and was about to call Rick when another wave of violent nausea overcame him. He made it to the bathroom just in time.

Eventually he made it into bed, sliding gratefully under the covers. He found himself curling into a huddled ball of misery as a pervasive ache overwhelmed his body. He had almost fallen asleep when he heard the front door open.

"Ed?" Rick called from the living room.

"In here," he whined.

Rick appeared at the bedroom door looking as miserable as Ed felt. Rick gulped as he viewed the sight of Ed twisted among the bedclothes and the basin he'd placed on the nightstand.

"Oh, no. Not you, too?" Rick choked out before he turned and stumbled into the bathroom.

As Ed listened to the sounds coming from across the hall, he reached for the basin and did some heaving of his own. *Puking in tandem,* he thought as he retched helplessly. *How's that for romantic?*

The next twenty-four hours seemed endless. They were both so miserable with aches, chills, and fevers that they couldn't even stand to share the bed, so they took turns stretching out on the sofa. Jett, usually a comforting presence, was kicked off the bed and the sofa so many times, he finally retired in high dudgeon to one of the easy chairs and refused to go near either of them for the duration. The answering machine filled up with messages for both of them, each one eliciting a groan of dismay from its recipient.

"Remember how we said we'd sign up for a new doctor when one of us got sick?" Rick mentioned at one point when they met in the bathroom. "Maybe it's time, you think?"

Ed clung to the sink. He caught a glimpse of himself in the mirror and moaned. "Doctors don't make house calls anymore, and I sure as hell can't go anywhere."

"Yeah. Guess you're right. Too bad our wills aren't signed yet, 'cause I don't plan on surviving this," Rick mumbled as he staggered down the hall to the sofa.

By the next morning, they were functional enough to return a few phone calls. Rick called in sick to work, and at Ed's request asked Vince if Susan had also come down with this horror. He couldn't imagine going through this hell and being pregnant at the same time. Much to Ed's relief, Vince reported that Susan had escaped their fate.

"But we're definitely not the only ones," Rick said after he hung up the phone. "Apparently this virus is all over Porterfield. Eunice is beside herself, afraid the home tour will be blamed for spreading it."

"Well, it did, didn't it?" Ed said resentfully.

Rick shrugged. "It's December. There's stuff going on almost every day. If it hadn't've been the home tour, it would have been something else. Anyway, there doesn't seem to be much we can do except ride it out."

"Yeah. And it's my turn for the bed again." Ed stumbled down the hall. He collapsed on the bed and managed to sink into the first peaceful sleep he'd had since awaking Monday morning.

By late afternoon they were both feeling well enough to sit up. Achy, restless, and cranky, they settled at opposite ends of the sofa as they silently watched reruns on television. When *The Patty Duke Show* came on, Ed began to sing along with the theme song but got such a glare from Rick that he trailed off in midchorus. Feeling most offended, he stalked to the refrigerator for the 7-Up Effie Maude had left outside their door along with some homemade chicken soup.

"I wonder why 7-Up tastes good after you've been throwing up." Ed settled back into his corner under an old quilt.

"I don't know," Rick responded listlessly. "I'd kill for some butter pecan ice cream."

"Oh, you always want that when you're sick." Ed sipped his pop, thinking butter pecan ice cream would just make him want to barf again.

Rick reached for the phone. He called the main house and in a pleading, whiny voice asked Effie Maude to go to the store and get him some ice cream before she finished her day. Ed rolled his eyes. Rick was not the best patient in the world, and somehow he always managed to get on Ed's nerves when he was sick. His only solace was the thought that if they were beginning to irritate each other, they were probably over the worst of it.

"Isn't that Jimmy Dean?" Rick asked once his attention returned to the TV screen.

"Yeah. Patty wants to enter a songwriting contest he's got. I think she's gonna steal Cathy's poem."

"I tell you, that Cathy had the patience of a saint, putting up with Patty's bullshit."

Ed snorted. "It's just a TV show." He decided to change the subject before Rick went off on one of his television tirades. "Doesn't watching Jimmy Dean make you think of sausage?"

Rick groaned and pulled an afghan over his head. Ed took another sip of 7-Up with satisfaction. He knew the thought of greasy meat would derail him.

"It's funny, though," Ed said. "I remember watching this show when I was a kid and wishing I could hang out with Patty and Cathy. I never wanted to hang out with Patty's younger brother, and he was about my age when this was on. Between that and lip synching with my Supremes records, you would have thought I would have known I was queer."

"Yeah." Rick pulled the afghan away from his face and tucked it around his shoulders. "The same way I only watched *My Three Sons* 'cause I thought Robbie was cute."

"Robbie *was* cute," Ed said thoughtfully. "And Bobby Sherman on *Shindig*. Remember that?"

"Oh, man," Rick sighed. "I remember beatin' off over him once when he was on *Here Come the Brides*. I thought I was going straight to hell, or if someone found out I'd be locked up somewhere. How did we survive all of that?"

"I don't know." Ed thought back to his own fear and self-disgust. He'd been well into his twenties before he was brave enough to completely accept the reality of his sexual orientation.

"I don't know," he repeated, sinking back into the gloom of being sick along with remembering how miserable he had been for so long. "Do you suppose it's any easier today?"

"I doubt it." Rick tucked the afghan tightly around his body as though protecting himself from the world. "That'll probably never change," he said bitterly, obviously allowing gloom to overtake him as well.

Ed's eyes were on the TV screen, where a noisy Christmas commercial aimed at children was in progress, but his mind was on the older boys, the young teens who were struggling the way he and Rick had struggled years ago. He wondered whether there were boys out there sighing over Duran Duran the same way he had sighed over the Rolling Stones. *I wish there was something we could do, but even if we tried to reach out, we'd probably be called child molesters. Life just stinks sometimes.*

Ed rummaged through his mind for any kind of pleasant thought. "Hey, I just remembered," he said suddenly. "I think *A Charlie Brown Christmas* is on TV tonight."

"Oh, thank God," Rick groaned as his head rolled back against the sofa. "If that doesn't make me feel better, nothing will. Thank God for *Peanuts*. At least Charles Schulz understands what it's like to feel left out."

"Yeah," Ed said, almost cheerful.

Feeling a sense of comradeship with Charlie Brown, who never got Christmas cards or Valentines, he went to the kitchen for more 7-Up. He thought about how lucky he was to have Rick, who not only loved him and gave him holiday presents and cards, but also understood him. Having someone who could empathize with his deepest hurts and fears made up for a lot in life, even the whiny voice Ed knew he'd be hearing from Rick until he was truly well again.

"You know what? I think we're gonna live to sign those wills," Ed said as he poured his pop.

Rick gave him a weak version of his warm and tender special. "Yeah. How 'bout that?"

❧•❧

By Wednesday morning they were both willing to take a stab at returning to work. Ed took it easy but still managed to get through some of his backlogged appointments. Early in the afternoon he decided to go home for a bowl of Effie Maude's chicken soup and at least an hour's rest on the sofa. He was surprised to see Rick's car in the garage and shocked to find Rick back in bed, coughing and blowing his nose.

"I think I caught a damned cold on top of that fucking virus," he said in his most aggrieved tone of voice.

"Aw, crud." Ed sighed. He turned on his heel and went to the kitchen for the notepad they used for grocery lists.

"What's that for?" Rick asked when he returned to the bedroom.

"This is for the list of stuff you're going to send me to the drugstore for."

That elicited a brief grin from Rick. "Well, I guess you've solved some of my mysteries, huh?"

"Yeah, sick boy. I have. You know what else? I'm gonna call Stratton County Medical and get you an appointment. I'm sure Paul Klarn is accepting new patients, so we might as well add ourselves to the list."

"I'm not sick enough to go to the doctor," Rick bitched as he threw a wad of tissue at the wastebasket. "I'm sure I'll get over this in a day or two."

A look of distaste on his face, Ed picked up the gooey wad and deposited it in Rick's intended target. He marched into the bathroom, washed his hands, and returned to the bedroom doorway, hands on hips.

"This is getting ridiculous," he lectured. "You are going to the doctor to see if there is anything that can be done. I don't think you'd have a cold after that stupid virus if you weren't so run-down. You've been pushing yourself like crazy all fall, and every time I told you to take it easy, you just went out and did some more. How the hell are we ever going to get any work done on that house if you're gonna feel crummy all winter? Not to mention that we haven't even started our Christmas shopping, *and* we have to go to Indy this weekend to help Gordy move. I'm making an appointment, and I'm taking you to the doctor. Got it?"

Rick scowled. "Are you finished, Marcus Welby?"

"No, I'm not. I'm also gonna chain you to that goddamned bed until you get some rest and feel better!"

"Bondage, huh?" Rick shifted in bed and smirked at him. "Now, there's a mystery I would have never suspected about you."

"Yeah, right. Make all the cracks you want." Ed threw the notepad and a pencil on the bed next to Rick. "Write down what you want for your dungeon while I go call the doctor."

⊰•⊱

Later that afternoon, Ed's truck rolled to a stop in the parking lot of the brand-new medical building next to Porterfield General on the south side of town. It seemed strange to Ed not to be visiting Dr. Weisburg's old office on Commerce Street as he had his whole life. He led Rick inside, and they stopped at the reception area for directions to Dr. Klarn's office.

After they'd been seated in the crowded waiting room for almost a half hour, a perky young nurse called Rick's name. She looked puzzled when Ed followed him to the examining room but didn't protest.

Dr. Paul Klarn walked in a few minutes later. Ed blinked at the sight of him. He was so accustomed to the shy, awkward boy enshrined in dozens of framed photos at Althea Klarn's house that the adult version came as a surprise.

Paul Klarn was a good deal shorter than Ed's six feet, slim framed, but well filled out for his size. Ed suspected he had spent time in a gym. His brown hair was cut in an acceptable eighties style, and his glasses were also an updated improvement over the seventies-style frames featured in those photos. The ugly duckling had grown up to be not a swan, perhaps, but a reasonably attractive man.

Ed also noted that the boyish awkwardness—so obvious from those pictures—had disappeared as well. However, instead of the arrogance Ed had sensed in some doctors, there was a distinct kindness in Paul's manner. Ed responded to it immediately, and some of his inhibitions about having a new doctor abated.

During introductions, Ed mentioned that he occasionally worked for Dr. Klarn's mother. The doctor eyes brightened with interest.

"Oh, so you're the handyman? Althea raves about what a good job you do for her." He chuckled. "You also save me a lot of time and grief as well. I'm indebted to you."

"You call your mom by her first name?" Ed asked curiously.

Dr. Klarn gave him a wry grin. "Wouldn't you?"

Ed laughed, pleased to know Paul Klarn had a healthy sense of humor where his overbearing mother was concerned.

"So what seems to be the problem"—Dr. Klarn consulted his file—"Richard?"

"Please, call me Rick," Rick began as he explained what had brought them to his office.

"We live together," Ed said boldly when Rick finished, "so I'm the one who'll be taking care of him, and making sure he finally gets some rest. I think he's been working too hard."

Rick glared at Ed while Dr. Klarn smiled. "I see," he said, not batting an eye at Ed's information. "Well, it's good you have each other for that."

The doctor gave Rick a brief examination, nodding his head. "I've been seeing a lot of this all week. We seem to have two different but very nasty bugs loose in town these days. What a way to start a new practice! I'm getting to meet all of my new patients at once.

"I'm sorry to say, Rick," he continued, "that you're not the only one who's been bitten by both of them. There's not much I can do, as they both seem to be viral in nature, but I'll prescribe an antibiotic just in case. I'll give you a strong decongestant and cough syrup as well. In addition, I'll second Ed's prescription for lots of bed rest. You do seem run-down to me, and if you're going to kick this, you need to take it easy."

Ed gave Rick a triumphant look.

"Okay, okay," Rick grumbled.

"It was a pleasure meeting both of you," Dr. Klarn said as he warmly shook their hands. "Rick, don't hesitate to come back if you're still feeling this way by early next week. We need to get you healthy before winter comes along."

When Ed and Rick were back in the truck, Ed thoughtfully said, "He seems nice, doesn't he? He's not Dr. Weisburg, but I think I can deal with him."

Rick shifted on the seat and coughed. "Yeah," he sputtered. "I'll tell you something else," he said once the spell had passed. "I think he's one of us."

"Really?" Ed slammed on the brakes as the light at Main and Cedar turned red in front of him. "What makes you think that?"

Rick cleared his throat and coughed again. "Damn! I feel like shit. I'm gonna wait in the truck while you get those prescriptions filled. At least that health insurance we pay for is finally coming in handy. I don't know why I think he's gay. I just picked up on something. You know how sometimes you know another man's gay without saying anything? Something in his eyes, I guess," he finished vaguely.

"I'll be damned," Ed muttered. He'd been too busy thinking about the boy in Mrs. Klarn's pictures to even consider that possibility. "If that's true, then why do you suppose he moved from New York City back to *Porterfield*? That's just weird."

"Well, if he is gay, doing his residency in New York makes sense," Rick said reasonably. "But maybe he's like Gordy. Maybe he had a boyfriend who dumped him and he decided to come home."

Ed's mind pondered the possibilities. "Well, if he does turn out to be gay, maybe we should introduce him to Gordy."

Rick groaned. "Do you even want to think about that, considering you're the one who introduced Gordy to *Doug*?"

"Oh. Yeah." Ed's face went red. He had in no way been playing matchmaker when Gordy and Doug met, but he did feel some responsibility for it. "I guess I'd better keep my mouth shut, huh?"

"Yeah. You'd better."

Ed sensed the usual Mr. Hyde persona Rick adopted when he was sick and miserable coming to the surface. He remained quiet on the rest of the short trip to Hook's Drugs.

Once home, Ed deposited Rick in bed with a Mary Higgins Clark paperback he'd picked up at the drugstore and told him to behave himself for the rest of the day. Still feeling exhausted from his own bout with the first vicious virus, he called Norma on an impulse and asked if she might be willing to cook dinner for them. He expected her to say that she was too busy being a liberated woman to do such a thing, but she affably agreed, insisting only that Ed meet her in the driveway to collect the food.

"I'm not about to set foot in that germ-filled apartment. The last thing I need to be at that bakery is Typhoid Mary."

When Ed met her downstairs, he smelled Norma's meatloaf and scalloped potatoes in the grocery bag she handed over. He gratefully thanked her.

"It wasn't any fuss," she said, waving away his gratitude. "I was cooking for myself anyway, so this would have just gone to waste. You both need to get better, though, because I'm not making a habit of this. I have a job, you know. I swear we're busier at that place than we were when I worked there for Christmas thirty years ago. Oh, and speaking of Christmas, I convinced that sister of yours to have Christmas dinner at my house this year, so you plan on that. And make sure Hilda knows she's welcome to join us."

"She'll like that," Ed said absently, his eyes on the across-the-street neighbors happily stringing lights on their evergreens. "Christmas," he said, sighing. "Only three weeks away and I'm totally not ready. This is going to be a long month."

"It's not easy when people are sick at Christmastime," Norma agreed, walking back to her car, "so you boys take care of yourselves, you hear? Three weeks is plenty of time to get well. I expect you both at my dinner table on Christmas Day, and healthy, too!"

"Yes, Mom," he said as she slammed her car door. "We'll be there, even if we have to hose ourselves down with Lysol before we come in the house!"

⁂

By Saturday morning Rick was still a long way from what could be called his best. As Ed moved about the apartment, preparing for the trip to Indianapolis, he felt that Rick should stay home and continue to rest. He made the mistake of saying as much.

"I'm going," Rick said flatly. "We're going to need all three vehicles to get Gordy's stuff back here in one trip, and furthermore, I am sick of lying in this bed and staring at these walls. I'm going stir-crazy, so I am getting the hell out for the day."

His statement ended with a severe coughing fit. When he was finished hacking, Rick gave Ed a look that dared him to say anything. Ed just rolled his eyes and made no further protest. He was glad, however, that they had to drive separately. At least he didn't have to spend the next two hours listening to Rick piss and moan. And cough.

When they arrived at Gordy and Doug's apartment on the north side of Indianapolis, it was apparent that Gordy had been working hard. Almost everything he was taking with him was boxed and ready to go except for a few pieces of furniture that would be loaded into Ed's truck.

Rick was genuinely tired from the long drive, and this time he meekly agreed when Ed insisted he rest in the apartment with a cup of coffee. Much to Ed's embarrassment, Doug was home. Ed had somehow assumed he would be at work, but he was there and eager to help. Ed couldn't decide whether Doug was feeling guilty or just wanted to get it over with as quickly as possible. The atmosphere was tense, and conversation was at a minimum.

When they were almost finished, Rick went downstairs to help Gordy arrange things in the trunk of his car, while Ed went back up for an armload of Gordy's clothes. As he was about to enter the bedroom, he saw Doug sitting on the edge of the bed, head in his hands. Ed realized he was crying. He turned to leave, but Doug heard him and looked up.

"I suppose you blame me for all of this," he said, wiping his eyes.

Frozen in the doorway, Ed stared at him, unsure of what to say. "Yeah, I guess I do," he finally said, deciding honesty was the best way to go.

Doug nodded. "I guess I don't blame you for blaming me. I feel like such an asshole."

"Maybe that's 'cause you are. An asshole, I mean. Only an asshole would throw away a guy like Gordy."

"You've only heard his side of it." Doug got up from the bed and went to the window, his back to Ed.

"So what's your side? It's not like you haven't had time to tell me or Rick what's going on."

"What's the use? I knew it wouldn't make any difference. You guys are so tight, I knew I'd end up being the bad guy no matter what I said. I've known all along that you were just waiting for me to fuck up. I've always been the weak link in this little foursome."

"Oh, Doug, that's not true."

"I think it's truer than you think. I began to realize a long time ago that I wasn't ready for this kind of a relationship. It's been tearing me up for months. Do you think I want to hurt Gordy? Do you think this isn't killing me? What would you have done if I had confided in you before we moved away?"

"Probably would have told you to move here without him," Ed said honestly.

"Exactly. And I was so afraid of letting him go, thinking that if we moved away somehow it would all get better. Well, it didn't. I was wrong. But you know what? If I had left Porterfield without Gordy, you would have kicked me out of your life to protect him. Shit, Ed, don't you realize I'm not just losing him; I'm losing you and Rick, too?"

Ed squirmed with embarrassment. "You'll still be our friend," he mumbled.

"Yeah, right!" Doug said bitterly. "Will you look at me as a young guy who's not ready to settle down to the kind of thing you have with Rick, or will you just think of me as the guy who ruined your best friend's life?"

"Geez, I don't know." Ed ran a hand through his hair in frustration. "Right now I don't know what to think." He paused. "Yeah, you're right, my first concern right now is seeing that Gordy is okay. Maybe I should have been there for you, too. I don't know. There's a part of me that understands how you feel, and there's another part that's mad as hell, thinking you're a total fool, that in all the guys you'll meet downtown at the bars, you'll never find someone who's as ready to love you and be with you as Gordy. Or at the bathhouse either," he added cruelly.

Doug winced. "Okay, okay. You think this is all about sex and fucking around. I figured as much."

"Well, isn't it?"

"There's a lot more to it. Now *I'm* mad that you can't see that, but it doesn't surprise me. You think Gordy's so great that you can't see that he's a long way from perfect. He's got his faults, too."

"Well, take it from me: Rick's not perfect either. We've had to learn to accept each other, faults and all, and do a lot of compromising. Every couple has to do that."

"I know that. But you have to be ready to do that stuff, and I'm not ready. Not now. Maybe I still have some growing up to do."

"Maybe," Ed said quietly.

Doug sat down again. "Look, I don't want to fight. I don't want you to leave here any madder at me than you already are. I just hope you can forgive me someday, like I hope Gordy will forgive me."

He turned pleading eyes to Ed. "And I want you to know how grateful I am to you."

"Grateful?"

"Yeah, really grateful. When I moved to Porterfield I was scared, even if I didn't show it. You were one of the few people who genuinely welcomed me. Even when I was lying about being gay, you were there for me, and I was glad to think you weren't just my landlord, but my friend. I really appreciate that."

"I wanted to be friends. I really liked you, Doug. Hell, I still do."

On an impulse Ed went to the bed and sat next to Doug. He put his arms around him and hugged him hard. "We're still friends. Friends get mad at each other sometimes. You've got my phone number and my address. You know where I am if you need me, okay?"

"Okay," Doug whispered, clinging to Ed.

Ed heard footsteps in the living room. He quickly got up, went to the closet, and grabbed the last of Gordy's clothes. He paused at the door and glanced at Doug, who was still on the bed, looking at the floor.

"Take care. Okay?" Ed tried to smile.

"Okay. I will," Doug responded without looking up.

Gordy walked into the room. "I think that's the worst of it," he said, looking from Ed to Doug.

"I'll meet you downstairs." Ed got a tighter hold on his armload and got the hell out.

Rick helped him arrange the clothes in the backseat of his car. When they were finished, they leaned against the Regal and waited for Gordy and Doug to finish their good-byes, Rick shivering a bit in the cool, damp air as he sipped the last of his coffee.

"So, did you talk to him?" Rick asked.

"Yeah."

"What'd he say?"

"I don't want to talk about it." Ed sighed.

Ed was once again glad for solitude on the drive home. He shifted around in his seat for a comfortable position, eventually realizing that it was guilt that was making him squirmy, not muscle fatigue.

Doug was right. Ed had not bothered to see his side of it. He had flown immediately to Gordy's side, determined to let Gordy know he had Ed's full and unqualified support. He supposed that was a natural reaction considering how close he was to Gordy, but he also realized it was the easy way out as well. If he were truly Doug's friend, he would have made more of an effort to understand his torment as well. Ed had grown to care for Doug, and perhaps even love him, in the past two years. It didn't really matter who was wrong or right. In the end, Ed had stood steadily by one friend at the expense of another.

"Aw, crud," he yelled, pounding the steering wheel. "Why does this stuff have to be so fucking hard?"

He didn't know why; he just knew it was, and somehow he'd have to muddle through it like any other human being. His only hope, at this point, was that time might heal some of the hurts for everyone involved. Maybe there would come a day when his friendship with Doug could be reestablished, and perhaps even nurtured.

He hoped so. The sight of Doug sitting on the bed looking at the floor wouldn't leave his mind, and it was breaking his heart.

He fumbled a cassette out of the glove compartment, hoping Diana Ross's greatest hits would put him in a better frame of mind. The first song to play was "Remember Me." He groaned and hit the steering wheel again. He snapped the stereo off, hunkered down in his seat, and counted off the mileage markers on the highway, just wanting to be home.

It was close to dusk when the three vehicles rounded the corner of Spruce and Race streets. The Christmas lights Ed had strung on the front porch and the evergreens the day before were lit. There was also what looked to be a large fir tree by the parlor window. Ed, who hadn't even thought about Christmas trees yet, wondered where it had come from.

Mrs. Penfield and Effie Maude had indeed been busy. The smell of Effie Maude's wonderful fried chicken was in the air when the three men, weary from the long drive, trooped into the main house. Gordy wasn't the only one surprised by the banner hanging in the doorway between the dining room and parlor that read, WELCOME HOME, GORDY. Both women came forward with warm hugs and greetings for all three of them.

"It's so good to have you with us, Gordy," Mrs. Penfield said with a firm grip around his midsection. "Now that you're here, you must think of this as home for as long as necessary. We're all delighted to have you here."

"Even Jett," Ed said, hoping for a laugh, as Gordy seemed near tears from the enthusiastic welcome.

"Aw," Gordy mumbled, embarrassed but obviously grateful.

"I got your room all ready," Effie Maude said heartily. She'd grown just as fond of Gordy as she had of Ed and Rick over the past few years. "We're puttin' you in Junior's old room at the back, upstairs. It's good to have a reason to make up that room again. You need anything, you just give me a holler."

"I don't know what to say." Gordy sent a sheepish grin around the beaming faces.

"I do," Rick piped up. He looked quite tired but happy. "When do we eat? I'm starved!"

Everyone laughed, and Effie Maude went to the kitchen to check on the meal. Rick and Mrs. Penfield relaxed in the parlor while Ed and Gordy began hauling Gordy's stuff from their vehicles, deciding what needed to go upstairs and what could be stored in the carriage house.

"What's up with the tree?" Ed asked Mrs. Penfield on one of his trips through the parlor.

"Isn't it wonderful?" Mrs. Penfield admired the eight-foot Douglas fir standing tall and proud by the bay window. "Effie Maude's brother is running a tree lot for the Lions Club this year. I told him to bring me the best tree he had, and he did this afternoon. He even wrestled it into that old Christmas tree stand. Now all we have to do is decorate it. Perhaps tomorrow evening, when everyone is rested, we can do so. Or some evening this week."

"That is one heck of a tree." Rick admired it as well as he sipped the hot tea and honey Effie Maude had forced on him. "All of your old ornaments will look beautiful on it, Mrs. P."

Ed sized it up. "I may have to buy some more lights for it," he murmured, last weekend's negative thoughts about Christmas decorating forgotten. "This is a lot bigger than the one we had last year."

"Well"—Mrs. Penfield flashed him her mischievous grin—"since I now have three huge men living here, it seemed appropriate to have a tree to match."

After everyone had thoroughly enjoyed Effie Maude's chicken and mashed potatoes, Gordy retired to the front porch for a smoke. Ed followed him. He put his arm around Gordy's shoulders and gave him a squeeze.

"Welcome home, bud."

Gordy returned the squeeze. "Thanks, bud. You guys, and Mrs. P.—you're all the best. I really appreciate all this."

"You're welcome. Anytime."

Gordy watched the smoke from his cigarette drift toward the colored lights wound through the garlands on the porch pillars. He turned to Ed with a sad smile.

"I just wish Doug was here, too."

Ed put his arm around him again and leaned against his shoulder.

"Me, too."

CHAPTER THIRTEEN

Ed had planned to spend most of Sunday doing nothing, but when Laurie called midmorning and asked him to accompany her on a Christmas shopping trip to Fort Wayne, he changed his mind. He knew his sneaky sister was looking primarily for someone to help her carry bags, but he decided he could be her caddy and get a good deal of his own Christmas shopping done at the same time.

Ed was peering out the living room window, watching for Laurie's car, when Rick wandered into the room with a sheet of notebook paper. He held it out to Ed with the closest thing to a teasing grin Ed had seen on his face in almost a week.

"Since I'm much too sick to be fighting crowds at the mall, do you suppose you could do some of my shopping, too?"

Ed snorted in disgust but couldn't stop a grin of his own. "Boy, you sure know how to play that sick card when it's convenient for you, don't you?" Ed scanned the list. "I don't see my name on here," he said indignantly.

"I arranged for an early delivery of your gift with Santa Claus while I was still in Indy. It's well hidden; don't even try to go looking for it. If you do, I'll send it right back to the North Pole."

Ed was about to make a smart-ass reply when a car horn pierced the Sunday quiet. He looked out and saw Laurie's sedan in the driveway. "I'm comin', Shortshit," he bellowed.

After a quick kiss good-bye, Ed scurried downstairs and into the passenger seat of Laurie's car.

Ed and Laurie had seen very little of each other all fall, so the thirty-mile drive north was a good time to get caught up on each other's lives. After family news had been exhausted, Laurie reminded Ed that their paperwork was finished at the office, and he and Rick needed to stop by and sign it sometime that week. Ed asked Laurie if she knew anything about Matt Croasdale's date with Claire. He suddenly realized he'd been so busy, he'd never heard any of the details.

"If must have been pretty good," Laurie said as she roared out of Porterfield well above the speed limit. "Unless I missed something, they've been out together at least two times since. The women on Commerce Street are furious that Claire somehow snapped him right out from under their noses."

"I'll be damned."

"Yeah. When Matt realized Claire and I are kinda related through you and Rick and that our daughters are friends, he started pumping me for info."

"What kind of info?"

"Oh, mostly about Claire's ex-husband. I told him the truth, didn't see any reason not to. It must not have bothered him too much, but since his ex-wife was apparently quite a horror, he probably decided they just had something in common."

"I wonder how the kids are taking this."

Laurie shrugged. "Okay, I guess. Apparently he's spent time with them. Jane seems to like him. She and Lesley have gone from planning Barbie's wedding to plotting Matt and Claire's."

"Girls," Ed said in mock disgust. "Don't you think that's jumping the gun a bit?"

Laurie giggled. "Yeah, I suppose, but we can dream, can't we?"

"What? You're in on it, too?"

"I think they have potential. They really are well suited for each other, but right now all we can do is sit back and watch the show. When you've been married as long as I have," she said, sighing, "you have a tendency to live vicariously through other people's romances."

"That's not always so great," Ed said, thinking of Gordy and Doug.

"True," Laurie admitted, "but it gives a girl something nice to think about when her stupid husband is too busy watching football to help her with the Christmas shopping."

"I'm filling in for Todd today? I knew you had an ulterior motive other than wanting to spend time with your big brother."

"Yeah." Laurie smirked. "I was desperate."

"Hey!" Ed hollered as she barreled through a yellow light a little too late. "Watch it! I don't want to be a holiday traffic statistic. Geez, you still drive as rotten as you did in high school."

"Oh, calm down. And don't start any of that crap about women drivers either."

"Dad said I was lots easier to teach to drive than you were." Ed's smug look matched the tone of his voice.

"That is such a lie!"

"Is not. He told me that when you got your license."

"Yeah?" She reached to jack up the radio volume and managed to slap his leg at the same time. "Well, he said the exact same thing to me, only in reverse, saying how awful you were and how easy I was."

They glared at each other briefly, and then began to laugh.

"Boy, the old man was smarter than I thought he was," Ed choked out.

Laurie shook her head, still giggling. "Yeah, he sure had us figured out."

Ed turned down the radio volume. "I am so sick of this song."

Laurie cranked the sound of "Total Eclipse of the Heart" even louder than before. "I like it."

"You always did have shitty taste in music," he shouted over Bonnie Tyler. He turned it down again.

"Me?" She snorted, turning it back up.

She glared at him as he reached again for the volume knob. "It's my car. Don't even think about it unless you want to walk home. As for bad taste in music, look who's talking! You're the only person I know who has a copy of 'Disco Duck'!"

Ed crossed his arms and pouted. "I got caught up in the moment when I bought that. I haven't played it since."

"Yeah, I'll just bet."

"Still got your crush on Davy Jones?" Ed jeered. "Still playing your Monkees records, and the 1910 Fruitgum Company?"

"Those were good songs!"

Yeah, until you made the whole neighborhood sick of 'em. I can still remember you and Vicky Gibson playing 'Daydream Believer' over and over and screaming, pretending you were at a Monkees concert."

"Hah! Said the boy who used to sing 'Leader of the Pack' when he was mowing yards and thought no one was listening."

"No one *was* listening, except you. I always knew you were a sneak, Shortshit."

"I know lots of other stuff, too," she said in her best bratty sister voice.

"Yeah? Like what?"

"I'm not telling," she said loftily.

Ed shook his head, thinking he'd fallen into a time warp. It seemed to be 1964 all over again. "It's a good thing Mom isn't in the car," he said, trying to return to 1983. "She'd be slapping us both and telling us Santa Claus is watching."

"Give up?" she asked with a smug glance.

"Yeah." He surrendered, slumping in his seat.

Laurie relished her victory by turning the radio volume even louder. Ed sighed. "Sisters," he muttered under his breath.

But as the car approached Fort Wayne, they were both smiling.

Ed arrived home late that afternoon, tired but satisfied with the day's results. Since Rick wasn't in sight, he hid his gift for him in his workshop. It was a beautiful lamb's wool overcoat that Ed felt would look great over Rick's suits all winter. It had been expensive, but in a rush of holiday felicity, Ed had decided Rick was worth it.

He lugged the rest of the bags, including some presents Laurie wanted to keep out of her kids' sight, up the stairs and found Rick stretched out on the sofa, contentedly reading Mrs. Penfield's copy of *A Christmas Carol*.

Rick tossed his book aside and dived into the bags. "What'd you get me?" he demanded.

He pulled out a girl's skirt-and-blouse set. "Not exactly what I wanted," he confessed, falling back on the sofa.

"Your gift is under lock and key, so don't worry about it until at least Christmas Eve," Ed said, separating the bags. "Right now you need to be worried about what you're giving, not getting."

"And wrapping them," Rick said glumly.

"Oh, don't worry. I'll help you like I always do. How are you feeling?"

Rick began to sort through the bags Ed was putting next to him. "Actually, I feel a lot better. I think I'm gonna go back to work tomorrow."

Ed frowned. "Are you sure?"

"I have to go back sometime. Vince keeps getting more and more distracted the closer it gets to the due date for the baby. He's so excited about being a daddy for the first time that he's counting on me to keep things running smoothly at the office after it's born."

"Oh, first babies are always late." Ed echoed what Norma had always said about him.

"Try telling that to Vince. He's convinced it's going to be a Christmas baby. He's already planned to close the office for the two weeks after Christmas."

"Then it probably won't show up until late January."

"Probably," Rick admitted. "Still, I need to be completely up to speed on everything that's going on. It'll be good experience for me, and I'd feel pretty good if Vince was confident enough in me to relax when the baby's born and let me run the place."

"Okay. Do you at least promise to take it as easy as possible?"

"I promise." Rick kissed Ed's forehead. "I want to be over this by Christmas, and not just for Norma's sake. I'd like to enjoy the holidays, too. Oh, it looks as though we're decorating that big tree tomorrow night. Mrs. Penfield asked me about it when I walked over to borrow this book. That okay with you?"

"Oh, sure. That'll be fun, especially with Gordy around. But we still need to have our little tree here in the apartment, too. I hope you don't mind, but since I was in Fort Wayne I decided to get this year's ornament. I think you'll like it."

Ever since the first Christmas they'd spent together, Rick had bought a special glass ornament for their tree. The first year it had been a snowman; after that there was a Santa Claus, and last year he had found a polar bear wearing a jaunty Christmas scarf.

"I don't mind," Rick said. "I don't know when I would have gotten out to look for something special. What'd you get?"

Ed rummaged through his bags and found the white box containing the ornament that had caught his eye. He handed it to Rick.

"Ooh," Rick breathed as he pulled out a delicate glass pinecone. It was painted red and had a drift of glittering snow on its top. "It's beautiful, baby."

Ed smiled nostalgically. "My grandma had some ornaments like that on the tree at the farm when I was little. I don't know whatever happened to them. I remember lying under the tree, staring up through the branches at the pinecones, thinking that pinecones grew like that—red and snow covered—on Christmas trees."

Rick had a faraway look in his eyes. "Yeah, I remember stuff like that. One time I asked my grandma how Santa Claus could keep track of all the kids in the world. She told me the Santa ornament on her tree was watching Claire and me, and that's how Santa knew if we were naughty or nice. I used to really behave myself in her living room, no matter what Claire did to make me mad."

"Does the Santa ornament on our tree do that?"

"Yep! Maybe we should put our tree up tonight so he can get busy checking up on us, and Jett, too." Rick pulled a catnip mouse out of another bag and shook it teasingly at the cat.

Ed was about to say that he was tired from the busy weekend and wasn't in the mood to lug the tree box upstairs from the storage area. (They had switched to an artificial tree after they had moved into the carriage house to save the trouble of sweeping up loose pine needles from the stairs.) However, seeing the genuine, childlike excitement in Rick's eyes, Ed relented. It was so good to see Rick feeling better and looking forward to something that he agreed to fetch their tree after he had the fruits of his shopping trip put away.

So after a quick supper, they assembled the tree and decorated it, all the while being serenaded by a Carpenters Christmas album. When they were finished they turned off all the lights except those on the tree and admired their work.

"It looks even better than last year," Rick remarked.

"Yeah." Ed peered out the window into the gloomy night. "Now, if it would just snow." It had been cool and damp all month but not cold enough to snow.

"Well, we've got two weeks yet." Rick collapsed onto the sofa, pulling Ed down with him. "Merry Two Weeks Until Christmas, baby," he said softly, stroking Ed's face.

"Merry Two Weeks Until Christmas to you too, darlin'." Ed sighed in contentment. "I think it's gonna be a good Christmas after all."

The next evening, they met Mrs. Penfield and Gordy in the front parlor of the main house. Gordy was bringing the last of several boxes full of tree trimmings down from the attic.

"These kind of ornaments never survived at my house growin' up," he said as he gingerly put the boxes on the sofa. "My mom finally got disgusted and switched to those dumb satin-covered ones that were so hot in the late sixties."

"Some of these ornaments date back to before I came to live at this house." Mrs. Penfield eagerly rummaged through ancient tissue paper to locate old favorites. "I've no doubt some of them would fetch a pretty price at a good antique store."

"You sure you trust us with 'em?" Gordy asked with a teasing glance.

Mrs. Penfield looked thoughtful. "I believe you've all matured enough to handle them properly."

Ed was pleased to see Mrs. Penfield and Gordy getting along so well. As Ed checked the old-fashioned bulbs on the light strings, Gordy, Rick, and Mrs. Penfield debated whether to wrap garlands around the tree or use the icicles Ed had picked up at Woolworth's. Icicles were finally agreed upon, and as Rick and Gordy stood on tiptoe to begin winding the lights around the top of the tree, Ed went to Mrs. Penfield's hi-fi for some appropriate music. He found several albums of traditional carols, and soon everyone was humming along with "The First Noel" as the lights began to cover the tree.

"It looks skimpy on the left side," Ed complained.

"Then get over here and help," Gordy grumbled good-naturedly.

As Ed joined Gordy, Mrs. Penfield declared that tree-trimming parties were nothing without hot chocolate, so even though the weather was unusually warm, she went to the kitchen to make some.

The men took that opportunity to discuss in low tones the gift they had decided to go in together on for Mrs. Penfield: new sets of sheets and blankets and a quilt for the bed she kept in the study. Mrs. Penfield's arthritis increasingly made it difficult for her to climb the stairs to her bedroom, so more and more she spent her nights in the study. She'd never bothered to have the bed made up nicely, so they all agreed that it would be a perfect gift.

By the time the hot chocolate was ready, the lights covered the tree in a blaze of color. They all took turns resting with their mugs of rich chocolate while the others carefully hung the fragile ornaments on the tree. Ed found one he remembered from previous years, a cluster of grapes, the deep purple paint faded with age. Rick found a Santa's face he especially liked, and Mrs. Penfield hung one of her favorites, a faded blue ball with the words *Merry Christmas* printed on it in fancy script.

When Mrs. Penfield and Rick began to shower the tree with the tinsel icicles, Gordy stepped outside for a smoke break. Ed followed him.

"There's something I've been meaning to tell you," Ed said as Gordy lit up. "I talked to your mom during the holiday home tour."

"Yeah?"

"Yeah. You were right. She had you and Doug figured out."

"Well, shit," Gordy said in disgust.

"Shit nothing. She's worried about you and wants to know how you're doing. Being honest and talking with her is probably the best Christmas present you could give her."

Gordy slumped against the porch railing. "Hell, couldn't I just give her a new microwave oven?"

Ed rolled his eyes. "You know what I mean."

Gordy looked uncertain.

"Look, it freaked me out when my mom told me she knew about me and what was really going on with Rick. It took a while for both of us to get comfortable talking about it, but we did. Now I don't even think about it anymore."

"But my dad—"

"She's not going to tell your dad," Ed interrupted. "She told me that. She just wants to be your mom, and make sure you're happy."

"Who said I'm happy?"

"Oh, c'mon, Gord. Here's one more person who understands, or is trying to understand, what you're going through. Will you make an effort? I really think it would mean a lot to her."

Gordy silently smoked as he stared out into the night. Ed gave him a few minutes to think it over.

"Well?"

"Oo-kay." Gordy sighed. "She told me she wants to see this place, and Mrs. P. said it'd be okay if she came over some night this week. I'll see if she wants to come over on dad's bowling night. Might as well get it over with."

"It won't be so bad." Ed patted him on the back.

"Yeah! Merry fuckin' Christmas." Gordy managed a weak grin as he stubbed his cigarette out in the standing ashtray near the door.

Once inside, Gordy waved his empty hot chocolate mug. "Who's for some more of this?"

"I am." Mrs. Penfield began to pull herself out of her chair, but Gordy laid a gentle, restraining hand on her shoulder.

"Don't sweat it, Mrs. P. I'll get enough for everyone." He walked toward the kitchen whistling "Jingle Bells."

Ed and Rick exchanged smiles across the tree as they fussed with the icicles.

"It seems to me," Rick said, squatting low to cover the bottom branches, "that perhaps a formerly rowdy, C-minus football player may actually learn a thing or two living here."

Mrs. Penfield chuckled. "I may have retired, but I haven't given up. I've never been able to correct Effie Maude's grammar, but she's far from the raw country girl who first came to work here forty years ago. I believe there's hope for our Gordon yet."

They all laughed.

"What's so funny?" Gordy demanded, coming back with the chocolate pitcher.

"Oh, nothing," Mrs. Penfield purred innocently.

Gordy first scowled, and then smirked at all of them in turn. "You bunch of elves are up to somethin'."

"We were remarking on our good fortune regarding your height, Gordy," Mrs. Penfield smoothly lied. "I believe you're the only one who will be able to place my mother-in-law's gilded star on the top of our tree without the need of a chair."

Mrs. Penfield carefully pulled away the tissue paper surrounding a delicate golden glass star. She handed it to Gordy with a warm smile and a twinkle in her eye, while Ed and Rick turned their backs and tried not to laugh.

Gordy gave her a suspicious look as he accepted the star, but nonetheless took it to the tree. Tall though he was, Gordy could not reach the top of the eight-foot tree, so Ed pulled a dining room chair next to the tree for him. By carefully stretching, he managed to secure the star on the top branch.

"There," Mrs. Penfield said in satisfaction. "It's finished, and I do believe it's the most beautiful tree to ever grace this room."

"It is nice," Gordy said with a pleased nod.

"Beautiful," Ed and Rick agreed.

They stood in a semicircle admiring the tree while the strains of "Joy to the World" mingled in the air with the pungent aroma of the fir tree. Mrs. Penfield motioned them to move closer together. She put her arms around their waists and gave them all a soft squeeze.

"Thank you, gentlemen, for bringing so much joy and holiday spirit into this home. To quote Tiny Tim: 'God bless us, every one.'"

⋖⋗•⋖⋗

As the week progressed and Ed's responsibilities seemed to increase, he looked upon their little tree-trimming party as the last quiet moment he was likely to have before Christmas. As usual, the bulk of his older clients shifted into high gear with what he called their "pre-Christmas hysteria." Every year, as it got closer to the big day, he found himself doing chores that had little or nothing to do with being a handyman.

He spent most of Tuesday Christmas shopping with Mrs. West. He had to call Norma that afternoon for her foolproof method of roasting a turkey for Mrs. Klarn, who "wanted everything to be just perfect now that Paul is home." On Wednesday he decorated another Christmas tree, this time for the Rinkenbergers, who were hosting a Sunday-school-class holiday party. He spent most of that afternoon addressing Christmas cards for elderly Mr. Abbott, a former Porterfield mayor, whose handwriting had become almost illegible due to an uncontrollable palsy. Ed almost fell asleep at the kitchen table that evening over his own Christmas cards.

On Thursday night Ed and Rick picked up Norma and went to Porterfield Elementary School for the annual Christmas pageant. Rick was compulsively sucking on cough drops to keep himself quiet during the show, while Norma shot him suspicious glances every time his dry, hacking cough slipped through his defenses. Ed had spent the bulk of the day decorating yet another house for Christmas; this time for an elderly couple who usually didn't bother but were excited about a potential grandchildren invasion. He was so burned-out on Christmas that he reacted to the usual display of children's holiday performances with something less than enthusiasm.

Rick gave him a sharp nudge when the third graders took the stage and began to form the outline of a Christmas tree while singing "O Tannenbaum." Rick pointed out Jane near the top of the tree, and Lesley somewhat farther upstage.

"I'm the one who's supposed to be sick and tired," Rick whispered. "Pay attention!"

Ed smiled and gave a thumbs-up to Lesley, who had spotted them. "I'm sick and tired of Christmas," he hissed back through his smile.

"Then pretend," Rick hissed through a smile of his own.

Fortunately Norma nudged Rick and distracted him by handing him her camera and asking him to get a picture of the human Christmas tree. Ed slumped back in his seat and returned to his Grinch-like thoughts.

Gwen Hauser called on Friday morning. Since it was such a nice day, she said, could he come over and clean all the leaves out of the gutters? Ed was so thrilled to have a non-Christmas-related job to do that he was out of the apartment and hauling his ladder out of his truck at the Hausers' before someone else could call and ask him to put up another Christmas tree.

Ed was so pleased to be a handyman again that he intended to spend most of Saturday at the Elm Street house. He had a copy of the home inspector's report and wanted to put together a specific list of projects and some sort of a timetable for getting them done.

Ed's usual energy had returned, and he bounced around the apartment Saturday morning, looking forward to the day ahead. Rick, however, was tired from a busy week at the real estate office. He was sluggish and listless, and his cough seemed to be worse, not better. Ed was amazed when Rick insisted on accompanying him to the Elm Street house. Not wanting to ruin his good mood with an argument, Ed patiently waited for Rick to pull on jeans and a sweatshirt for the day.

At the house, Ed wandered around, mumbling to himself and making notes. Rick sat at the bottom of the stairs, drinking coffee from a thermos and occasionally coughing. Ed couldn't understand why Rick had even wanted to join him.

Ed yanked at the oh-so-seventies gold shag carpet in the living room, deciding it had to go. "You know what, though," he called to Rick. "Gordy's had some experience laying carpet, so if I can con him into helping me, we should be able to get this chore done for just the cost of the carpeting."

"That's good," Rick responded in a disinterested voice.

Ed walked into the front hall and looked at Rick huddled over his coffee. "Darlin', you look miserable. Why don't I take you home?"

Rick withdrew even further into his jean jacket, the one Ed had given him for Christmas three years earlier. "Cause this is my project, too," he said sullenly.

"But I'm not really doing anything today. I'm just making notes and figuring out the best way to get things done for the least amount of money."

"Yeah, I know. And then you've got Gordy to help you with the carpet, and Gene to help you with the plumbing, and a whole host of other people will be parading through here to help you with other stuff. What do I do?"

Ed sat next to him on the stairs. "I know what you've already done," he said softly. "You put yourself through those real estate classes, got a license, and spent a year and a half in Indy learning everything you needed to about buying and selling places like this. You've worked your ass off for over two years. Now it's time for me to start working hard."

"I thought we'd be working on this together, not apart."

"You think I'm gonna paint the whole interior of this house by myself? Think again! I'll have a paint roller in your hand before you know it."

Rick shrugged. "I just feel so useless right now." He was seized by a spasm of coughing.

"Darlin', you're sick. And tired. You're not useless."

"I'm sick of being sick," Rick whined, tears coming to his eyes. "I'm sitting here wondering what the hell I got us into with this. Right now I don't feel like I'll ever get better, and we'll never get anything done on this place. Right now it just feels like money down the drain."

Ed pulled Rick to him and put Rick's head on his shoulder. "You're run-down and depressed. That's natural when you feel so crummy. Yeah, we haven't got anything done here yet, but so what? It's Christmas! It's hard to get anything done. Once January's here and things calm down, we'll get to work. You'll feel better, and then you'll be bitchin' at me about having better things to do than paint this damned house."

Rick relaxed against Ed and sighed. "You think so?"

"Yeah, I think so. I even promise. You always say the day will come when I'll get mad at you and throw a hammer at you. Well, I promise that day will come before we're done with this."

Rick gave him a tired grin. "Do you also promise to miss me when you throw that hammer?"

"Yeah, I promise. It'll just be a warning shot." Ed grinned back at him and kissed his nose.

That sat silently for a few minutes, Rick's harsh breathing the only sound in the empty house. Ed was uneasy about Rick's condition and plotted how to get Rick to another appointment with Dr. Klarn. He also wanted to get Rick out of the musty, damp air of the long-neglected house, so he got to his feet, pulling Rick up with him.

"C'mon," he said. "Let's go home and wrap Christmas presents. That's something we can do together. And I think Effie Maude's baking Christmas cookies today. Maybe we can go over to the main house and help her decorate them. I haven't done that in years."

Rick brushed off his jeans. "I thought you were sick of Christmas," he teased.

"I'm sick of *working* for Christmas. This is stuff we can do for fun. There's a big difference."

"Yeah." Rick looked around the house. "I was hoping this would be fun for us, too."

"It will be. Just give it time. I swear I'm gonna have to spend the rest of my life getting you to slow down and enjoy stuff."

"Oh, I'll learn someday."

"If you say so." Ed gave him a mock punch to the face.

Rick put his arms around Ed and kissed him. "I love you, baby," he whispered. "Thanks for putting up with me."

"Just call me Saint Ed." Ed giggled, then kissed Rick. "I love you, too, darlin'. Now, let's get out here."

They shut off the lights and locked the front door behind them. Ed paused for a moment on the porch and observed the overcast skies.

"Not cold and not warm," he grumbled. "Just damp and yucky. When's winter gonna get here?"

⋄•⋄

When is winter going to get here? It was a question on the lips of many Porterfield citizens that December. There were those who thought back to Christmas the year before, which had been so unseasonably warm that many people celebrated outside wearing T-shirts and shorts.

"Going to be another warm one," they said sagely.

Others, however, who were dreaming of a white Christmas, crossed their fingers and wished for cold and snow. Still, the weather continued to be, in Ed's words, "not cold; not warm; just damp and yucky."

Ed was more aligned with the white Christmas camp. The balmy Christmas of '82 had been a novelty, but Ed was enough of a traditionalist to think Christmas felt more like Christmas when it was cold and snowy. He kept his thoughts to himself, as Rick was more inclined to hope for a warm Christmas weekend. They were scheduled to spend most of Christmas Eve with John and Vera in Indianapolis, and then return to Porterfield for dinner at Norma's on Christmas Day. The weekend would be hectic enough, he said, without having to worry about ice and snow-covered roads.

Ed had to agree with him, but he still hoped for a least a *little* snow; not enough to mess up the roads, but just enough to make everything look festive.

Ed had pretty much resigned himself to another tropical holiday when, less than a week before Christmas, the weather suddenly changed. Gusty winds began to blow out of the northwest, and the rain that had been falling changed to snow. It didn't stick at first, but as the winds gathered strength and the temperature began to plummet, the snow quickly accumulated. The thermometer dropped even further, and the heavy, wet snow froze into a hard, icy glaze across yards, exposed vehicles, and outdoor Christmas decorations.

Still the temperature fell, and eventually the streets and highways acquired the same icy covering. People shivered as the bitter wind found its way into cracks and crevices and became drafts most folks had forgotten about during the previous mild winter. Rugs were rolled up and shoved in front of doors; electric blankets were hauled out of closets; drivers rummaged through car trunks looking for that ice scraper they hadn't needed in almost two years; and children glued themselves to the radio for school-closing announcements, hoping the storm would be bad enough to bring an early start to Christmas vacation.

And in the midst of that storm, Susan Cummings went into labor, surprising everyone except her husband.

Vince called Rick early the next morning. Susan was still in labor but doing fine, he said. He expected to be a daddy within the next hour or so, and could Rick keep an eye on the office and tie up as many loose ends as he could? Vince promised to be in by late afternoon, and together they would officially close the office for the holidays. Rick agreed, congratulated Vince, and hung up the phone with a sigh.

Ed had been looking out the windows, which were almost opaque with frost. He turned at Rick's sigh and saw Rick standing motionless by the sofa in his bathrobe. His breathing was harsher and obviously more painful than it had been over the past several days, and he looked even worse than he had when they'd both been in the grips of that intestinal virus earlier in the month. Instinctively Ed went to Rick and felt his forehead; he was dismayed by how warm he was.

"Darlin', I think you've got a fever. I really wish you were going to Dr. Klarn's office instead of yours."

Rick shrugged. "What can I do? Vince is counting on me. At least this is the last day I'll have to work until January. I'll get through this, and if I still feel this lousy at the end of the day, I'll call Dr. Klarn."

"Okay," Ed relented, still quite troubled by Rick's appearance.

The phone rang again. It was one of Ed's clients wanting to know when Ed would be clearing their walks that day. It was only the first call, and soon Ed became so involved in scheduling snow-removal chores that he stopped worrying about Rick and began to worry about taking care of himself in the suddenly savage weather. The snow had ceased overnight, but the temperature had fallen to near zero, and the winds were still howling out of the northwest. He pulled on his cold-weather gear and went downstairs to fire up his snowblower.

Ed gasped when the wind hit him. The preceding winter had been so warm that this first arctic blast was even more of shock than it usually was. He hunkered down and did his best to clear his clients' walks and driveways. Fortunately only about two inches of snow had fallen, but it seemed to be frozen into a solid mass. He soldiered on and was almost done for the day when he arrived at the Hauser house by midafternoon.

He'd just begun on the driveway when he noticed darker clouds rolling across the sky. The wind blasted him again, and the next moment, new snow was falling in a sudden squall. He groaned as he started his snowblower, wondering whether he'd have to go back and start his day all over again.

Herb Hauser, who worked at home as an accountant, appeared at the front door. The tinsel garland around the door had come loose and was flapping in the breeze. Herb tried to tie it down, but the wind was so persistent in pulling it away that he finally gave up. He hollered at Ed and motioned for him to turn off the snowblower.

"TV says we're in for lake-effect showers off and on all night," Herb called to him. "There's no sense in you trying to clear that driveway now. Why don't you go home and get some rest? As cold as it is, I'm not going anywhere unless I have to anyway."

Ed leaned against the snowblower and let out a tired sigh. "Sounds good to me, Herb. I'll be back tomorrow."

He loaded up his truck and headed for home, hoping the rest of his snow-removal clients would be as practical about the new snow as Herb. Once inside the apartment, he began to shed his snow-chore clothes, then lit the fire under the teakettle. Jett, who was obviously feeling the cold as well despite his thick fur, settled in Ed's lap when he finally sat down with his tea. The warmth of both the tea and the cat was comforting, and as his gaze wandered over the Christmas tree and he listened to the wind beating against the carriage house, he relaxed into the comfort of home.

The phone rang. Ed groaned and pushed the cat aside to get up and answer it, assuming it was a client bitching about the new snow. To his surprise, the caller was Vince Cummings.

"What's up, Vince? How's Susan? Is everything okay?"

"Susan is fine, and so is Ethan Michael Cummings, seven pounds, six ounces," Vince said proudly.

The tone of his voice changed. "I'm here at the hospital, Ed, but not with Susan and the baby. Can you come out here? They've just admitted Rick. They think he has pneumonia."

CHAPTER FOURTEEN

Vince was sitting in the lobby of Porterfield General Hospital when Ed burst through the front doors fifteen minutes later. He was red faced and winded from the cold and his mad dash across the parking lot.

"How is he?" Ed panted. "What happened? Can I see him?"

Vince stood up and put an arm around Ed's shoulders. He guided him to a seat by the wall.

"Relax, Ed. I'm sure Rick will be fine. Sit here and catch your breath and I'll tell you what happened."

Vince sat down and chuckled. "What a day! First the weather, then the baby, and then Rick collapses on me. I'm sure we'll be laughing about this on Ethan's first birthday next year.

"Anyway," he continued, "I went to the office to check on things and found Rick at his desk. It looked like he was asleep, so I made a joke about him sleeping on the job while the boss was away. He looked up, and I realized he was really sick. He mumbled something about his chest hurting and how hard it was to breathe. Next thing I knew, he passed out right there at his desk.

"I managed to revive him, and somehow I got his coat on him and got him out to the car. I drove here to the emergency room. Rick was conscious enough to tell me that Dr. Klarn was his new physician, and fortunately he was in the emergency room with another patient. He took a look at Rick, ordered a chest X-ray and some blood tests, and said he was going to admit him. The minute they wheeled Rick off for the X-ray, I called you. The nurses told me to wait here, that when Rick had been placed in a room upstairs the front desk would be notified."

"Aw, crud," Ed muttered. "I knew he was sick this morning, but not this sick."

Vince smiled. "It's been a rough month for Rick. He's been pushing too hard, and it got to him. I'm sure a few days of forced bed rest here will take care of it. I'm not going to reopen the office until after New Year's, so he doesn't have to worry about work. Hopefully this will scare him enough to make him realize he's not Superman."

The warmth of the overheated hospital began to seep into Ed. He realized his head was sweating under his stocking cap. He pulled it off and shrugged off his down coat as well. Vince's calming presence had helped to decrease his panic and slow his rapid heartbeat, but fear and worry had settled into his stomach. He wanted to be with Rick right that moment, but he told himself over and over again to be patient. Freaking out in the lobby wouldn't do Rick any good.

He noticed an aluminum Christmas tree decorated with red ornaments near the registration desk. Every time the front doors opened, the shiny branches and glittering balls would gently bob in the breeze.

"Merry Christmas," Ed sighed, slumping against the wall.

"Now, Ed, just relax. Christmas is still four days away. I'm sure Rick will be doing a lot better by then."

Ed thought of all of their holiday plans and groaned. "I should call Claire," he said as he got to his feet.

Vince put out a hand and urged him to sit down again. "Why don't we wait until we have some news? I'm sure it won't be much longer."

A nurse dressed for the bitter weather walked into the lobby. "Hi, Vince." She smiled. "That guy you brought in has gone upstairs. Third floor."

Vince thanked her and motioned to Ed to follow him to the elevator. Once they arrived at the third floor, they were about to inquire at the nurse's station when Ed spotted Dr. Klarn coming down the hall. He had a lab coat thrown over his usual office attire. He was studying a chart, and Ed couldn't help but notice that he looked tired.

"Oh, good," Dr. Klarn said after he spotted Ed. He gave him a brief smile. "I was just about to page and see if you were here."

"How is he?"

Dr. Klarn ran a hand through his hair. "Rick is a pretty sick man, but I'm sure he'll pull through. He has pneumonia, and I suspect there's a secondary infection as well. Once we bring his temperature down, I think we'll be out of the woods."

"Can I see him?" Ed asked anxiously.

Dr. Klarn gestured behind him. "He's in room 309. You can look in, but keep it brief. He's resting and shouldn't be disturbed."

Ed hurried down the hall. He pushed open the door of room 309 and saw two beds inside. The one near the door was empty. Rick was lying in the other, a plastic tube in his nose and an IV drip attached to his left arm. He seemed to be asleep. In fact, if it wasn't for his raspy breathing, Ed would have almost allowed himself to think he was dead.

Ed let the door close behind him. He walked over to the bed and gently put a hand on Rick's pale cheek. He stroked Rick's beard, noticing yet a few more gray hairs. Fear and worry continued to churn in Ed's stomach, but being able to see and feel Rick finally allowed a small wave of calmness to sweep through Ed for the first time since Vince's phone call.

"I love you, darlin'," he whispered. "I love you, and you're gonna be fine. Just rest and beat this thing."

"Ed?"

Ed turned and saw Dr. Klarn at the door. He gestured for Ed to join him in the hall. Once the door had closed, Dr. Klarn smiled at Ed with the same kindness that had comforted Ed earlier that month.

"I'm sure Rick will be fine. We need to give the medication a chance to work." He glanced at his watch. "In the meantime, do you think you could meet me in the cafeteria in half an hour? I need to grab some supper, and I'd like to ask you a few questions about Rick's medical history. The bulk of Dr. Weisburg's files are still in storage. Fortunately Rick was able to tell me he has no known allergies to medication and other pertinent details, but I'd like to know a few more things as we continue treatment."

Ed nodded. "I'll be there." He bit his lip and willed himself not to cry. "Is he really gonna be okay?"

Dr. Klarn laid a hand on Ed's arm. "Yes, Ed. He'll be okay. I'm not going to promise you he'll be home for Christmas, but I'm sure you'll be bringing in 1984 together."

"Thank you," Ed whispered as a few tears seeped out of his eyes. "I'm just scared."

"I know," Dr. Klarn said in a low voice. "These next few hours will be tense, but I'm optimistic."

Ed drew a shuddery breath. "When can he have visitors? I'm sure his family will want to be here."

"Hopefully tomorrow. I'd like to keep all visits as brief as possible until his temperature is down and his breathing returns to normal, but there's no reason why you can't take turns sitting with him quietly."

"Okay." Ed's legs suddenly felt very weak, so he leaned against the wall. "I guess I should make some phone calls."

"Fine. I'll see you downstairs in half an hour."

Dr. Klarn went to the nurse's station with his chart. He spoke briefly with Vince, who walked over to where Ed was slumped against the wall.

"You okay, Ed?"

Ed nodded. "Yeah, I guess I'm just freaked-out. I'll be okay, though. I've got to make some calls. As long as I have something to do, I'll be okay."

"Good. I'm going to see Susan and the baby. If you need me for anything, you'll find me in Maternity." Vince gave Ed a cheerful smile. "It will be a merry Christmas, Ed. Rick will be fine, okay?"

Ed managed a tentative smile. "Thanks, Vince. We're really lucky that Rick has a boss like you."

Vince laughed. "No sweat. You just get him healthy and back to work next month. I'll be needing him by then."

As Vince made his way to the elevator, Ed walked to a nearby alcove where he had spotted a pay phone. Grateful for the change in his pocket, he first called Claire, who said she'd be at the hospital as soon as possible. Then he called Mrs. Penfield, who also insisted on being with him.

"No," Ed argued. "You don't have any business coming out in this weather. Send Gordy out here. He can keep you up to date on what's happening."

"Very well, Ed," she said gently. "I'll have Gordy on his way as soon as I speak with him. Is there anything you need aside from my prayers and best wishes?"

"No." Ed leaned against the wall and let out a tired sigh. "At some point I'll need some of Rick's things, but I can't think about that right now. Gordy can take care of that, I guess. Right now I need to meet with the doctor."

"All right. Don't worry, Ed. We'll do everything we can to help. I'm sure Rick will pull through this."

Ed thanked her and hung up. He looked at his watch. It wasn't quite time for his meeting with Dr. Klarn, but he decided to go the cafeteria anyway. After a quick look at Rick, he slowly walked down three flights of stairs and found his way to the cafeteria. He bought himself a can of Pepsi from a vending machine and seated himself at a corner table in the noisy, busy room. He sipped his pop and tried to think positive thoughts.

Rick is going to be fine, he told himself. *He let himself get run-down, and now he's paying for it. This is the best place for him. He'll get medicine and rest, and everything will be okay.*

He almost believed it. He knew he wouldn't really accept it until he saw Rick sit up and smile at him. Ed's exhaustion from the long day finally caught up with him, and he laid his head on the table and closed his eyes. He jerked upright when he felt a tap on his shoulder.

"It's been a busy day," Dr. Klarn said as he put a tray on the table. He seated himself across from Ed and gave him a glance of understanding. "I wouldn't mind laying my head down as well. I thought the pace would let up for me, moving from New York to Porterfield, but I sure didn't see this month coming."

The doctor bit into a ham and cheese sandwich. "Thanks for agreeing to meet with me here, Ed," he said after he swallowed. "I know this isn't terribly professional, but it seemed the best time for me. And I do want to talk confidentially with you."

Ed felt a new stirring of panic within. "Is Rick sicker than you told me?"

Dr. Klarn shook his head. "No. I haven't kept anything from you. I have no reason to believe Rick won't make it through this.

"However," he said after a long gulp of coffee, "I do need to ask you a few questions. I'll grant you, these are probably not questions any other doctor here would think to ask, but since I know the truth about your relationship with Rick, and with things I've seen myself, I feel it's my responsibility to dig a little deeper."

The doctor set aside his coffee and gave Ed a solemn look. "Ed," he said softly, "I need you to convince me not to order a test for pneumocystis pneumonia."

"Pneumocystis?" Ed mumbled, looking puzzled. "I've heard that before, but I can't think where."

Dr. Klarn nodded. "As a gay man, I'm sure you have. Pneumocystis is the sort of pneumonia people with AIDS generally have."

Ed's eyes flew open as a jolt of terror spread through his body. "You're trying to tell me Rick has AIDS?" he whispered in horror.

"No, not at all." Dr. Klarn reached across the table and touched Ed's arm. "Don't panic. I couldn't think of any other way to ease into this. As a . . ." He hesitated.

"Yes?"

"As a gay physician," Dr Klarn said steadily, "I would feel negligent if I didn't talk about this. I saw some AIDS cases during my residency in New York, and I spent a little time at the Gay Men's Health Crisis, so I know what I'm talking about."

Ed gave him a feeble grin. "So Rick was right about you."

Dr. Klarn chuckled. "Yes. I wondered if you both figured it out that day in the office. I'm hoping I can count on your discretion now that I've been honest about it."

Ed nodded. "I understand." He put a hand to his heart as though perhaps he could stop its wild beating. "Just please tell me Rick doesn't have AIDS," he whispered. "Now I'm even more scared than I was."

"Let me ask you a few questions. First, how long have you been together?"

"Three years."

"Are you monogamous?"

Ed nodded. "Yes. We don't play around."

"Three years," Dr. Klarn mumbled thoughtfully. "Nineteen-eighty? How about before that."

Ed shifted uncomfortably. "Well, we weren't celibate, but we weren't sluts either."

"To your knowledge, were any of your sexual partners extremely active, or perhaps from New York or California?"

"I don't think so. Anyone I met would have been from around Fort Wayne, and Rick lived in Indy."

"They are discovering that AIDS can have quite a long incubation period, so that doesn't let you off the hook as well as I'd like," Dr. Klarn said honestly. "Let's look at Rick's recent health. Has he had any significant loss of appetite or weight loss?"

"No, not until he got that bug earlier this month."

"Understandable. How about any unusual sweating at night?"

"No."

"Other than the normal fatigue that comes with the illnesses he's had this month, has he complained of fatigue?"

"Well, yes and no," Ed admitted. "He's been run-down, but he's been working so hard. So, yeah, he's been tired, but he still gets up and does what he has to do."

"Okay. Any changes in his skin, or unusual discolorations?"

"No," said Ed in relief, assuming the doctor was referring to Kaposi's sarcoma.

"Good. Has he had any other sort of medical complaints before this month? I don't mean just recently, but anything out of the ordinary in the time you've known him."

"No. He has back trouble that bothers him occasionally, and he's had a few colds, but that's it. There hasn't been anything until we both got that stomach thing this month."

Dr. Klarn nodded. "How about you?"

Ed shook his head. "Nothing. Oh, I had the flu a few years ago, and a cold or two, but that's it."

"Well, it sounds good," said the doctor, mostly to himself. "Ed, I'm going to ask again. Has there been any unusual sexual activity outside of your relationship? Please be honest with me."

"I am being honest," Ed insisted. "We've talked about it. We haven't cheated on each other. In fact, we made a promise to each other not to. I don't have any reason to believe that Rick would lie to me about it. If you knew him, you'd agree with me."

"I'm sure," Dr. Klarn said in a reasonable voice. "And that's why I'm asking these questions—to get to know Rick and make sure I'm giving him the best care."

"Everybody just assumes all gay guys screw around," Ed muttered. "Well, we don't."

"I'm sorry, Ed. I didn't mean to offend you, but do you see the necessity of my questions?"

"Yeah," Ed sighed, slumping in his chair. "I do. I'm sorry as well."

"That's okay. Look, from what you've told me, I have no reason to believe Rick has AIDS. I'll proceed with the usual treatment for viral and bacterial pneumonia, and hopefully that will be all that is needed. Believe me, the last thing I want to do is raise a red flag by ordering a pneumocystis test."

"Red flag?"

Dr. Klarn sighed. "Ed, you and Rick are obviously keeping informed on the AIDS epidemic. That's good. All gay men should. So I'm guessing you're aware of the AIDS hysteria that has swept the nation this past year. In the short time I've been here, I've heard some unbelievable things from otherwise rational and excellent health-care providers. This hospital simply isn't prepared medically or emotionally to deal with an AIDS case."

"Geez," Ed said as the truth of the doctor's words sank into him. "You're right. People would be freaking out all over the place."

"Exactly. Therefore, we need to keep our concerns to ourselves. For a physician, that's problematic; I could get myself in a lot of trouble, but as a gay man I see it as necessary protection for both you and Rick at this moment. I'm going to keep a very close watch on him, even after he leaves the hospital. Unfortunately there isn't a specific test for AIDS at this point, so the best I can do is monitor his condition. Again, I genuinely do not believe Rick has AIDS. I promise I am not holding anything back from you, Ed, but all gay men must be both cautious and concerned these days. That's really all we can do."

"And don't fuck around." Ed laughed ruefully.

"Yes, that, too." Dr. Klarn busied himself with his food while Ed glanced around the cafeteria, hoping no one had overheard the conversation.

Ed reached out a trembling hand for his pop can. He still wasn't completely reassured, but he didn't know quite how to phrase his concerns. "Dr. Klarn," he began tentatively.

The doctor smiled. "Why don't you call me Paul? After all my nosy questions, I feel more like a concerned friend than a doctor. In fact, I'm hoping we'll all be able to become friends."

"Yes, I'd like that, too. I'm realizing how lucky Rick and I are to have you for both a doctor and a friend. But . . . but how will you know Rick doesn't have pneumocystis without that test?"

"If he doesn't respond to the usual pneumonia treatment, I'll have the test done. At this point I'm inclined to believe that Rick simply pushed himself too hard and allowed himself to get sick. It's an old story, and the only one we'd be discussing if we both didn't have a healthy fear of this awful plague that has affected so many men like us."

"But when will you know if he's responding to the medicine?"

"I'll know within the next day or so. Just sit tight, Ed. I know that's easy to say, but it's really all we can do right now."

"Okay." Ed finished the last of his pop and realized that hunger was mixing with the emotions in his midsection. He looked at the food on Paul's tray and almost recoiled. He couldn't eat anything, he decided. Not yet. Maybe later.

"Paul? There's one more thing I'm curious about. Actually, both Rick and I have been wondering. Why did you leave New York City for Porterfield?"

Paul laughed. "Yes, that does seem a bit strange, doesn't it? I've been telling people it was merely to pacify Althea, but that's not the real reason. I suppose I can tell you the truth."

He set his sandwich aside and leaned across the table. "I went through a bad breakup with the man I had been seeing. Unlike you and Rick, he did feel it was a gay man's right to screw around, and with what I had seen, I couldn't accept that. That in itself wouldn't have sent me back to Porterfield, but I'll be honest: AIDS was probably the real reason I came home.

"It's bad, Ed, really bad," he said softly. "Even from what you may have read, you can't even begin to imagine how bad it is, and how bad it will become. There will come a day when this hospital will have AIDS cases, and hopefully by then they will be prepared for it. AIDS will come here to northeast Indiana. It will come everywhere. And when it does, I hope I can help.

"Oh, I could have done a lot in New York, but I kept thinking of how terrible it will be when it hits here. I finally decided that as a gay man and a doctor I could probably do the most good here, in my home state, where life is a lot tougher for gay men. I wanted to be someone they could trust and count on.

"I'll admit," he said, laughing, "I didn't expect to be dealing with it quite so soon, but again, I'm confident Rick is okay in that respect. But when that first man with AIDS walks through the doors of this place, I want to be here."

"Wow," Ed breathed. "That's pretty noble."

"Is it? I don't know. Maybe it's just a stall. I had no intention of ever returning to this town before all of this. It wasn't easy for me growing up here. That's something I'm sure you understand quite well. But I knew my life would become consumed with AIDS in New York. Maybe by coming home I'm just delaying the inevitable, telling myself that I'm doing a good thing in order to avoid it a while longer. There are no easy answers, and I believe the questions will only get tougher over the next few years."

Ed's concern for Rick shifted to all the men who had been stricken with this terrible disease as he thought of what he had read in the last two years, and the few news reports he had seen on television. He had to admit that he had felt safe from AIDS by remaining in Porterfield, but Paul's questions and concerns let him know in no uncertain terms that there really wasn't anyplace to hide.

"It's going to get worse, then, right?" he asked as a feeling of dread joined his already overloaded emotions.

"Much worse."

"Are they ever gonna find a cure?"

Dr. Paul Klarn sat back in his chair and stared into space. He seemed to age at least ten years in front of Ed's eyes.

"I don't know."

◆

Ed trudged up the stairs to the third floor. Since no one was around, he snuck into Rick's room. Rick was still asleep and seemed no better or worse than before. Ed kneeled by the bed and softly stroked Rick's arm as he tried to send all of his positive thoughts into Rick's lungs, willing him to beat the illness that had brought him here.

He noticed that Rick's gold neck chain was missing. Rick always wore the neck chain Ed had given him; Ed remembered watching Rick put it on that morning. Some nurse had probably removed it when Rick was admitted. Ed assumed that the chain, along with Rick's other personal items, was locked up for safekeeping. He thought about asking for it, but after his conversation with Paul, he didn't want to say or do anything that might draw more attention to the fact that Rick was his spouse, or give the hospital staff any reason to hesitate about treating a gay man.

Instead he took his ring—the ring Rick had given him—off his left hand and slipped it onto Rick's ring finger. Rick never wore rings, so Ed hoped the feeling of the gold band on his finger would somehow tell Rick that Ed was with him even if he wasn't in the room.

After a quick kiss on Rick's cheek, Ed slipped out of the room. He walked to the waiting area and saw Claire and Gordy huddled together in quiet conversation. Claire jumped up when she spotted Ed. She came over and gave him a big hug, laying her head on his shoulder. They stood there for a few moments taking what comfort they could from each other.

"I called Mom and Dad," Claire finally said. "They wanted to come up here tonight, but I told them to wait until daylight. With the way it's snowing, there's no sense in them risking a wreck just to be here."

"Is it snowing?" Ed asked in surprise. He'd forgotten all about the weather.

"Hell yeah, it's snowin'," Gordy said, walking over to them. "Been snowin' for the past couple of hours. Streets are a mess."

Gordy put an arm around Ed's shoulders and gripped him as tightly as he could. "How you holdin' up, bud?" he whispered.

"Okay, I guess." Ed leaned into Gordy and felt a little of the tension ebb away. It was good to know that he and Rick were not alone.

"Is there anything I can do?" Claire wanted to know.

Ed thought for a moment. "Actually, there is. Can you call Matt Croasdale?"

Claire blushed. "Yes, I can call Matt. What do you need?"

"In all those papers Rick and I signed, there's a thing that makes me Rick's health-care representative. Dr. Klarn told me the hospital needs a copy of it on file. Can you tell Matt? Maybe he can give a copy to Laurie, and she can bring it over in the morning."

Claire nodded. "Okay. I'll call him right now."

"Glad I could give you an excuse," Ed joked feebly.

She smirked at him and walked off to the pay phone.

Gordy watched her go. "So those two are getting all hot and heavy, huh?"

"Looks that way."

"Well, least it'll be a merry Christmas for someone."

Gordy led Ed over to a beige sofa in the waiting area. They sat down and stared out the window, where the whirling snow could be seen in the glow of the streetlights.

Gordy nudged Ed. "So is my bro really gonna be okay?"

"I hope so. We won't know anything until the medicine starts to work."

"And that's all there is to it, right?"

Ed looked at Gordy and saw both skepticism and worry on his face.

"Gordy!" he hissed, realizing what Gordy was alluding to. "Don't even think about that! Crud, I just went through all of that with Dr. Klarn. Rick's just got pneumonia and nothing else. You hear me?"

"Can you blame me for worryin'?" Gordy said defensively.

Ed sighed. "No."

Gordy made a fist and slammed it against his knee. "I just fuckin' hate all of this. So that Klarn guy knows about you guys?"

"It's no big deal. He told me he's gay, too. He asked me to keep it to myself, but I guess it's okay if you know."

Gordy looked surprised. "No shit? Well, I guess that's a good thing. He'll know what to do if . . ."

"Gordy!"

"I know; I know. I'm just scared. Scared for all of us. And pissed off that no one else seems to be scared, except that they'll get this shit from us. I worry about Doug . . . Shit, I worry about me, and now I'm worryin' about Rick. This just sucks."

"Yeah, it does, but all we can do is wait. Rick's gonna be better tomorrow. I have to believe that."

"Yeah." Gordy leaned his head against the wall and let out a long sigh. "Yeah, he's gonna be better, even if I have to go in there and threaten him."

"Like he's ever taken you seriously before?" Ed managed a chuckle.

"He will this time," Gordy said with a grim smile.

They both chuckled. Ed decided it was a good time to change the subject.

"So, do you think you can help me get Rick's car home tonight? It's at the real estate office. I don't want to leave it on Clark Street with the snowplows going through."

"Yeah. I'm supposed to bring you home for at least an hour. Effie Maude's stayin' at the house until you come home and eat a good meal. If you don't show up, she'll probably come here and feed you herself."

"Okay. Maybe when—"

"Gordy!"

Ed and Gordy looked up. An older, short, heavyset man bundled up against the weather was standing in front of them.

"What the hell are you doin' here?"

Gordy nodded to the man. "Hey, Roger. I'm just waitin' for news on a sick friend."

Roger glanced at Ed and a look of disgust came over his face. "Shit, Gordy, your dad told me you were hangin' out with those fags, but I didn't believe it. What's the matter? One of 'em got that AIDS shit?"

Gordy's face went deadly pale. "No," he said quietly.

"Yeah, don't believe it. They all do. Bunch of human scum, all of 'em. AIDS is gonna get rid of all of 'em." The man smirked at Ed.

Ed felt his hands clench. He was about to stand up when Gordy leaped out of his seat and slammed into Roger. One of Gordy's big hands closed around the man's throat and pinned him to the wall.

"You dirty bastard," Gordy hissed. "Don't you fuckin' talk about my friends that way. You worthless, no-good son of a bitch. If there's any scum in this room, it's you."

Roger's eyes bugged out in horror. "C'mon, Gordy, let me go. You know I'm right. You shouldn't be hangin' around those guys. You'll get it, too."

Gordy's hand tightened around his throat. Roger moaned. "Let me go, Gordy; someone's gonna call the cops."

"Fuckin' bastard," Gordy whispered. "You don't know shit. I'm scum, too. Yeah, fucker, I'm a faggot, and I'm touchin' you. You good and scared now? You pissin' in your pants? I sure the fuck hope so."

Roger stared at him in disbelief. "Geez, Gordy—"

"Geez what? You want me to beat the shit out of you here or down in the parking lot? I don't care. You decide."

Ed stood up. "Gordy, let him go. If that nurse comes back, she probably will call the cops. We've got enough trouble already."

"Yeah, listen to your fag friend there, Gordy."

Gordy slammed a fist into Roger's stomach. "Fuck you! Now, if I let you go, are you gonna get out of here quietly, without sayin' another word? I don't fuckin' care who you tell when you get out of here, but if you ever, *ever*, say anything about me or my friends to my face again, I'll fuckin' make sure you end up here as a patient. Want that, old man? Want a faggot to put you in the hospital? Don't think I won't do it."

Roger was trembling but stared Gordy down and said nothing.

"You listen, old man. I don't have AIDS, and my friends don't have AIDS. If you tell anyone that we do, I'll hunt you down and finish this. That's a fuckin' promise you can take to the bank. And I'm gonna outlive ya, too. I can't wait 'til I fuckin' dance on your grave."

Gordy took his hand away from Roger's throat. "Now, get out of here. Go over to that elevator and get the hell out of here. Run tell my dad. See if I give a fuck."

Roger scampered away. He didn't stop at the elevator but headed for the stairs. Gordy collapsed on the sofa with a sigh.

Shaking from the surprise of the encounter, Gordy's anger, and the things he had said, Ed sat down next to him.

"Damn, Gord, I—"

"Fuck it," Gordy muttered. "I'm just so sick of all of this shit. So he tells my dad. I don't care anymore. My life's in the goddamned toilet, and one of my best friends is down the hall probably fightin' for his life. I don't care what those sacks of shit think of me anymore. It ain't worth it."

"I-I know, but . . . ," Ed stammered.

"I don't wanna talk about it. You think your mom'll care if I come over on Christmas? I don't think I'll be too welcome at my folks'."

"Uh, sure. I guess."

"Good." Gordy stood up. "I need a smoke."

He zipped up his coat and walked to the elevator, where he impatiently jammed his finger against the call button. Claire walked back into the room as the elevator arrived. She looked from Gordy's grim face to Ed's shocked one and shook her head.

"What happened?"

Ed's head fell into his lap as he moaned. "You wouldn't believe me if I told you. I can't believe this day. I'll bet this all beats anything that happened on *All My Children* today."

Claire sat next to him. "Ed, why don't you go home for a while? I know Effie Maude's waiting supper for you, and I promise to call if there's any change. I think maybe you need to get out of here."

Ed reached for his coat. "Yeah, maybe you're right. I better go track Gordy down before he slams his fist into a utility pole or something."

Claire gave him a puzzled look. "Is he okay?"

"He will be," Ed said briefly. "He's just taking this hard. I guess we all are. Promise to call me? I'll be back in an hour or so."

Claire hugged him. "Don't worry. Big sister is here, and she'll keep an eye on her little brother. Go take care of yourself."

"Okay."

Ed stood up and gave her a weak smile. "So things are goin' good for you and Matt, huh? Any fireworks yet?"

Claire groaned. "Maybe a sparkler or two. Now, get out of here. I'll tell you about it when we get my dumb brother back to normal, okay?"

Ed found Gordy hunched over an ashtray outside the parking lot entrance to the hospital. He walked up behind him and hugged him.

"I love you, bud," he whispered.

Gordy turned around and hugged him hard. "I love you, too, bud."

He ground his cigarette into the snow-covered ashtray. "You got a set of Rick's keys?"

"Yeah."

"Okay. Let's go get his car."

Hunched over against the stinging wind and snow, they walked to Gordy's car. Ed huddled in the passenger seat, shivering uncontrollably, while Gordy brushed the snow off the windows. He jacked up the heater fan, wishing it would hurry up and blow out some warm air. He turned the radio on and sighed as Andy Williams happily sang about the most wonderful time of year.

Gordy jumped in and slammed his door. He carefully backed out of the lot and onto Cedar Avenue, then turned left at Main and headed for downtown. The pavement, despite the best efforts of the Porterfield Street Department, was slick and snowy. Gordy drove slowly, and Ed was silently grateful for the lack of traffic. Apparently people had decided to stay home, where it was warm and dry.

The Romantics followed Andy Williams on the radio with "Talking in Your Sleep." Ed, still shivering, lowered the volume.

"Gord, what the hell is going on? Why is everything so crazy?"

"I don't know."

Ed began to cry. "I'm scared. I'm scared about Rick and I'm scared about you. Are we ever gonna be able to relax and be okay again?"

Gordy took one gloved hand off the steering wheel. He reached across the car and grabbed Ed's hand.

"We'll be okay, bud. Rick's gonna be fine, and we'll get through this." He squeezed Ed's hand tighter. "I don't know how, but we'll get through it."

Ed sniffed and clutched Gordy's hand. He nodded and wiped at his nose with his other hand. Through the melting snow being pushed back and forth by the windshield wipers, he could see the lit Christmas garlands swinging in the wind over Main Street. He glanced at the time-and-temperature sign hanging from the Porterfield First National Bank building. According to its thermometer it was minus seven degrees.

"Man, this is gonna be the coldest Christmas ever, isn't it?"

Gordy took his hand back to turn the car onto Clark Street.

"Yeah, it is."

CHAPTER FIFTEEN

The Romantics had set up their equipment next to the dresser and were playing their big hit. Ed tossed and turned in bed as the lead singer chanted the chorus over and over. The words were somehow different from what Ed always heard on the radio. The guy seemed to be singing about the secrets that *Rick* was keeping in his sleep. It was loud and annoying, and he wanted them to turn the volume down on their amplifiers, but he didn't want to be rude. He rolled over and asked Rick if he would politely tell them that he needed his sleep because he had to go see Rick at the hospital.

"But I'm right here," Rick said.

"No, you're not, you're sick in the hospital."

"I was at the hospital, but I'm not anymore."

"Why are you here?"

"I'm dead. I wanted to tell you I lied to you. If you'd listened while I was asleep, you would have known that I had an affair in Indy. That guy gave me AIDS, and I'm dead now."

Ed peered across the bed at Rick. He was nothing but a talking, grinning skeleton. Ed gasped and the skeleton laughed at him.

"But you promised!" Ed shouted.

"Sorry, baby. I was talking in my sleep, but you didn't listen."

"No!"

"Sorry, baby. You're gonna croak, too, now."

"No!"

Ed flailed under the covers and sat up. The music was playing only in his head, and there was no skeleton in bed with him, only Jett curled up against Rick's pillows.

Ed slumped down and pulled the covers over him, and then pushed the sheet, damp with cold sweat, away from him. He threw his equally wet pillow on the floor and wiggled to a dry place on the mattress. Jett blinked at him and yawned, then pulled his tail tighter around himself and went back to sleep.

"Geez," Ed whispered, shivering from both the nightmare and the cold.

Their bedroom usually remained nicely warm on even the coldest of nights, so Ed assumed the temperature had dropped even further. He could hear the northwest wind still beating against the carriage house and shivered again, imagining just how dangerously frigid it must be outside.

He turned and squinted at the clock: 5:25 a.m. It wouldn't be light for another three hours. He rolled over and petted the cat, trying to reorient himself.

Ed had left the hospital late the night before. Paul Klarn had insisted that Ed needed to rest in his own bed, and the head nurse on the third floor had promised to call Ed if there was any change in Rick's condition. Ed didn't think he'd be able to sleep at all but had fallen into a sound sleep minutes after he crawled into the chilly bed.

He'd probably still be asleep if that awful dream hadn't awakened him. He shook his head, trying to dislodge the terrible images and words from his brain. Why would he dream such a horrible thing? Did he subconsciously think Rick had lied to him?

No, he decided as Jett began to purr. No, he was just overstressed and worried. He hadn't lost his confidence in Rick. He didn't believe for a moment that Rick had lied to him about anything.

But he also knew that no matter how strongly he believed in Rick, in some dark place in his soul, he'd continue to worry until Rick responded to treatment and Dr. Klarn had no reason to order a test for pneumocystis pneumonia. As Dr. Klarn had said, it didn't matter if they had been faithful to each other these past three years. It could have happened long before that. No gay man who had been sexually active during the past several years could rest easy. Not yet.

Ed slid out of bed and reached for his bathrobe. He tried to look out the window, but it was completely frosted over. He shuffled down the hall and into the living room, turning on a lamp when he got there. As he went to plug in the Christmas tree lights, he almost tripped over several gaily wrapped boxes underneath the tree. After the lights were on, he examined the packages. There was a square box exquisitely wrapped in gold foil paper and tied with a shiny bow and ribbon. The tag read MERRY CHRISTMAS AND LOVE FROM RICK TO ED. Ed smiled. Knowing what an inept gift wrapper Rick was, he could only assume Claire had wrapped it for him.

Ed's package for Rick was under the tree as well, the heavy woolen coat he'd bought earlier that month disguised in a box wrapped with paper featuring a snow-topped pine-cone design, similar to the ornament he'd bought for their tree.

He settled on the end of the sofa nearest the tree, pulling his feet under him. As he stared at the snowman ornament Rick had bought three years earlier, which they had rather unoriginally named Frosty, he could remember his excitement that Christmas, how thrilled he was to be suddenly in love with the man of his dreams. The only thing that had bothered him was that Rick had to spend Christmas in Indianapolis that year. He'd resigned himself to being without Rick on December 25, but Ed had wished on Frosty that somehow Rick could be with him. And sure enough, Rick had surprised him late on Christmas Eve, after Vera had sent him back to Porterfield to be with Ed.

Ed stood up and gently stroked the jolly snowman ornament. "Well, it worked once before," he mumbled.

He concentrated as hard as he could as the wind whistled against the windows. "Frosty," he whispered, "even if he can't be here for Christmas, will you just make sure he's okay? That's all I want. I don't care about the presents under the tree. The only thing I want is for Rick to be okay."

There was a muffled rumbling under his feet. Ed's eyes grew large as a light breeze set the ornaments to bobbing on their branches. Then he sighed as he realized it was only the furnace kicking into gear.

"Aw, crud," he hollered.

He turned away from the tree and headed for the bedroom, where he began to pull together the warmest outfit he could find. Wishes or not, he knew he couldn't just sit in the apartment and wait. He needed to be with Rick.

Ed was sitting in a chair next to Rick's bed when the door opened. Ed jumped to his feet with a guilty look on his face, and then relaxed when he recognized the nurse walking into the room. It was Geraldine Zeigler, the daughter of the late Agnes Heston. Mrs. Heston had been one of Ed's most loyal handyman clients until her death two years earlier, and Geraldine's opinion of Ed was equally high.

"Ed Stephens," she softly scolded as she bustled across the room. "What are you doing in here? We're a long way yet from visiting hours."

"I couldn't sleep, so I decided I'd feel better if I was here."

Geraldine frowned at him, but then smiled. "I understand. I won't tell anyone, but don't let our Head Scrooge, Nurse Corbett, find you in here."

She fussed over Rick and checked his temperature while Ed watched. "Well?" he said as she examined the reading.

"One-oh-two." She sighed. "That's certainly better than the 104 he had when he was admitted. We're making progress."

Ed looked at Rick. He was still quite pale, but his breathing seemed a little easier.

"Why doesn't he wake up?"

"Sleep is the best thing for him right now," Geraldine said as she smoothed the sheet around Rick's shoulders. "Don't worry, Ed. It may not look like it, but he's fighting this like a trooper. I've seen lots of pneumonia in my years here, and I'm sure Rick will be just fine."

She smiled fondly at the sleeping man on the bed. "I remember after Mother died when Rick wanted to buy Mother's desk for your birthday. He was so sweet, insisting I take some money for it, when I wanted to just give it to you. I remembered Mother telling me how glad she was that you had found such a special companion, and I saw how right she was."

"Thanks." Ed settled back in his chair. "That means a lot, you not making a fuss the way some people would."

"Yes, I know." Geraldine looked at him solemnly. "Not everyone can see that what may be right for them isn't right for someone else. It's a shame, and I do hope people in town haven't been cruel to either of you."

"I feel better knowing you're keeping an eye on Rick here. I have to admit I'm kind of worried about . . ." He trailed off.

"Don't worry." Geraldine briskly pulled the curtains open and looked outside. "My, can you believe this weather? I'll keep an eye on Rick while I'm on duty. If anyone gives you any nonsense, you just let me know. I'll take care of it, and I'm sure Dr. Klarn feels the same way."

More than you know, Ed thought with a grin.

"Speaking of Dr. Klarn, I'm sure he'll be through on rounds in an hour or so. Why don't you go downstairs and get yourself some breakfast? If Mildred Corbett finds you here, she'll give you the dickens. I can't protect you from her! Go have something to eat, and I'm sure Dr. Klarn will have good news for you after his rounds."

"Okay." Ed reluctantly got to his feet. "Thanks again," he said, smiling.

"You're welcome." She patted him on the shoulder. "Now, get out of here."

⋘●⋙

Ed managed to choke down some eggs and toast in the cafeteria and made it back upstairs to meet with Dr. Klarn.

"How's he doing?"

Paul looked at Rick's chart. "I'm optimistic. His temperature is still high, but I believe the medication is taking hold. The first twenty-four hours are always the toughest. I'm sure he'll continue to improve throughout the day."

"Do you think it's safe for me to leave? I've got a hell of a lot of snow to clear away for my clients."

Paul nodded. "Go ahead. I think work will help you pass the day. Although I don't envy you being outside." He shook his head ruefully. "The wind chill was thirty below when I came in this morning."

"Yeah," Ed said with a sigh. "It sucks, but I'm used to it, more or less. I just wish someone else was here."

No sooner had Ed expressed that thought than he saw Effie Maude striding off the elevator. She barged up to Ed and Paul and grabbed Paul's arm.

"How's he doin', Doc?" she demanded.

"Uh, better," Paul said, obviously startled by the large woman in the navy blue parka. "I think Rick will be fine, Mrs. uh . . ."

"Miss Sanders," she rasped. "Miss Effie Maude Sanders. Glad to know ya." She gave Paul's hand a quick, firm shake.

She turned to Ed. "You scamp! I went over to the carriage barn to see about gettin' you some breakfast and you weren't there. I figured you'd be out here causin' trouble. Did you eat yet?"

Ed smiled at Paul's reaction to Effie Maude. "Yeah, I had something in the cafeteria."

"Hospital food," she scoffed. "Well, at least you had somethin'. Your phone was ringin' when I was up there. Your people are carryin' on about gettin' their walks cleared, so you'd better get busy. I'll stay here and watch Rick. Oh, and I fed the cat, too. You ran off and left his dish empty."

"Aw, crud," Ed mumbled, ashamed.

"Don't fret it. I'll take care of everything 'til we get Rick home. You get to work. What room is Rick in?"

"Three-oh-nine." Ed grinned, taking great comfort in Effie Maude's bossiness. "But watch out for Nurse Corbett," he warned.

"Mildred Corbett?" Effie Maude sniffed. "She don't scare me."

"She scares me," Paul admitted.

"Men!" Effie Maude huffed. "Always takes a woman to straighten things out. You both get back to work, and I'll take care of things here."

"Yes, ma'am!" Paul saluted her with a smile and went back to his rounds.

Ed gave her a quick hug and went to the elevator, zipping up his coat. He allowed Paul's optimism about Rick's condition to flow through him and help to brace him against the bitter cold, along with Effie Maude's take-charge attitude. He knew he was leaving Rick in the best hands possible.

⟨⟩•⟨⟩

Ed worked as hard and as fast as he could in the brutal cold. The wind continued to blow and undo a lot of the snow removal he accomplished, so he resigned himself to clearing the north-south sidewalks and driveways every day until the wind finally subsided.

He returned to the hospital by midafternoon. He walked casually by the nurse's station and the formidable Nurse Corbett and slipped into Rick's room. He was disappointed to find Rick still asleep, but his breathing was softer than it had been earlier in the day. He snuck back to the waiting area when Nurse Corbett's back was turned and was surprised to see Judy sitting on the beige sofa, the headphones of her Walkman perched on her head as she flipped through an old *Newsweek*.

He waved a hand in front of her face and grinned as he sat next to her. "So, whatcha listening to? Quiet Riot? The Eurythmics?"

Judy smiled and slipped her headphones off her own head and put them over Ed's ears. He was surprised to hear Abba's "S.O.S."

"Abba always makes me feel better when I'm worried," Judy told him as she took the headphones back and clicked off the tape.

"Everything's okay, isn't it? I mean, nothing's changed since I left, right?"

"Uncle Rick is the same," Judy admitted, "but I'm still worried. Aren't you?"

"Of course! But everyone keeps telling me to be patient, so I'm trying to be."

"Yeah, me, too." She sighed. "Oh, Effie Maude was here. She left when I got here to go home and see about Mrs. Penfield's lunch. She said to call her if you need her. Grandpa and Grandma will be here pretty soon. I asked Mom if I could come out here and meet them."

"Why aren't you in school?" Ed asked with a mock frown.

Judy smirked. "They closed school today because it's so cold. My friend Angie's older brother dropped me off here on his way to work. Josh and Jane wanted to come, but Mom said they were too young, and they probably wouldn't allow them to hang around here. I've already called them, but I think they'd like to talk to you."

"I'll call them," Ed promised. "Any other bulletins?"

"Let's see," Judy frowned. "Oh, yeah. Your mom was here on her lunch break. She said she'd be back tonight sometime, and if you weren't eating right and taking care of yourself in this cold she was going to spank you, even though you're thirty-one years old. And Gordy stopped by. He told me to tell you everything was cool at work, whatever that means."

"I know what it means," Ed said with relief.

"I think that's it. I feel like a receptionist," she cheerfully complained.

Ed gave her a playful punch. "It just shows how important it is for you to be here and keep everyone up to date. And it shows how much everyone loves your uncle Rick."

"You, too," she said, punching him back. "I think they're as worried about you as they are about him."

"Yeah." Ed felt a warm glow that had nothing to do with the overheated hospital.

"So what's up with your mom and Matt?" Ed asked to get both their minds off of Rick.

Judy rolled her eyes. "They're sure spending a lot of time together. Mom even got him a Christmas present."

"How do you feel about that?"

She shrugged. "Oh, it's okay, I guess. I thought a lot about what you said at Thanksgiving. You were right. Mom's been through hell, and there's no reason why she shouldn't be seeing a nice man. And Matt is a nice guy. I can tell. Jane's crazy about him. She hopes they get married. Josh is about ready to kill her."

"He's not so thrilled with the idea?"

"No. He keeps saying that Matt's okay, but he doesn't need to marry Mom, 'cause you and Uncle Rick are around."

"We'll still be around, even if they get married." *I hope*, Ed added to himself, thinking of Rick lying so still down the hall.

"I'm guessing the idea of marriage is still a long way off," he told her. "If it does happen, Rick and I will talk to Josh. Are you okay with it?"

"Yeah. I'm not all that crazy about having a stepfather, but if Mom does decide to get married again, she could do a lot worse than Matt."

"Ed?" Geraldine Zeigler popped her head into the waiting lounge. "Do you want to see Rick? Visiting hours have begun."

"Thanks, Geraldine." Ed got to his feet. "Judy, why don't you go see him first? I'll call Josh and Jane while you're in there."

Ed was just hanging up the phone after doing his best to reassure the younger kids that Uncle Rick was going to be okay when John and Vera came down the hall. They spotted Ed and hurried over to him. After hugs and worried greetings, Ed led them to Rick's room.

"Oh, dear," Vera whispered at the sight of Rick. "I just feel so helpless. He's going to be fine, isn't he?"

"We should know more by tonight," Ed said, trying to keep his own worry out of his voice.

He put his arm gently around Judy and led her to the door. "C'mon, kid. Let's go back to the waiting area. Nurse Corbett will throw a fit if she sees us all in here at once."

Once they were in the lounge, Judy went back to Abba and her Walkman, and Ed stood at the window watching a snowplow clear more of the drifting snow away from Main Street.

He began to fantasize that Rick was better. It was Christmas, and they were getting ready to go to Norma's for dinner. Rick was wearing his new overcoat. Ed was busy stuffing family presents into a shopping bag. Jett was playing with his new catnip mouse, racing down the hall as Rick threw it for him.

"Stop playing with that cat and help me."

"Some elf you are! Can't even get those presents in a bag without smashing the bows."

"Well, get me another bag, then, Mr. Best-Dressed Real Estate Agent."

"Man, I am too cool to touch in this coat. Thanks again, baby."

"You're welcome, hot stuff. Merry Christmas again. Now, get me another bag!"

"Uncle Ed." Judy's hand on his arm snapped him back to reality. "Look at that!"

He turned and saw a cart loaded with flowers, plants, and balloons at the nurse's station.

"They're all for Uncle Rick," Judy said excitedly.

"I don't want these placed in Mr. Benton's room until his condition has stabilized." Nurse Corbett gave the volunteer pushing the cart a steely glare. Her arms were crossed against her bony bosom, and her gray hair, piled in a bun under her old-fashioned nurse's cap, seemed to make her appear taller and even more terrifying. "You can just arrange those in the corner of the nurse's station until tomorrow."

Ed walked to the nurse's station. "Mrs. Corbett," he said politely, "may I look at the cards? I'd like to see who was thoughtful enough to send so many nice flowers to Rick."

Nurse Corbett's glacial frown melted a bit. "I suppose," she muttered. "Since we're not busy at the moment, you may examine the cards. Just don't take them to the patient's room! We can't risk having flower pollen in that room until his breathing is back to normal."

"Yes, ma'am," Ed said respectfully.

Judy joined him, and together they read the cards. There was a planter from Mrs. Penfield, another one from Effie Maude, and a huge poinsettia from Vince and Susan. Ed felt badly reading that card, as he'd been too distracted to send anything for Susan and the baby. He vowed to visit her the moment he knew Rick would be okay.

Laurie and Todd had sent the balloon bouquet, and there were floral arrangements from Vince's secretary and Eunice Ames, and another one bearing the names of several other historical society members. Ed was astonished to see that another floral arrangement was from the Hausers, and that a small planter featuring a Styrofoam snowman bore the name Althea Klarn. He was so used to his clients tactfully ignoring his relationship with Rick that he was amazed and touched that they would go to this sort of trouble.

"Mrs. Penfield's right," he murmured. "I guess a lot of people in this town do know how to live and let live."

Judy laughed. She knew what he meant. "I think it's awesome."

"Me, too, kid; me, too."

"My goodness!" Vera exclaimed behind them. "Are those all for Rick?"

Ed grinned at her. "Yep!"

John was grinning as well. "That's wonderful. It does my heart good to know Rick is well liked here in Porterfield."

"Oh, Grandpa," Judy groaned.

"Hush, Judy." Vera was smiling as well. "Your grandfather is right. It *is* good to know Rick is respected."

"You people need to clear away from the nurse's station." Nurse Corbett was glowering at them. "Either return to your patient's room or sit in the waiting area."

Vera quickly turned in the direction of Rick's room as though afraid the imposing woman behind the counter might change her mind. Ed and Judy returned to the good ole beige sofa.

John remained at the desk. "I'm John Benton, Richard's father," he said to Nurse Corbett. "I'd like to know about his specific treatment, and when I can meet with the doctor."

"I suggest you speak to Mr. Stephens." Nurse Corbett didn't bother to look up from the pills she was rattling into paper cups.

"I'm sorry?" John looked puzzled.

"According to my file, Mr. Stephens is Mr. Benton's official health-care representative. It's my job to keep Mr. Stephens informed of Mr. Benton's condition. Therefore, I suggest you talk with him."

"But I'm Rick's father," John protested.

Nurse Corbett looked up from her task. She gave John a frosty smile. "I'm very happy for you, sir. Congratulations. However, Mr. Stephens is responsible for Mr. Benton's treatment until such time as Mr. Benton is able to make his own treatment decisions. Now, if you'll excuse me, I have medication to distribute."

John turned from the desk and looked across the room at Ed. Ed looked John right in the eye, prepared for an argument. However, John shrugged and disappeared down the hall in the direction of Rick's room. Ed sagged against the sofa in relief. He had a feeling, though, that he hadn't heard the last of John's thoughts on the matter. He just hoped John would keep those thoughts to himself until Rick was better.

The afternoon dragged by. At dusk Vera went to the pay phone. She returned and collapsed on the sofa next to Judy with a tired sigh.

"I've spoken to your mother. She'd like us to drop you at home so you can get supper started for Josh and Jane. She plans to come here to the hospital as soon as she's finished with her last cleaning." Claire was a dental hygienist for Dr. Wells on the north side of town.

"How grody," Judy grumbled, but got to her feet.

"I've also spoken to Hilda," Vera said to Ed. "She's graciously invited us to stay in her guest room, bless her heart. Apparently Effie Maude has supper waiting for us as well. My, both of those women are such a blessing! You and Rick are so lucky."

"I know," Ed said, nodding. "Please go to Mrs. Penfield's and get some rest. I'm sure it was an awful drive up here in the snow. I promise to call if anything changes."

John gave Ed a look of genuine concern. "Ed, why don't you come home with us? Claire will be here shortly, and I'm sure you could use some rest and a good meal as well."

Ed shook his head. "I don't want to leave until Dr. Klarn looks in on Rick after his office hours."

John clapped him on the back. "If you're sure. You give me a call if you want me to come and get you."

Vera gave Ed a hug, as did Judy. "Promise to call me, too, if anything changes?" Judy pleaded.

"I will." Ed hugged her back.

The three of them pulled on coats, gloves, and hats and walked to the elevator. Ed walked down the hall to Rick's room and took up his post in the chair by Rick's bed.

He didn't realize how tired he was until he caught himself nodding off. He stood up and shook himself, trying to stay awake. His hand covered a huge yawn as he glared at Rick.

"Dammit, Rick," he whispered. "Wake up and talk to me! Let me know you're gonna be okay."

Rick remained still.

"Aw, crud," Ed muttered and flopped back in his chair.

Paul came in a few minutes later. He asked Ed to step out into the hall while he checked on his patient. Ed leaned against the wall, trying to subdue the impatience rising within him. He just wanted this to be over with, just wanted Rick to wake up and be "all better." He began to pace in the hall and was making his second lap when Paul emerged from Rick's room.

"Well?" Ed stopped in front of him.

Paul looked concerned. "It seems Rick's temperature has risen again," he said carefully.

"What?" Ed whispered.

"Don't panic, Ed. This sometimes happens. It's clear to me that Rick's body is fighting the infection. A rising temperature can be a sign of this. Still, I'm going to instruct the staff to keep a very close watch on him for the next few hours."

"And if his temperature doesn't come down?"

Paul laid a gentle hand on Ed's arm. "If his temperature continues to rise and he continues to be unresponsive, then I'll have to consider additional tests and different medication. I'm sorry, Ed, but that's all I can tell you right now."

Ed stood still, feeling as though his heart had fallen into his stomach. He gulped. "Okay," he whispered.

"I'll be back to check on Rick in two hours." Paul patted Ed's arm. "Is there anything I can do for you?"

Ed shook his head.

"Hang in there, Ed. I know this is tough, but I'm still convinced Rick will come through this."

Ed nodded, and Paul walked on to another patient's room. Ed watched him disappear behind the door. Ed tried to swallow his fear as he hesitantly pushed open Rick's door. He stared at Rick for a few moments, and then abruptly turned away. He grabbed his coat from the waiting lounge and ran for the stairs.

Once he was outside, the cold air slapped him in the face and he gasped. He hurried to his truck, praying it would start. After a few noisy groans, the engine rolled over and caught. Ed jumped out and began to scrape away at the frost on the windshield. It was so cold that frost had even begun to form on the inside of the windows. He doggedly scraped away until the windows were clear enough for him to drive safely.

He pulled onto Main Street and headed north. As they were the night before, the streets were almost deserted. Obviously the citizens of Porterfield had taken the dire warnings of deadly windchills from the radio and television weather forecasters to heart and had decided to remain indoors.

Ed glanced at the Porterfield First National sign as he drove through downtown. It read minus fourteen.

He turned east onto Stratton Avenue and didn't slow down until the Porterfield town cemetery came into view. The narrow lanes through the burial grounds had not been plowed, and the tires of the truck spun as they sought traction on the snow and ice. Ed carefully navigated the truck around the twists and bends until he reached a familiar grave site.

He put the truck in park and contemplated the bleak graveyard. The truck's headlights illuminated the snow-covered tombstones. The wind whipped and rattled the Christmas greenery decorating some of the graves; a red satin ribbon, barely attached to a wire arrangement, ripped free and caught briefly on the front of the truck before it blew away into the night.

Leaving the truck running, Ed jumped out. The frozen snow crunched under his boots as he walked, by memory, a few feet to his father's grave. With his glove he tried to brush the snow and ice away from the marker, and managed to uncover his father's first name: TIMOTHY.

Shivering, he slumped to his knees and raised his eyes to the sky. To his surprise there were no clouds, and the stars were glittering on high as though someone had thrown ice chips into the heavens.

"Help me, Dad," he whispered.

A gust of wind almost knocked him over. He pulled his stocking cap tighter around his ears and regained his balance.

"I guess other people would pray to God," he said in a louder voice, "but I trust you more than him right now."

Ed ran his gloved hand over the etchings on the stone. "Maybe the Bible-bangers are right. Maybe God hates fags. I don't know anymore. Maybe that disease is a punishment. I don't know, but I do know that you wouldn't punish me for loving Rick. I know you love me unconditionally, and you'd love Rick the same way.

"Remember when I told you I thought you sent him to me? I still think that. I think you knew Rick was the perfect guy for me, so you sent him to my front door three years ago. If you did . . ."

Ed gulped. "If you did, don't take him away from me. Not yet."

The fear he had tried so hard to keep in check for the past twenty-four hours finally overwhelmed him. He began to cry as he beat his fist on the granite marker. The hot tears scalded his cold cheeks and ran off his face onto the tombstone.

"Dammit, Dad," he cried wildly. "Don't let him go! Not yet. We're just getting started. If he has . . . aw, crud, I can't even say it. If he has that thing, please make him better. Help those assholes who are doing nothing find a treatment. Do something! Just don't take him away from me."

Ed lay on the ground and sobbed. His toes, inside his heavy boots and two pairs of thick socks, went numb, and then began to tingle with pain. His tears froze in his mustache. And still he cried as he begged his father to do something, and he cried as he cursed God for taking his father away from him, the one person he'd always known was there for him no matter what.

"Please?" he whispered. "Do something."

The arctic wind blew against him with no mercy. He shivered uncontrollably and tried to wipe the frozen tears from his face as he gazed skyward, trying to interpret some sort of sign from his father, from God, from anyone or anything, that Rick was going to be okay.

Ed wearily stopped his truck in the hospital parking lot. He made a feeble attempt at fixing his appearance. He found a paper napkin in the glove compartment and wiped his face. He winced as the harsh paper stung his raw, frozen skin.

He looked toward the hospital and groaned. He didn't want to go back inside, but even if the building did not seem to be a safe harbor on this bitter night, at least it was warm, and he knew for his own sake that he needed to get warm.

When the elevator let him out at the third floor, he was surprised to see Norma seated on the beige sofa, staring out the window. She sensed his presence and turned, and as she looked him up and down, her eyebrows rose.

"Been to see your father?"

Ed gave a shaky laugh. "I guess it's true what they say: mothers do have eyes in the backs of their heads."

She shrugged. "It's where I go when I get scared. Why should you be any different?"

Ed flopped on the couch beside her. He stamped his feet, willing the tingling pain to go away from his toes. It wouldn't do anyone any good if he were admitted for frostbite.

"Where's Claire?" He sighed.

"Downstairs with that lawyer friend of hers. She was pretty shaken up when the nurse told her Rick was doing worse."

"Oh, Mom," he groaned, putting his head in his hands. "How am I gonna get through this?"

"By being the son your father raised," she said crisply. "Tim Stephens didn't raise a quitter, and neither did I. You just hold on until Rick is better. He will be."

"How do you know?" he asked bitterly.

"I just do. Sit up straight!" She jabbed her elbow into his ribs. "You're going to ruin your spine slumping around like that."

Ed rearranged himself on the sofa. "So you still talk to Dad, too, huh?"

"All the time," she said softly. "I miss him as much as you and your sister do. Don't ever think that I don't."

"I know, Mom."

Norma snorted. "If you did, you'd stop trying to fix me up with Clyde Croasdale."

"What's that got to do with missing Dad?"

"Ed Stephens! Use your head. That you and your sister even think I could marry another man after your father is ridiculous. Why, no one could compare with Tim Stephens."

"I know, but people do remarry even after they've lost someone that special."

"Do they?" She stared hard at Ed. "Do you honestly think you could find someone else if something *did* happen to Rick?"

Ed looked at the floor. "Probably not."

"Of course not. Although I still don't understand why you're with a man and not a woman, I'm no fool. I see how you two are together. I know how much you care about him, and how much he cares about you. Why, if something happened to Rick, I'd never nag you about finding someone else. I know something that special can't be replaced."

Ed glanced around the quiet waiting area. He read over and over the brightly colored foil letters hanging over the nurse's station: MERRY CHRISTMAS—HAPPY NEW YEAR. He looked out into the night and finally back at his mother, and thought how odd it seemed, having this conversation with her at this place and time.

"You and Dad were that special, huh? Tell me about it, Mom. Somehow I always knew you were, but you were so different, I always wondered why you were so crazy about each other."

Norma looked at her hands in her lap. "I may have been sweet on Clyde Croasdale when I was a girl," she admitted, "but I forgot about him and any other boy I'd ever seen the first time I saw your father. That day he walked into the bakery? I knew. I just knew he was the one for me. And he knew it, too.

"I know we were different, but that was part of the attraction. I loved how gentle he was, and he loved my spirit, loved how I would fight for anything I thought was right. Sure, that caused some problems sometimes. But we always worked it out because we loved each other so much. We knew it was worth the compromise. I see you and Rick doing the same thing.

"Other than that," she said, raising her hands helplessly into the air, "I don't know. We just loved each other."

"Was it a mystery?"

"I guess it was."

"Mrs. Penfield says love is a mystery, and we shouldn't try too hard to figure it out."

"She's a wise woman," Norma said softly.

They sat in silence for a few minutes.

"Ed," Norma finally said. "If love is a mystery, then so are things like this, Rick being sick and all. You'll drive yourself crazy trying to figure out why things like this happen. I had to stop asking why your father had to die so young. I realized I was never going to get an answer, and if I kept asking I'd just end up in the funny farm. I don't know if I'll ever accept it. I guess some mysteries don't ever get solved."

"And some questions never get answered," Ed said, thinking of all the questions he'd been asking the past few months that didn't seem to have answers.

"Yes. I guess that's true."

Ed stood up. The burning sensation had eased from his toes, and suddenly he felt like Tim Stephens's son again, a man who didn't quit.

"I'm going to go look in on Rick."

He walked down the hall and opened the door to Rick's room. Rick was just as he had left him an hour earlier. Ed kneeled next to Rick's bed and took his hand. On an impulse, he lay his other hand on Rick's forehead, frowned, and then stroked his forehead. Maybe it was his imagination, but Rick seemed cooler now than he had all day.

"Darlin'," he whispered, "this has gone on long enough. You need to wake up and start getting better. We're all worried about you. It's almost Christmas, and we need you to get better so we can all open our presents and celebrate. We can't do it without you, so you need to get your ass in gear and get over this, okay?"

Ed rubbed Rick's hand against his cheek. Rick's skin was very dry, but again he felt cooler to Ed's touch.

"I love you, darlin'. I guess it's a mystery why I love you so much. God and anyone else knows you make me crazy sometimes, but I do love you with all of my heart, and I need you to keep sharing this mystery with me."

Rick's hand moved against Ed's cheek. Ed held his breath and willed the hand to move again.

"Baby," said a raspy voice, "why the hell I am wearing your ring?"

Ed looked up. Rick's eyes were open and blinking. He was looking not at Ed, but at the ring on his left hand. He then noticed the IV drip in his arm, and his eyes opened wider.

"Shit! I'm in the hospital, aren't I?"

Ed began to laugh as he slumped to the floor, taking Rick's right hand with him.

"Yeah, darlin', you are."

"Damn, I must really be sick."

"Yeah." Ed laughed. "You are."

Rick blinked some more and moved restlessly on the bed. He looked both puzzled and surprised, but when he looked into Ed's eyes, he smiled, that beautiful warm and tender special smile Ed had been waiting for.

"Am I gonna be okay?"

Ed, his laughter now mixed with tears, kissed Rick's hand. "Yeah, darlin'. I think you are now."

CHAPTER SIXTEEN

The sun was shining so brightly through the carriage-house windows that Ed had to squint to tell if the Christmas tree lights were on or not. He settled on the sofa with a mug of tea, contemplating the tree, pleased to have his snow-removal chores done for the day. It was two days before Christmas, and now that Rick was firmly on the road to recovery, he could at last relax and enjoy the holiday season.

The wind was still blowing and the bitter cold had not let up, but the sunshine encouraged Ed toward optimism as much as Rick's progress had. Hopefully the wind would die down, and Ed would be able to take the entire weekend off to celebrate—not Christmas so much as the fact that Rick was going to be okay.

He watched Jett sniffing around the presents under the tree. Jett seemed wise to the idea that something under that tree was for him, and Ed looked forward to Jett's foolish pleasure when the catnip mouse was unwrapped. As for his own gifts, he didn't care. He meant what he had told Frosty the day before; the presents didn't mean a thing as long as he knew Rick was coming home where he belonged.

The phone rang. Ed sighed and hoped it wasn't a call for more snow-removal work.

"Hello?"

"Hey! How's the cutest snowman in Porterfield, Indiana?"

Ed smiled. "He's a lot better now that the cutest real estate agent in this town is awake and breathing easier."

"That he is, baby; that he is." Rick's voice was low and weak but steady. Ed realized it would be quite a while before Rick was back to his old, ornery self.

"So, when're you coming out here to see me? They won't let me out of bed, and I'm going stir-crazy."

"You stay in that bed! I want you to completely beat this thing. Dr. Klarn says you'll have to take it easy for a long time, and, by God, I'm gonna see that you do."

"Okay, okay, but could you at least bring me some books to read? You know what a low tolerance I have for daytime television."

Ed rolled his eyes. Yeah, Rick was definitely on the mend if he was bitching about TV.

Ed heard someone stomping on the carriage-house stairs. The door opened and Gordy appeared. He kicked the snow off his boots and began to pull off the layers of heavy clothes he'd worn to walk his mail route that day.

"Speaking of snowmen," Ed said to Rick, "an abominable one just walked in the house."

Gordy threw a glove at him.

"Gordy's there? Put him on."

Ed handed the phone over to Gordy, who sniffed at Ed's tea mug and made a face.

"No coffee?"

"Make it yourself, dork."

"Damn, Benton, you're gonna have to come home soon," Gordy said into the phone. "Your husband doesn't know jack shit about what to drink on a cold day. Tea!" He snorted.

Ed threw Gordy's glove back at him and got up from the sofa. He walked toward the kitchen to make Gordy think he was going to make coffee but wandered back to the stereo by the Christmas tree. He was suddenly in the mood for some festive music.

"It's good to have you back in the land of the living, bro," Gordy was saying into the phone. "You had us pretty scared there for a minute. I'll come see you when Ed goes out today, okay?"

He handed the phone to Ed. "Now I'm gonna go make some coffee," he said loudly, "since your lazy-ass husband won't do it for a man who's been delivering mail in the cold all day!"

"Hey," Ed hollered at him as he stomped into the kitchen. "I was out in the cold all day, too, ya know!"

"Maybe I'll just stay here," Rick said dryly. "I'm not sure I want to go home if all I have to look forward to is listening to you two bitch at each other."

"Oh, we're just happy you're better," Ed said with a laugh. "That's our way of showing it."

"If you say so." Ed could imagine Rick rolling his eyes. "Anyway, speaking of going home, I asked Dr. Klarn if he'll spring me tomorrow for Christmas Eve."

"So soon? Are you sure?"

"Well, he's not too enthusiastic about the idea," Rick admitted. "He says this cold air will, in his words, 'wreak havoc' on my lungs. Still, I'd much rather be there with you for Christmas instead of stuck here."

"Well . . ." Ed was undecided. Yes, he wanted Rick home for Christmas, but he didn't want to risk any sort of relapse. "We'll see what Paul says tomorrow, I guess."

"Paul? My God, you *did* get close to our new doctor while I was conked out, didn't you?"

"He was wonderful," Ed gently scolded. "He did his best to keep me from freaking out, and I appreciate it. I can't believe how lucky we are to have a gay doctor. I mean, what are the odds?"

"You're right, baby. He does seem like a genuinely nice guy. Oh, Mom and Dad are here. They're downstairs getting some coffee. We've decided to postpone the Benton family Christmas until New Year's Eve, here in Porterfield instead of Indy. So we don't have that to worry about for another week."

"Oh, good," Ed said absently, wondering if Paul had said anything to Rick about his fears of pneumocystis pneumonia.

"Mom and Dad just walked back in," Rick said, "so I'll let you go. When are you coming out?"

"As soon as Gordy and I have had a chance to thaw out, we'll pull all those clothes back on and come see you. I love you, darlin'."

"I love you, too. I'll see you in a little bit."

Ed hung up the phone and settled back on the sofa with his tea. He was grateful that Paul had found no reason to test Rick for pneumocystis, but he knew Rick needed to be told anyway. As Paul had said, he planned to keep a close watch on Rick for quite awhile to make sure there was no threat of a more serious illness.

"Man, I haven't heard this in years," Gordy said as Leroy Anderson's version of "Sleigh Ride" began to play. He settled himself in an easy chair with a loud, tired groan. "So everything's gonna be cool?"

Ed looked at him for a moment. "Yeah, I think so." He didn't want to dwell on the possibility that Rick could still be sicker than he seemed to be. "How about you, tough guy? You seem pretty cool considering that scene the other night."

Gordy looked thoughtful. "Well, I sure as hell put the fear of God into that asshole. I know that much."

"Yeah? You see him again?"

"No, but I had a surprise visitor on my mail route today."

"Oh? Who?"

Gordy smirked and shook his head. "My dad. Can ya believe it? Tracked me down in the cold and snow on Michigan Street. I about fell over a snowbank."

Ed sat up, clutching his tea. "What happened?"

Gordy went to the kitchen for his coffee. "Well, first he bawled me out for scarin' the shit out of his worthless buddy Roger."

"He deserved it."

"Yeah! I pretty much told him that. He said that Roger said I'd gone completely loco, and what was this queer business about? So I said to Dad, yeah, it's true. Wanna make somethin' of it? Dad got all red and said the least I coulda done was tell him first, instead of hearin' it from that idiot. Then he said I didn't have any business bein' some 'goddamn queer,' but if I was, he respected me for standing up for myself. Go figure."

"Wow. So then what happened?"

"He said he and Mom were expecting me to show up for dinner on Christmas, and I'd better be there or he was gonna beat the shit out of me. Then he said he was glad I'd dumped Doug, that the bastard wasn't good enough for me, and I could do better. Then he shook his head at me, called me an asshole, and got in his truck and stormed off."

Ed looked at Gordy in amazement. "You know, in all the things I imagined, that wasn't one of them."

"I know. I guess Mom really put her foot down for once. That's all I can figure."

"Well, maybe it'll be okay after all."

Gordy shrugged. "Maybe. I'm not holdin' my breath, but I gotta tell ya, I'm glad he knows. I didn't realize how much I hated bein' in the closet. Now if anybody looks at me funny I know it's 'cause they know, not just me bein' all paranoid."

"Yeah." Ed nodded. "In some ways it's a lot better knowing exactly where you stand. You find out who you friends really are."

Gordy sipped his coffee with a thoughtful frown. "Yeah, I s'pose you're right."

"And after the scare you gave that Roger, I don't think anyone's gonna mess with you. They know better now."

Gordy nodded. "Yeah. I hate actin' like that, but if I have to, I have to. It drives me nuts that no one will stand up for us, so I guess we gotta stand up for ourselves. I've just hit a point in my life where I'm not about to take any shit from anybody."

They both lapsed into silence, each thinking his own thoughts. Ed knew the struggle for all of them would always be there, but for the moment he was glad that Gordy seemed to have accepted the situation for what it was. It would probably never get any easier, but at least they had one another. The bonds between them had grown only stronger in the past few days. It may have been small comfort in an often cruel and unfriendly world, but Ed knew that he, Rick, and Gordy didn't have to face it alone.

The record changer clicked and the phonograph needle landed on Ed's scratchy copy of "White Christmas."

"Well, Bing, ole boy," Gordy said, stretching in his chair. "Looks like we got ourselves a white Christmas; now we just have to see about making it merry."

Ed stretched out on the sofa as well with a contented sigh. He allowed the familiar strains of the old song, the presence of his dear friend, and the warmth and coziness of the apartment to ease him into the quiet comfort of holiday tradition. He smiled at Gordy.

"I don't think we're gonna have to work too hard on that."

◆

When Ed and Gordy arrived at Rick's room that afternoon, they found John and Vera comfortably settled among the flowers, plants, and balloons. Ed was amused to see a new addition to the greenhouse—a tiny, homely Christmas tree, rather reminiscent of Charlie Brown's Christmas tree. Vera explained that Josh and Jane had put it together so Uncle Rick would have some Christmas in his room.

"Come along, John," Vera said, reaching for her purse. "Let's let the boys have a visit. If that Nurse Corbett catches us all in here at once, she may permanently ban us from the premises."

"Go ahead, dear," John said as played with his unlit pipe. "Gordy, would you mind stepping outside for a few minutes? I'd like to have a word with the boys."

Gordy nodded and left while Ed and Rick exchanged glances, Rick's puzzled and Ed's pessimistic. He had a pretty good idea what John wanted to talk about.

"Boys," John began, "I'm hoping you can explain this 'health-care representative' business to me. I was quite taken aback when that Corbett woman refused to talk with me about Rick's treatment."

Rick settled himself in the bed. He lay back and looked at the ceiling. Ed knew he was doing his best to compose himself and remain calm for both the sake of his health and family harmony.

"Well, it's this way, Dad," he said in his still weak voice. "Ed is my spouse. Therefore, it makes sense that he should be the one to make my health-care decisions if I can't."

John looked nonplussed.

"Since we can't get legally married, we've done everything we actually can to protect ourselves," Ed explained.

"Is that really necessary?"

Rick glanced at Ed, and then returned his gaze to the ceiling. "Yes, Dad, it is. The fact that you don't see the necessity makes it necessary. Our society doesn't recognize the relationship that Ed and I have, so we've done what we can to see that they do."

"But as long as your mother and I are here," John protested, "why should you have to do anything?"

Rick snorted. "For crying out loud, you make it sound like I'm retarded, not gay."

"Richard . . ." John glowered at him.

"Look at it this way. If your dad were still alive, would you want him making your decisions? Or what about Mom? If Mom's dad were still alive, would you want him to take over if something happened to Mom? Would you want him to assume that your relationship with Mom didn't mean anything?"

"But we've welcomed Ed into our family," John argued. "We consider him a part of the family. Do you suspect we somehow think any less of him because he's a man and not a woman?"

"I think maybe you do." Rick raised his left arm and looked at the ring that was still on his finger. Struggling a bit, he pulled it off and reached for Ed's hand.

"With this ring, I thee wed. Again," he said as he slipped it onto Ed's finger.

"See, Dad? I can put that ring on Ed's finger, and we can recite marriage vows until we're hoarse, but since there is no marriage license to go with it, you don't take it seriously. Neither does anyone else. Can you blame us for wanting you and other people to respect the relationship we have? Since no one does, we're doing what we can to make sure they do respect it."

John looked at his hands as he rubbed his pipe. "I see," he said quietly.

"Do you?"

"Yes, I do. I'm also a bit ashamed of myself. I've always considered myself a liberal man, a champion for the rights of all, but it's taken this incident for me to see how narrow-minded I can be."

He looked up at Ed and Rick. "I also see that if my own thinking is so faulty, what must it mean about the thinking of others? I see that you boys—

men—have done the right thing. I can only imagine how much education it would take to bring the rest of the world to this reality."

"That's why we did what we did," Ed said, "in case no one ever tries to understand."

"Perhaps they will someday, Ed." John smiled optimistically. "Attitudes have changed dramatically in the past ten years."

"And a certain disease seems to be pushing those attitudes right back where they were before," Rick muttered.

John looked troubled. "Boys, I've never spoken to you about AIDS. I haven't wanted to worry . . ."

"Don't worry, Dad. Ed and I are fine. We know how to take care of ourselves in that respect."

Rick smiled confidently at Ed, who smiled back, realizing that Rick had no idea about the concern both Ed and Paul Klarn had shared over the past few days. Now, however, wasn't the time to go into it.

"That's good to know." John stood up. He gripped Rick's shoulder affectionately. "I'm proud of you, Son. You're doing a great job with your life, and your spouse selection was certainly inspired."

"Thanks, Dad." Rick grabbed his hand and squeezed it.

John gave Ed's shoulder a similar grip as he walked to the door. "You're both good men, and if no one else respects that, please know that I do. Now I'm going to send your friend in here while I find a place to light my pipe."

Rick lay back with a sigh. "Well, that wasn't so bad."

Ed leaned over and kissed his forehead. "It went better than I thought it would."

Rick reached for Ed's hand. He pulled it to his chest and rubbed a finger against the ring. "Changing one mind at a time . . ."

"If that's what it takes."

Ed pulled his chair closer to Rick's bed. Together they stared out the window at the beautifully bright but bitterly cold day.

⋄──●──⋄

Ed was parked on the beige sofa, watching the traffic ebb and flow by the nurse's station as Gordy visited with Rick—no doubt filling Rick in on his own drama of the past few days. A woman about Ed's age got off the elevator and glanced around. She was obviously pregnant, and there was something vaguely familiar about her. Ed stared at her, trying to place where and how he knew her, when she caught his eye. She cocked her head and smiled.

"Ed?"

That voice brought it all back to him. It was Cathy Carroll, his high school girlfriend, the last female he'd ever dated.

He stood up and grinned. "Cathy Carroll?"

She walked over to him. "Actually, it's Cathy Stillman now." She put an arm around him and gave him a brief hug. "How are you? Boy, the years have been good to you, Ed. You look great!"

"So do you!"

She did. In high school Cathy had always been just a little too uptight, always fretting about her clothes and her appearance. Her girlfriends had called her the Aqua Net Queen behind her back because of her oversprayed, stiff hair. Now her dark blond hair was hanging loose and her general attitude seemed relaxed and casual.

Cathy smiled wryly. "It's amazing how motherhood will knock the bullshit out of you."

Ed's eyebrows rose. Cathy never would have used such a word fifteen years ago.

"Is this your first?"

"Oh, no. Second. We have a hellion of a two-year-old named Adam at home. He'll have a little brother or sister sometime around Valentine's Day. Actually, he and his father are at my folks' house right now. I dropped my mom off here to visit a friend recovering from hip surgery while I did some last-minute shopping. Why are you here? Is everything okay?"

"Oh, yes. I mean, it is now. So, tell me about your husband, and where you're living." Ed found himself extremely curious to know about this radically different Cathy.

"My husband's name is David. We've been married for five years now. He's a chemistry professor at Purdue, so we live in West Lafayette. Chemistry!" She smirked at him. "Can you believe that?"

They both laughed. Cathy had detested Mr. Stieglitz's chemistry class in high school even more than Ed had.

"So, what are you up to, Ed? Still here in Porterfield, I take it?"

"Yeah. I have my own handyman business. I have for eight years now. Can't believe it's been that long! Most of my clients are elderly, so I do all sorts of stuff for them. It can get hectic sometimes, but I like it."

"Well, you always were good at that stuff." She smiled warmly. "Still single?"

Ed took a deep breath and decided to be completely honest. "No. I'm married to a wonderful guy named Rick. He's a real estate agent here in town."

Cathy's eyes widened. "Rick," she repeated, blinking. "Oh!"

She looked away for a moment, and then began to laugh.

"Well, that explains a lot!" she finally choked out, still chuckling.

"What do you mean?" Ed smiled at her.

"Why I never had to fight you off when we were dating!" she roared, cracking up again. "Shoot, all this time I thought it was me!"

Ed began to laugh as well. "Sorry about that!"

"Oh, God," she wheezed, clutching her belly. "All these years and it never occurred to me."

She finally managed to calm down. "I'm sorry, Ed. That just really took me by surprise."

"That's okay. It freaks out a lot of people."

"I can imagine," she said, settling onto the beige sofa. She pulled him down next to her. "Still, I think it's great that you found someone. It must be hell living in this town, so I give you a lot of credit."

"Thanks," he said giving her a curious look. He was just as surprised by her easy acceptance of his sexual orientation.

She seemed to understand. "One of David's best friends in the science department is gay," she explained. "I've learned a lot from talking with him."

She shook her head. "Oh, Ed, it must have been hell growing up here."

"Yeah, it was."

She took his hand. "At least you're doing okay. From talking with Bart, I know there are so many guys—women, too, for that matter—that don't make it. And now with this AIDS—oh, Lord, is your lover okay? That's not why you're here, is it?"

"No," he assured her. "Rick's been down with a bad case of pneumonia, but it's not AIDS. He's going to be fine. He might even get to come home for Christmas."

"Well, that's a relief. I hope you guys are taking care of yourselves."

"We are."

"Good." Cathy squeezed his hand.

She looked thoughtful for a moment. "You know, I'd like to apologize. I was pretty snotty when I broke up with you right after prom. I was so involved in my own shit, I never stopped to think about what you might be going through."

"Yeah? Well, then, I apologize, too, for being a lousy boyfriend who wished he had a boyfriend and not a girlfriend."

She sighed. "God, adolescence sucks. Apologies all around, then. I understand, Ed, really. Funny thing, though: as frustrated as I got with you in high school, I really missed you in college. I dated so many creeps. I always remembered how shy and polite you were, how you didn't seem to need to prove anything to anybody. I had pretty much given up when I finally met David. In some ways I guess he's a heterosexual version of Ed Stephens."

Ed chuckled. "Thanks. I guess things worked out for both of us."

"Yes." She sighed again.

Cathy pulled herself up from the sofa. "Well, I need to rustle up Mom and get out of here. I want to get back and get these presents wrapped before Adam wakes up from his nap."

She pulled Ed up and gave him a warm hug. "It's so good to see you. Best of luck to you and your Rick. I hope you have a great life."

"You, too. Good luck with the new baby."

"Thanks! Take care, now."

Cathy disappeared down the hall with a wave.

Ed settled back on the sofa feeling at peace. He realized he'd been carrying around a lot of guilt where his relationship with Cathy was concerned. He'd always maintained that she had used him for status and a ticket to the senior prom, but Ed had used her as well, dating her to pass himself off as straight.

Cathy was right. Adolescence did suck. In their individual struggles to grow up and understand themselves, they had managed to hurt each other. But they'd survived it. And with their mutual apology, they could both let go of any leftover bad feelings once and for all.

He thought of Rick down the hall and the life they were building together. He realized they would not have accomplished what they already had if it weren't for their willingness to move beyond the hurt and horrors of those earlier years. He suddenly knew that Mrs. Penfield was right when she referred to Ed and Rick as strong men. They were. It took a strong man to be honest with himself and others, and to accept both the past and the present for what they were. Oh, he'd been a basket case the night before, wailing at his father and at God, but wasn't part of being a strong man admitting your fear? He smiled, making a mental note to ask Mrs. Penfield about that sometime.

Gordy wandered into the waiting lounge. He jerked a thumb toward the elevator. "Isn't that Cathy Carroll?"

Ed glanced over and waved at Cathy as the elevator door closed. "Yeah, that's her," he said, feeling rather nostalgic for a time in his life that had been absolutely miserable.

"Didn't you go out with her?"

"Yeah."

"Hmmm." Gordy stroked his beard thoughtfully. "We've come a long way, haven't we, baby?" He asked, paraphrasing an old cigarette slogan.

Ed smiled at his friend. "Yeah, we sure have."

⋘•⋙

Ed returned to the hospital one last time at dusk on Christmas Eve. Paul had reluctantly agreed to discharge Rick for the holiday. He gave both Ed and Rick strict orders that Rick was to do nothing more strenuous than open gifts, stay indoors as much as possible, and report to Paul's office first thing Monday morning. If Paul detected any backsliding in Rick's condition, he threatened, he'd put him right back on the third floor.

It was still quite cold, but at least the temperature had begun to rise above zero during the daylight hours. The wind had finally died away as well. Rick, looking like a mummy in all the heavy clothes Ed had bundled him in, contentedly looked at the Christmas decorations lighting many of the houses along the way as Ed concentrated on getting him home as quickly as possible.

"It seems like this is all new," Rick said, waving to a bunch of carolers when they were stopped for a red light. "There's nothing like being in the hospital to change your perspective."

Ed cracked his window so they could hear the festive group singing "Oh, Come, All Ye Faithful." "You think you've learned a lesson about slowing down and taking care of yourself?" Ed smirked at him.

"Yes, sir. I don't want to go through anything like this again. I promise to behave."

Ed gave Rick's leg a quick squeeze as the light turned green. He didn't quite believe Rick but decided to take him at his word for the moment.

Once they were home, Ed settled Rick on the sofa under the afghan. He gave Rick a mug of hot tea to keep him busy while Ed did his best to place all the flowers, planters, and balloons.

"You keep away from that," Ed scolded Jett, who was sniffing the poinsettia. "The last thing we need is for you to get sick, too."

He put the poinsettia out of the cat's reach on top of the fridge. When he had everything arranged to his satisfaction, he flopped on the floor next to the sofa with some tea of his own. The refrigerator was full of good things to eat, thanks to Effie Maude, and they had Norma's turkey dinner to look forward to the next day. At the moment, though, Ed was so full of gratitude to be spending a quiet Christmas Eve with Rick, he wasn't in the least hungry. He let out a happy sigh and took Rick's hand in his.

"Man, is it good to have you home. I know it's only been four days, but it feels like a lifetime since Vince called me Wednesday afternoon."

Rick gave his hand a weak squeeze. "I'm sorry, baby. I realize now that if I hadn't've been so pigheaded, I might have gotten through this without scaring you so badly. Do you forgive me?"

"Yeah. I have to admit, I never thought you were that sick. If I did, I would have made you do something."

"Well, then, hopefully we've both learned a lesson."

They sipped their tea and stared at the Christmas tree, enjoying the silence, each other's presence, and that indescribable magic that seemed so much a part of Christmas Eve for both of them.

"I have to admit, despite how awful this week was, I'm glad we're here and not in Indy with your folks."

"Me, too. This is the first Christmas Eve we're spent alone together since that first one, three years ago."

Rick grinned at Ed. "So, what do you think? Should we open our presents?"

"You don't want to wait until tomorrow morning?"

Rick snorted. "Shit, for all I know, you'll have to haul me back to the hospital in the morning. No, I do not want to wait."

"Okay, okay," Ed grumbled, crawling over to the tree. Actually, he was eager for Rick to see his new coat.

He pushed boxes aside and took the heavy box with Rick's coat and carefully placed it on Rick's stomach. Jett jumped up and began to paw at the bow.

"Hey! This is my present, cat. Give Jett his present, too. I'm surprised he hasn't sniffed it out already."

"Oh, I wrapped it pretty tightly, but you're right. He knows something is up."

Ed pulled out the box with Jett's catnip mouse. While Jett poked at the box, Ed and Rick unwrapped it for him. Jett was more than pleased with both the mouse and the box. He batted them both around and finally retired to a quiet corner to maul his new mouse.

"That cat is stoned," Rick declared with a chuckle as Jett rolled onto his back and let out a blissful meow. "We are a bad influence on him."

Ed laughed. "Well, I say screw Nancy 'Marie Antoinette' Reagan and her Just Say No crap. As long as he uses in moderation, I'm sure it's okay. So, who's going first? You or me?"

"Me," Rick said firmly. "I've been sick."

Ed rolled his eyes at that logic and sat back to watch as Rick struggled to unwrap the large coat box.

"Need some help, darlin'?"

"Maybe," Rick muttered as he finally sat up to get a better hold on the box. "What have you got in here, anyway? A load of coal?"

With a little assistance from Ed, Rick managed to get the paper off and the box open. He gasped when he pulled out the coat.

"Baby, this is gorgeous! Help me stand up so I can try it on."

Ed pulled Rick to his feet and went behind him to slide the coat over his arms. Rick stroked the soft lamb's wool and the satin lining in admiration.

"Can you believe it?" Ed stood back and admired the coat as well. "I actually bought this before you got so sick, and I knew how much you were going to need a really warm coat this winter."

Rick pulled Ed to him for a kiss. "I love it. It's perfect."

"Well, I figured you were probably tired of wearing that hand-me-down from your dad over your business clothes."

"Yeah," Rick said gratefully. "Thanks, baby. Can you help me into the bedroom so I can see myself in the full-length mirror?"

Ed put an arm around Rick and guided him into the bedroom. Rick smiled at his reflection in the mirror attached to the closet door.

"I guess it's not so great over pajamas, but I'm gonna look great when I go back to work next month. It almost makes me wish it would stay this cold."

"It'll be cold enough." Ed hugged him. "Now, let's get you back to the couch, okay?"

They returned to the living room. Rick reluctantly gave up his coat to settle under the afghan again. Ed greedily reached for his present and began to go to work on the gold ribbon. When he opened the box he gasped in surprise as well. There was a Walkman inside, something he'd been wanting ever since Judy got one.

"Merry Christmas, baby!" Rick grinned at him. "I noticed those envious eyes of yours whenever Judy strapped hers on. Now you can listen to the radio or your tapes while you're working to tune out those obnoxious clients."

"I don't know if I'll be able to get away with that." Ed busily inspected the buttons and dials. "But it'll be great when I'm working alone or at the new house, or working in the yard. Thanks, darlin'!"

"The batteries are already installed. Crank it up and see how it sounds."

Ed turned the radio on and dialed through the stations. He smiled as he landed on the Carpenters' "Merry Christmas, Darling." He put the headphones over Rick's ears so he could hear. Rick smiled and listened for a moment, and then put the headphones around Ed's neck.

Rick settled against the sofa pillow with satisfaction. "Looks like we both did pretty good this year."

"Yeah." Ed carefully sat on the edge of the sofa and gently kissed him. "Merry Christmas, darlin'," he whispered. "You know, just like the song, I was afraid I'd be alone here tonight. I'm so glad you're here, not just tonight, but always. I don't know if I can even say how grateful I am for that."

"I know. Me, too. Every Christmas I think of how lucky we are to have found each other, and still be together. When I think of all the men out there who are fighting for their lives right now, well, I realize just how blessed we are. I love you, baby."

"I love you, too, darlin'."

Ed smiled at Rick, and then looked at the tree. His eyes rested on Frosty. He winked at the ornament and mouthed the word *thanks*.

Apparently there was still some magic in that old black, glass hat on the snowman's head after all.

CHAPTER SEVENTEEN

The bone-chilling cold left after Christmas as abruptly as it had arrived. It was still cold when Ed took Rick to his Monday morning appointment with Paul Klarn, but by the end of the day the temperature had risen above freezing. By the next day Ed was storing his snowblower in the carriage house and shedding the extra layers of clothes he had worn for the past week. The snow quickly melted as the temperature continued to rise, and the sound of cars sluicing through puddles replaced the noise of tires skidding on ice.

Paul saw no reason to readmit Rick to the hospital as long as he continued to take his medication and rest quietly at home. Mrs. Penfield had given them a VCR for Christmas, and Gordy and Effie Maude had gone into together on a stack of tapes, so Rick contentedly read and watched movies, usually falling asleep on the sofa midway through every feature. Ed was relieved that none of those Mr. Hyde qualities that usually surfaced when Rick was sick had made an appearance. Rick seemed genuinely chastened by the seriousness of his illness and hospital stay. He did as he was told and actually relaxed and did his best to enjoy his convalescence.

He had plenty of visitors as well. People who had not ventured out in the cold to see Rick at the hospital took advantage of the warmer weather to drop by the carriage-house apartment. Ed was glad there were plenty of leftover Christmas goodies to serve as refreshments.

Clyde and Claudine Croasdale stopped by Tuesday afternoon. While Rick and Claudine chatted, Ed and Clyde puttered in Ed's workshop downstairs.

"I've been thinking," Ed said as they debated a new project. "Rick's going to have to take it really easy all winter. I don't want him doing anything that will put a strain on his lungs, so the last thing I want is him insisting on helping me with projects at the new house. What do you think, Clyde? Would you like to be my assistant over there? I'll have a lot easier time talking Rick out of being underfoot if he knows you're around to help."

Clyde smiled. "I was just waiting for you to ask. I won't be doing anything but twiddling my thumbs until spring when I can put my boat back in the water. Tell me when, and I'm good to go."

"Awesome!" Ed shook his hand to seal the deal. "With your help I know I can get that house ready to go back on the market by the time you're ready to hit the lakes again."

Ed came home from work late the next afternoon to find Rick sprawled on the sofa snickering at *Tootsie*, a movie they'd seen in the theater a year earlier and had thoroughly enjoyed. Ed had sat down to watch for a few minutes before he got their supper together when the doorbell rang.

"Aw, crud," Ed muttered. "You sure are popular."

"Just when it was getting good, too." Rick hit the Stop button on the VCR remote. "I wonder who it is."

The visitor turned out to be Paul Klarn. Ed ushered him into the apartment. While Ed hung up Paul's coat, Paul handed a gift-wrapped bottle of champagne to Rick.

"Shouldn't we be giving *you* a present?" Rick asked after he fervently thanked Paul.

Paul waved his hand in dismissal. "Not at all. You'll be getting my bill soon enough."

Everyone laughed. "Seriously, though, I wanted to congratulate you both on Rick's recovery, and wish you a happy New Year. Rick seems to be doing very well. I couldn't be more pleased. Also, I wanted to thank you for being my new favorite patients. It's been a huge relief for me to know that I'm not the only gay man in Porterfield."

"Now, that's something we can understand," Rick said wryly as he handed the gift box to Ed. "You'll have to come over sometime when our friend Gordy is around. That puts the known gay population of this town up to four. I'm sure there are others, but they seem to be firmly in the closet."

"I suspect you're right. I, too, am in need of a certain amount of discretion where my career is concerned, but it's good to know I'm not alone. Perhaps when you've fully recovered, we could all meet for dinner sometime."

"Sounds good." Rick nodded. "You think so, Ed?"

"Absolutely." Ed grinned. "As Gordy always says, we Porterfield fags need to stick together."

Paul laughed. "Wonderful. Thank you."

His face took on a decidedly solemn expression. "There's something I wanted to talk to you about as well. Since my concern is that of both your doctor and a potential friend, I thought it might be better if we talk away from the hospital. Ed, have you said anything to Rick about what we discussed after he was admitted?"

Ed shifted uneasily. "No. I guess I was waiting until he was better."

Rick looked mystified. "What?"

Paul nodded at Ed. "Well," Ed said slowly, "if you didn't respond to the usual pneumonia treatment, Paul was gonna order a test for pneumocystis pneumonia."

"*What?*" Rick sat bolt upright, tightly clutching one of the sofa pillows to him. "You thought . . . you think I have—"

Paul put up a hand and vigorously shook his head. "No, Rick, not at all. Nothing I've seen in your tests and blood work leads me to believe in any way that you have contracted AIDS."

Rick let out a deep breath as he slumped against the sofa arm. "It's a good thing you didn't tell me this last week," he muttered. "I might have had a heart attack."

"I felt you should know. You see, Rick, since I wasn't acquainted with either you or Ed, I felt it was my responsibility to ask Ed some rather intimate questions. I needed to be sure I wasn't dealing with anything other than routine pneumonia. With what I've seen in New York and the general climate of gay men's health, I felt it was in your best interests."

Rick released his grip on the pillow and sighed. "I understand."

"He scared the shit out of me," Ed said frankly. "But once I thought about it, I knew he was right to ask about that stuff. That's one of the reasons I was so relieved when you started to get better."

Rick glanced at Ed. "Oh, baby," he whispered. "How scared you must have been. Now I really understand why you were crying when I finally woke up."

Ed felt himself getting choked up again. He went and sat next to Rick on the sofa. Rick put his arms around him and hugged him.

Paul watched their display of affection with a wistful smile. "This is a terrifying disease," he said quietly. "As I told Ed last week, every gay man needs to be cautious these days."

Rick pulled Ed closer to him. "So you really don't think I have it?"

"No, Rick, I don't. However, with your permission, I'd like to sit down and talk seriously about your sexual encounters before Ed, and I'd like to do some more specific blood work. If you agree, I'll ship the blood to a lab out of state. I have an old friend who understands the need for discretion and confidentiality."

Rick's eyes narrowed in suspicion. "Why do you want to do that if you don't think I have it?"

"For your peace of mind. I know this will continue to disturb you, and I don't want the stress of it to interfere with your recovery."

"Then why did you even bring it up?" Rick grumbled.

Paul smiled at Ed. "For Ed's peace of mind as well."

Rick looked at Ed, who nodded.

"Okay." Rick sighed. "I can give you the dirty details of my sex life pre-Ed, but what do you hope to find out with these tests?"

"As you probably know, they have yet to discover what actually causes AIDS. However, with what I learned at the Gay Men's Health Crisis in New York, I have a good knowledge of the entire range of opportunistic infections that routinely affect people with AIDS. I can test for those. Unfortunately, there isn't a specific test for AIDS, and I doubt that there will be for some time. But I believe if we can determine that you are a completely healthy man, aside from your recent illnesses, you'll both rest a lot easier."

"But if I had any of those infections, wouldn't you know it already?"

"Probably," Paul admitted, "but again, I'm more concerned with being able to show you concrete proof of your good health. That will have to do until there is a specific AIDS test.

"There are a great many men who have something to fear, and I strongly doubt that you are one of them. However, Ed shared with me some of the details of your life together, and the plans you've made. I think it would be a shame if you allowed any of that, or your relationship, both emotional and physical, to be blighted by fear."

Rick gave Ed another squeeze. "You two must have had one hell of a talk while I was out of it."

"We did, that night you were admitted. I needed someone to talk to. I couldn't really talk to Gordy because he was so upset. I needed to talk to someone calm who knew more about it than I did."

"All right, you vampire," Rick said with a feeble smile. "When I come in for my next appointment, you can draw some more blood if it will make Ed feel better."

"The important thing is, it will make you both feel better in the longer run. You understand that, right? I also hope you don't feel I'm overreacting. A good many doctors would feel that I'm looking for smoke where there is no fire, but if you could see what I have seen in New York . . ." Paul trailed off with a grim shake of his head.

Rick held out his hand for the doctor to shake. "No, I get where you're coming from. I'm also realizing that Ed was right; we are lucky to have you for a doctor. Yes, I'm a little disturbed, but I'm also grateful for your concern."

Paul warmly shook Rick's hand. "All gay men have reason to be disturbed these days. Unfortunately, no one is crying 'wolf.' This is a deadly situation, and we have to do everything we can to take care of ourselves, since our government and society in general don't seem to have much interest in doing so."

"Don't get me started on the Reagan administration," Rick groaned.

Paul chuckled, but there was little mirth in it. "Oh, I'm sure we could hammer away at that all evening, but I should be on my way. I still have rounds to do."

He stood up. "So we're okay on this? Are you sure you'd still like to have that dinner sometime?"

Rick smiled weakly. "Yeah, sure. I'll see you Friday morning for my next appointment."

Ed walked Paul to the door. "Thanks, Paul," he said with a hug. "We both really appreciate it."

"My pleasure." Paul grinned at them both and headed for the stairs as he shrugged on his coat.

Ed closed the door. He turned to look at Rick, who was staring at the Christmas tree with a sober expression.

"You okay, darlin'?"

Rick let out a very heavy sigh. "Yeah, I guess so. Come sit next to me."

"The truth is," Rick said as Ed settled in beside him, "I was worried about this before I ended up in the hospital. I couldn't help but think of it when I couldn't shake that cold."

"Why didn't you say anything to me?"

"I was scared. I know that's no excuse, but it's hard to be rational about something so scary."

"I understand." Ed reached over and stroked Rick's beard. "It is scary. You can't imagine what I went through while you were unconscious. I even went to the cemetery and screamed at Dad. I just wanted you to get better so Paul wouldn't have any reason to do that test."

"Well, at least you had the good doctor to talk to," Rick teased, grabbing Ed's hand. "I think he's got a crush on you."

"What?"

"Yeah, I think Dr. Klarn is a little sweet on you."

"Oh, brother," Ed groaned. "He just wants to be my friend; your friend, too. Remember when Gordy wanted to be friends and you thought he was after me? Now you think of him as your big brother."

Rick gave him a sheepish grin. "Okay, okay. Maybe I'm overreacting, seeing something that isn't there."

"We only had that one long talk while you were sick," Ed scolded. "And that was in the hospital cafeteria. It's not like we were sneaking off for a romantic rendezvous."

"Well, there's nothing rational about jealousy either." Rick gave him a soft kiss. "I still don't want to share my handyman with any other guy."

"You don't have to." Ed returned the kiss.

"Good."

Rick made a motion to stretch out on the sofa. Ed got up and put the afghan over him.

"You look tired after all of that. You want to take a nap before I fix our supper?"

Rick reached for the VCR remote and started the movie again. Dustin Hoffman in drag flashed onto the TV screen. "No. Why don't you heat up some leftovers and we can eat while we watch this?" He grinned wryly. "I think we both could use a laugh about now."

The atmosphere in the apartment remained rather subdued through the next day. Neither of them talked about it, but Ed knew that the reality of AIDS had entered their lives. His gut told him that both he and Rick were fine and had nothing to worry about, but he knew the state of their health wasn't the only concern. As Paul had said the week before, a certain amount of AIDS hysteria had swept across the United States that year, and people who might have been on the verge of tolerance where gay men were concerned were now looking askance at them once again. Ed knew that awful scene with Roger in the hospital was the kind of scene being repeated all over the country. He could only hope it was the first and last one he had to witness in Porterfield.

Happily, Mrs. Penfield provided a distraction late Thursday afternoon. She was making one of her rare trips to the carriage-house apartment to visit with Rick. Ed happened to be home, so they were both present when she unfolded that day's edition of the *Porterfield Courier* and pointed to a headline on the society page.

"I'll be damned," Rick muttered as he read it. "What do you suppose that's all about?"

Ed looked over his shoulder and read the headline: EUNICE AMES RESIGNS HISTORICAL SOCIETY POST.

"I don't know," Ed said, shaking his head. "But I'll bet that awful Harriet Drinkwater has something to do with it."

"I suspect you're right." Mrs. Penfield nodded. "Read the article, Rick."

Through a series of quotes, Eunice conveyed deep regret at resigning her presidency, but due to an overwhelming slate of obligations, she felt it was in the best interest of the historical society that she step down at this time. And indeed, Rick read, Harriet Drinkwater would assume the presidency at the monthly meeting in January.

"Something major must have gone down while I've been sick," Rick declared. "Eunice would no sooner give up her iron grip on the historical society than she'd fly to the moon."

"It does seem rather out of character." Mrs. Penfield chuckled.

"Well, I know one thing," Ed stated adamantly. "If that nasty woman is in charge of next year's holiday home tour, we aren't having anything to do with it. After the way she treated me that day I was putting up that Christmas tree, I wouldn't throw water on Harriet Drinkwater if she was on fire!"

"No arguments from me." Rick handed the paper to Mrs. Penfield. "I don't want to work with her either. I wonder what happened, though."

"I've no doubt that Eunice's resignation is at the heart of a great scandal among the society ladies of Porterfield," Mrs. Penfield said wisely. "I'm sure our individual sources will be eager to fill us in as the details leak out."

Mrs. Penfield was right. There was a great deal of talk after that article appeared. Ed and Rick didn't have much time to speculate on what little they heard, however. Eunice Ames herself showed up the very next day.

Dressed for a formal afternoon call, Eunice regally entered the carriage-house apartment, her rather wide form giving her the appearance of a majestic steamship cutting through the waves. An appropriately holiday-themed hat was upon her head, and she gracefully handed Ed her mink stole. Ed stowed it in the hall closet, afraid Jett would get his paws on it.

While Eunice expressed her joy at Rick's recovery, Ed made tea. He handed Eunice a cup and saucer and offered her some of Effie Maude's Christmas cookies and fruitcake as well. She politely refused any additional refreshment as she remarked on the weather and asked about their New Year's plans.

"Okay, Eunice," Rick said once Ed had sat down with his own tea. "Cut the chitchat. What's up with you resigning from the historical society?"

Eunice delicately stirred her tea. "That is an unpleasant situation at best. I'd prefer not to dwell on it."

Rick narrowed his eyes at her and said nothing.

"Oh, all right. If you insist." She parked her teacup and saucer on the coffee table. "That dreadful Harriet Drinkwater forced me to resign. She's wanted to take over the society for years now, and she has finally gotten her way."

"But you're the heart and soul of the society." Rick flattered her to get her to reveal all the gory details. "How will it function without you?"

Eunice sat upright, her pale blue eyes snapping. "Very poorly, I'm sure! That Drinkwater woman has no organizational skills whatsoever. The rest of the board will be *begging* me to return within a year. Hah! What a satisfaction *that* will be.

"Harriet Drinkwater is a sloppy, vain, self-centered woman. They will find that out soon enough. Why, that woman started a whispering campaign against me. She holds me and me alone responsible for our poor profits from this year's holiday tour. She also seems to hold me personally responsible for that virus that spread through town earlier this month!"

"That's ridiculous," Rick said. "Ed and I both got sick, and we certain don't blame you, do we, Ed?"

"Uh, no, not at all," Ed said less than truthfully.

"She claims I should have postponed the tour and has somehow convinced other members of that as well. Postpone the tour! Why, those dates are carved on the town's calendar in stone. When else could we have had it? She's just a troublemaker. She's even hinted darkly at some sort of misappropriation of funds. The nerve!

"I suppose I could have fought her accusations, but I felt the most dignified thing to do was step down. The board seems to feel that some new blood in the presidency might attract more interest in local history, and perhaps increase the fund-raising. I can understand that, but believe me, they will rue the day they allowed Harriet Drinkwater to take over. That miserable cow!"

Ed choked on his tea and began to snicker. Rick shot him a disapproving look, but Eunice began to laugh as well.

"I suppose it is funny, Edward." She shook her head. "I mustn't take myself too seriously. And perhaps it is time for a new breeze within the society. Unfortunately Harriet Drinkwater will race through it like a typhoon, but when the damage is done, it can be rebuilt, and hopefully become even more vital than before. I have no regrets, and I don't intend to worry about it.

"However, I have a new project that I'm most excited about." Eunice reached for her tea and smiled brightly at both of them. "I've been talking with Mayor Forrest about his plans to beautify the downtown area. He's put me in charge of his committee. We'll be talking with business owners and raising money for planters and urns for the downtown area this spring. We also hope to install them on the Stratton Creek Bridge. In addition, we'll be doing our best to coax building owners into restoring the original facades of the buildings. Oh, there are a great many other ideas brewing, but we must start somewhere. We'll need a fund-raising project. I'm thinking of a local variety show at the high school auditorium."

Ed managed to keep himself from rolling his eyes. To his knowledge, there wasn't much in the way of talent in Porterfield, and he could only imagine what sort of nightmare production they would be able to throw together.

"There will be much to do over the next few months, but I'm eager to jump in and get started. We must do what we can to see that our downtown district remains a vital area of commerce."

Personally, Ed felt it would take a hell of a lot more than a few flowers and plants to save Porterfield's dying downtown, but he wasn't about to say so in front of Eunice.

"Might I assume you're busy these days sniffing out appropriate committee members?" Rick coyly asked.

Eunice giggled. "Oh, Rick, you do have an uncanny ability to read my mind." Eunice, it seemed, was not above using a little soft soap of her own to get what she wanted. "What an asset that would be on this new committee! And think what meeting and talking with local business owners would do for your own career. I do hope you're as excited about this as I am."

Rick smiled. "It does sound like fun, actually. And you're right: it wouldn't hurt me at all professionally."

"Now, wait a minute." Ed thumped his teacup on top of the television. "Have you forgotten that you are getting over a serious bout of pneumonia? Do you think you have any business taking on any new projects?"

"Oh, Dad, please?" Rick mock-whined.

"Ed, I assure you I wouldn't do anything to jeopardize Rick's health," Eunice hurriedly said.

Ed tapped his foot against the floor as he silently debated the matter. The other two looked at him in suspense.

"Okay, here's the deal," he finally said. "If Eunice sticks to her word and keeps your involvement to a minimum, at least until warmer weather, I guess you can join the committee. There's a condition, though," he added craftily. "You'll have to leave all the work at the new house to me and Clyde in exchange for the time and energy you'll be giving to Eunice."

"Hmmm." Rick thought for a moment. "Okay. That works. It's a deal."

Eunice jumped up and hugged Ed. "Oh, that's wonderful! I promise to treat Rick like fragile glass until his health is restored. And, Ed, I'll be counting on you when we get ready to hang those planters on the streetlight poles this spring! We'll certainly need the town's finest handyman for *that*."

Ed groaned. "I should have known I'd get dragged into this one, too."

Later, after Eunice had left and Ed was washing the teacups at the sink, Rick walked into the kitchen and hugged him from behind.

"You know, baby, I think we were both had on that deal."

"What do you mean?"

"Well, I didn't want to let you do all the work at the new house without me, and you didn't want me to join that committee. So we both gave up something we wanted to get what we really wanted."

Ed started to laugh. "Yeah, you're right."

Rick kissed his neck. "And you thought you were being so sneaky, getting me to agree to that. I knew exactly what you were up to."

"Yeah?" Ed flipped some water from the sink at him. "Well, you know what? I guess that's just how smart married people make compromises."

CHAPTER EIGHTEEN

John and Vera returned to Porterfield on New Year's Eve. That evening, the whole family went to the Wood Haven restaurant for their belated Christmas celebration. Ed was surprised and amused to see that Matt Croasdale had been invited as well.

After dinner they returned to the Penfield house for the gift-opening ritual. When they all felt they were comfortably caught up on Christmas, they shifted gears and turned the festivities into a New Year's Eve party.

At one point Ed and Rick were in the kitchen together getting wineglasses ready for the traditional midnight toast. Rick glanced into the dining room, where Claire and Matt were engaged in intimate conversation.

Rick nudged Ed. "How much you wanna bet Claire gets a ring by next Christmas? I think I'm gonna have a new brother-in-law."

"Geez, you're as bad as the girls," Ed groaned. "What makes you think so?"

Rick shrugged. "Just a feeling."

Ed took a peek into the dining room as well. "How do you feel about that?"

"Okay, I guess." Rick frowned at a bottle of sparkling grape juice. In theory it was for the kids, but since he wasn't allowed to mix alcohol with his medication, he would be bringing in 1984 with it as well. "Glad and sad, if you know what I mean."

"No, I don't know what you mean."

"Well, I'm happy for Claire. After all she's been through, she deserves a nice guy, and from what I've seen, Matt is great. I think he'd be great with the kids, too. That's the sad part. If they get married, it means I'll be giving up my honorary daddy role."

Ed grinned. "I remember three years ago tonight when you told me you were gonna be involved in raising those kids for as long as it took. Maybe it's time for that to come to an end."

"Maybe." Rick's warm and tender special flashed across his face as he teasingly flicked Ed with a dish towel. "I guess that just means we'll have more time to concentrate on our own plans and dreams, huh?"

"Yeah." Ed thought that wasn't a bad thing to consider at the start of a new year.

Mrs. Penfield and Gordy joined them as they gathered in the study near the television to watch Dick Clark usher in the New Year from Times Square. When 1984 flashed on the screen, everyone clinked glasses, hugged, and wished one another a Happy New Year. Rick dragged Ed into the front hall for a private kiss.

"Happy New Year, baby," he whispered. "The best is yet to come."

"Happy New Year, darlin'. I love you."

"I love you, too." Rick proved it with another kiss, a very long, romantic one. "You s'pose when we're finally alone we can bring in 1984 in style?"

Ed giggled. "You sure you're up to it?"

Rick glanced down. "Oh, yeah. I'm up to it."

"Hmmm. Looks like my Dream Man is raring to go."

"He is. Is my handyman ready for the ride?"

Ed kissed him with a passion and aggression he hadn't allowed himself in weeks. "Trust me. When the train pulls out of the station, I'll be on board."

⋖⋗•⋖⋗

New Year's Day passed quietly, and on Monday everyone went back to work, even Rick. Vince was reluctant to leave home and his enchanting new son but decided to reopen the office. Rick, with Paul's permission, would be working half days for at least that week.

Ed looked at his calendar and realized that the usual January slump in his business was in progress. Although he was enjoying the milder weather, he couldn't help but hope for a snowfall or two. Since there was no snow in the forecast, he called Clyde and arranged to spend most of the week at the Elm Street house. On Monday afternoon, however, he walked across the yard to the main house to check on Mrs. Penfield. Effie Maude was taking an extended holiday break to visit with family, so Ed thought he should look in on Mrs. Penfield and see if she needed anything. While he was at it, he thought, he might as well deal with that Christmas tree as well.

When Ed let himself in the back door, he heard music coming from Mrs. Penfield's hi-fi in the front parlor. He found her sitting quietly on the sofa, contemplating the Christmas tree. Ed couldn't help but grin.

"Aw, don't worry, little girl. Christmas will come again, sooner than you think."

Mrs. Penfield shook herself out of her private reverie. "Yes, it will indeed. I, however, have been thinking over this holiday season, and Christmas past as well."

"You ready for me to get that dried-up thing out of here?"

She nodded. "Of course. I'll even gladly help put away the ornaments."

Ed went to the attic for the boxes, and with Mrs. Penfield's help began to carefully wrap the fragile ornaments in tissue as she stowed them away in their boxes until next year. Ed turned up the volume of the song playing on the hi-fi, Henry Mancini's "Moon River."

"What a great song."

Mrs. Penfield smiled. "Yes, it was a favorite of George's and mine. I always enjoyed Audrey Hepburn, and I do believe *Breakfast at Tiffany's* was one of my favorites."

Ed glanced at the LP cover featuring a glammed-out Audrey, complete with black cigarette holder. "If I find some old Hepburn movies on tape, would you like to watch them with our VCR?"

"Yes, I would." Mrs. Penfield looked nostalgic. "George and I would go to the Strand for the new feature almost every Friday for years. It was wonderful relaxation for both of us after a busy week. It would indeed be a treat to see some of those old movies again."

Ed handed her an ornament shaped like a snow-covered cottage. "I haven't seen much of Gordy the past few days. Is he doing okay?"

"I believe so." Mrs. Penfield reached for more of the aged tissue. "We've had several long talks of late, and he's decided to take my advice and talk with someone at Sloan Mental Health Center."

"What?" Ed almost dropped an ornament. "Really? Gordy?"

"There is no shame in talking with someone when you're troubled," Mrs. Penfield gently chided him. "I think it will do Gordy some good."

"I know. I'm just surprised that he would go."

"These past few months have been rough for Gordy. I felt a professional might be of assistance in helping Gordy deal with both his anger and his depression. I must admit I was bit surprised as well when he agreed with me. I also suggested that he remain here through the winter as opposed to moving out at the end of the month as he had originally planned. I think it would be beneficial for him to be close to us until he regains his confidence."

"Well, I hope he does. Stay, I mean."

"I believe he will. Gordy is a good deal more intelligent than he gives himself credit for. The fact that he wants to work through his problems is a sign of that."

Mrs. Penfield gave Ed a confident smile. "He'll be fine once he accepts the realities of his life. How about you, though? Rick gave you quite a scare over the holidays. Have you recovered from that?"

Ed chuckled. "Yeah. I kind of lost it for a while, but I'm okay now."

He told her about his trip to the cemetery at the height of his worry about Rick. "I felt a little stupid when he starting getting better that night, but who knew, right?"

Mrs. Penfield adjusted the hook on an ornament. "Perhaps your father or God answered your prayers. Did you ever consider that?"

"No. I was so bitter and freaked-out, I didn't think anybody was actually listening."

She settled back in her chair with a sigh. "Spiritual matters are as mysterious as love. Even at my age, I still have no real understanding of God or the mysteries of our universe. However, I do believe in forces we can't see. I believe there is a spiritual world beyond this one. There have been times when I've implored George for help, and the help has arrived in some form or another."

"Really?"

"Oh, yes." She smiled at him. "When I began to worry about my health and advancing age, and how on earth I was going to continue living in this house, I asked George for guidance and inspiration. It was around that time that you and Rick began to plan a future together. I knew George, or someone or something, had provided the help I needed. And it's worked out beautifully, hasn't it? You and Rick enjoy living here, and my burden of worry has been lifted since the day you took up residence in that apartment."

Ed smiled. "Yes. We love it here. I guess I should be thanking Mr. Penfield for that as well as you."

"I believe George would be as proud of you both as I am. I also believe he would second my decision to leave this house to you. I can rest comfortably knowing that after I'm gone it will remain the dignified yet warm haven it's always been."

"You don't think we'll hire a wrecking ball to knock it down?" Ed teased.

She chuckled. "Oh, I strongly doubt that. Your feelings, and Rick's feelings, for this home have grown stronger over the years. I've become very aware of that. You've also become stronger, even more mature men. I suspect you'll be here for many years to come."

"I hope so. I do love it here. I was thinking about that over Thanksgiving, and again when we put this tree up. Do you really think we're stronger, though? I mean, after that scene I pulled at the cemetery, I really began to doubt myself. Is part of being strong admitting you're scared to death?"

"Absolutely. There's no shame in admitting your fear and doing something constructive to cope with it. You chose to speak to your father and confront the Almighty. History is full of strong, wise men who have done the same."

"So you really think we've grown since we've been here?"

"Of course! Why, that separation you endured would be the ruin of a good many marriages, but you both came through it with an even greater determination to remain together. I've had the satisfaction of watching you learn and grow and become obedient to the mystery of love. Not only are you there for each other, but your love is strong and large enough to be there for your friends and families as well. You may think you're lucky to have accepting families and good friends, but believe me, Ed, we all bask in our good fortune at having you and Rick in our lives as well."

Ed blushed. "You've been a good teacher."

"Perhaps. However, you and Rick have done the hard work yourselves. If I still had my grade book handy, I'd happily mark an A-plus next to both of your names."

He bashfully turned toward the tree to hide his red cheeks. "Thanks, Mrs. Penfield."

They quietly continued with their work for a few minutes. The record on the turntable repeated, and "Moon River" began to play again.

"I do believe that when you and Rick reach the rainbow's end they refer to in this song, you'll be hand in hand, a long journey full of wonders and good work behind you. Oh, rainbow's end is quite elusive. Some people spend their entire lives longing for the treasures supposedly waiting there, but the intelligent people enjoy the journey and the lessons along the way. You are one of those people, Ed. You aren't afraid to admit to ignorance, nor do you accept our world on blind faith. You ask the hard questions, and you work at understanding situations and people. You've learned a lot and gained in your own wisdom. Why, I've no doubt that someday you'll inspire someone as I know I have inspired you."

"Kind of like passing a torch?"

"Yes." She smiled warmly at her young friend. "Along with this house I shall pass the bright light of my knowledge to you so you'll be able to do for someone else what I hope I've done for you and Rick."

That seemed like an incredible responsibility to Ed, but realizing he had Mrs. Penfield's complete confidence, he brushed away his doubts and mentally accepted her gifts and the challenge implied in them.

Ed pushed the ornament box aside so he could hug his dear friend and mentor.

"Thanks, Mrs. Penfield. I promise Rick and I will always do our best to make you proud of us."

"I have no doubt, Ed," she whispered.

⋞⋅●⋅⋟

As the week progressed, Ed and Clyde put in long days at the Elm Street house while Rick regained his sure footing at Cummings Realty. Rick even survived Eunice's first enthusiastic and lengthy meeting of the Downtown Beautification Committee. Rick met Ed at home Friday afternoon looking tired but happy.

"What do you say we go out for a nice dinner tonight and celebrate?" he asked Ed, giving him a kiss and a hug before he even removed his coat.

"Celebrate? What are we celebrating?"

"Well, I took a certain lawyer we know on a house tour. He was pretty taken with a comfortable old four-bedroom place about five blocks from here on the corner of Maple and Ohio."

Ed grinned. "Four bedrooms? For a currently single man? That sounds promising."

Rick laughed. "Yeah, I can see his wheels turning. My real estate agent's instinct tells me he'll be putting an offer on that place within the next week. And if the sale goes through, my commission will repay all that legal work he did for us, and then some."

"Okay, then I guess we can do some early celebrating. You sure you're up to it, though?"

"Yeah, baby. I feel better than I have in weeks. Oh, I'm a little tired, but I'm at peace as well. Paul Klarn called me today. All of those tests came back negative. He says that neither of us have anything to worry about right now, and that as long as we take the proper precautions, we should be okay."

Ed hugged Rick tightly. "Now, *that's* good news. We definitely need to celebrate. Where do you want to go?"

"How 'bout that Mexican place in Fort Wayne with the great chorizo? I'm even feeling reckless enough to eat some spicy food."

"Don't push it too far, buddy," Ed said severely. "Don't come bitchin' to me tonight if you end up with heartburn."

"Yeah? Okay, I won't, but I bet you'll fetch me the antacid if I ask nicely."

Ed kissed him and rubbed the gold chain around his neck. "Yeah, I probably will, you big dork. I'm always here when you need me."

"And I'm here for you, baby." Rick slapped Ed's ass. "Now, go get dressed. I'm hungry!"

The next day Rick was busy with an open house and Clyde had plans with Claudine, so Ed spent most of Saturday in his office getting caught up on his records. He put his cherished Walkman aside and cranked up the portable stereo on the shelf above his desk. He bopped to the beat of a new dance song he loved, Shannon's "Let the Music Play." He made a mental note to get the record the next time he was shopping. He was amazed that dance music seemed to be making a comeback of sorts. He had also being hearing a fun, bouncy song from some girl named Madonna these days, and he hoped there were more good grooves coming in 1984.

Gordy wandered into the workshop, still dressed from walking his mail route. He glanced at Ed banging the song's beat on his desk with a pen, and then at the stereo.

"Now, that's what I call a good faggot jam."

Ed laughed. "Yeah. Almost makes me want to go to a bar. Almost, but not quite."

"Yeah, me, too."

"You okay, bud?"

Gordy lit a cigarette and looked around for the ashtray Ed kept for him. "Yeah, I guess so. You?"

"I'm good."

Shannon faded out and the Romantics came on. Ed turned the volume down with a shudder. He didn't think he'd be able to listen to "Talking in Your Sleep" for a long time without remembering that awful nightmare he'd had when Rick was sick.

He turned back to Gordy. "I talked to Mrs. Penfield the other day. She says you're not gonna move out at the end of the month."

Gordy blew out a long stream of smoke. "Yeah. She also tell you I'm seein' a shrink?"

"Yeah, she did."

Gordy snorted. "Who ever thought I'd live to see that happen? But it's a good thing, I guess. This woman has her shit together, and hopefully she can help me get my shit together."

"I hope so, bud. I'm still worried about you."

"Yeah, me, too. I gotta get a handle on stuff, you know? Things are still tense between me and Dad, and Mom's caught in the middle. And Doug . . . I keep thinkin' about him, too. I gotta get over that."

"You still miss him?"

Gordy nodded. "Yeah. Stupid, huh?"

"I don't know if it's stupid. I think it's natural, though."

Gordy sat back and took a deep drag on his cigarette. "I keep wonderin' what I'd do if he moved back here, if he wanted to try again. Shit. That ain't gonna happen."

Ed twiddled his pen. "I think he still loves you."

"Maybe, but so what? He's not gonna move back here, and I sure as hell ain't goin' to Indy, or any other big city. I've learned my lesson. I'm just a hick from the sticks. Now I gotta accept that and move on."

Ed got up and put his arms around Gordy. "I'll bet there are a lot of other hicks out there who'd be just crazy about you."

Gordy looked down and smiled. "You think so?"

"Yeah, I do. Maybe when enough time passes, and when you're ready for it again, some guy'll walk into your life just like Doug did. Only this time it'll be an older guy who's settled, and who wants all the same things you do."

Gordy stubbed out his cigarette. "Yeah. I suppose it could happen. Maybe I should just clone you or Rick."

Ed laughed, and then groaned. "Geez, what a thought. No, there's a better guy out there for you somewhere. I have to believe that. Someone as special as you won't be on the market forever."

"My therapist said something about my experience with Doug bein' a life lesson, or some sort of bullshit. Maybe she's right. Maybe after what I've learned I can get it right next time."

Ed smiled at the sound of optimism in Gordy's voice, the first time he'd heard anything like it in months.

"You will. Get it right I mean. Hell, if I can do it, anybody can do it."

Gordy slapped Ed upside the head. "Don't underestimate yourself, bud. You and Rick have worked hard to make things work out. I think I've learned a lot just from watchin' you guys.

"So yeah, I'll know what to do next time," Gordy said with a faraway look in his eyes.

"As long as there's hope, there's possibility."

Gordy pulled himself back to the present and gave Ed a scrutinizing look. "Damn, that sounds like something Mrs. P. would say."

Ed thought of that passed torch and grinned at his friend. "Yeah? Well, maybe that's where I got it from."

◆

Paul Klarn called the next day. He wanted to know if Ed, Rick, and Gordy would be interested in joining him for brunch in Fort Wayne. Ed and Rick agreed, and Ed twisted Gordy's arm a bit to get him to go as well, swearing over and over again that he had no intention of trying to fix him up with Paul.

The four men chatted amiably during the car ride and during their meal. Paul laughed at Gordy's nonsense, and Gordy roared at some of the stories Paul told of his experiences in New York, but Ed could tell there was nothing sparking between them other than potential friendship. He was a bit relieved, but also pleased, thinking of the old adage that a person couldn't have too many friends. Ed suspected that Gordy occasionally got tired of hanging around a couple as tight as he and Rick were and thought it would be good for him to have a single friend in town as well.

The next day Ed met Clyde at the Elm Street house. As they began to gut the kitchen for its remodel, Ed asked Clyde about the house Matt was looking at on Maple Street.

"He seems pretty serious about it," Clyde said, fishing a crowbar out of a jumble of tools on the floor.

"Does that mean he's also serious about Claire? And her kids? What do you think about that?"

Clyde handed the crowbar to Ed. "I'm okay with it. Claire's a good woman, a breath of fresh air after his ex-wife. If Matt decides to ask her to marry him, I'm all for it."

Ed grunted as he used the crowbar to pry the metal cabinets away from the walls. "But what about the kids? Are you ready to be a step-grandpa to her three monsters?"

Clyde laughed. "They're not monsters. From what I could see at Thanksgiving, they're all good kids, and considering that my other grandchildren are all in Wisconsin, I think I'd like having a few to spoil closer to home. They seem relatively happy and okay as far as I can see, considering what they've been through."

Ed stopped to rest for a moment. "Yeah, they've been through a rough time, but they've come through it okay."

"Claire did a good job," Clyde said approvingly. "I also hear from Matt that you and Rick are just as responsible. She told Matt she would have never made it without your help. You and Rick did a good job, too."

"Geez," Ed grumbled. The weight of all the compliments he had been receiving of late was making him blush again, along with his inability to work the cabinets loose. "Now all I need to do is perform a few miracles, die, and then they can make me a saint."

Clyde laughed and took the crowbar from him. "Don't get too big-headed, kiddo. You sure aren't performing a miracle with that crowbar. Step aside and let a professional do it. Why don't you get ready to clean up the mess?"

Ed handed the crowbar to Clyde with a grin and went to get his Shop-Vac.

Ed and Clyde worked hard the rest of that day, eager to get the kitchen ready for Sam Carmichael, the cabinetmaker. Sam was due later in the week to take measurements and hopefully give Ed some kind of estimate on the work involved. Ed was pleased at how things were progressing at the house. He brought home a book of carpet samples that evening to show Rick, along with some paint swatches. There was a good deal of work to be done before Ed would be ready to paint or lay carpet, but he thought they might as well be in complete agreement about what would be best before the time actually arrived.

"You know, now that I'm into the work," Ed told Rick, "I don't see any reason why we won't be done by mid-spring. The furnace-and-AC guy is coming next week, and I've got some roofers scheduled for estimates, too. Once spring is here, that new roof can go on, and we can clean up the landscaping just in time for those factory executives to show up in town."

"Ah, my wonderful, efficient handyman." Rick's warm and tender special was glowing over the carpet book. "I know you'll have that place whipped into shape. Then I'll slap a good price on it, sell it, and you and me will be in the gravy, baby."

"Gravy?" Ed wrinkled his nose. "Don't you mean rolling in dough?"

"Your mom rolls dough," Rick said firmly. "We are going to be swimming in financial gravy."

"Well, then I guess I'd better get a new swimsuit," Ed teased as he went to the fridge for a Pepsi. "What color goes best with this financial gravy?"

Rick rolled his eyes. "Green, baby. Green!"

⋆●⋆

The next morning Ed woke up feeling more confident and optimistic than he had in weeks. He peered out the bedroom window at the sun rising in the east. A light fog was beginning to burn off, and it looked as though it would be another sunny, mild day.

"C'mon, snow," Ed grumbled. "Ed could use a little of that gravy now to help pay for some of that remodeling."

Rick got up and began rushing around to get ready for a breakfast meeting with Eunice and some downtown business owners. He showered and shaved and was dressed and out the door before Ed had done anything more than let the cat out. Ed wasn't meeting Clyde at the house until ten, so he took his time eating breakfast, then strapped on his Walkman as he made the bed and sorted through their dirty clothes for the laundry.

When he went downstairs to let Jett back in, he blinked at the bright sunlight, grateful that his sunglasses were in his truck. He glanced at Effie Maude's pickup. She had returned to work the day before, so Ed decided against making a trip across the yard to see if Mrs. Penfield needed anything.

He was just getting ready to get his truck out of the carriage house when the back storm door on the main house slammed. Ed glanced over and saw Effie Maude slowly making her way down the walk.

"Something wrong?" he called, thinking she must have forgotten something in her truck.

Effie Maude said nothing. She continued to trudge toward him, her head down.

Uneasiness swept through Ed. He hurried across the driveway and through the back gate to meet her on the walk.

"Effie Maude, what's up? You look like you saw a ghost."

She looked up at him, her face gray and horror-struck. "Oh, Ed," she whispered. "She's gone."

Effie Maude threw her arms around Ed and began to wail. "Mrs. P. is dead! She's gone! She's gone!"

CHAPTER NINETEEN

Ed sat in a chair he'd pulled over to one of the living room windows in the apartment. When he turned his head he noticed the sun fading quickly in the west; the shadows in the backyard were deepening with its descent.

He'd been sitting there since the hearse from Reimer and Bayless had carried Mrs. Penfield away late that morning. Rick had come home in the afternoon and was now bustling around the kitchen making chili soup from Norma's recipe.

"This'll be ready in a few minutes," Rick called.

"I'm not hungry."

"Well, then walk over and tell Effie Maude. She's been cleaning that house like a woman possessed all day. It's about time I fed her for a change, so tell her to come over here and eat."

"I don't think she's hungry either."

"Dammit, Ed!" Rick threw a spoon in the sink and burst into tears. "I didn't make this soup so no one would eat it!"

Ed got up from his chair and walked to the kitchen. He put his arms around Rick as he sobbed.

"Oh, God, what are we going to do without her?" Rick choked out through his tears. "I can't believe this is happening; no warning, no nothing. She just dies in her sleep. I'm not ready for this."

"I know," Ed said quietly.

Rick clung to him. "I knew when we moved in here that she would be gone someday, but I thought . . . I thought . . . oh, years and years. Not so soon!"

"I know."

Rick sighed. "Oh, baby, I'm gonna miss her so much."

"Me, too."

Ed handed Rick a paper towel. He couldn't seem to look at Rick, so he grabbed his jean jacket from the clothes tree near the door.

"I'll go get Effie Maude."

Ed walked to the back door and hesitated. He wasn't at all sure he wanted to go in, but he knew he had to face the house sometime. He pushed the door open and stepped inside. The house felt cold. Already Mrs. Penfield's warming presence was fading, just as the sunlight was disappearing from the day.

Effie Maude was seated at the kitchen table, an untouched cup of coffee in front of her. She looked up when Ed entered the kitchen. Her eyes were red and swollen.

"Oh, Ed, what am I gonna do? I've been comin' here every day since I was seventeen years old. I'm an old woman now. What am I gonna do?"

Ed sat next to her at the table. "Keep coming here every day."

He burst into tears. "You have to keep coming every day. We can't run this place without you."

Effie Maude threw her arms around Ed and sobbed as well. "Are you sure you want this raw ole country gal working for you?"

"Yes," Ed said through the tears he had been holding in all day. "You've got a job here as long as you want."

They clung to each other, sharing their grief. When their tears had finally ceased, Ed pushed back his chair and held out his hand to her.

"C'mon. Rick's got supper ready for us. I didn't think I could eat a bite, but maybe I can now."

Ed put his arm around Effie Maude, and they slowly made their way out of the house and across the yard and driveway to the carriage house.

"I thought the world of that woman," Effie Maude whispered. "She was the greatest lady who ever lived."

"I know." Ed shivered in the chilly dusk. "She *was* the greatest. What are we going to do, Effie? I haven't been this scared and sad since my dad died. What are we going to do without her to keep us together and flying right?"

"I don't know," Effie Maude said miserably.

Rick appeared at the top of stairs and saw them huddled in the doorway. He thundered down and threw his arms around both of them, and then they all cried together.

⋄•⋄

They tried to eat. Effie Maude managed to eat spoonfuls of soup between loud, large sniffs. Ed pushed a cracker around in his soup bowl with his spoon. And Rick, who seldom drank anything harder than beer or wine, had poured a shot of whiskey into his Pepsi and was paying more attention to that than to his soup.

They all looked up at the sound of a car in the driveway. Ed pushed himself from the table to go to the window and see who could possibly be visiting. He squinted into the gloom at the car to make sure his eyes weren't deceiving him.

Ed turned to Rick and Effie Maude with a look of disbelief on his face. "It's Doug!"

Doug came into the apartment with warm hugs for all of them. "I'm so sorry, you guys," he murmured, not as a funeral director but as a friend.

He looked around a bit apprehensively. "Where's Gordy?"

Ed and Rick looked at each other. Gordy was at his regularly scheduled therapy appointment, but Ed didn't feel it was necessary to tell Doug that.

"He had an appointment," Rick said smoothly, hanging Doug's coat on the rack. "He'll be home later."

"But what are you doing here?" Ed asked. "You didn't have to come up from Indy for this."

"No, I guess not, but I wanted to." Doug grinned at them. "Sometime after Gordy and I started dating, Mrs. Penfield came to see me about her prearrangements. She wanted to make sure everything was completely taken care of so you guys wouldn't have to make any decisions."

"Isn't that just like her?" Effie Maude shook her head with a trembling smile.

"Stuart Reimer called me this morning with the news. I told him I would take a few days off work and come here and handle everything. I wanted to make sure every last detail was what she wanted."

"Thanks, Doug." Ed gave him a grateful hug. "That means so much to us."

Doug returned the hug. "Hey, I loved her, too. It was hard not to."

Rick glanced at the leather satchel Doug had put on the table. "Is there anything we need to know now?"

Doug nodded and began going through papers and a folder. "Yes, there is. I don't know if she told you this, Rick, but she wanted you to give a brief eulogy before the minister's final prayer."

Rick looked stunned. "I had no idea," he whispered.

"I think that's wonderful," Effie Maude said, her voice sounding happier than it had all day. She slapped Rick on the back. "That's quite an honor!"

"Yes, it is." Ed grinned for the first time that day. "That just shows how much she thought of you, darlin'."

Rick shook his head. "Well, I guess I'd better get busy putting some ideas together. Hell, I've never given a eulogy before!"

"She'd also like you to be a pallbearer," Doug said, looking at his notes. "You, too, Ed, and Gordy. She also requested your brother-in-law, Todd, and Clyde Croasdale. She wanted her friend Dr. Weisburg as well, but his health is too poor to handle it right now. Do you have a suggestion for a replacement?"

"How about Matt?" Ed asked the table at large.

Rick and Effie Maude nodded.

"Who's Matt?"

Ed shook his head. "Boy, are you out of the loop these days. Matt is Clyde's son and Claire's boyfriend. We think he's gonna ask her to marry him."

Doug grinned. "Works for me. Do you have his number?"

Rick wrote Matt's phone number on the folder as Doug asked Effie Maude to locate the specific dress Mrs. Penfield wanted for her burial.

"That's pretty much it except for the music. Mrs. Penfield requested some traditional hymns, but for some reason she also wants us to play Simon and Garfunkel's 'Bridge Over Troubled Water' at the service. Do you have a copy of that, Ed?"

Ed nodded. "Sure. I think I know why she wants it at her service. I remember when that song came out during my senior year. She asked me who sang it because it made her think of George Junior. She said there was a lot of comfort in that song."

"Oh, and one other thing." Doug frowned at a scrawled note. "She apparently called Reimer and Bayless recently and requested 'Moon River.' According to this note, it's to remind both of you to enjoy the journey on the way to the rainbow's end." Doug gave him a puzzled look. "Do you know what that's about?"

Ed put a hand to his heart, stunned. "We just listened to that record and talked about it last week," he whispered. "I can't believe it. It's like she knew this was going to happen."

"Maybe she did," Rick quietly said, looking as though he was going to cry again.

Effie Maude gave Ed a curious look. "You mean that song from the record with Audrey Hepburn on the cover?"

Ed nodded.

Effie Maude sniffed and wiped at her eyes with her napkin. "She knew, the poor dear. She listened to that record over and over again after Mr. P. died. She must have known she was goin' to join him, bless her heart."

Ed rubbed furiously at his own eyes; afraid he was going to cry again, too. "I'll get 'Bridge Over Troubled Water' for you," he mumbled, going to the record cabinet.

Effie Maude got up and said she'd go to the house for the *Breakfast at Tiffany's* LP and Mrs. Penfield's dress. Rick sat at the table and stared at his soup bowl while Doug busied himself with his notes.

Ed handed the record to Doug, who quietly thanked him. He gave both Ed and Rick another hug and said he was going back to the funeral home.

"You can call me there if you have any questions. If not, I'll see you for the calling hours."

"Do you have a place to stay?" Rick asked. "I mean, you could—"

"No, that's okay," Doug said with a smile. "I've got a room at the Evergreen Lodge near the hospital. I think that's the best thing, considering."

"Okay." Rick hugged him and then kissed his cheek. "You're wonderful to do this, Doug. We won't worry about a thing knowing you're in charge."

"Please don't worry, but do call me at the funeral home or the motel if you need anything."

Doug put his coat on and walked to the door. "I'll meet Effie Maude downstairs for the other things. Thanks, guys. Oh, and . . . tell Gordy I was here, and . . . well, tell him I said hello."

Ed hugged him again. "We will."

Doug smiled and waved as he pulled the door closed behind him.

"Wow." Ed sighed as he slumped into his chair.

"Wow what?"

"Wow everything, I guess."

"Yeah." Rick sighed, too, as he returned to his chair. "A eulogy! Can you believe it? I guess she thought having to write that would keep me too busy to cry."

"So what'll keep me from crying while you're writing it?"

Rick reached across the table and took Ed's hand. "You'll be busy helping me write it, baby. I may be the one to deliver it, but it'll come from both of our hearts."

Ed slept fitfully that night. He woke up at around four thirty convinced he heard someone in the shower. Rick was snoring next to him, so Ed puzzled over the running water until he remembered: Gordy had crashed on their couch, saying he felt uncomfortable spending the night in the main house. Gordy probably couldn't sleep either and had obviously decided to get up and get ready for work.

Ed rolled over and tried to go back to sleep, but he was wide awake. With a sigh he crawled out of bed and shuffled to the kitchen. He was at the table, huddled over a mug of tea, when Gordy appeared ten minutes later. They glanced at each other but said nothing. Gordy poured his morning coffee and slumped into a chair across from Ed with a soft groan.

Apparently they had made enough noise to wake Rick. He silently entered the kitchen, poured his own coffee, and joined them at the table. Jett, disturbed by this break in the usual morning routine, stood by the table and meowed a few times. Ed pulled the cat into his lap and petted him, rubbing his face against the top of Jett's head.

Gordy lit a cigarette. Rick glanced at him, grinned briefly, but said nothing. He even reached for the ashtray on the counter and handed it to Gordy, who grinned back in gratitude.

It was Gordy who finally broke the silence. "I've been thinkin'," he said, exhaling. "With you guys movin' into the big house, you'll probably need to rent this apartment to help with expenses for a while. Instead of me tryin' to find a new place, how 'bout we just kinda swap?"

Ed's head jerked up. "Who said anything about us moving?"

"Well, that's the plan, isn't it?" Gordy asked defensively.

"I don't know if I can ever live in that house," Ed muttered.

Rick reached for Ed's hand. "Yeah, that was the plan. The house belongs to Ed and me now, but we don't have to talk about it yet. As far as I'm concerned, Gord, this is your home, and you can stay here as long as you like. We'll work out the details when we're not so upset."

Ed didn't want to think about moving into the main house, although they had agreed with Mrs. Penfield years ago that they would do so upon her death. But he didn't want Gordy to feel any uncertainty either. He reached for Gordy's hand. "Yeah, bud, you need to stay here. You may think you need us right now, but we really need you, too. Rick's right. This is your home, no matter what."

Ed shuddered. "I just can't face that house right now. I feel like I'm dancing on her grave, and it's not even dug yet."

Gordy reached for Rick's hand, connecting the three of them. "Man, this sucks."

"Yeah, it does." Rick sighed. "I don't know how it's all gonna shake out. All I know now is that we have to get through the calling, the funeral, and that funeral dinner at the First Presbyterian Church. Maybe after that we can have a collective nervous breakdown. Right now we're still in shock . . . in mourning. Shit, I feel like someone has smashed our world to pieces."

"Me, too," Ed mumbled into Jett's fur.

"Me three." Gordy let go of their hands to stub out his cigarette. Then he stood up and said, "Well, hell, I might as well go over to the house and get dressed for work. Old Don'll probably pass out when he sees me showin' up early, but I need to keep busy."

Rick looked up. "You want any breakfast?"

"Naah. Maybe I'll run over to Dottie's before I start my route. I'm not hungry."

"Don't forget to ask Don for the next two days off."

"I won't. I'm sure he'll be okay with it. I'm the one who has to deal with Mrs. P. bein' gone, and seeing Doug again. Fuck!" He snorted as he shrugged his coat on over his sweatshirt and pants.

Jett jumped off of Ed's lap and joined Gordy at the door.

"C'mon, cat! Let's go face what's left of the world." Gordy shooed Jett ahead of him as he closed the door.

"Poor Gordy," Ed murmured as he reached for his tea.

"Yeah. But you know what? I don't think his seeing Doug is such a bad thing. I just wish it was under different circumstances."

"Yeah, I suppose you're right. I just want this week to be over with for all of us."

Rick pulled his chair closer to Ed's so he could lay his head on Ed's shoulder. "I know. I kept hoping I would wake up and find out this had all been a bad dream. But it isn't. So I guess the only thing to do is deal with it like the strong men Mrs. P. said we were."

Ed put an arm around Rick, trying to find some comfort in his presence. "I didn't know until now how much of my strength came from her approval, and from her keeping an eye on us."

Rick smiled wistfully. "Maybe it was all a big lesson. Maybe she was teaching us how to cope with it all when she was gone."

"Yeah? Well, if this is the first test, I wish I had studied more. I'm not convinced I'm gonna pass it."

Ed took a sip of tea. "There's one thing that's really been bugging me since last night."

"What's that?"

"Well, remember when Effie Maude said Mrs. Penfield must have known her time was coming because she was listening to 'Moon River'? If that's so, how come she encouraged me to find some Audrey Hepburn movies for her to watch, and talked about how she was looking forward to having Gordy around all winter?"

Rick shrugged. "Beats me. Maybe she knew; maybe she didn't. Maybe she was just in the mood to listen to that album. I guess we'll never really know for sure."

"Yeah." Ed sighed. He thought about the day ahead. He had purposely not canceled any of his handyman appointments. Like Gordy, he felt the need to keep busy.

"I think I'll call Mrs. Klarn when it gets light out and see if I can move her appointment up to this morning. Who knew I'd be up so early?"

"What do you have to do for her today?"

Ed grimaced. "Oh, supposedly her bathroom faucet is dripping, so I'm gonna take a look at it."

"Ah." Rick nodded wisely. "Fixing a drip for a drip, huh?"

Ed groaned, and then shocked himself by laughing. "Thanks, darlin'." He gave Rick a quick kiss. "That was really bad, but it was really good, too. I guess if I can still laugh, there's hope I'll get through this."

Rick returned the kiss. "We'll get through it. No matter what, we're still here for each other."

Ed smiled at Rick, grateful that he wasn't alone, and comforted by the thought that even if their world had indeed been smashed to pieces, he still had something for which to be grateful.

Ed managed to get inside Mrs. Klarn's house and into her upstairs bathroom with a minimum of her droning chatter. For once in her life, Mrs. Klarn seemed to understand that Ed was in no mood for conversation.

There was definitely a drip from the faucet. Ed twisted the taps back and forth and decided the hot-water side was probably the culprit. He turned the water off under the sink and was rummaging through his toolbox when he heard a car pull in the driveway. He peeked out the window and saw Paul getting out of his car with a loaded laundry basket. A few moments later he heard Mrs. Klarn open the front door for him.

"Good morning, Althea! Since you insist on doing my laundry, I thought I might as well drop it off on my way to the office."

"That's what mothers are for, Paul. There's no reason for you to worry about such things."

Ed rolled his eyes. He could just imagine what Norma would have to say if he dropped his dirty clothes off at her house on his way to work.

"There's no reason why I can't do my own laundry, but if it makes you happy, I'm certainly willing to let you do it."

"Oh, brother," Ed whispered, pulling a screwdriver out of his toolbox.

"Is that Ed's truck parked out front?" Ed heard Paul ask his mother.

"Yes. He's taking care of that leaky faucet for me."

"Oh, good. I'll just run up and say hello."

"Paul, before you do that, I need to ask you something about him."

"About Ed?"

"Well, yes. I'm concerned. You know I read all the medical and science news in the paper and pay attention to those segments on the *Today* show so I can keep up with you and talk intelligently about your work."

"What could that have to do with Ed?" Paul sounded amused.

"Well, this AIDS disease. I just don't know about having him work here anymore."

Ed quietly laid his screwdriver on the sink. *Doesn't she know I can hear this?* he thought, a grim look on his face. *But then maybe the old bat wants me to hear it.*

"Althea, why would AIDS have anything to do with the excellent work Ed does for you?" Paul's voice was stern.

"It's such a terrible disease," she droned in her usual monotone. "I certainly wouldn't want to expose myself, or you, to it."

Ed picked up his screwdriver and clenched his fist around the handle as his heartbeat accelerated. *That rotten old hypocrite*, he thought. *Why, she even sent Rick a plant when he was sick! I wish to hell I could take back that thank-you note we wrote.*

"And why would having Ed work here possibly expose you to AIDS?"

"He's a gay man, Paul. You know that."

"And I'm a gay man, too. You know *that*."

"But you're my son, and a doctor."

"I'm still a gay man, same as Ed. You have as much chance of getting AIDS from me as from him. Really, Althea, I'm ashamed of you for even thinking such a thing. If you had been paying attention to those medical reports, then you would know your chance of acquiring AIDS through casual contact is nonexistent."

"But you can't be too careful."

"Yes, you can. When caution becomes paranoia and hysteria, you're being too careful. At that point, all you're doing is contributing to the lies and misinformation that are spreading about this disease. Ed does not have AIDS. Neither does his partner. They are both healthy, hardworking men, and you have nothing to fear from either of them."

"That Rick was so sick at Christmastime—"

"Rick had a bad case of pneumonia. I seem to recall a similar case of pneumonia my father had when you were still married to him."

That silenced Mrs. Klarn. It even distracted Ed for a moment. He still wondered what had ever happened to Paul's father.

"Well, I'm not the only one who's concerned," Mrs. Klarn said. Obviously she didn't like discussing her ex-husband with Paul any more than she did with Ed. "Maxine Ilinski has been wondering the same thing."

Ed's mouth fell open. Mrs. Ilinski was one of his longtime and most faithful clients. She had never said or done anything to lead Ed to believe that she was uncomfortable with him. Why, she was even responsible for Jett becoming Ed and Rick's pet. Ed had taken the stray tomcat off her hands nearly three years earlier. She still asked about him and occasionally sent cat treats home with Ed when he worked for her.

"This is ridiculous," Paul said impatiently. "This is just the sort of thing that stirs up trouble. Althea, I assure you, you have nothing to fear from Ed, nor does Maxine Ilinski. Not only am I ashamed of you, I'm very angry as well. I can't believe my mother would actually be a party to ruining a good man's reputation based on misinformation and fear."

"I'm sorry, Paul. I guess I just didn't understand." Ed noted a tone of contrition in her voice. He was sure it had more to do with pissing off Paul than with what she had said about Ed.

"You understand now." Paul's voice was harsh. "I want you to promise me that you'll tell that woman she has nothing to fear from contact with Ed, and that if anyone else says one word about this, you'll correct them and see to it this nonsense is stopped dead. You hear me?"

"Yes, Paul, I hear you. Now, let me get this laundry sorted."

"Althea? Do you promise me?"

"Yes, Paul. I promise. I'll speak to Maxine."

Ed heard someone coming up the stairs. He quickly went to work dismantling the hot-water tap. Paul appeared in the bathroom doorway, a troubled look on his face.

"Did you hear that?" he quietly asked.

Ed nodded, not looking up.

Paul sighed. "I'm sorry, Ed. You've worked for my mother long enough to know what a dingbat she can be."

Ed managed a weak smile. "Yeah."

"This won't . . . I mean . . ."

Ed put down his screwdriver and laid a hand on Paul's arm. "No, don't worry about it. I'd hate it if people held me responsible for all the goofy stuff my mom says."

"Good," Paul said, relieved.

"I may think twice, though, about coming over here the next time she calls."

Paul grinned. "I don't blame you a bit. I promise I'll keep her quiet about this bullshit. Don't worry about it, okay?"

"Okay." Ed returned to his work.

"Ed? I also wanted to tell you how sorry I was to hear about Mrs. Penfield. She was a great teacher and a wonderful woman."

"Thanks."

"When are the calling hours? I'd like to stop by and pay my respects."

Ed glanced at him. "Tonight from six to eight, and tomorrow from two to eight. The funeral is Friday morning."

"Okay. I'll try to stop by tomorrow."

Paul walked to the sink and put his arms around Ed. "I'm really sorry, Ed," he whispered. "About Althea, and about losing your friend. I understand what you're going through in so many ways."

Ed turned from the sink and hugged Paul. He knew Paul understood. As they stood in each other's arms, it occurred to Ed that they didn't know each other all that well, but as gay men who had grown up in the same town, they did indeed understand things about each other that most people could never begin to comprehend.

⋄⋅●⋅⋄

Ed was huddled on the corner of the sofa near the stereo when Rick burst through the apartment door late that afternoon, tossed his coat on a chair, and began going through the mail on the kitchen table. He glanced over at Ed.

"Baby, you need to get dressed. We need to be at the funeral home before six."

Ed reached over and turned down the volume on the Mamas and the Papas. "I know. I'll get to it."

"We don't have to worry about supper," Rick murmured as he frowned at a bill. "Doug called from the funeral home. Dunlap's Market sent over a huge deli tray."

"Yeah. The Dunlaps always do that when one of their favorite customers dies."

"How 'bout that? Mrs. Patterson sent over a box of doughnuts, too. That's the nice thing about living in a small town. I can't imagine people doing anything like that in a big city."

"Yeah."

The record changer clicked, and "California Dreamin'" began to play again. Rick looked up from the mail and grinned wistfully.

"Comfort music?"

"Yeah."

"I remember when we were getting ready to go to San Francisco. You played that record over and over again."

Rick sighed. "This sure is a good day for doin' some California dreamin'. It's winter and the sky is gray, and I wish to hell we were somewhere else. California sounds damned good right now."

"It sure does."

Rick plopped himself on the sofa next to Ed. "Maybe when this is all over we can take a trip. I think it would do us both good to get the hell out of here for a few days. Maybe we should take what money we have and blow it on a trip to Southern California, where it's warm right now."

"Maybe." Ed reached under Rick's shirt collar to stroke the gold chain. "Maybe we should go permanently."

Rick's eyebrows rose. "Permanently?"

Ed shrugged. "I'm just sick of worrying what this town thinks of us."

Rick put an arm around Ed. "Something happen at work today?"

Ed shrugged again. He'd already decided he wasn't going to tell Rick about the conversation he had overheard until after the funeral.

"No," he lied. "I guess I'm just not ready to think about what anyone might say or do without Mrs. Penfield's seal of approval to protect us."

"We'll protect ourselves, just like she taught us," Rick said quietly. "Still, I understand. You wouldn't believe the crazy thoughts that have been going through my head since yesterday. I've just put myself on autopilot to get through all of this."

Ed smiled at Rick. "Crazy thoughts?"

"Yeah. All sorts of stuff. I made up my mind to ignore it until after the funeral. This weekend—who knows? I may spend it crying and screaming and slamming doors. Maybe I'll get drunk. Or maybe I'll call the airlines and book two tickets to paradise. I don't know. I just know we owe it to Mrs. P. to get through this all as gracefully and respectfully as possible."

Ed nodded. Rick was right. They did owe that and a lot more to Mrs. Penfield, and he blushed as he thought of how disappointed she would be to find him moping on the sofa like a scared little boy instead of behaving like the strong man she believed him to be.

Rick's arm squeezed Ed's shoulders. "Now. You ready to get dressed and go to the funeral home with me?"

Ed sniffed at his T-shirt and frowned. "I'm kinda smelly from all the work I did today. I think I should take a shower first. Why don't you go ahead without me? I promise I'll be there as soon as I get myself cleaned up."

"Okay." Rick kissed him and stood up. He grabbed his new overcoat from the chair and put it on, adjusting the scarf Laurie had given him for Christmas to go with it. He hesitated at the door.

"I love you, baby. We're gonna be okay, okay?"

Ed grinned at him as he took the phonograph needle off the record. "Yeah, we'll be okay. I love you, too, darlin'."

Ed slid the record into its paper sleeve and carefully put it in the record cabinet. After shutting off the stereo, he headed for the bathroom, peeling his shirt off as he went, thinking how proud he was of Rick for doing what he needed to do without a lot of whining. He was just as grief stricken as Ed, but he was behaving like the strong, mature man Mrs. Penfield had nurtured over the past three years. Ed decided it was time for him to do the same.

He was wiping the steam from his shower off the bathroom mirror when he heard someone pounding at the apartment door. He put his bathrobe on and stuck his head into the hall as Norma opened the door and barged in. She put her hands on her hips at the sight of him.

"Edward Timothy Stephens!" she barked. "Why aren't you at that funeral home?"

"I'm working on it, Mom." He sighed. "I'm just running a little late."

She glared at him suspiciously. "Is that all? Rick told me you were upset about something. Honestly! We're all upset, but you need to be at that funeral home and show some respect for the woman who was so good to you. We're the closest thing to a family that woman had, and I won't stand by and watch you be disrespectful!"

"I know; I know. I just need to get dressed."

Norma kept her eyes on Ed's. "What's bothering you?"

Ed pulled his bathrobe belt tighter as he looked back at Norma. Before yesterday he would have said nothing was bothering him, or made up some story to get her off his back. And then he probably would have gone to Mrs. Penfield and told her what had happened. Mrs. Penfield wasn't around for him to confide in anymore, but he realized that his mother, who had a lot to do with making him the man Mrs. Penfield had admired, was.

He thought back to their quiet conversation that night in the hospital when he had been so worried about Rick. He realized that Norma, despite her reservations about him being with another man, had come a long way in understanding. Maybe it was time to begin showing her the respect he had shown Mrs. Penfield.

"I overheard Mrs. Klarn telling her son that she was worried about me working for her because of AIDS," he said bluntly.

Norma snorted. "For Pete's sake! Is that what's bothering you? Honestly, you should know to take anything that woman says with a grain of salt. Your father always said she was a silly, annoying woman, and that she drove her husband off with her foolishness."

Ed looked at her in surprise. "Dad knew Mr. Klarn?"

Norma nodded. "Yes, they worked together. Apparently Luther Klarn had a drinking problem, and your father said living with that woman only made it worse. He finally sobered up and moved far away to stay sober. Probably the smartest thing he could have done. How that son turned out so well is beyond me, having to put up with her for a mother."

"Hmmm." Ed scratched his head. "Well, that's one mystery solved."

"Good. So just forget it about, and get dressed."

Ed walked into the living room and leaned against the wall. "That's not all, Mom. Apparently Mrs. Ilinski was concerned as well. If someone who's been such a good client is worrying, what could other people be saying?"

Norma rolled her eyes in disgust. "Maxine Ilinski's always been a worrywart. Honestly, Ed, don't make a fuss about this. People always overreact where disease is involved. They're just scared. Why, I remember the polio epidemics back in the forties and fifties. Fortunately you're too young to remember how terrified people were back then. And the silly things they did and said? Why, sometimes it was downright disgraceful. But eventually Jonas Salk came up with a vaccine, and you don't hear a thing about it anymore. The same thing will happen with this AIDS. Until they know more about it, people are going to act foolishly. It's just human nature."

"Yeah, but I feel like I'm wearing a big target on my head 'cause I'm a gay man, and everyone still thinks AIDS is a gay man's disease."

"So what? From what I've read you can't get it from breathing the same air, or from some germ floating through the air like polio or smallpox. As long as you and Rick behave yourselves, your clients don't have anything to worry about. They'll figure that out eventually."

"What'll I do until then?"

"You just ride it out. Remember a few years ago when that tramp Ruth Dorsey made such a fuss about you? Sure, you lost a few clients from the awful things she said, but you picked up new ones. If some people are dumb enough to let go of a good worker like you because they're scared of some disease they can't even catch from you, well, good riddance. There are still plenty of sensible people in this town who know a good handyman when they see one."

Ed smiled. "You think I'm a good handyman, Mom?"

Norma sniffed. "Of course you are. I don't say it very often because it's my job to keep you humble. Despite what *some* people say, you have a good reputation in this town, and you're respected for what you do. So don't let any of this nonsense worry you. It'll blow over, just like everything else does."

Ed fiddled with his bathrobe belt as he looked at the floor. "Even without Mrs. Penfield around to defend me?"

Norma put a finger under Ed's chin and lifted his eyes to hers. "I never let you hide behind my skirts," she said firmly. "And I don't think Hilda would like to picture you hiding behind hers. It's your responsibility to go out in the world and be the man your father and I raised, and be the man Hilda respected so much that she left her home to you. I thought you knew that."

Ed shrugged. "Yeah, Mom, I know that. I guess I'm just so . . . so freaked-out that she died. I just wasn't expecting it. I guess I didn't realize how much I depended on her."

Norma sighed and sat on the sofa, a tired look on her face. "Edward, even if you knew she was going to go, it wouldn't be any easier. And as for depending on her, well, you never realize how much you truly depend on someone until they're gone. I learned that when my parents died, and when your father died. It's terrible, but adjusting to death is a big part of life."

Ed sat next to her. "Funny, isn't it? From the time we're born we have to learn to accept death. Almost makes me wonder what the point is."

"I don't think there is a point." Norma said with a snort. "You just do your best and hope for the best. Everything else you can leave to the philosophers and the Bible-bangers."

She turned to him with a critical look. "Now, are you going to get dressed, or am I going to have to dress you like the big baby you are?"

Ed jumped up with a grin. "No, I can dress myself. But you can help me tie my tie since Rick isn't here."

Norma moaned. "It's a good thing I'm still around. What would you do without your mother to keep you marching forward?"

"You always say Laurie and I are going to send you to your grave," Ed shouted from the bedroom.

"Well, you can just forget about that!" she shouted back at him. "I've changed my mind. I'm not going anywhere until the two of you start behaving like the adults I thought I raised. Honestly!"

Ed chuckled to himself as he pulled his suit out of the closet. For the first time since Tuesday morning he realized he would find a way to survive the loss of Mrs. Penfield.

He thought of Norma in the living room and laughed out loud. Yeah, he'd survive, whether he wanted to or not.

CHAPTER TWENTY

The snow Ed had wished for earlier in the week arrived the morning of Mrs. Penfield's funeral. He peered out the bedroom window, watching the light, fluffy flakes slowly cover the barren ground. Several inches had been predicted, and as grateful as he was for the work it would bring him, he now hoped the worst of it would hold off until after the funeral.

He turned from the window, glancing at his dark suit hanging on the closet door. He braced himself for the day ahead, grateful that it probably wouldn't be as bad as he had originally feared. The two days of calling had gone much better than he had expected. The funeral home had been filled with floral tributes from Mrs. Penfield's friends, admirers, and past students. Those who came to call had nothing but words of kindness and praise for Ed, Rick, and Effie Maude in regard to everything they had done to make Mrs. Penfield's last years easier. Ed had relaxed, and the darker thoughts that had been churning in his mind where the citizens of Porterfield were concerned abated.

He had been a bit surprised, however, when he first entered the viewing room Wednesday evening. Mrs. Penfield's casket was closed, and next to it on a large easel was a framed enlargement of her picture from the Porterfield High School yearbook the year she retired.

"That's what she wanted," Doug said when Ed asked him about it. "She said she thought it was unduly morbid to make people stare at a dead body in a box, and she didn't want anyone to have to go through that for her sake."

Ed grinned. "That sounds just like her."

Eunice Ames arrived at that moment, leading her entire Downtown Beautification Committee into the viewing room. Ed and Rick were swept into the middle of the crowd with hugs and words of condolence.

While Ed was listening to Eunice reminisce about her feuds with Mrs. Penfield during her school board years, he noticed Gordy and Doug in quiet conversation in a far corner. Ed smiled. He didn't know what they were talking about but was pleased to see they were obviously comfortable with each other.

After Eunice and her committee members took their leave, Ed and Rick settled on a sofa near the casket while Effie Maude and Norma went to the kitchen to help themselves to the food from Dunlap's Market. Ed was just catching his breath and thinking about making a sandwich of his own when a man he didn't recognize approached them.

"Are you Ed Stephens?"

Ed looked up. He guessed the man standing in front of him was about his age. He was of average height and had a strong and powerful-looking build. His black hair was slightly receding, and there was a friendly smile on his rugged face. Ed couldn't help but think he knew him from somewhere.

"Yes, I'm Ed," he said, holding out his hand.

The man gave it a good shake. "I guess you don't remember me. I'm Pete Carmichael, Sam's nephew? Sam the cabinetmaker? He told me he canceled an appointment with you at your new house because of a death close to you. When he told me it was Mrs. Penfield, I knew I had to come down from Fort Wayne and pay my respects. She was my favorite teacher in high school."

"Oh," Ed said, still shaking his hand. "That's where I know you from—school. Geez, I don't think I've seen you since . . . since . . ."

"Probably 1967, when I graduated." Pete chuckled.

"Yeah! You were on the football team, weren't you?"

Pete rolled his eyes and grinned. "For what's it worth. I don't know if I contributed much to the Porterfield Bobcats, but I gave it my all."

Ed glanced at Rick, who was following their conversation with interest.

"I'm sorry," Ed said, nodding to Rick. "This is my, uh, this is Rick Benton."

"Your partner?" Pete grinned as he shook Rick's hand. "I was hoping I'd get to meet both of you. When Sam explained your relationship, I knew I had to come down and meet another gay man who had survived growing up in Porterfield."

"Nice to meet you." Rick gave Pete's hand a vigorous shake. He glanced at Ed with a smile. "Your old schoolmates have been coming out all over the place lately, haven't they?"

"Yeah," Ed said, looking at Pete with both surprise and admiration.

"There's more?" Pete asked with interest. "You know, I left Porterfield for Fort Wayne right after graduation. Haven't lived here since. I always knew I couldn't be the only one, but I didn't stick around to find out."

Ed laughed. "Oh, there's a few of us running loose. In fact, here comes one now."

Gordy was walking toward them. Pete turned around and a look of astonished pleasure came over his face. "Gordy!" he exclaimed. "Is that you?"

Gordy's mouth fell open. "Pete?"

Pete grabbed Gordy for a big bear hug. "You old son of a bitch! I haven't seen you since I graduated. Where have you been hiding? These guys your friends?"

Gordy, looking absolutely stunned, glanced at Ed and Rick. "Yeah, they're my buds. I don't do much hiding anymore."

Pete let go of Gordy but kept a hand on his arm. "Well, that's sure good to know."

Gordy's eyes brightened. Ed could tell he'd figured it out. "I'll be dipped in shit," he roared, slapping Pete on the back. "So I wasn't the only one in the locker room, huh?"

"No, sir!"

All four of them began to laugh.

"Geez, now I'm beginning to wonder about the rest of the Bobcats," Ed managed to choke out.

"Hell, me, too!" Gordy slapped Pete again. "Man, if we'd only known . . ."

Pete shrugged. "Yeah, but what the hell? Things were a lot different back then. I'm just glad I decided to drive down here tonight. Oh, shoot," he mumbled, a guilty look on his face. "I mean I came down here to pay my respects and all of that . . ."

Rick put a hand out to halt Pete's apology. "Don't worry about it. I may be the only one here who didn't have Mrs. Penfield for English, but I can tell you she would be loving every minute of this."

Gordy glanced behind them at some newcomers entering the room. "I guess we'd better calm down. Pete, you still smoke like a chimney?"

Pete pulled a pack of Marlboros out of his pocket. "Yeah," he said ruefully.

"C'mon, then. Let's go out back for a smoke and get caught up." Gordy led him through the back entrance of the room, pulling his own cigarettes out of his pocket.

Ed and Rick looked at each other and giggled.

"I tell you, will wonders never cease to amaze?" Rick shook his head. "What is it with Gordy hooking up with guys in this place? This is where he and Doug first really connected, ya know."

Ed, still giggling, nodded. "Yeah, I know. I just hope this one turns out better than the last."

"Ah, hell, who knows? I just think it's great he ran into an old teammate. Meeting Pete should do wonders for cheering him up, one way or the other."

"Yeah." Ed looked over at Mrs. Penfield's casket and smiled. "Looks like the old girl did it again. Even in death she's still watching out for us."

Ed thought about that now as he slid his suit jacket on and inspected his appearance in the mirror. He smiled as he recalled seeing Gordy leave the funeral home Thursday evening. Gordy had been on his way to Fort Wayne to spend time with Pete. There had been a light in Gordy's eyes Ed hadn't seen in a while, and a certain swagger to his step. And Ed knew Mrs. Penfield would be delighted to know that two of her former students were discovering they had more in common than they had ever expected.

Gordy walked into the bedroom. He stood next to Ed at the mirror and adjusted his own suit. "Couldn't tell you the last time I looked this good," he grumbled. "Wish it was for a happier occasion."

"It won't go to waste if you see Pete today," Ed teased.

Gordy smirked at him. "Nope. You know he's a manager at an auto parts warehouse on the north side of Fort Wayne."

"Yeah, I believe you told us that two or three times already."

Gordy gave Ed an affectionate shove. "Well, he couldn't get the day off, but I'm gonna go up to his place tomorrow night."

"Should we be waiting up for you?"

"Hell no! If things go the way I think they will, I won't be home until Sunday."

Ed chuckled. "Good. I'm glad."

"Yeah, me, too." Gordy's face sobered as he looked at himself in the mirror. "It's kinda like a final present from Mrs. P., ya know?"

"I know. I hope it works out."

"We'll see. Right now I'm havin' a good time. I always did like Pete a lot. If nothin' else, I've got a new bud. If it turns out to be something more . . . well, we'll just see, okay?"

Rick entered the bedroom. He looked them both up and down and grinned. "I gotta say, you two do clean up nicely."

Ed and Gordy looked at each other in disgust. "You wanna hit him, or should I?" Ed asked.

"You do it. I got better things to think about." With a dignified lift to his head, Gordy marched out of the room.

Rick shook his head. "Man, he's going to be one big pain in the ass for a while, isn't he?"

Ed laughed. "Yeah. Ain't it great?"

⟨⧫⟩

When they arrived at Reimer and Bayless, Ed was surprised to see cars already overflowing the parking lot. He thought the snow might keep people away, but apparently everyone who knew and respected Mrs. Penfield was determined to be a witness to her final farewell.

Once inside, Ed picked up a funeral program from the podium near the door. Mrs. Penfield's picture was at the top of the front page. Underneath it read:

HILDA JEAN BRENT PENFIELD

1907–1984

BELOVED TEACHER AND FRIEND OF THE COMMUNITY

HER LEGACY WILL BE CHERISHED BY MANY

"That's nice, isn't it?" Ed whispered to Rick.

"Yeah. I guess the wording was Reverend Norris's idea. He seems like an okay guy. I think he'll do right by Mrs. P. today."

"How about you? Nervous about that eulogy we wrote?"

Rick shrugged. "Yeah, but I got my note cards in my jacket pocket. I just hope I can get through it without crying."

"You'll be fine." Ed discreetly squeezed Rick's hand. "Cry if you want. I don't know if I'll make it through this day without crying."

Rick returned the hand squeeze. "Thanks, baby," he whispered as he turned away to greet Claire and the kids, just coming through the door. The Croasdale family was right behind them. Ed was about to go over to them when he felt a tap on his shoulder. He turned around and saw Bob Mason, Mrs. Penfield's attorney.

"Good morning, Ed. I'm sorry to see you under such sad circumstances."

"Good morning, Bob. Yeah, I was just telling Rick I hope I can make it through this day without breaking down."

Bob nodded. "That will be difficult for all of us who knew and loved Hilda. Anyway, I wanted to remind you to make an appointment for next week to go over the will. You know all of the details; there are no surprises, but we'll need to start the machinery for probate and such."

"Okay." Ed sighed.

"Oh, and one other thing." Bob reached inside his suit jacket. He pulled out an envelope and handed it to Ed. "Hilda wanted me to make sure you and Rick received this on the day of her funeral."

"What the . . ." Ed looked at the envelope in disbelief. His name and Rick's were written across the front in Mrs. Penfield's shaky but very legible teacher's handwriting.

Bob shrugged. "Some final thoughts or best wishes, I suppose. Hold on to it until after the funeral and read it when you're ready. Those were her instructions."

"Thanks, Bob." Ed put the envelope in his own suit pocket, wondering what Mrs. Penfield could have possibly wanted to tell them after she died. He didn't have time to dwell on it, however. Norma came through the door with Laurie and Todd and their children, and they walked over to greet him. Ed ushered them into the room and made sure they had seats in the front.

The room full of people and the solemn music from the organ began to get to Ed. Pretending he had to go to the bathroom, he ducked out the side entrance and wandered into one of the offices. Doug was there, putting a cassette tape in the funeral home's stereo system.

"The special music Mrs. Penfield requested," Doug said as he closed the cassette deck. "I put the songs on a tape. I'll give you the records back before I leave today."

Ed walked over to him. "You're going home after the funeral dinner?"

Doug nodded. "Originally I thought I'd hang around for another day, but . . ."

Ed smiled wistfully. "But you didn't know Gordy was going to be busy, right?"

Doug blushed. "Yeah. Stupid of me, wasn't it?"

"No, I don't think so. This whole Pete thing took us all by surprise. I'm happy for him. I just hope you're cool with it. Did you guys get a chance to talk things out?"

"Yeah, we did. We're cool, really. And believe it or not, I'm actually happy for him. Pete looks like the kind of guy Gordy needs."

Ed leaned against the stereo cabinet and nudged Doug. "What about you?"

Doug shrugged. "I think I might move again. Indy is always going to remind me of how I fucked up with him. One good thing about being a mortician is it's easy to find work almost anywhere. I'm thinking about the southwest . . . maybe Arizona or New Mexico. I spent a little time there when I was in the army and loved it. I think it may be time to move on and see if I can do some more of my growing up."

Ed grinned. "If you do move out there, can we come visit?"

"Just try and get out of it!" Doug hugged Ed. "Hell, if things work out for Gordy with this guy, I hope they come visit, too. Believe me, Ed, he may never be my lover again, but I sure want him as a friend."

"That's good to know." Ed hugged him back. "Thanks, Doug, for everything. I hope we'll know each other the rest of our lives."

"Me, too. Thanks for being my friend. No matter what, we'll always be in touch."

Doug looked at his watch. "It's almost time to begin. You'd better go sit down."

"Okay." Ed took a deep breath and returned to his seat between Effie Maude and Rick in the front row. Every chair in the room was filled, and some latecomers were being seated in the hall. Claire leaned forward and whispered to him that John and Vera sent their condolences; they had been unable to take the day off but planned to call later. Ed nodded and faced the podium, where Reverend Norris, the pastor of Porterfield First Presbyterian, Mrs. Penfield's church for many years, was adjusting the microphone.

The organ music came to an end and "Moon River" began to play. Listening to the melancholy music, Ed felt tears come to his eyes. He reached into his pocket and pulled out a handkerchief with the initial *S* embroidered on it. The handkerchief had belonged to his father, and Norma had given it to him just the day before in case he needed it during the service. He dabbed at his eyes and composed himself as the song came to an end. He noticed, with grim amusement, that Rick and Effie Maude were doing the same thing.

"A good woman beloved by us all has reached her own rainbow's end," Reverend Norris intoned into the microphone. "Let us pray in memory of Hilda Penfield."

Heads throughout the room bowed. Ed's mind wandered during the prayer and through the rest of the minister's eulogy. He was too busy thinking his own thoughts about Mrs. Penfield and watching Rick out of the corner of his eye as he fidgeted nervously with his note cards. Ed knew how much Rick wanted to make Mrs. Penfield proud of him, so he concentrated on sending his positive vibrations to Rick.

Reverend Norris concluded his comments and nodded at Rick, who cleared his throat and walked to the podium. Ed's heart swelled with pride at how tall and confident he looked, and what a dignified appearance he projected in his best dark suit. Rick glanced at him, and Ed smiled broadly and gave him a discreet thumbs-up. Rick gave him a quick grin and looked down at his notes; then his eyes scanned the crowd.

"For those of you who don't know me, my name is Rick Benton," he began. "I didn't grow up in Porterfield, and I didn't have the privilege of experiencing Hilda Penfield in the classrooms of Porterfield High. However, for the past three years I've been an avid pupil in her classes of life."

Rick's chin quivered a moment. He took a deep breath and composed himself.

"My parents are teachers," he continued in a steady voice. "I've been around teachers all of my life. I know that it can be a difficult and often thankless profession. But those who are drawn to the teaching profession are usually those with a desire to help others learn and understand. Comprehension in a student's eyes is sometimes the only reward for a teacher, but I know from my parents that it can be the biggest and best reward a teacher receives.

"As a teacher, Mrs. Penfield gave of herself without restraint or reservation. She was amply rewarded for her work over the years through her numerous awards, the devotion of her students, and endless praise from grateful parents. I've been told more than once that Mrs. P. was tough in the classroom. She didn't win the deep respect and admiration she had by going easy on her pupils; she earned it through excellent teaching, and her enthusiastic desire to not just help her students learn the basics of our language and literature, but open their eyes to the world around them.

"And for those of us who were her students in or out of the classroom, the rewards are numerous, almost too numerous to mention."

Rick smiled. "Mrs. Penfield was simply the greatest teacher I have ever known. I knew the moment I met her that I was in the presence of a woman who could teach me many things. And she did. Mrs. P. was generous with her time and her wisdom, not just with me, but with all who knew her. Those of us fortunate to be close to her learned of compassion and tolerance. We learned humility. She shared her observations and insight into the human race. Her wisdom enabled us all to deal with our shortcomings, and also shed light on our many blessings. Of course, the biggest blessing of all was Mrs. Penfield herself. How blessed we all were to have her in our lives."

Rick looked at his notes on the podium. He wiped a shaking hand across his eyes and cleared his throat. Ed felt his hands clenching together in his lap. He looked at his hands, and then up at Rick, willing him to continue.

"Mrs. Penfield had no living relatives left in her last years." Rick's voice was calm but commanding. "However, she was wise enough to know that a family isn't restricted to blood kin, or necessarily created through traditional wedding vows. Mrs. Penfield created her own family, a family of people who loved and deeply respected her. This family, of which I am proud to be a member, looked to her for guidance, comfort, and nurturance. She never let us down. She was always available when we needed her. Today, as we honor this woman who touched our lives in such a special way, we also thank her.

Our good fortune in having known her, and having been her students in the classroom of life, is a priceless keepsake."

Rick paused. He smiled at the people assembled in the first two rows: Ed, Effie Maude, and Gordy; Claire, Judy, Josh, and Jane; the Croasdales; and Norma, Laurie, Todd, Bobby, and Lesley. They all looked back at him, and Ed could sense in their families and friends the same pride he felt for Rick as he spoke the words in all of their hearts.

"Thank you, Mrs. Penfield." Rick's voice was almost a whisper, but the microphone picked it up and delivered his fervent gratitude throughout the room. "Thank you for being mother, teacher, mentor, friend, confidant, and benefactress. Those of us whose lives you touched so deeply and sincerely promise to move forward on our own journeys using the lessons and tools you so unselfishly gave us. We'll miss you, but we'll never forget you or your gift of wisdom shared."

Rick bowed his head. Reverend Norris joined him at the podium with a nod of respect as he turned to the assembled mourners.

"Would you please join us in a moment of silence for our dear friend, Hilda Jean Penfield."

Heads bowed once again. The silence was almost deafening in its significance. Ed snuck a look at Rick and thought, *I don't think I've ever loved you more than I do right now.*

As the piano introduction of Simon and Garfunkel's "Bridge Over Troubled Water" began to play, Rick returned to his seat next to Ed. He looked at Ed, and his warm and tender special spread across his face as he acknowledged the love and respect in Ed's eyes.

Effie Maude leaned over Ed and grasped Rick's hand. "Oh, Rick, she would be so proud of you," she whispered. "That was just beautiful."

"Thanks," Rick whispered shakily. His nerves seemed to get the best of him as he slumped in his seat and let out a deep breath.

The song's powerful orchestration and Art Garfunkel's soaring tenor poured through the room. Ed reached again for his father's handkerchief as the tears began to fall. Mrs. Penfield had indeed been his bridge over troubled water, and Ed couldn't even begin to count the times she had, as Art sang, eased his mind. From the sounds of sniffing and purses being opened behind him, he knew he wasn't the only one profoundly moved by Paul Simon's lyrics and by the wonderful gift of having known Hilda Penfield.

When the song reached its climax, the ushers began to escort the mourners from the room. Reverend Norris nodded at Ed and Rick, and along with the other pallbearers they took their assigned places at the casket. Doug opened the double doors that had been specially built into the side of the room that led to a short flight of stairs and the driveway. Ed could see the black hearse, quickly acquiring a coat of white, parked outside. Ed, Rick, Gordy, Clyde, Todd, and Matt gently and carefully carried the coffin containing the remains of their beloved friend through the doors and into the swirling snow.

Once the casket was safely stowed in the back of the hearse, the men backed away.

Clyde brushed at the snow on his balding head. "I think we're going to need our overcoats for the cemetery."

"Yeah," Ed said, his eyes red and blinking but dry. He smiled at them all in thanks. "Let's get our coats and find our cars in the procession."

Rick's car, with Rick at the wheel, Effie Maude riding shotgun, and Ed and Gordy in the backseat, slowly followed the hearse out of the parking lot and onto Coleman Street. The hearse turned right onto Main, and the long funeral procession began to snake out behind them.

"Oh, my stars," Effie Maude whispered. "Look!"

At every intersection there was a Porterfield police car, lights flashing, blocking traffic from the cross streets. By each car a police officer stood tall and proud, hands clasping his cap at his waist. Ed's respect for local law enforcement increased as he realized they probably had more pressing matters to attend to on such a snowy day, but he understood that most of these men, former students of Mrs. Penfield, wanted to pay their respects to her.

"Wow," Gordy breathed, nudging Ed as they entered the downtown area. At the post office Don Hoffmeyer and all of his employees were lined up on the sidewalk, oblivious to the snow and cold. All along Main Street merchants and shoppers lined the curbs in silence as the hearse carrying one of Porterfield's most beloved teachers made its way to the cemetery. Everyone in the car gasped as they saw the broad, steep steps of the Stratton County Courthouse filled with county employees. Ed felt tears come to his eyes once again as he witnessed this outpouring of respect and admiration.

Maybe Porterfield's not such a bad place after all, he thought, wiping away his tears.

The funeral procession turned onto Stratton Avenue and entered the sprawling Porterfield town cemetery. Once again the pallbearers assembled to carry Mrs. Penfield to her final resting place next to her husband and son. Ed, Rick, Effie Maude, Gordy, and their families were directed to seats under the canvas tent covering the grave site, while other mourners stood silently in the blowing and drifting snow for Reverend Norris's prayer.

While the minister spoke, Ed concentrated on the banks of flowers atop the coffin to keep himself from crying again. Effie Maude lost her own battle and broke down. Ed put an arm around her shoulders, and Rick handed her a dry handkerchief from his breast pocket. Effie Maude's tears seemed to be a signal to several others. Ed heard muffled sobs from behind him as Reverend Norris's voice rose in intensity.

Ed was startled by the touch of a hand on his shoulder. He turned his head slightly and saw Norma smiling gently at him. Ed smiled back at her in relief and gratitude before he turned his eyes once again to the flowers, which, despite the protection of the tent, were beginning to acquire a frosty covering.

Ed shivered. He hoped Reverend Norris would wrap things up quickly for the sake of everyone trembling from the cold and their sadness. Fortunately Reverend Norris concluded his comments and invited everyone to a dinner in Mrs. Penfield's honor at the First Presbyterian Church. Mourners began to walk to their cars, and Ed could hear the sound of windshield wipers scraping over ice-covered glass.

Rick and Gordy led Effie Maude back to Rick's car. Claire and Laurie herded their kids away as well. Todd escorted Norma back to his car, but when he had her safely inside he returned for Ed, who was still sitting under the tent.

"Ed?" Todd put a hand on his shoulder. "You coming?"

Ed looked up at his brother-in-law. Snow was clinging to his dark hair and his black coat, and concern was in his eyes. Ed felt a flash of gratitude that his sister had married such a good man.

"Yeah, I'm coming."

Ed glanced at the coffin. Snow was beginning to collect on the exposed sides.

"It just doesn't seem right to leave her here where it's so cold."

Todd put his arm around Ed's shoulders and gently pulled him out of the folding chair. "You know the Mrs. Penfield you loved isn't in that box. She can't feel the cold anymore, so it'll be okay. You *can* feel the cold, though, and the last thing she'd want is for you to get sick. So let's go to that warm church and have lunch, okay?" Todd grinned at him.

Ed grinned back. "Okay."

The two of them walked toward the waiting cars.

"By the way," Ed said, snow crunching under his dress shoes. "Have I ever thanked you for marrying my sister?"

Todd's eyebrows rose. "I don't think so. You grateful I took the beast off your hands?"

Ed chuckled as he kicked snow onto Todd's own dress shoes. "Yeah, something like that."

Ed eased into the backseat of Rick's car, trying to knock some of the snow off his shoes.

"Oh, hell, don't bother with that." Rick thumped the driver's seat into place and jumped in the car. "The last thing I'm worried about today is snow in the car."

Rick slowly piloted the car along the slippery lane to the street. Ed looked to the north toward his father's grave, and behind him at the tent covering Mrs. Penfield's.

Accepting death is a part of life.

He shook his head. *Maybe Mom's right. Maybe there isn't a point. Or maybe Mrs. Penfield was right, and it's a big mystery, and we don't get the answer until we're dead. Geez, maybe we never get the solution. Who really knows?*

The car entered the slow-moving traffic on Stratton Avenue. Ed looked out the snow-frosted back window one last time.

"Good-bye, Mrs. Penfield," he whispered.

CHAPTER TWENTY-ONE

That weekend was quiet at the Penfield place. There was no crying or screaming; no one overindulged in alcohol; and there were no calls to airlines or travel agents. Gordy spent most of his time at Pete Carmichael's home in Fort Wayne; Rick kept his nose buried in an assortment of lengthy historical novels; and Ed, when he wasn't busy with snow-removal chores, puttered around in his workshop.

On Monday Ed set about disposing of the many plants Stuart Reimer had delivered from the funeral home. He was still amazed and touched at the outpouring of floral tributes for Mrs. Penfield, but he didn't feel he could add the care and maintenance of twenty-seven planters to his usual routine. He dropped off plants at Norma's, gave a few to both Laurie and Claire, and even took one to Mrs. Ilinski when he stopped by her place to deal with a new dusting of snow. He hoped killing her with kindness would help him deal with the negative thoughts he was still harboring for her.

That evening Ed and Rick went through the box of cards that had been attached to the flowers and planters and began the time-consuming chore of writing thank-you notes. They had their first laugh of the day when Rick commented that the cost of the stamps alone would probably keep the U.S. Postal Service in the black for 1984.

Oh, they kept busy and they did what they had to do—with one exception: neither Ed nor Rick had gone near the main house since before the funeral. They had given Effie Maude the entire week off to absorb the shock of losing her longtime friend and employer, and also to adjust to the idea of working for the two of them instead. Aside from Gordy's comings and goings, the main house remained empty and silent. They didn't mention it to each other, but Ed was sure it was troubling Rick as much as it was him. Still, he just couldn't seem to face it, so he continued to say nothing and cowardly waited for Rick to broach the topic.

Their appointment with Bob Mason to discuss Mrs. Penfield's will was Thursday morning. When Ed walked into the bedroom after breakfast to get dressed for the ordeal, he found Rick sitting on the corner of the bed looking out the window. Ed could tell from Rick's position that he was staring at the back of the house. He looked up when he heard Ed pull open a dresser door for clean underwear.

"You know," Rick said quietly, "from what little I know about the probate process, I think Bob will want to send an appraiser to the house to go through Mrs. P.'s things. He'll have to have an accurate dollar amount for the entire estate."

Ed said nothing as he laid a pair of jockeys on the dresser and slowly closed the drawer.

"Aside from the jewelry and stuff she left to Effie Maude, and her bequests to the historical society and the library and such, all the stuff in that house belongs to us now."

Ed sighed. "How 'bout that."

"Yeah. How 'bout that. I'm thinking we'll have to go through the house and maybe sell a few things we don't really want or need to help meet the expenses. Financially we weren't prepared for this yet."

"Yeah, I guess not."

Rick pulled Ed next to him on the bed. "Baby, what you said last week about leaving permanently—was it just the shock of Mrs. P. dying so suddenly that brought that on? How do you feel about it now?"

Ed took Rick's hand and told him of the conversation he had overheard at the Klarn house, and Norma's thoughts on the matter.

Rick smiled. "Well, thank God for Norma's fuck-'em attitude. That at least got you through the week. How do you feel now, though?"

Ed shrugged. "I don't know. I felt better about things when I saw all those people lined up on Main Street for Mrs. Penfield, but that didn't have anything to do with us. I know I'm tired of walking around waiting for someone to say something mean. But it's like I always said: I don't want them running us off either."

"Yeah, I know." There was a thoughtful frown on Rick's face. "I've kind of been thinking about that myself lately. Since Mrs. P. is gone, we have to make a real decision on this. When I got that job in Indy, I think we both would have packed up and gone under different circumstances, but it wasn't practical. Mrs. P. needed us, and Claire still needed us. Now Mrs. P. is gone, and it looks like Claire and the kids will be taken care of. The awful truth is, we're free to do as we please now."

Ed shuddered. "Who knew freedom could be so scary?"

"Yeah. And what about that house sitting over there? We haven't gone near it for over a week. You know what I think? I think we feel guilty."

Ed grinned as he realized Rick had accurately nailed his feelings. Yes, he felt overwhelmed with guilt that they now had their dream house, thanks to the death of Mrs. Penfield.

"You're right. I feel guilty as hell."

Rick chuckled. "Me, too. I keep telling myself it was what she wanted, but I feel like we won some kind of macabre lottery. What are we gonna do, baby? Are we gonna settle down in that house like we always planned, and build our life here in narrow-minded old Porterfield, or are we gonna move away like Doug and seek greener and gayer pastures?"

Ed put his head on Rick's shoulder. "I don't know, darlin', but do we have to decide right now?"

"No, we don't. But we have to deal with our fear and guilt about that house. I had an idea before we went to bed last night. I wanted to see how it looked in the morning, and then bounce it off you."

"What?"

"Well, what do you say we have kind of our own memorial service for Mrs. P.? Gordy will be at Pete's most of this weekend, and Effie Maude isn't due back until Monday. What do you say we spend Saturday kind of honoring her in our own way? We can go through the house, share our memories of her, and do some talking. Maybe that way we can sort out our feelings, and maybe even come up with a game plan."

Ed nodded. "I think that's a great idea. Aw, crud!" he exclaimed, jumping up from the bed. "I completely forgot."

He went to the closet and fumbled through the jacket of his suit for the letter Bob Mason had given him. He handed it to Rick.

"He gave me this right before the funeral, and I was so distracted I forgot all about it."

Rick turned the envelope over and over in his hands. "Well, what do you know? Some last thoughts from our wonderful mentor. I don't know why I'm surprised. This is just the sort of thing she'd do. You know what? Let's wait until Saturday and open it together in the house."

Rick did a dead-on imitation of Mrs. Penfield's mischievous grin. "I have a feeling that in addition to that house, she may have left us one last piece of advice that'll help us figure out what to do."

<♦●♦>

Ed came home Friday afternoon with something hidden under his coat. Rick was in the kitchen making a baked macaroni-and-cheese casserole from Norma's recipe and immediately spotted the bulge and demanded that Ed reveal his surprise. Ed pulled out the videotape he'd picked up at the library.

Rick squinted at the title. "*Wait Until Dark?*" he exclaimed.

Ed's grin was a bit sheepish. "*Breakfast at Tiffany's* was checked out. Still, it's Audrey Hepburn. I thought we could watch it tomorrow afternoon before we tackle the house."

Rick laughed as he shook his head. "Instead of watching Audrey be romanced by George Peppard we get to see her be terrorized by Alan Arkin. Oh, baby, that's great."

"I think Mrs. Penfield would think it's funny." Ed slapped Rick with the hard plastic video case.

"Yeah, you're right." Rick's warm and tender special brightened his face as he shoved the casserole dish in the oven. "I think she would, too."

Gordy stopped by the next afternoon on his way to Fort Wayne.

"Well, look at him," Rick said from the sofa. "All showered and shaved and lookin' good, ready for a weekend of love, romance, and physical pleasure."

Gordy smirked at him. "If I didn't know better, Benton, I'd swear you were jealous."

Rick threw a magazine at him. "Well, it's like Ed's sister says: we old married farts have to live vicariously through our single friends."

"Yeah," said Ed, who was getting ready to put some popcorn in the microwave for their movie. "Besides, Pete's kinda hot."

"He's very hot." Gordy moaned. "Damn! Not only that—he's a good euchre player."

"Yeah?" Rick picked up the magazine Gordy had thrown back at him. "Well, then get his ass down here for a card night, okay?"

"I will. I was just waitin' for you two assholes to get moved to the other house so I can set up my stuff. I think my leather couch will look great in here."

Rick smirked at him. "Your leather couch is a piece of shit and it will look hideous in here, but if it'll make you happy, I'm all for it. I have a feeling some decisions will be made before the end of the weekend."

Gordy went to the fridge to grab a Pepsi for the road. He pulled the flip top off the can and quietly looked at them both for a moment. He hadn't been told of their doubts about remaining in Porterfield, but he seemed to realize they had more on their minds than just moving from the carriage house to the main house.

"Whatever you guys decide to do, it'll be the right thing," he said tentatively. "And you know I'll do whatever you want to help make it easier."

Ed walked over and hugged him. "We know, bud."

Rick joined them in the kitchen for a hug as well. "You're the big brother I always wanted," he said softly. "Knowing we can always count on you makes this all easier already."

"Shit," Gordy mumbled, squeezing Rick. "I'm gonna get out of here before this gets sloppy. I got me a hot man to get naked tonight."

He let Rick go and walked to the door. He paused and grinned at both of them.

"See you guys tomorrow night, okay?"

"'Bye, Gord," Ed and Rick said more or less together.

They listened to his boots stomp down the stairs. Rick, smiling, went back to the sofa, while Ed slammed the microwave oven shut and punched in the time. He was smiling as well.

Good old Gordy, he thought. *He's like my big brother, too. If we move away, we'll still be friends, but we'll lose him, and everyone else who makes our lives so good here. Maybe we've lost enough already.*

Ed put those thoughts aside as he was swept into the suspense of *Wait Until Dark*. When the movie was over, it was dark in Porterfield as well. The early winter dusk had descended, bringing with it a flurry of light snow. Ed watched it fall as the tape rewound, thinking of the snow falling on the cemetery. He repeated Todd's words to himself and reminded himself that Mrs. Penfield was free from her painful arthritis and no longer had to worry about the cold.

"You know," Rick said as he ejected the tape from the VCR, "I think I understand now why Mrs. P. liked Audrey Hepburn so much. They didn't look or act alike, but they both have class and elegance, a certain kind of dignity. Mrs. P. never forgot she was a lady, but she didn't let it stop her from doing what she wanted. If you think about it, that was kind of unusual before the women's lib movement. Audrey Hepburn always comes off like a free spirit, even though she never seems to forget that she's a classy woman."

"Yeah," Ed replied absently, still watching the snow quietly falling.

"So, what do you say? Shall I call Gino's for a pizza? We can eat it in the kitchen over at the house, or hell, even eat it in the dining room on the Havilland that belongs to us now."

Ed turned from the window. "Why don't we wait on that a little bit? I'd kind of like to go to the cemetery first."

Rick frowned. "Do you really think that's a good idea?"

Ed grinned. "No, not *that* cemetery. *Our* cemetery."

"Oh!" Rick grinned back at him. "Okay."

Ed was referring to a little country cemetery located several miles west of Porterfield where some of his ancestors on his mother's side of the family were buried. Ed had first taken Rick there shortly after they had met, and ever since, it had been a special place for them. Whenever they were troubled or had decisions to make, they would go there, individually or together, and think.

So they piled into Ed's truck and headed west. Ed drove slowly as the snow continued to fall. The county roads were slick, and oddly deserted for an early Saturday evening. They encountered few vehicles, and when Ed drove through the gates of the cemetery they both had the feeling that they were the only two people out and about for miles around.

Ed drove over the hill, and the truck's headlights illuminated the nineteenth-century graveyard at the rear of the cemetery. The long-neglected tombstones—some leaning to one side, others completely flat on the ground, thanks to a century's worth of aggressive tree roots—always made Ed feel both wistful and proud as he thought of his ancestors, who had moved to this part of Indiana 150 years earlier to establish a home on land they could call their own.

The snow stopped falling as Ed parked the truck behind a huge, spreading pine tree near the circular path. As they jumped from the truck and walked to the edge of the burial ground, Ed noticed a half-moon shining through the clouds scudding across the sky.

"I remember the first time you brought me here," Rick said nostalgically.

"Yeah, we made out in my truck like high school kids." Ed smiled at the memory.

"Uh-huh. You know what, though? It was also the first time I began to see how you fit into the landscape of Stratton County, how long your family had been here and all that. I think it was the first time I really considered staying here myself, and allowing my own roots to grow here. It's funny. Some places are prettier, or maybe they're more sophisticated, or whatever, but there's something to be said for the quiet tradition, the security of a place like Stratton County."

Ed moved closer to Rick. "Even for people like us?"

Rick shrugged. "I don't see why not. When your ancestors came here they only had a vague idea of what they were really getting into; we know exactly what we're facing in Porterfield, both the good and the bad."

Ed looked to the sky. The clouds had moved away, revealing the moon and a cluster of stars. He remembered a much colder January night three years earlier, when he and Rick had stood in this same spot and made decisions about their future.

Ed reached for Rick's hand. "Remember that night we came out here after Mrs. Penfield gave you her strength-through-adversity lecture? She told you we needed to go out and look at the stars and put everything into perspective."

Rick looked up as well. "Yeah. I'll never forget that night. That was when I knew beyond any doubt that I wanted to spend my life with you."

"And we decided to stay in Porterfield and fight if we had to."

"Right. Has that changed for you, baby?"

Ed sighed. "No, I guess not. Standing here, I remember what Mrs. Penfield said, that no matter where we were we'd have things to worry about, or things that would scare us. The fighting part makes me sad, though."

"Me, too. But I've been thinking. Maybe our problem is that we're concentrating on defense instead of offense. Oh, we've done a good job of building our financial security, thanks in no small part to Mrs. P., and we've both earned a lot of respect in that town, but yet we still worry about what some people will think. You know what? I think maybe it's time to stop worrying about them and see what we can do to make things better."

Ed looked at Rick curiously. "What do you mean?"

"Well, as I said, we've both earned a certain amount of respect in Porterfield. A lot of people either don't have a problem with us being gay, or overlook it because they respect us. Maybe being openly gay in that town is the best way to change attitudes.

"Think about it. When you were in high school, if you had known about a gay couple like us in that town, would you have felt so lonely? What about Gordy, or Pete? Just think how many other gay men you went to school with and didn't know it. I can't help but think that despite the setbacks AIDS has brought, things are gonna change, and change for the better. Maybe there are men in that town, or even boys in high school, who would be willing to risk coming out of the closet if they see us living our lives, open and proud, doing our jobs, working in the community, and making one of the nicest Victorian homes in town even more of a showplace than it already is."

Rick squeezed Ed's hand. "We've both done a lot for Porterfield in our own ways. Maybe by continuing to do that, we can help men like ourselves. And then there's the AIDS thing. Paul says it's going to get worse before it gets better. Maybe when the time comes we can show our gratitude for being okay by helping the men who will need it here close to home."

Ed remained silent as he contemplated Rick's words.

"In other words," Ed said slowly, "instead of worrying about any fighting we have to do, we keep on loving each other, and hope our love sets a good example. That sounds kind of sappy, but I think I get what you mean."

"Yeah! The hell with the assholes in that town who don't approve of us. Let's make ourselves available to the people who do, especially the men, and even women, who are still living in fear. Look at how we've totally been there for Gordy. Where would he be if we hadn't've become friends? I'm not saying we rent rooms and start a halfway house, but just *be* there, kind of like Mrs. P. was there for us when we needed her.

"Oh, sure," Rick continued. "There's a lot we could do in any big city. But I think about Paul moving back here so he'll be available when AIDS hits northeast Indiana. Maybe staying here in gay no-man's-land is the best thing we can do for when we're needed."

Rick shrugged. "That sounds all noble and altruistic, and I may be full of shit, but I do know we've been blessed over and over again, whether by fate or by Mrs. Penfield. I'd like to share some of that if we can."

Ed grasped Rick's hand, thinking of how proud he had been of him at Mrs. Penfield's funeral, and how much love he had felt for Rick when he had spoken the words that came from both of their hearts. *This is my Dream Man,* he thought now. He looked at Rick, who was staring at the stars, an eager smile on his face. *This is my husband, the man I've chosen to share my life with. Not only am I lucky, but I'm also a damned good husband picker.*

Ed turned Rick to him and kissed him, a kiss filled with every bit of that love and pride he felt.

"I love you, darlin'," he whispered. "And I think you're brilliant. I say we stay and become the official poster guys for gay Porterfield."

Rick's laugh rang out through the cemetery. He grabbed Ed and squeezed him tightly. "Oh, baby, I love you, too. Three years. Three years and I'm still crazy about you. What do you say we go back to that house and start the next chapter of our lives?"

Ed's smile was as eager as Rick's.

"Okay. Let's go."

⟡●⟡

They drove back to town and stopped at Gino's for a pizza. A short time later, Ed pulled into the driveway and they both looked at the big house, lit only by a light Gordy had left on in the kitchen.

Rick clutched the pizza box on his lap. "Well, here we go. How 'bout you put the truck away and run upstairs and get that letter while I take the pizza in?"

Ed nodded.

"Oh," Rick said, as he was about to slam the door shut. "Why don't you get Jett, too? He might as well start getting used to his new home."

They ate their pizza off the Havilland china in the dining room, using the sterling silver for utensils, and drinking their Pepsi-Cola from crystal glasses. Rick had lit the tapers on the table, so they dined in candlelight. Ed chuckled to himself, thinking Mrs. Penfield would get a kick out of the scene.

Jett ran from room to room, sniffing and investigating. He galloped up the stairs, then galloped back down and charged into the dining room with a meow. Rick dropped a piece of sausage on the floor for him. Jett gobbled it down, and then wandered into the study, where he settled in one of the wing chairs by the fireplace to wash his whiskers.

"Jett seems to approve of this place." Ed smiled at the sight of the cat curled up in the chair where Ed had spent so much time warming himself by the fire.

"I think he likes having more running room." Rick looked fondly at their cat; like Ed, he seemed to be enjoying the cozy picture Jett created by the fireplace. "How 'bout we build a fire and read Mrs. P.'s letter in there?"

Ed picked up his plate and headed for the kitchen. "After we clean up," he said primly. "We shouldn't leave a mess for Effie Maude."

Rick laughed and gathered the other plates from the table.

"I know one improvement I'm gonna make in here," Ed said as he ran water in the sink.

"A dishwasher?"

Ed firmly nodded. "A dishwasher! One that isn't named Ed Stephens."

"Speaking of names," Rick said as he carefully rinsed their glasses. "What do you think we should call this place? I mean, people just refer to it as the Penfield place. Why don't we give it an official name?"

Ed thought as he scrubbed the forks. "How about Penfield House, or Penfield Manor? That way we won't let people forget who built it and owned it for so long."

Rick smiled, a faraway look in his eyes. "Penfield Manor. I like that. It sounds like some big, beautiful estate in a mystery novel. Maybe we can get a plaque made with that name and 1898 on it. We can put it on the front porch so anyone who comes to the door will know they're entering a historical home."

"Yeah, and we won't let Harriet Drinkwater near the place. We'll wait 'til Eunice is back running the historical society, and then we'll open the doors so everyone can see what *real* Stratton County history looks like."

When they were finished in the kitchen, they wandered through the first-floor rooms, and then went upstairs to the master bedroom.

"I think we should put our bed right there." Rick pointed to an inside wall near the door. Then we can roll over in the morning, look out that east window, and watch the sun rise through the spruce branches. What do you think?"

Ed giggled. "I think Mrs. Penfield would probably think it's as hideous as you think Gordy's leather couch is, but I like it. We can watch the oak leaves turn color every fall out those southern windows, too."

They walked across the hall to the bedroom Mrs. Penfield had made over into a library many years before.

"This would make a great home office for me," Rick said, looking around. "See? We could move Mr. Penfield's desk up from the study. It would look great under the window, and I could enjoy the view of the garden in the warm months. We're getting a new computer at work. I might ask Vince if I can have the old one. I'll bring it home, and we can both learn how to use it. He's convinced everyone will have a home computer within the next ten years."

Ed nodded. "And just think how nice it will be to have all of your books in one place."

Rick smiled at him. "Not all of them. I want to keep that bookcase you made for me filled, too. I was thinking about putting it on the stairway landing. There's plenty of room."

They descended the stairs and agreed that a cozy nook could be created on the landing with Rick's bookcase.

"I love this banister," Ed commented as he stroked the finely carved oak. "Maybe next Christmas we can wrap a garland around it, with maybe a wreath on the post at the foot of the stairs."

"Yeah. Maybe we could even string some lights, or some gold beads through it."

They slowly walked down the stairs and entered the back parlor, where the first Mrs. Penfield had received company, usually afternoon calls from ladies wearing hats.

"What should we do with this room?" Ed wore his handyman frown as he rubbed his chin. "Even Mrs. Penfield didn't use it much. Effie Maude dusts in here, and that's about it."

"We'll think of something," Rick said confidently. "Somehow I don't see either of us sitting here in the afternoon pouring tea for Eunice Ames."

Ed laughed. "Hey! I just thought of something. Why don't we take that enlargement from Mrs. Penfield's funeral and hang it up where the first Mrs. Penfield's portrait is? That picture will go to the historical society, so we'll just have a blank wall there. Then we can sort of redecorate in here, and make the whole room kind of a tribute to our Mrs. Penfield."

Rick's warm and tender special was glowing. "That's a great idea, baby. If we do that, we'll never forget her, or how we came to live in such a grand place."

They concluded their tour in the study. Ed frowned at Mrs. Penfield's bed in the corner; neatly made up with the sheets and quilt they had given her for Christmas.

"I think that bed is one of the things we should sell," Ed muttered as he arranged kindling in the fireplace.

Rick shook his head. "No, let's just move it upstairs into that tiny spare bedroom. It might come in handy if we have company. Think of it: not only can we have houseguests now, but we have room for a house full of 'em."

Ed deposited some logs on the grate. He nodded. "Okay. That works."

Once the fire was blazing away, Rick ceremoniously opened the envelope Ed had left on the mantel. He unfolded several sheets of Mrs. Penfield's stationary and spread them on the slate in front of the fireplace. With Jett comfortably asleep in his new nap chair, they settled themselves on the floor so they could both read Mrs. Penfield's last words for them.

January 3, 1984

My dearest Ed and Rick,

I have been collecting various thoughts and composing this letter in my mind for quite some time. Ed, after our little talk yesterday, I've decided it is finally time to put pen to paper.

You see, I have been aware these past few months of a weakness within me, a weakness my intuition tells me is a sign that my time left in this world may be brief. Oh, I suppose I could have gone to your Dr. Paul for confirmation, but it did not seem necessary. As my determination to continue the battle with this demon arthritis grows fainter, I simply do not feel the need to poke and prod and investigate possible health regimens that might prolong my existence. I have lived a full and glorious life. If my time is near, I am ready to surrender with grace and dignity, and with the knowledge that my years have been both bountiful and beautiful. Yes, there has been great sadness and disappointment, but I realize that is primarily due to the loss of people who have meant so much to me. If indeed there is a heaven, I eagerly look forward to my reunion with them.

It pains me, though, to leave the two of you. Can mere words express my gratitude for the joy and happiness you've brought to my life these past few years? Please know, both of you, what a blessing you have been to me at the end of my life. Watching your love for each other grow stronger as you both have become stronger men has been a great satisfaction. I leave this world knowing I leave behind two mature men, capable of dealing with both life's hardships and its rewards.

I also suspect that my death may leave you with feelings of guilt. Ed, Rick, do not give in to these feelings. You know how very much I want you to continue your lives in this house. If you feel there is something you must do in regards to the easy rest of my spirit, please do this: create a home within these walls filled with love, joy, and laughter, as you have done in the carriage-house apartment. That is all I ask, so move forward with your plans knowing you have my strongest blessings and encouragement.

I have been thinking about your future together in other ways as well. Perhaps it is time to take the strength and wisdom you have acquired and use it to the benefit of others. I am aware of the fact that my acceptance of your homosexuality is something you both see as a great gift. Perhaps it is. As we know, it shouldn't be. All of God's children should be accepted as they are without qualification. I have seen some progress made in this regard, but I fear the journey to full acceptance will be a long and occasionally painful one. I am hoping you can find it in your hearts to take the gifts I have given you, and perhaps find a way to use them to ease the struggle for others who haven't been blessed with your good fortune. I have always given of myself as fully as possible. As more is learned of this terrible new disease casting a shadow over your brothers, and the path for all gay men becomes rockier, I challenge you both to do the same.

One last thought: Please remember, both of you, to enjoy the journey; savor the highs and the lows of your walk through life together. My gift of this cherished home is not your rainbow's end. As I have said, rainbow's end is elusive. I suspect the treasures for the two of you will not be found in a golden pot at the end of the rainbow; rather, I believe you will come across them one by one as you continue the fascinating journey of life. Go forward with my best wishes for success.

Much love from your friend and teacher,

Hilda Penfield

Ed and Rick looked at each other and grinned. For a moment Ed was afraid he would cry, but the time for tears seemed to have passed. Instead he began to chuckle.

"How do you like that?" Ed shook his head. "The old girl is still one step ahead of us. She knew exactly how we were going to feel. Geez, it's even like she was at the cemetery with us, still prodding us forward to do the right thing."

Rick threw back his head and laughed. "Yep! But you know what? We read this letter *after* we made those decisions tonight. That means her lessons and wisdom have seeped into our brains already. It just proves she's right: we are ready to move on without her."

Ed's smile was wistful. "Yeah. I don't want to, but since we have to go on without her, we will. Now I feel like we can."

Rick leaned over and kissed Ed. "Me, too. Mrs. P.'s death may be the end of one chapter in our lives, but it's also the beginning of a new one, and right now I'm feeling pretty good about what we'll find written on its pages."

Ed carefully folded the pages of Mrs. Penfield's letter and slid them into the envelope. He stood up and gently placed the envelope on a table away from the fire. Then he turned to Rick.

"I think we should put this letter in that keepsake box Mrs. Penfield kept on her dresser. We can put the box in the back parlor, under her picture, and whenever we get scared or stupid we can read it and get our courage and our smarts back."

Rick nodded as he stood up. "Another great idea, baby."

Ed grabbed Rick's hand and led him into the front parlor to Mrs. Penfield's hi-fi. While Rick watched him, Ed reached for the record he had brought over from the carriage house and had hidden in the cabinet when Rick wasn't looking.

Rick smiled. "'Moon River,' baby? For Mrs. P.?"

Ed started the turntable. "Nope. This one is for you and me, darlin'."

Rick laughed as their song, Three Dog Night's "One Man Band," began to play.

"I always said this was a rockin', happy song," he said as he began to move to the beat. "Crank it up, Edward; crank it up."

As Ed turned the volume knob farther and farther to the right, music began to fill the house, their home. They moved into each other's arms and began to sway back and forth. Rick took Ed's left hand in his and stroked the ring he had given him.

"My wonderful one-man band," Rick whispered in Ed's ear. "Ed, will you let me keep holding your hand as we walk through life? If you do, this one-man band promises to keep making the best music he can for you."

Ed reached under Rick's sweatshirt and rubbed the gold chain around his neck. "Yeah, Rick. You can hold my hand forever, and this one-man band promises to make our soundtrack the most beautiful one in the world."

And as Ed pulled his Dream Man even closer to him, and they danced together through the rooms of their dream home, he smiled with confidence, for he knew that was a promise he could keep.

John Gevers Photography— www.newmediabrew.com

ABOUT THE AUTHOR

Nick Poff currently lives in Fort Wayne, Indiana. *The Handyman's Promise* is his third novel. To learn more about the author and his books, visit www.nickpoff.com or www.writermen.com. Imixes of the music featured in his novels can be found through Itunes.

Printed in the United States
110166LV00003B/158/P